The fat man Bender came up, his thick fingers grabbing the front of Cynthia's dress. With a strong jerk, the robber tore the garment away. Cynthia screamed in terror as his claw-like fingers grabbed the top of her petticoat. There was a ripping sound and Cynthia stood naked to the waist. It was then that he raised the butt of his pistol and let it drop with a thud on her husband's head.

"Quit screaming," he ordered, his eyes roaming over her breasts. "Just do as I say and no one'll get hurt. Just gonna take a little pleasurin', that's all."

Twisting her arm, he forced her down to the ground. Cynthia struck at his face, but his thick arm deflected her blow. Her hand fell down ineffectually and, in that instant, brushed against a knife holstered to his belt. As Bender lunged forward, Cynthia freed the knife and slashed out. Bender felt a numb sensation in his lower abdomen. Dumbly he looked down and then screamed in horror, "You've cut off my—you filthy bitch!"

Blood gushed from the wound between his legs. When the pain came with a solid, forceful jolt, he cried out in agony. Cynthia stood behind him holding the pistol in her hand, but she had no intention of using it now; he would be dead by the time she reached her husband and the wagon.

They would have to put this incident behind them if they were to complete the long journey west...

THE
FRONTIER RAKERS

BY
DAVID
NORMAN

ZEBRA BOOKS

KENSINGTON PUBLISHING CORP.

ZEBRA BOOKS

are published by

KENSINGTON PUBLISHING CORP.
21 East 40th Street
New York, N.Y. 10016

First Printing: April, 1979

Second Printing: July, 1980

Printed in the United States of America

Do not stain the glory of your worthy ancestors; fight to retain your God-given rights.

—Jefferson Warren; 1772

ONE

They hanged the boy after breakfast. The site of the hanging was a quarter mile east of the wagon camp. Men, women and children walked across the muddy field. They waited beneath a large oak tree. They murmured approvingly when a rope was thrown over a high limb. A man from Kentucky stepped forward and tied a noose.

A woman cried out, "He's a-coming!"

The crowd turned toward the circle of canvas-topped wagons. Four grim-faced men came across the field, pushing a thin boy in front of them. His bony hands were tied with rawhide. Tears rolled down his face. Halfway across the field, the boy slipped and fell in the mud. One man grabbed the collar of the boy's ragged shirt. He jerked the prisoner to his feet.

The crowd parted when the men drew close. The man from Kentucky slipped the noose around the boy's neck. Several men grabbed the youth and thrust him up on the back of a mule. The Kentuckian tied the other end of the rope to a nearby tree.

A bearded man raised his hand for silence.

"This skunk is named Elijah Bender," the man said. "He killed Emily Gilbert last night. Sneaked into camp to steal grub. Says he's fifteen years old. Told us he killed the little Gilbert girl when she caught him. Reckon that's enough for us. We voted for hanging. We'll leave him swing here as a warning to anyone else with thieving ideas."

Steve Wellman stood on the edge of the crowd, shifting his weight from boot to boot in an agitated manner. He was bothered by the look of stark terror on the boy's face. The slightness of the prisoner's body indicated he was malnourished. Wellman pushed forward and asked, "Do we have to hang him?"

"That was the vote." The bearded man seemed surprised that anyone would question the order. He studied the man who stood before him. Wellman was about twenty-eight years old, dressed better than the average immigrant in new canvas trousers, polished black boots and a freshly laundered wool shirt. The bearded man looked into Steve Wellman's icy blue eyes, and averted his stare.

"We don't like hanging a young'un, mister," the bearded man said. "You got to remember we ain't back home. We ain't got time for a lot of folderol with this thing. Rule of the committee is law on a wagon train."

"Hang him," yelled a man.

"Get it over with," shouted another immigrant.

"Got to start our wagons rolling."

Wellman stepped back into the crowd. The bearded man looked up at the boy.

"You got anything to say, son?"

The boy trembled. "I ain't a bad 'un. Paw made me do

8

it. Paw'd kill me if I come back without any grub. Said I should knife anybody who saw me. I ain't a bad 'un. Jesus is my savior, but my Paw—"

With a hoarse cry of anguish, a middle-aged man stepped up and slapped the mule. The animal leaped forward. Elijah Bender went backward over the mule's haunches. The boy's feet dangled in the air, kicking for support. His face took on a distorted appearance, mouth open, tongue hanging out. Bulging eyes threatened to burst from their sockets. His skin took on a blue-black coloration.

"Burn in hell!" screamed the man who had struck the mule. He was Albert Gilbert, the dead girl's father.

The boy's body was still jerking when the crowd crossed the field and walked to the top of a small knoll. They gathered beside a freshly dug grave that contained a homemade wood coffin. A man took a position at the head of the grave, opened a Bible and read a few verses of scripture. He spoke quietly about the brief life of Emily Gilbert, and about the grief of her parents. As the man closed the Bible, several men and women began to sing a hymn. Men took up shovels and, working quickly, began to fill the grave. Another man pounded a wooden cross at the head of the grave. A hand-carved inscription read:

EMILY GILBERT
1838-1848
With the Angels

As the last words of the hymn sounded, Steve Wellman took his wife's hand and started away. Cynthia Wellman resisted for a brief instant, then realized that other families were hurrying back to their wagons. She fell in step with her husband, hoping the faintness she felt would go away. She was horrified by the death of little Emily, the hanging of the boy. She thought, I am twenty-one years old and scared of this violent world. Going to Oregon is a mistake. But Steve has the Oregon fever and I must not show my true feelings. Vaguely, she heard Steve's voice.

"Got to move out quick this morning," he was saying. "Another fifteen miles to Independence and we're leaving late."

"I've got most things packed in the wagon," Cynthia said.

Ten minutes later, they sat on the front seat of their wagon. Steve shook the reins and the oxen moved forward. Cynthia looked across the muddy field. The boy was a dead weight on the end of the rope. A robin was perched on the shoulder of the corpse.

Steve Wellman sensed his wife's despair.

He said, "I did my best to stop it."

Cynthia shivered.

"Things are handled fast out here," he added.

"I'll never forget the look of fear on his face."

He nodded. "Think about the little Gilbert girl."

"Well, I shouldn't clutter up my mind," Cynthia said. "Worry won't help anything."

"He was old enough to know better." He patted his wife's hand. "Nothing we can do now, honey. I would have felt better if he'd been turned over to the law for a regular trial."

Wellman pulled back on the reins as his wagon rolled to the edge of the campground. He halted until a Conestoga wagon, iron-rimmed wheels pressing deep into the red clay earth, rolled past. A tall emigrant in a red flannel shirt was perched on the front seat. The man smiled and waved as his wagon went past. A hand-scrawled sign was painted on the side of the wagon's canvas top: *Oregon or bust!*

Cynthia giggled. "Two to one he goes bust!"

Steve smiled and clucked at the oxen. The animals plodded forward at a slow gait, pulling the wagon over a small incline onto the road. A dozen wagons were spread out ahead of Wellman, their white tops shining in the morning sun. Every man was anxious to reach Independence that night. They wanted to camp in the great rendezvous outside the town, join the hundreds of emigrants headed west along the Oregon Trail. Trains were being organized, committees elected to govern the caravans, guides hired to lead the settlers on the 2,000-mile trip. As soon as the grass greened up, the trains would strike out for the Willamette Valley of Oregon. Upon arriving there, a man would be given a donor grant of 160 acres of fertile cropland. The government required a cabin be built, that a man live on the grant acres for a year. When these two conditions were met, the title to the land passed to the emigrant.

When the wagon started up a small hill, and the oxen slowed to a deliberate gait, Cynthia leaped down from the wagon. She ran into the ditch and picked a bouquet of daisies. She hurried along beside the wagon, commenting to Steve on the great patches of wild flowers.

"Look at those violets over there." She pointed across a small valley. "Must be a million of them."

Near the top of the hill, she picked a handful of budding wild roses. As she climbed back on the wagon, the sound of laughter came from a wagon ahead.

"Sounds like someone has Oregon fever," commented Steve.

"Isn't it something?" Cynthia held the flowers close to his face. "Just like a picnic. A great big picnic with hundreds of people joining together."

"May be rougher than that."

"We'll manage," Cynthia smiled. "Are we going to stop for lunch?"

"Have to let the oxen rest."

"Let's don't stop with the others."

Steve smiled. "What do you have in mind?"

"Our very own private picnic." She smiled happily. "Just the two of us. No one else around. I've got ham left over from breakfast this morning. It won't last 'til tonight. Neither one of us ate much this morning. I kept some biscuits. We can have ham sandwiches, one of those jam cakes I made last night, and some cool water from a creek."

"Your jam cake is nice," he said, eyes on the road ahead, "but I figure you could serve a better dessert."

Cynthia cast him a look of mock severity. "You mean . . ."

"Been more than a week."

She smiled. "Poor baby. We'll have to do something about that. Maybe tonight. I don't relish pleasuring outdoors in front of God and everybody."

"Maybe I'll fix a place in the wagon."

The sun was at its zenith when Steve looked for a quiet place off the road. They passed several groups of wagons gathered for the noon meal. At last, Steve caught a glimpse of an opening leading off the road. He guided the wagon through a forest of oak, elm, poplar and pine trees, lofty and tall, rising up from the vast sea of prairie grass. He pulled up by the edge of a small brook. Cattails, bulrushes, and broad-leafed water lilies filled a violet

12

pool of stagnant water.

"Nothing to drink here," said Steve. He stepped down from the wagon, unhitched the oxen. "I'll run them upstream for a drink."

Cynthia was busily pulling pans and boxes out of the wagon. "Food will be ready when you get back."

Steve had barely started down to the creek when Cynthia heard a loud crash in the woods. She wheeled in his direction, heard someone running through the brush. The forest went silent. Mouth dry, heart pounding with fear, Cynthia ran toward the creek. A loud argumentative voice drifted through the woods. The hostility in the man's tone drew her up short. She stopped, then crept forward as quietly as possible.

Steve was down by the creek. Two men stood across the stream from her husband, their faces hidden behind makeshift masks. A tall man with long blond dirty hair pointed a pistol at Steve's stomach. A short man with a large stomach hanging over his belt held a shotgun cradled in his thick, fat arms. The gun was pointed toward Steve's head. She could see the gleaming baldness of the fat man's head and, on the bicep of his arm, the tattoo of a serpent.

The fat man spoke angrily as he stepped across the creek.

"You're just plain unlucky, emigrant. We want your gold."

Steve asked, "What gold?"

"The gold you're carrying to Oregon." The fat man's voice was muffled by the mask. "The gold you're carrying to buy supplies in Independence."

Steve lied. "Sorry, mister. My Paw's got another wagon. He's got the money."

"Don't be funny," growled the fat man. He cocked his gun. "Search him and see if he's got anything."

The blond man stepped forward. His dirty hands roamed over Steve's body, dipped into the front pocket of his trousers. He came up with a five-dollar gold piece. "This is all he's got."

"Where's your wife?" growled the fat man.

"I'm traveling alone."

The blond man laughed. "Bet his wagon's full of money."

The fat man grinned. "Get back to your wagon, pilgrim. We'll see where you hide your money."

Cynthia's mind raced with confusion. She was paralyzed by the guns pointed at her husband. Then the fear passed and she acted on instinct. She slipped from her hiding place, raced through the woods toward the wagon. She was crawling up into the vehicle when she heard someone rummaging in the back. She opened the front flap of canvas, saw a dark figure moving inside. She grabbed for Steve's rifle.

"Ain't there, missy."

Cynthia looked in the direction of the voice. Gradually, her eyes adjusted to the dimness inside the wagon. A woman in ragged clothes held Steve's rifle. She was bent over their lunch, gulping down ham as if she was starved.

The woman cocked the rifle. "No need getting excited, girlie. Paw's got your man by now. No need to get your blood boiling. Just take things as they are." The woman stopped talking, shoved another piece of ham into her mouth.

Cynthia heard a noise outside, turned and saw the terrified expression on his face as Steve came up to the wagon. The fat man's eyes glistened brightly when he saw

14

Cynthia standing on the wagon seat.

"Well, what have we here. My oh my." The man's lips spread into a broad, leering grin.

"'Nother one for you, paw." The old woman leaped down from the back of the wagon. She came walking around the vehicle. "Ain't she a purty one?"

"Better'n the last one." The fat man eyed Cynthia with lustful eyes.

"I found her, paw," cried the old woman. "I get to pleasure her 'fore you-all tear her up."

The fat man grinned wolfishly. "You can work her up for me. Get her good and excited."

The woman took another bite of ham. "Maybe just a little funning a-fore you get her."

The blond man stepped forward. He spoke with disgust. "We come here for money. I joined you 'cause you"—his thumb jerked toward the fat man—"said there was money to be made robbing these pilgrims. I ain't seen anything 'cept this five-dollar gold piece in the last month. We've been eating ever'thing 'cept grub worms. Let's get the money and be on our way."

The old woman smiled at Cynthia. "Ain't he the strong one? Always wanting money. Just like Paw used to be 'fore he took to drink."

The fat man growled. "Watch your tongue, wife, or I'll cut your throat."

While the blond man crawled up into the wagon, rummaging in the boxes, the woman came close to Cynthia. Her dirty hand touched Cynthia's arm. "I'm Beulah Bender and this here is my husband, Paw Bender."

Cynthia gasped. "The boy's folks."

"You seed Elijah get hung?" asked the woman.

"I did."

"Did he die like a man?" The woman's beady eyes roved up and down Cynthia's body.

Steve interjected. "He died like a boy."

"Tole Paw he wouldn't 'mount to much." The woman slipped her arm around Cynthia's waist.

Steve stepped forward. "Leave her alone," he said firmly.

The blond man looked out of the wagon. "Where'd you hide the money, pilgrim."

"Told you my Paw had it." Steve stepped between Cynthia and the old woman.

Paw Bender shoved his gun into Steve's stomach. "Don't get smart, pilgrim. I'll blow you to kingdom come. If Maw wants some funning, we'll let her have it."

The woman grinned wolfishly and pulled Cynthia toward her. Although Cynthia yelled, kicked and scratched at the woman's face, she was driven back against the side of the wagon. The fat man came up, his thick fingers grabbing the front of Cynthia's dress. With a strong jerk, he tore the garment away. Cynthia screamed with terror as the old woman's clawlike fingers grabbed the top of her petticoat. There was a ripping sound and Cynthia stood naked above the waist. She began to sob incoherently.

The fat man slapped Cynthia's face.

"Quit screaming," he ordered. His eyes roamed over Cynthia's breasts. "Quite a little woman, ain't she?"

The old woman's mouth pursed. "Nice and firm."

Paw Bender chuckled. "Just don't bite off her nipples."

The old woman growled. "She's mine, Paw. Going to keep her for a week or two. I ain't had no funning in a

16

long time. Nobody lets me get pleasure."

The blond man came out of the wagon. He cursed. "Can't find a damn cent."

As the blond man turned his back to step off the wagon, Steve Wellman saw his chance. Maw and Paw Bender's eyes were fixed on Cynthia's breasts. With a quick leap, Steve moved forward, grabbing for the blond man's gun. The robber cried out, trying to hold onto the weapon. Then his grasp loosened and he fell into the grass. Steve wheeled, pointing the gun toward the Benders and the barrel swept past Cynthia's head. He started pulling the trigger. Paw Bender gave a loud cry, threw his arm up to deflect the shot. The roar of the gun was deafening. A sheet of orange flame spurted from the barrel. The buckshot struck the old woman full force in the face, ripping away her features. Something white shot out of the back of her head. She stood for an instant, her face a mass of raw meat, and stumbled backward. She fell into a crumpled heap beside the wagon.

Cynthia screamed as Paw Bender's pistol came down on Steve's head. With a loud cry, Steve fell onto the ground.

"Jesus Christ!" The blond man pulled himself to a standing position. He looked over at the old woman's body and shuddered. "She's dead."

Paw Bender slapped Cynthia in the face. "Just quiet down, honey. Maw ain't been right in the head lately. Kept her around too long. Should have kilt her a long time ago. 'Pears your husband done me a favor."

The blond man adjusted his mask. He looked down at Steve's body. He asked, "He dead?"

"I ain't no fool," Bender replied. "He knows where the money is. You keep a-looking 'til he comes to. I'm going

17

to fun this little girl in the woods."

The blond man shook his head. "Might be somebody heard the shot."

"They're always shooting around here." Exasperation edged the fat man's voice. "Sighting in guns. Killing rabbits. People shoot at anything moving. Naw, anybody heard that shooting'll think somebody was after rabbit. While I'm pleasurin' this one"—the fat man's mouth moved close to Cynthia's lips—"you tie her man up."

"Let's just get the money and go," persisted the blond robber.

Bender's gun came around with the barrel pointed toward his partner's head. "Do as I say or I'll lay you out there with maw. She wasn't much for pleasuring these past few years. But she was around when you needed her. Pity she liked women better'n men when she got older."

"Whatever you say." The blond man turned and started wrapping a leather harness around Steve's arms.

"Tie 'im good," said Bender. He turned and eyed Cynthia with a leer. She shrank back as his hands grabbed for her breasts. "Don't be trying to save it. Ole Bender ain't going to hurt you. Just a little pleasurin' and you won't miss it."

"Don't touch me, you . . . you . . . animal!"

Bender grinned. He grabbed Cynthia's arm and began to pull her down into a patch of weeds. Twisting her arm, he forced her down to the ground. She started to roll away, but his heavy boot came down hard on her stomach.

"Stay there, sweet thing! You ain't running off. My oh my! look at them two pretty ones. Sticking straight up like two purty mountains. Bet you're nice and tight. Prob'ly the tightest I've had in a long time."

Cynthia looked up, saw Bender unbuckle his belt. His trousers dropped down over his boots.

"Please . . . please . . . " she whimpered.

Bender's body came down upon her, rising slightly when he pushed her dress up to her waist. She tightened her legs. He moved to a kneeling position and a hand gripped each of her thighs. Slowly, with a twisted smile on his face, Bender began to pull her legs apart. She shuddered when he pushed her legs wide apart. She felt his hardness stab once, twice at her. She twisted to avoid him. He cursed and pulled her body closer to him.

Cynthia struck at his face, but his thick arm deflected her blow. Her hand fell down ineffectually and, in that instant, brushed against a knife holstered on his belt. The blade was snapped into the holster and, realizing she needed time, Cynthia gazed up into the fat man's face.

"Please . . ." she whimpered.

"Lay still, damn you!" His breath came fast and heavy.

"You're . . . you're too big."

Bender grinned. "Never had a real man, eh?"

"Let me guide you." Her hand came out and grasped his swollen member.

He grinned. "Might keep you for a few days."

As he lunged forward, Cynthia freed the knife. The blade glistened in the sunlight. Bender caught sight of the weapon, made a loud sucking sound and tried to move away. His escape was hampered by his boots and trousers. He felt almost safe when, eyes closed, Cynthia slashed out with the knife.

Bender felt a numb sensation in his lower abdomen. Dumbly, he looked down.

The bitch! The dirty stinking little bitch!

He screamed with horror.

"You've cut off my pecker," he screamed with disbelief.

Blood gushed from the wound between his legs. He stared down at his appendage on the ground. He screamed when the pain came with a solid, forceful jolt, like a hot poker was being rammed up inside him. He looked around for the girl. She held his pistol in her hand. She was running toward the woods. She disappeared into the trees.

Cynthia watched from the woods as the tall blond man came running up. Howling like a banshee, the fat man stooped down and picked up his member. He held the appendage in his hand to show his partner.

"She . . . she . . ." began Bender.

The tall man laughed. "Hell, Bender, she cut off your pecker."

"Help me . . . get a doctor!" The man's face was contorted with pain.

"You're dead, old man!"

"Kill her for me."

"Where'd she go?"

"Into the woods."

The tall man looked around. "Where's your gun?"

"She took it."

The tall man looked toward the woods. "She's got your gun?"

Bender pointed his joint in Cynthia's direction. He spoke with a liquid, gurgling sound.

"Get her for me," he gasped.

"Not a chance, old man!" The blond headed man cocked his pistol. "I'm not going out in the woods hunting that wildcat."

Bender's hands opened. His member dropped to the

grass. He looked down with dismay.

"Kill . . ." he gurgled.

"You ain't going to make it, friend," said the tall robber. "I ain't even going to make it easy for you. Not worth wasting a bullet. We could have had the money and gone. Nosiree! You and your crazy old lady had to put pleasure before business. Well, I'll take the money you carry in your poke. See you in hell, Bender!"

The fat man squealed as his partner slit his pockets.

"Quit crying," said the blond man. "Else I'll stuff your pecker in your mouth. Wouldn't that be a way to die? Suffocating on your best part?" He laughed, shoved a money bag into his pocket and looked around. The surrounding area was quiet. He tipped his hand to the man on the ground. "See you around, you dumb cluck!"

Cynthia watched as the blond man, still masked, headed down the road to Independence. He walked swiftly, then—as if frightened,—began to run. Within a few moments, he was gone from view. She hurried past Bender, now lying in the grass and groaning from pain. She came up to the wagon, saw Steve was still unconscious. A slight bruise colored his cheek. She was surprised to see he wasn't bleeding. She applied a rag to his head. He groaned. She ran back and dipped the cloth in the water barrel. She laid the cloth on his forehead, untied his bonds. He was still groaning when she came back to the creek with the oxen.

After Cynthia recounted what had happened, Steve walked over and looked down at the dying fat man.

He came back to Cynthia.

"Suppose we should shoot him?" he asked. "Put him out of his suffering."

She gritted her teeth. "Leave him be."

21

Groggily, Steve hitched up the oxen. Cynthia checked the wagon, saw a jumbled mass of supplies tossed around in the interior. Hastily, she began to clean up the mess. Steve came back, checked the ground for articles thrown out. He carefully averted his eyes from the dead woman's body.

"Come on up with me," he said, crawling up on the wagon seat.

Cynthia sat close to him as they pulled back on the road. They were out on the trail to Independence before she started trembling. Steve tried to calm her, talking soothingly, holding her in his arms. At last, with a great rush of tears, all the fear swept across her mind. She cried.

TWO

The sun had started to rise when the alarm clock went off. Grumbling sleepily, Steve Wellman pressed down on the alarm button. He fell back on the bed, grateful for the silence, and looked up at the canvas top of his wagon. Cynthia moaned sleepily and moved over to him. The top of her nightgown had become unbuttoned during the night, exposing a red-tipped mound of white flesh. Steve wanted to touch his tongue to her breast, to taste the warm muskiness of her flesh.

Instead, he pulled the blanket up to his chin. He slipped his arm under Cynthia's neck and drew her face into a three-quarter profile. Still asleep, she snuggled closer. Her arm moved over his bare chest, pushing the blanket down again. He looked at Cynthia with a feeling of wonderment. She would always be a beautiful woman, despite the passing of years. Her skin was tanned by the sun, even though she'd worn a bonnet from morning until sunset. Her long blonde hair was tied in a severe knot behind her neck. He used to wonder about the color, finally deciding her hair was the same shade as honey. He knew that Cynthia would always have that vulnerable child-woman expression, although her looks hid a gritty inner toughness like high-grade iron.

The murdering Benders had misjudged Cynthia's capacity for survival. They had not taken into account her gritty determination to live. That error called for the supreme payment—their lives. After they had gotten back in the wagon, heading west again, Cynthia had broken down. Anger gave way to fear; a violent trembling wracked her body. She cried out against the terror back in the woods. Sobbing loudly, she crawled back under the wagon top, lay on their pallet, and drew herself into a tight ball. She slept for two hours, got up and yawned, wiped her eyes, blew her nose and came up front to sit beside him. Steve said very little during the trip to Independence. They pulled in late that night. Cynthia handled the reins during the last three miles to the rendezvous. Steve carried a lantern and walked ahead of the oxen to light up the trail. They parked on the edge of the mass of wagons. Another emigrant, a man from New York, helped unhitch the oxen, feed and hobble the animals. The man accepted Steve's thanks, left for his wagon. Steve and Cynthia crawled up into their wagon, lay on the pallet and tried to sleep.

Cynthia awoke several times during the night. Her sleep was disturbed by nightmarish images of the Benders, visions of faceless corpses and blood flowing out onto new green grass. She awoke once with a strangled scream, flailing her arms wildly about the wagon. Steve calmed her down with soothing whispers, wiped the cold sweat from her face. She mumbled something about people, then fell back into a deep sleep.

Cynthia still slept. She moved closer to Steve, feeling the firmness of his body. Steve drew her closer and marveled at her body. Although Cynthia gave the impression of being slightly built, there was an aura of physical well-being beneath her deceptive exterior. The slenderness of her body was often mistaken for weakness. Gradually, observers detected the details of her strength. A sensual pair of lips, a bit too thin, were evident. Her blue eyes, strong and deep, were a subtle mirror of her lively personality. Most men in time realized that Cynthia Wellman was an exciting woman. Many wives were disturbed by Cynthia's presence. Women realized she was a possible threat to their marriages. Instinctively, they realized Cynthia could have any man she wanted. She never did anything to cause talk; her actions were those of a properly married woman. Yet, men slavered like hound dogs when she walked by.

"Something about that Wellman woman."

"You feeling it, too?"

"Bet my best horse that she's not satisfied."

"Been thinking that myself. Can't figure out what there is about her that makes me think that way."

"She's looking for something she ain't found."

"That's Steve Wellman's wife. Been married some time and ain't no young'uns."

"Something about that woman . . ."

Six years before, as the daughter of an Indiana homesteader, Cynthia lived placidly on the isolated prairie. She had been educated by her mother and, that summer, made plans to attend the female seminary in Vincennes in the fall. These plans were changed when a dozen Indian braves sneaked off a reservation in Ohio and rode west on a raid. They were led by an elderly medicine man, Running Bear, who claimed to have fought with Laulewasikaw the Prophet at the battle of Tippecanoe. Running Bear claimed to know the Prophet's secrets for turning bullets away by magic charms. The young Indians had heard of their fathers and uncles being killed by white man's bullets at Tippecanoe. They questioned the power of the Prophet's magic. Running Bear explained the magic had been ruined when a squaw touched one of the Prophet's magic amulets.

Satisfied with this explanation, the Indians bolted the reservation. They stole horses and rode west into Indiana, killing whoever they met along the trail. Cynthia's father was clearing land out back of the cabin when the raiders came riding up. He was killed with a single blow from an Indian tomahawk. While an Indian remained with his body, planning to remove his scalp, the remainder of the Indians lay siege to the cabin.

Helga Horstman, Cynthia's mother, was a stout woman of German ancestry. Although she had misgivings about leaving western Pennsylvania, Helga came west in a wagon with her husband. They filed a claim on a homestead north of Albany, Indiana. Their first home was a small dugout in the side of a hill. The first year, working from dawn to dust, they cleared eleven acres of land of the trees, brush and undergrowth. The second year they built a log cabin.

Helga was boiling clothes in the yard behind the cabin when the Indians came riding up. She looked around for Cynthia, saw the girl was inside the cabin. At that moment, an eager brave leaped off his pony and ran toward Helga. His tomahawk was raised high above his head, ready to strike. Helga grabbed a pail, dipped it into the iron kettle of boiling lye water. She threw the hot liquid onto the Indian's face. Screaming with pain, the Indian sprawled down on the ground. His fingers clawed at his burning eyes. Before the main group of Indians could reach her, Helga knocked her wash kettle off its stand. Thirty gallons of scalding water splashed over the fallen Indian brave. He was whimpering with pain when Helga ran into the cabin, bolted the doors and picked up her husband's hunting rifle.

The Indians eyed their fallen comrade. Running Bear had promised his magic amulets would protect against the white man's bullets. They looked down at the scalded brave and wondered about the medicine man's protection. When Running Bear suggested easier prey could be found elsewhere, the group rode west. They left the fallen Indian in the back yard of the Horstman cabin.

Helga waited until the Indians passed out of sight over the western prairie. She took Cynthia's trembling hand and hurried on foot to the cabin of their neighbor, Lars Jensen, a distance of eight miles. Midway there, Helga began to complain of chest pains. When they stopped and rested, Helga's breath came in hard, tight gasps. She complained of pains in her forearms, a dull throbbing in her lower neck. With darkness falling, Helga sent Cynthia ahead to the Jensen homestead. Helga leaned back against the trunk of a small elm tree. She watched Cynthia run across the flat land toward the Jensen farm. Without emotion, but wishing her life had a better ending, Helga closed her eyes, dropped her head forward, and died.

Lars Jensen refused to return for Helga that night. He paced the floor of his dugout, talked about the spirits of

Odin, night beasts and death from Indians. Cynthia lay awake most of the night, praying for her mother. The next morning, Jensen saddled his mule and rode off. He found Helga Horstman's body and, with a pick and shovel, dug a shallow grave. He went on to the Horstman farm and buried Cynthia's father. He milked the Horstmans' cow, fed the pigs and closed the door to the cabin. When he returned home, Jensen drew his wife aside.

"I buried them both," he whispered. "Wolves got to them last night. Their bodies were awful. We must never tell their girl about that."

"Poor orphan child," clucked Mrs. Jensen in her native language.

That morning, Lars Jensen rode into Albany and reported the Indian raid. The local men formed a militia troop and headed west after the marauders. They were led by a middle-aged storekeeper, Raymond Detwiller, who rode at the head of the column on his black and white horse. Detwiller owned the only store in Albany that extended credit to the homesteaders. Few men argued with the merchant when he put out a call for volunteers. One homesteader had refused to join Detwiller on a chase after two river pirates the previous summer. The reluctant homesteader lost his credit at the store and, within a few months, gave up his claim and headed home to New Jersey.

Three days later, Detwiller led his men into the yard of the Jensen farm. While the volunteers watered their horses, the storekeeper went inside the dugout to talk with Jensen.

"Got every last one of them," Detwiller said proudly. "Caught them camping down in a draw about twenty miles from here. Killed all of them except the old hoodoo man. He was too drunk to fight. Passed out. Slept right through the whole battle. We took a vote and decided to hang him. Got what he deserved. Now everybody can get back to work."

Lars Jensen asked, "What about the Horstman young'un?"

Detwiller stared at the homesteader. "Ain't she got relatives?"

"Not any she knows about."

"Can you take her in?"

Jensen gestured around the dugout. "We ain't got enough room as it is."

"Well, she can't live alone out here." Detwiller frowned. "That's a nice place the Horstmans got. Too bad you ain't got a boy old enough to marry the Horstman girl."

"I mentioned she ought to get married."

"How'd she feel about it?"

"Said everyone around here is smelly and dumb."

Detwiller nodded. "I can't argue that with her. How old is she?"

"Fifteen next month."

"Right pretty woman, I'd say." Detwiller stroked his chin. His mind traveled over the options available. "I got nine kids at home. We sure can't take in another mouth to feed. Maybe she'll have to be sent to an orphan's home."

Jensen smiled with relief. "Fine with me. You handle it, Mister Detwiller. You know how these things are done."

The storekeeper got up and walked out of the dugout. Cynthia was in the yard, playing with one of the small

Jensen children. He called the girl to the side of the yard, explaining she would have to leave the homestead and go to a home for orphan girls.

"I'll find you a nice one," Detwiller said. "Presbyterians have a place back in Ohio that's supposed to be real nice."

"I got a home," Cynthia said.

"You can't live there by yourself."

"I'll manage."

"Wouldn't be fitting for a young girl out here." Detwiller's expression indicated certain subjects were better left unspoken between a man and woman.

"I'll get along," said Cynthia.

"You need a man."

Cynthia shook her head in an obstinate gesture.

"They're dumb," she said. "they don't take baths."

Detwiller noticed the glint of determination in her eyes, the forward jut of her chin.

"You'll do as I say, young lady," he declared. He grabbed Cynthia's arm and started toward the dugout, pulling her behind him. "You need a talking to, for sure."

Cynthia screamed, her hand coming around, nails raking Detwiller's face. The storekeeper cursed. His grip loosened on her arm. He stepped back and stared speechlessly at the girl. He wiped the blood on his face with the back of his hand. He stared with wonder at the liquid redness of his hand.

"You . . . you . . ." he stammered, lurching toward Cynthia.

"Keep your distance." The man's voice was soft.

Detwiller whirled around. "Don't butt in, Wellman. This girl needs taking down a peg or two. She's got to go to an orphan's home."

"Keep your hand off her," the man said.

Detwiller frowned. "I'm leader of this militia troop and—"

"You're not being fair to the girl."

Her face pale and luminous, Cynthia moved away from the two men. She noticed the young man who had accosted Detweiller was a shabbily dressed, yet neat, youth about eighteen years old. He wore a black hat over his sandy hair. He moved with a peculiar graceful flamboyant manner. She studied the stranger a little closer, noticed the muscular strength of his shoulders beneath his homespun shirt, the dancing laughter in his blue eyes. His eyes provided a focal point for his tanned face. It was not a handsome face. His square nose, wide lips and heavy sandy eyebrows looked slightly awry. His forehead was tanned and, on the side, was peeling from the sun. It was apparent that he spent much of his time in the outdoors. His hands were long, the fingers callused, and yet the nails were clean.

In turn, the stranger appraised Cynthia and smiled. She was not as buxom as most girls, yet there was a determined stubbornness in her expression. He said, "I'm Steve Wellman, ma'am. What seems to be the problem?"

"I . . . I . . ." Cynthia faltered.

Detwiller wiped his face with his handkerchief. "She can't stay on her folks' homestead."

Wellman asked, "You want to stay there?"

"No place else to go," answered Cynthia, "except an orphan's home."

Detwiller's smile was cunning. "You've been thinking about homesteading," he said tentatively to the young

31

man. "The Horstman place is the finest in this area. A man could move on there and get a head start. Why don't you marry this girl?" His hand gestured toward Cynthia.

Wellman smiled. "Ain't sure I want to get married."

"Me neither," Cynthia said defiantly. She dropped her head, looked down to the ground.

Detwiller giggled nervously. "Solves a lot of problems, it does. Miss Horstman gets a husband. You get yourself a going homestead."

Cynthia glanced shyly at Wellman. "I got certain requirements for a husband."

"Spell them out," Detwiller said heartily.

"He's got to take a bath at least once a week."

Detwiller stared at the girl. "Even in winter?" he asked.

Cynthia nodded. "Whenever he starts smelling."

Detwiller turned to Wellman. "What about it?"

"'Spect I could do that."

"What else?" The storekeeper looked sharply at Cynthia.

"My man should be smart."

Wellman frowned. "I didn't get much schooling. Guess that leaves me out."

Cynthia added hastily, "Or be willing to let me teach him some book learning."

"That sounds fair," said Detwiller.

"I'd like to know how to write my name," said Wellman.

Detwiller rubbed his hands together. "Sounds like we may be having a wedding."

"One more thing," said Cynthia.

"You're awful fussy." The storekeeper's tone was stern.

"My man has to be gentle," Cynthia went on. "I don't ever want to be hit by my husband."

Detwiller's expression was that of utter bewilderment.

"A husband has to run things," he said. "Women get funny ideas sometimes. They start nagging a man and have to be put in their place. Women and kids require a strong hand—"

"Fair enough," interrupted Wellman. He smiled at Cynthia. "You have any more rules?"

Cynthia blushed under his gaze. "You willing to have me?"

"Yes ma'am."

"I reckon we better get married," Cynthia replied.

Detwiller clapped his hands. "You-all come into town and we'll hunt up the preacher right away. No need to delay things. We can have some little celebration after the ceremony. If there's time, my wife will bake a wedding cake."

"That would be nice," Cynthia said. "I'm sorry to have scratched you, mister . . ."

"Detwiller." He laughed with mock gaiety. "Figure your husband will have a time with a little ball of fire like you. Now, let's get started—"

"I have one more question," Cynthia interrupted.

"What's that?" asked the storekeeper.

Cynthia looked into Steve Wellman's face.

She said, "I need to know my husband's name."

Detwiller laughed. "Guess I forgot to introduce you folks. This is Steve Wellman. And your bride is Cynthia Horstman, Steve."

"Pleased to meet you," Cynthia said, extending her hand shyly.

Steve shook her hand with elaborate care. "Glad to

know you, ma'am. I hope we can get along."

"I'll do my best." She smiled.

He nodded. "A man can't ask for anything more'n that."

They were married that afternoon in Albany and, after a brief reception, borrowed a carriage from Raymond Detwiller to go back to the Horstman farm. As dusk approached, they rolled into the yard. Cynthia rushed inside to clean up the house, while Steve unhitched the team. After the horses were watered and fed, he walked around the homestead, inspecting the barn, judging the condition of the fields, checking out the garden. When darkness made it impossible to see, he walked shyly into the log cabin.

Cynthia blushed when he stepped into the house.

"Dinner's cooking," she said quietly.

"Smells good."

"I barely had time to meet your folks this afternoon."

He nodded. "You'll get to know them."

Cynthia's face reddened to a deep crimson. "I'd better get your supper," she said, moving off toward the large cast iron stove.

She busied herself with preparing food. Her mind dwelled on her ignorance about what took place between a man and his wife. Cynthia knew surprisingly little about marriage. She had never received instructions from her mother and, living out on the prairie, seldom had contact with other girls her age. She had some clue as to what rituals transpired in the marital bed. The interior walls of the cabin were thin. On certain nights she could hear the heavy rustle of movement in her parents' bed. Once, she had slipped out of bed and crept through the darkness to peek into their room. Dimly, she saw the vague form of her mother lying on her back in the featherbed. Her nightgown was pushed up around her waist. Her father's body loomed over her mother, pumping up and down vigorously for several minutes. With a sudden heavy sigh, her father stopped moving and rolled over on his side of the bed.

Cynthia knew men and women probably coupled like animals. She had seen roosters mount their hens, pecking menacing at squawking heads. She knew there was something about horses and cows, although her parents had forbidden her to watch. As she finished cooking their first dinner together, Cynthia wondered where Steve would put his thing. Was she supposed to lay back like her mother? Maybe that was just for older people. She wouldn't like doing it like the two dogs that had got together in the churchyard that Sunday morning. She didn't think being stuck together would be much fun. The preacher and male members of the congregation had chased the dogs away, while the ladies properly averted their faces.

Surprisingly, Cynthia's fears were without basis. After dinner, Steve Wellman told her to forget cleaning up the dishes. He drew her to his side, kissing her lips gently and chastely. He took her in his arms and stroked her hair. "You've had a hard time," he whispered with solicitude.

"Steve, Steve!" She told him. "I'm lucky to have found you. I wish I knew more about being a proper wife."

He kissed the tip of her nose. "We got plenty of time for that."

She almost cried. "But I don't want to ruin your wedding night."

Later, Steve went outside while she undressed, put on

her gown, and slipped into bed. She pretended to be asleep when he came into the room and undressed. She lay still and rigid when he lay down beside her. She trembled when his arm came over and lay gently on her stomach. Suddenly, her awful fears vanished. Cynthia opened her arms to the stranger who was her husband. With a great rush of affection, she helped him consummate their marriage.

Afterward, she asked, "Was I all right?"

"Beautiful," he said with sincerity. "How was I?"

She hesitated. "I've got no way of knowing. Maybe we should do it again."

Steve laughed and hugged her.

"I think we're going to do just fine," he said.

"Me too," Cynthia whispered.

THREE

Steve Wellman smiled as he jumped down from his wagon. He grabbed the iron rim of a rear wheel, inhaled the fresh morning air and looked around the encampment. At least a hundred wagons were parked on the campground east of the town of Independence. These wagons would remain parked there until the emigrants laid in their supplies, organized or joined a wagon train and prepared for the trip to Oregon. Horses needed to be shod for the last time. Salt, pepper, bacon, sugar or honey, needles, thread, a thousand things needed to be bought at the general stores in town. A man might buy an extra rifle, maybe go so far as to purchase a new dragoon revolver. Women laid in an extra mirror, some yard goods, hard rock candy for the children or a few toys to prevent the first bleak Christmas in Oregon from being without store-bought presents.

Once the wagons were outfitted, the train organized, the emigrants moved through Independence. They camped out in the Kaw Valley and waited for the grass to green up along the trail. Spring was late that year of 1848. Two thousand men, women and children were beset with anxiety. Everyone talked about the two thousand miles to Oregon, the best routes, the quickest way. The early wagons had arrived in March, when the wild turkey gobbled and strutted in the woods. Others had arrived in April, during the rainy season when the wild fowl flew north. It was now the first week of May and the upland plovers nested across the prairies. Each day, more wagons rolled into the campground. Neighbors ran out to greet the late arrivals, laughing at their tardiness in reaching the rendezvous. Steve Wellman noticed several wagons had pulled in behind his rig, although he had been parked for only a few hours. He saw men and women waving to each other, recognizing that friendships were formed quickly on the frontier. Families were becoming acquainted. Men were taking measure of their neighbors' abilities. The gradual sifting and shifting of social values had started. Knots and groups of men were gathered around the encampment, all discussing the opportunities to be found in Oregon.

Behind him, Steve heard Cynthia moving around in the wagon. She had awakened with a smile on her face, evidence of her determination to survive. In the six years since their marriage, he had learned his wife's mind was a unique and different phenomenon.

"I can push things way in back," Cynthia told him one afternoon. "Shove them off to the side and never worry about it. Saves a lot of time because I don't have to bother about something. I just accept things that come along and don't fret and chew over them like other women."

She was not fretting over the deaths of the Benders. That had happened yesterday afternoon and, after a

38

night's sleep, Cynthia had pushed the horror from her mind. After he watered his oxen, saddled his horse, Steve had returned to the wagon. Cynthia was bent over the wide plank wagon bed. Her slender fingers picked up an array of needles tossed down by the robber. She looked up when he came swinging under the canvas top.

"You going to town?" she asked.

"If you're feeling all right."

She glanced around the dimness for sign of a needle. "You said something about telling the law about what happened yesterday."

"It should be reported."

"Don't bring our names into it," Cynthia said quickly. "What happened out there was awful. No other way to describe it. But those people are dead now and nothing's going to breathe life into their bodies. Steve, I don't want people to know I killed a man. Something like that attaches itself to a woman, follows her until her dying day. We're starting a new life out in Oregon. I don't want people to whisper that I killed a man. Don't want little kids following me on the streets and asking about how I did it. When you talk with the law, you tell them you heard about this from someone else."

"I'll probably do that," he answered, thinking mostly of humoring her.

Cynthia raised her head. "Listen to me, Steve," she said with firmness. "We've been married for six good years. We had a good home back in Indiana, although I admit the money was tight."

"Ever since the panic in 1837." He recalled the expression on Raymond Detwiller's face when the merchant took title to their homestead. Six hundred in cash for the cabin, milk cows and thirty cleared acres.

"I wasn't fond of leaving there, but you already know that," Cynthia continued. "Maybe men have more adventure in their blood. Maybe they want to see what lays over the next mountain." She came close to him and held her head against his chest. "I'm being a dutiful wife. Don't do something to mark me for life."

Steve caressed the back of her head, gently running his hand across the fine long strands of hair. "I'll do it your way," he said. "Maybe we don't even have to report it. Might not even be any law in Independence."

Cynthia swallowed hard, raised her eyes to his face. "Then get out of here, Steve Wellman. Let a woman clean up her home—if this creaky old wagon can be called that. Now, shoo!"

Laughing, he slapped her on the hip and set out for town.

Wellman mounted his horse and turned the animal westward toward town. He rode easily, a born horseman astride a compact, short-coupled, cat-hammed steed of coal black color, with a dashing forelock reaching almost to his red nostril. The heavily embossed saddle with silver concho decorations was unfamiliar that far to the north. Few people had seen the thin leather braided bridle with a frontlet band and large bit, or the massive spurs with jingling rowel bells. Steve had captured the horse during the Mexican War when he had felt the call to march with Scott, Taylor and Doniphen. He was with the troops commanded by General Zachary Taylor when they fought and won the battle of Buena Vista on February 23, 1847. For several hours, a force of 5,000 Americans stood firm against the assault of General Santa Anna's 20,000 troops. When the Mexicans acknowledged defeat, Steve spied the black horse on the battlefield. The animal became his prize for the long hours of bloody fighting. Although he pretended otherwise, Wellman was always pleased by the attention given to his Spanish mount.

Riding toward town, he gave the appearance of being a flamboyant man of the saddle. Few observers would have guessed he was a dirt farmer from Indiana. He wore close-cut leather trousers, polished black boots, a broad black hat of brushed beaver. His clean-cut, laughing eyes, his impassive face stamped him as a gentleman.

Wellman noticed the weather was dark and menacing to the west. Great masses of black thunderclouds were moving from west to east, throwing a greenish pall over the landscape. The white canvas tops of wagons took on a greenish-gold cast. The earth, wagons, horses and people seemed to shrink under the towering dark mist. Westward beyond the Kaw Valley, Wellman saw jagged flashes of sheet lightning dart across the sky.

The road into Independence was more tumultuous than he expected. It seemed as if every man, woman and child in the east had gathered there that spring. Two thousand souls were headed for Oregon, the new *El Dorado*. Oregon was a land of fertile green valleys, warm weather and rich black soil. Or so everyone said. It was a place where a man could prosper, could sink his roots and become a part of a new land.

Wellman was still a half mile from Independence when he noticed a crowd of emigrants in a vacant field. Two men stood rigidly on opposite ends of the clearing. They were candidates to captain a wagon train to Oregon. Members of the train voted by lining up behind their favored candidate. Wellman smiled wryly at the long line of emigrants gathering behind a bearded man in homespun shirt and trousers. His opponent, on the other side of the field, had only a half dozen men standing behind his back. He looked sour and unhappy.

Past the clearing, Wellman came to a dirty tent erected beneath a large elm tree. A large keg of whiskey rested on two sawhorses in front of the makeshift saloon. Several emigrants lounged about the tent in various degrees of drunkenness.

A thin man with a pock-marked face waved to Wellman.

"Come on in, pilgrim," the man yelled. "Have a free drink on the house before you head to Oregon."

Wellman smiled at the man without breaking stride. He knew about the rascals and thieves who came to Independence each spring to prey on unsuspecting travelers. More than one emigrant, Wellman had heard, had lost their life savings to a rogue during a crooked gambling game. Seeking even easier prey, the charlatans and conmen offered drugged liquor to emigrants. When the pilgrims passed out, they were robbed and tossed into the Missouri River.

"Watch out for the crooks," an old-timer in St. Louis had cautioned him. "Some of them even have wagons. They ride along posing as emigrants to Oregon. Use their wives and girl friends to lure a man into drinking too much whiskey. A chile gets a little too much, they take his poke. Some folks say the fattest catfish in the world can be found downriver from Independence. That's because they've been fed so much pilgrim meat. So watch yourself out there, young feller, and don't mess with the bad ones."

Independence was a mass of confusion. Hundreds of

people, four times that number of animals, scores of wagons could be seen in the streets. The '48 Company, a group of wagons from Sangamon County, Illinois, were lined up along the edges of the street. Oxen bellowed, horses brayed. Lean boys in overalls, brown and barefoot girls in calico dresses ran through the crowd shouting gaily. Lean dogs yelped and raced through the turmoil. Chickens clucked from the coops attached to the side of wagons. Women in slatted sun bonnets gossiped on the sidewalks, in the stores, or sat impassively on the high front seats of wagons and looked down at the crowd.

The noise of bells, animals, creaking wagons and the ring of the blacksmith's hammer added to the din. On one corner, a group of Kansas Indians in ragged blankets danced for a crowd of amused emigrants. Hordes of men and women moved in and out of the stores and shops. They carried boxes, packages, bags and cartons of merchandise. U.S. Army soldiers moved through the teeming streets, talking with the emigrants, eyeing the young girls, laughing at jokes, telling the emigrants of their experiences on the plains. People laughed and giggled, raising their voices more than necessary, feeling the spirit of adventure. They would soon be on a journey through the wilderness that led to the land of milk and honey.

Wellman pulled his horse into a livery stable. He swung easily out of the saddle, his hand on the tall, broad Spanish horn. He tossed the bridle over the animal's head, which seemingly anchored the horse in spite of the noise. A stablehand eyed the mount with admiration.

"You're a good judge of horse flesh," the livery operator said, stepping from his office. "I'd be willing to buy him."

"Not for sale," Steve smiled. "Just want to leave him here until I see some people."

The man nodded. "That we got, pilgrim. More people than anybody knows what to do with. And the wagons just keep coming. If I wasn't tied down with my wife and kids, I'd head for Oregon myself."

Behind him, Steve heard a loud shout. He turned and saw a column of huge Santa Fe freighter wagons maneuvering through the street. Bearded bull-whackers hollered at their oxen, cracking long whips over the heads of their slow-moving animals. The wagons creaked under the load of supplies headed for the southwest along the Santa Fe Trail.

Dark-skinned Spanish cowboys on sleek horses rode alongside the wagons. They were the *caballeros* who guarded the Sante Fe caravans against raids by white renegades and hostile Indians. They rode easily on their Spanish saddles. Their faces were shaded by tall sombreros favored by the southwesterners. Inlaid silver glittered from the pommels of their saddles, spurs, gunbelts, pistols and rifles. Their trousers were worn tight to the legs, flaring out above their rich decorated boots.

A caballero reined in his horse and rode over to the livery stable. His dark eyes appraised Wellman's dress, then traveled along the lines of his horse.

"A beautiful animal, *senor*," said the caballero with a Spanish accent.

"Thank you."

"Are you a Texican?" The man leaned forward.

"Indiana. I'm headed for Oregon."

The man tipped his hat. "May the virgin be with you." He wheeled his horse and rode off after the caravan.

Wellman gave instructions to the livery hand to feed his horse. He left the barn and strode down the sidewalk. The front of each store was piled high with wooden crates and boxes. Sweating men struggled to load supplies onto the wagons. Somewhere a shot rang out, then a loud shout followed by angry curses. The saloons in Independence were full of celebrating emigrants drinking to their trip westward. Wellman moved aside quickly when two men in buckskins came rushing out of a dim tavern. Like rampaging barbarians, they bellowed lustily at the darkening sky. Each man carried a long-barreled rifle cradled in his arms, a Green River trapping knife on his belt. The youngest of the mountain men stepped deliberately into Wellman's path.

"Look at the fancy dude," the man cried out. He grinned wolfishly at Wellman, then bowed elaborately from the waist.

Wellman started to step around the man. The trapper moved his shoulder and bumped hard against Wellman's body.

"Didn't hurt you, did I?" The trapper grinned broadly.

"No problem." Wellman grinned nervously and started to walk away.

The trapper blocked his path. "Maybe I dirtied up your fancy clothes."

"You barely touched me."

The trapper grimaced. "You want to fight, pilgrim?"

The older of the two trappers stepped between them.

"Leave him alone, Paul," the man growled to his companion. "No need causing trouble."

"Shit, Sam," complained the young trapper. "Bunch of sissies here. Nobody wants to fight. Take a look at this here chile" —his hand gestured toward Wellman— "all

45

duded up like one of those Spanish cowboys from down around Taos or Santa Fe. Maybe this dude would like to go for a free-style romp."

The older man smiled at Wellman. "My friend's had a bit of lightning. Always gets in a fighting mood when he gets liquored up."

The young man drew himself fully a head taller than Wellman. His brown eyes danced with amusement at Wellman's discomfort. "Don't you like fighting, pilgrim?"

"Not unless I have to." Wellman paled under the young giant's stare.

"You going to Oregon?" asked the older man.

"I hope to get there."

"Then you'd better get into a fighting mood, pilgrim," interupted the blond giant. "There's a heap of trouble twixt here and there. Indians are meaner than a hound dog passing chain and getting ready to let loose with the hook. Rattlesnakes as big around as a whiskey barrel and longer'n those wagons parked over there. Two-legged and four-legged wolves wanting a piece of your tail. Deserts that ain't seen a drop of water since Noah's flood. Mountains so high they stop the clouds from going over. Mountain cats, panthers, enough buffalo to turn your backbone to jelly. And if that ain't enough, you got old Brigham and his Mormons. They got a crew called the avenging angels who protect their heathen faith. See this scar?—" The man pulled up the sleeve of his buckskin jacket. Steve Wellman saw a violent red spot just above the giant's wrist. "That was put there by one of Brigham's avenging angels. I got the cuss, skinned him with my Green River. So I figure you won't make it past the coast of Nebraska."

Steve's face was impassive. "I'll take my chances."

"You got a woman?" asked the older trapper.

"A wife."

The older man tugged at his bushy black beard. "Come on, Paul," he admonished his friend. "Quit bothering the pilgrim. He's a family man."

Suddenly, the tall mountain man leaped forward, throwing his arms around Wellman's body. He lifted Wellman off the sidewalk, gripping him in a tight bear hug. Without an outward sign of exertion, the trapper raised Steve high into the air. He looked up with a whimsical expression.

"You're all right, pilgrim," the young man hiccuped. "Like the rest of these Oregon doo-dad travelers. Greenhorns by the barrel. Maybe you'll be a lucky one and get to the promised land, get your little farm and grow turnips." He laughed with evident humor as he dropped Wellman down onto the sidewalk.

"No offense," the older trapper said quickly.

"None taken," Steve replied, straightening his shirt.

"My name's Paul Spurlock." The younger man extended his hand. Wellman took it. "My partner here is ole Sam Lawson, the best mountain man, trapper and general do-nothing that ever run a line of traps on the Siskedee River. We been away from civilization longer'n we can remember. Trapping what's left of the beaver."

Sam Lawson extended his hand. Wellman felt his palm disappear into the mountain man's grasp.

"Don't pay no attention to this young pup," Lawson said with sincere friendship. "He ain't spent much time in a civilized place."

Spurlock drew himself up with an expression of mock anger. He glared down at his partner with amusement.

"Dang, Sam. Just 'cause you were born in a house with a real roof on it," he sputtered. "That don't mean you can lord it over us poor folks."

"We're in Independence for a good time," Lawson said. "Been trying to drink these places dry. I must be getting old. Can't make a dent like I used to."

"Want to drink with us?" asked Paul Spurlock.

Wellman hesitated. "Some other time. I got some errands to handle."

Spurlock bristled. "You won't drink with us?"

"I got to get hooked onto a wagon train."

The young trapper's eyes narrowed. His face took on a foxlike craftiness. "Trains are all filled up."

"Maybe they'll let me tag along with one."

Sam Lawson belched. "Ought to think about making up your own train, mister . . . mister. . . ."

"Steve Wellman."

"That's a good idea," said Spurlock. He eyed Wellman with speculation. "Sam and me gave up beavering. Ain't enough peltries to make a decent living. We're in the guide business, letting our services out to a wagon train. Trouble is, we ain't had no takers this year. You don't find a train, look us up. We'll get you there before the snow flies."

"I'll remember that," Wellman promised.

"You get interested, look us up," Spurlock went on. "Might take a day to get us sobered up. We'll guide you all the way to Oregon City if you organize a train."

Lawson put his arm around Wellman's shoulder. Together, they turned toward the street teeming with emigrants and wagons. "Look at those fools anxious to get out on the trail," Lawson said gravely. "Ain't one in a dozen knows what's ahead. Going to Oregon is a giant task. A man could start the biggest store in the world with what's been dropped from the wagons. These fools travel so heavy they have to throw away most of their plunder. Me and Paul actually seen an honest-to-Jehoshaphat piano sitting on the side of the trail. Out by Scott's Bluff, it was. Some poor soul actually thought he could take a piano over the Oregon Trail. Funniest thing was an old squaw standing there playing that piano. Terriblest tune you ever heard."

Spurlock laughed. "Sam, I don't think that squaw ever had piano lessons."

Lawson looked around with mock bewilderment. "You suppose that explains her terrible playing?" He eyed Wellman with amusement. "What do you think?"

Wellman grinned. "He might have a point."

Lawson pulled up his buckskin trousers. "Look us up, Wellman. You need a guide, we'll get you there."

The two mountain men turned and shouldered their way back into the tavern. Wellman hurried along the sidewalk until his attention was attracted by a man standing on the back of an uncovered wagon. The man was dressed in a white dresscoat, red silk shirt and yellow cravat. The lower part of his black trousers were smeared with dried mud. He began to give a speech, raising his voice to attract a crowd.

"This is the greatest medical discovery of all time!" The speaker held an amber bottle in his right hand. "The greatest nostrum humanity will ever know. Yesiree, folks, this is the renowned medicine that everyone has been talking about in Europe. Dr. Honsetter's Golden Drops. Imagine being on the way to Oregon when your horse goes lame. An expensive piece of horseflesh that you have to leave on the trail. Friends, you can shoot that

49

horse, put the poor beast out of his misery. You can leave him alone in the great wilderness. Let the poor animal become the prey of wolves and mountain panthers. Or, friends, you can apply a single drop of Dr. Honsetter's medicine on the afflicted hoof. The animal will recover within minutes. God forbid! The plague may break out in your wagon train. A drop of this golden elixir will protect you and your loved ones from death by this dreaded scourge. If your baby has the colic—"

The speaker paused and eyed the growing crowd. "Step closer, folks," he smiled. "Yes, if your baby has the colic, your dog has distemper or your wife has those troubles peculiar to women, these mysterious and magical golden drops will relieve the symptoms. Sickness, plague, pain will disappear under the power of this marvelous medicine. Dr. Honsetter wants every emigrant going to Oregon to have the benefits of this golden medical discovery. He has—"

A man whispered in Wellman's ear. "Watch your purse!"

Wellman made a sudden motion, wheeling around as he felt heavy pressure on his hip pocket. He grabbed the arm of a man standing near him, saw the startled expression on the man's face.

The pickpocket was a short, fat man with crooked teeth.

"Robber!" screamed the pickpocket.

"You're the thief," Wellman said.

"Robber!" The man screamed again. He hissed a whisper, "Lemme go!"

The crowd parted to form a circle around the two men. Wellman held the man's wrist. The pickpocket sneered, his round face twisting into a grotesque expression. His free hand slipped into the pocket of his jacket. Wellman jumped back when a knife flashed into view.

"Try to rob an honest man," snarled the pickpocket. "Heard about your kind, mister. Robbing honest farmers. I'm going to cut your gizzard out and feed it to the buzzards!"

The knife flashed in an arc toward Steve Wellman's stomach.

FOUR

Steve Wellman leaped backward. The blade sliced through the air a scant inch in front of his stomach. The fat man wheezed, looked surprised, and grinned crookedly. He licked his lips and started advancing toward Wellman. The crowd of onlookers pressed forward, blocking Wellman's retreat. He looked around wildly, his face pale and lifeless. No one made a move to stop the fight.

Knife held at his hip, the fat pickpocket moved forward. The tip of the knife blade was pointed at Wellman's stomach. The pickpocket's eyes dropped for an instant to measure the distance between the two men. Instantly, Wellman's fist shot out against the fat man's mouth. The man grunted with pain, falling back against the crowd. Wellman slammed two more blows on the man's face. The pickpocket retched, spitting blood. He gave the appearance of being hurt. Suddenly he came up with a furious speed. He drew the knife back to cut Wellman.

A hand shot out of the crowd and locked on the pickpocket's wrist. There was a flurry of moving bodies, then a short man with curly black hair drove his fist into the fat man's chest. Before the man could fall, the stranger's knee shot up into the pickpocket's groin. Screaming like a wounded animal, the pickpocket dropped to the ground. The stranger bent over and picked up the knife.

"Nothing wrong with a fair fight," said the stranger. He glared down at the fallen pickpocket. "But I won't stand by and see a thief kill an honest man."

The pickpocket groaned. "He's the thief," he lied with a hoarse gasp.

"I saw it all," said the stranger. "I warned this pilgrim that your hand was in his pocket."

Wellman appraised his benefactor. The stranger was of medium height and dressed in plain brown trousers, a white shirt, a red bandanna tied around his neck. Curly black hair hung over his ears in an uncombed mass. His full lips were cracked from prolonged exposure to the weather. They contained the hint of a slight smile, almost as if the man viewed life as a human comedy. When he spoke, the stranger revealed large white teeth in even rows.

The stranger was now addressing the crowd.

"This sculpin on the ground preys on honest folks," he announced in a lilting voice. "Watch the likes of him when they get close to you. He's a pickpocket who dips his mitts into an honest man's purse."

Several men in the crowd made an ominous sound.

"We don't need his kind!" shouted a farmer from Ohio.

"Get a rope!" shouted an emigrant from Virginia.

The pickpocket looked up in terror. He rolled over on his knees, trying to crawl to safety. Several men grabbed his fat body, pulled him to a standing position. A short man in a brown suit, reported to be a preacher from New Orleans, stepped forward and slapped the thief's face. "That's for going against the Lord's wishes," the man said in a cracking voice. "Thou shalt not kill sayeth the Lord and you were ready to kill an honest man." The preacher spat into the pickpocket's face.

A stern voice sounded on the edge of the crowd. An army lieutenant and two soldiers pushed their way through the emigrants. The lieutenant, about twenty-five with a ruddy complexion and sun-bleached hair, said in a firm tone: "We'll take him now. Everyone step back."

The two soldiers stepped forward and clamped handcuffs on the pickpocket.

"We've been looking for this one," said the lieutenant. His voice was disciplined. "Came upriver on a steamboat last night. Heard he was coming but he slipped away over at Westport Landing. He and his partner are the best pickpockets in St. Louis."

The fat man looked at the lieutenant with disgust. "Where's Benny?" he inquired in a sullen manner.

"Your partner's dead," answered the lieutenant. "He was shot by a farmer who saw Benny coming out of his wagon."

The pickpocket looked dumbfounded. "Benny dead?"

"This isn't St. Louis," the lieutenant said.

The curly-headed stranger eyed the lieutenant. "What'll you do with this rascal?"

"Hold him for the law." The lieutenant motioned for the soldiers to take the prisoner away. "There's law around here. But we have a hard time spotting every thief and rascal who comes into town. There's two thousand people crowded in here waiting to leave for Oregon. Some are good. Others are bad. A lot are in between those two places. I advise everyone to watch who they talk to, don't drink with strangers and stay out of the gambling and drinking tents outside of town. Not even the U.S. Army can help a man if he's acting like a fool."

The crowd murmured approvingly and started to break up. The lieutenant hastened away, walking with military rigidness. Wellman walked over to where the curly-haired stranger stood.

"You probably saved my life," he told the man.

The stranger smiled impishly. "Forget it, bucko. Maybe you'll have a chance to do the same for me."

"I'll do my best." Wellman extended his hand and introduced himself.

"I'm Mike Gorman. Michael Earl Gorman, to be precise." The man shook Wellman's hand with enthusiasm. "You headed for Oregon?"

"Yep."

"Hooked up with a train yet?"

Wellman shook his head. "I just got in last night. Haven't started looking around for one."

Mike Gorman grinned slyly. "I've been here for three days. All the regular trains are full up. I'm getting worried that the grass will green up and I'll be stuck here. Seems I ain't proper to join some of the trains."

Wellman looked bewildered. "Not right?"

"I'm an Irishman," Gorman went on. "Seems like this is the land of the free—except for Irishmen. Some people figure a man from the auld sod is one of God's dumber creatures. You've probably heard, maybe even told, a few of those Pat and Mike jokes. Seems that some people take them to heart."

"That shouldn't stop you from getting a train."

Gorman shifted and glanced down at his boots. "My religion is a problem."

"You a Mormon?"

Mike Gorman laughed. "Worse than that. I'm Catholic."

"A Papist?"

"Don't say that so loud," Gorman said urgently. He glanced furtively around to see if Wellman's words had been overheard.

"Let's walk over to a saloon," said Wellman. "I'll buy."

They went out into the street, crossing the crowded thoroughfare to a small stone building standing on a corner. They went into the dimly lit interior, purchasing cups of whiskey, walking out the back door. They dropped down on a wooden bench and began to talk.

"Most people headed for Oregon are Protestants," said Mike Gorman. "They don't want a dumb Catholic Irishman in their caravan. It just never occurred to me that would be a problem. All I was interested in doing was getting out of the Ohio Valley. Too much fever there. We lost our boy last year to it. Figured I'd better get out now before it got my wife or me."

"Change your name and religion until you get to Oregon." Wellman took a sip of the bitter whiskey. He coughed when the fiery liquid went down his throat. "Jesus, they sure don't age this stuff."

Mike Gorman grinned. "Maybe I'm crazy but I don't want to change my name."

"Why not?"

"I've done nothing to be ashamed of," the Irishman went on. "I'm a better man than most of these yahoos heading West. I wouldn't trade one good priest for a wagonload of these whoop-and-holler preachers. I haven't done anything wrong so changing my name, or being quiet about my religion, doesn't sit right with me."

They sat out back of the tavern, slowly sipping their cups of whiskey and developed the ritual of friendship. The tradition was as old as humanity; men who wore furs and lived in caves exchanged the idle talk that helped get a stranger's measure. They talked easily about seemingly inconsequential things, yet each question or answer provided a clue to the other's character. They discussed farming, drought, blizzards, bankers, landlords and the fact that money was hard to get, even harder to hold onto. They gave their opinions on the guidebooks printed for emigrants, deciding that most were written by men who'd never been to Oregon. Maybe the best idea was to depend on a good guide, although some trains were heading west without them.

Eventually they got around to talking about the Mexican war. Mike Gorman was interested in finding out about Wellman's experiences in the conflict. Wellman had not been away from the battlefield long enough to idealize the events of battle. He could remember vividly the look of pained incomprehension when he shot a Mexican infantryman in the shoulder. Or the dying moments—had it really only been a few minutes?—of the little girl shot by mistake during the battle of Buena Vista. He didn't like to talk about the battle of Matamoras, the fight for Monterrey, or the other skirmishes with the Mexican army. He was confused by the simplicity of the Mexican people, their stoic acceptance of strong military leaders. He didn't like the grinding poverty endured by the average peasant, or the illiteracy that existed everywhere he'd been in Mexico. The country had great natural beauty, grand cathedrals that made a man stand in wonderment. Mexico was a strange land, Wellman said.

Mike Gorman told about the beauties of Ireland, the persecution of the Catholics under the British tyrants, the pitfalls of trying to earn a living on a small farm. He had stolen money for passage to the United States, took it one night from a tax collector's strongbox. It wasn't right. Yet, it wouldn't be right to stay in Ireland and starve to death. A potato blight had hit his small farm, coming silently one spring, turning the spuds to rotten mush. People were starving over in the auld sod right now. If the pestilence kept hitting the potatoes, thousands more would starve.

"So I come to the United States and let a land agent sell me a farm on the Ohio River," said Gorman. "Lovely place. Rich soil. Just right for my wife, Molly, and myself. Then our first baby arrived—a fine boy who would grow up to farm the land when I got old. Crops were good. Throw a seed in the earth down there and it would sprout overnight. But, we had another blight: river fever. Seems like I've been running from some sort of blight for the last ten years. At least in Ireland, the potatoes go first. Along the Ohio, the kids are the first to come down with fever and die."

They did not lie to each other that afternoon. They shared an openness—an examination of mind, character and philosophy—that could only lead to the bonding of friendship. Mike Gorman had proven his character by stepping into Wellman's fight with the pickpocket.

Somehow, and he didn't know the way it would happen, Wellman knew they would travel to Oregon together.

Wellman looked into his empty cup. He stood up.

"Let's look into latching onto a train," he told Gorman.

They went back into the tavern, a rude stone hut that was lit by two small windows in front. The interior was dim. Wellman sat their cups on the bar made from rough-hewn logs. The tavern had started to fill up with customers. In the back, around a scarred square table, men played cards by the light of a single sputtering candle. Several men stood at the bar, mostly emigrants, drinking whiskey from tin cups. The proprietor came waddling over toward Wellman and Gorman. He was a robust man with an enormous belly, a pleasant round face and bloodshot eyes.

"Refill?" asked the bartender.

Wellman asked if the proprietor knew of a wagon train forming up.

The man picked up their cups, wiped them with a cloth. "Gents, you're the smartest two men I've met this week," he said in a hearty voice. "You're actually asking advice from someone who knows the situation in Independence." He eyed them with hooded lids. "Do you figure on taking my advice?"

"If it's good," answered Wellman.

"Fair enough, gents." The bartender waddled over to a keg of whiskey, drew two scant cups. He set them before his two customers. "On the house. This is my prime stock, although the best here is worse than most in St. Louis. So you're heading for Oregon?"

"If we get a train," added Gorman.

"Don't hurry," advised the bartender. "A lot of trains

are heading west without a guide. Depending on maps and books published back east. A whole wagonload of them books won't get you to Oregon. Saw one map with the Green River clear over on the Nebraska coast. It was that bad. But this damned fool thought he was a wagon master, fixing to lead his caravan of schooners to Oregon. Maybe they'll get there. Maybe not. I wouldn't take chances like that."

Wellman asked, "What would you do?"

The bartender eyed them speculatively. "Don't hurry," he repeated. "Stick around Independence until you find the right train. Don't get panicky and grab the first column headed out. It might be led by a madman— or worse, a damned fool. There are guides here in town. Good men. Find a train with a good man heading it up. Hire the best guide that your money can buy. Pay him well. Don't let him feel you're crooking him. Your life depends on him getting you through before the snow flies."

"You heard of any trains like that?" Wellman asked.

"Just a minute." The bartender walked down the room, refilled drinks for two emigrants. He returned and leaned over the plank counter. He brought his head forward, whispering quietly.

"Jim Bridger's in town," he said. "Ole Gabe is getting himself a lot of merchandise laid in. He runs a fort way out west. He'll be pulling out in a few days. Best mountain man in the business. Used to be a trapper and guide until the fur business started dying out. I'd talk to him about hitching onto his wagons, heading west to Ft. Bridger. That's what I'd do."

Wellman asked, "What about the rest of the way?"

"Let Bridger find you a good guide."

60

"I've heard of Bridger," said Wellman.

"So have I," Mike Gorman chimed in. "Think he'd take us?"

"Ole Gabe's a square shooter," replied the bartender. "He might under the right conditions."

"What might those be?" asked Gorman.

The bartender spread his hands expansively. "You'd have to talk to Ole Gabe about that."

"Where do we find him?" asked Wellman.

"Like I said, he's outfitting his wagons." The bartender winked conspiratorially. "But he always comes in here every morning about an hour after sunup. I make up some breakfast. We sit around and jaw about the good old days. We were trapping beaver twenty years ago when this country wasn't overrun by emigrants."

Wellman asked, "You were with Bridger?"

The bartender warmed to his subject. "Gentlemen, I have stood on the shores of California and felt the warm waters of the Pacific Ocean on my feet. My bucket has been dipped in the Columbia River, the Snake and a few more. I have seen the most beautiful land that God will ever create: majestic mountains, great valleys, and meadows that run for a hundred miles. I have also seen land made by the devil. Without water. Deserts that extend for hundreds of miles. Living was a lot easier in those days. You set out your Newhouse beaver traps and got ready to pack the pelts."

Gorman inquired, "How'd you get involved in furring?"

"Went upriver with the Rocky Mountain Fur Company," answered the bartender, a distant glint in his eyes. "That was owned by William Ashley and Andrew Henry. They put an ad in the *Missouri Gazette and Public*

Advertiser, a newspaper in St. Louis. Requested the services of a few enterprising young men to go into the wilderness. Ashley told me a few years later he wanted young men. We were actually not much more than boys. Older men wouldn't take the chance of being scalped by the Indians, killed by bears, or be willing to face the hardships of the fur trade. Young Jim Clyman signed on. Quit a job of surveying to do it. He's out in California right now, supposed to be a power there. Jim Bridger was an apprentice blacksmith. Charlie Sublette was the constable in St. Charles, Missouri. His pay wouldn't stretch from payday to payday. Charlie had to sell his bedstead to have a dollar in his pocket before we left. His brother, Willie Sublette, was just a lazy boy who hadn't done anything. But he made a fine trapper.

"But we also had some tough men with us out there. Hugh Glass once whipped a grizzly she-bear in a bare-handed brawl. Ed Rose was part Cherokee Indian, part black man. Kind of an interesting sort of guy. He had been a pirate and bandit down the Mississippi someplace. Never found a better man to have by my side in a fight. I even met the son of a U.S. president out there. Good ole hard-drinking Benjamin Harrison had been sent west. His family couldn't stand him at home. Had a terrible drinking problem; his carousing around disturbed his family. He come west and fit right with the trappers. Jeb Smith was another good man and, sometimes, Bridger and I wonder what happened to Tom Fitzgerald and Jim Beckwourth. Kit Carson come through a couple years back. We had a good time remembering the good old days. But"—the bartender looked sheepish—"I sound like an old man bothering a couple of young pups. You boys will rule the West now. Don't figure we can go back to what it was. But sometimes I sure wish we could."

Wellman said, "We'll stop by and talk with Bridger in the morning."

"Don't hurry," cautioned the proprietor. "Better leave for Oregon late with a good man than early with a fool. See you boys in the morning." He hastened off to tend to his customers.

The mass of dark clouds had passed over Independence when they left the tavern. The late afternoon sun was shining thinly as Gorman and Wellman rode back toward the wagon camp. Midway to the rendezvous, they met a wagon train pulling out. Slowly, swaying, stately, the ox teams came down the rutted road, drawing their fleet of canvas topped schooners. The oxen did not hurry, nor did they lessen their speed, but moved in a steady fashion. Gorman and Wellman halted their mounts beside the trail. They watched the wagons roll past. Forty-seven covered wagons made up the column. Outriders on horses, with rifles in scabbards, pistols holstered on their hips, guarded the flanks of the caravan. When the schooners had gone past, a large herd of cattle moved slowly westward. These animals were tended by men with long whips.

A barefoot boy of fourteen rode past on a mule. His eyes danced with excitement.

"Oregon or bust!" he yelled to the two men.

"We're headin' out!" cried a man on a horse. A large sheepdog raced along beside his mount.

Wellman and Gorman remained silent until the caravan had passed. Even then, they gazed down the trail as the wagons formed a white-topped serpent pointed west.

Gorman broke the silence. "Awful late in the day to be heading out."

"They'll camp tonight in the Kaw Valley," said Wellman. "Get an early start tomorrow."

They rode into the wagon camp, parting company at Gorman's wagon. They promised to meet and hunt down Jim Bridger the following morning. Cynthia was chatting with a woman in front of their wagon when Wellman rode up. She smiled and came running over to him. He filled her in on the details of his trip to town, purposely not mentioning his fight with the pickpocket. She gave him a pleasing smile when he mentioned forgetting to inform the law about the Benders.

"Everybody's so excited about Oregon," Cynthia said with enthusiasm. "It gets contagious. Steve, do you suppose there really is a paradise like that?"

He started to unsaddle his horse.

"Maybe there is, honey. Maybe there is."

FIVE

Hundreds of emigrants were ready to hit the trail. Their wagons were parked from the east side of Independence, all through town and over into the Kaw Valley. Independence had quadrupled in population in three weeks. Over on the Missouri River, the arrival of steamboats had brought the new town of Westport Landing. The wharves were covered with cargo. Even with these massive supplies brought up the snag-infested river from St. Louis, some merchandise was in high demand. A number of shortages developed. Black pepper was scarce. Camp stoves couldn't be bought at any price. Sunbonnets were sold out. Liniment—for both horses and men—was gone from the storekeepers' shelves. Hundreds of mules, horses and oxen had been brought in for the spring rendezvous. Even so, there were not enough animals to supply the demand for brute power.

Rumors flashed through the emigrant camps like prairie fire. Although Governor Lillburn Boggs's militiamen had driven the Mormons from Missouri in 1838-39, the specter of the saints frightened the emigrants. Two thousand Mormon wagons were headed west this very minute, some men claimed. They were heading out from Council Bluffs. Old Brigham Young—that devilish prophet—was leading the columns personally. The Mormons' oxen would devour every blade of grass along the trail.

". . . Better leave this very minute! The Mormons will get the grass!"

". . . Them saints will poison the water!"

". . . Lord! I heard it from a trader in from Taos. There's a big army coming out of Mexico. They're going to invade California, then move up and take Oregon!"

". . . England ain't going to let Oregon get away!"

". . . Know it for a fact. The Indians have been paid by the British to ambush our trains."

". . . 'Pon my honor! I know them Indians are waiting to kill us all."

". . . The government's quit giving donor grants."

". . . Land office is closed in Oregon City!"

". . . Take all the iron you can carry, neighbor! Worth more than gold in Oregon!"

". . . Army closed down Ft. Kearney. Indians are killing everyone out there!"

Day or night, in taverns or around campfires, wherever people gathered, an exchange of rumors started. Each man swore his story was based on absolute fact. Cousins, traders, trappers in from the West were the shadowy sources of information. Doubt grew in people's minds. Apprehensive men and women condemned the circulation of rumors. At the same time they spread lies and half-truths as verified fact. An undercurrent of uncertainty swept through the camps.

This sense of doomsday was heightened by a handful of itinerant preachers. These men of the cloth, many of them spellbinding orators, shouted the gospel on street corners, in makeshift tents and under a shade tree out in the valley. They whooped and hollered, praised the Lord, and urged the emigrants to repent. Most of the preachers were God-fearing men who fervently hoped to baptize the multitudes before they left for the wilderness. A couple of the preachers were confidence men preying on the anxiety of the people.

One morning out in the wagon camp east of Independence, a young girl named Hattie Gill fainted during breakfast. She came back to consciousness and claimed she had received a revelation from God. Hattie was a sallow, pimpled girl with stringy brown hair and sunken eyes. She had been hearing a buzzing in her head for several years. Back home in eastern Missouri, her mother had dismissed the girl's complaints as the ramblings of a child. Now out on the edge of the world, Gladys Gill accepted Hattie's statements as the truth. The girl converted her mother within a few minutes. Her father, Clay Gill, didn't cotton to any religious talk from his daughters, preachers or anyone else. He considered such discussions to be a waste of time.

Together, mother and daughter wandered through the wagon camp urging the migrants to repent. From time to time, Hattie fell into a trance and uttered gibberish. Her mother interpreted this babble as the word of God. Their new gospel appointed Hattie as a prophet, an angel sent down from heaven to lead the wagons to Oregon. Clay Gill went about his business without comment. Gladys roamed the camp, ranting to whoever would listen, preaching to the women during the day, holding prayer services at night. She abused the people who laughed at Hattie, declared God would strike them dead before they got halfway to Oregon. Within a few days the two women had gathered a flock of people known as True Christians. The group held a nightly meeting on the edge of the wagon camp in a small clearing.

That night, Steve and Cynthia Wellman left their wagon and went to hear Hattie preach. A couple of hundred men and women had gathered there by a large bonfire. Hattie walked into their midst like an angry cat. Her eyes blazed with murderous rage. She leaped up on a makeshift stage consisting of several wood planks sitting atop two large barrels. She paced back and forth and anxiously eyed the assembly.

"I am Hattie the Revelator of the Lord's Word—" she began.

"Get out!" cried a man. "You're a false prophet!" He explained to the group that he was an ordained minister of the Methodist faith.

Hattie's followers leaped to her defense.

"Liar!" yelled a zealot.

"God talks to Hattie!" cried a middle-aged woman.

The minister stepped to the front of the crowd. "This girl is confused," he announced. "The Bible says to beware false prophets."

Hattie glared down at the preacher.

"You should know a false prophet," the girl cried. "You're one yourself."

"God will punish you!" screamed the man.

Hattie held her Bible as a shield before her bosom. "I work for the true Lord. He reveals his words to me."

"You're working for the devil."

Hattie's reply was high and shrill. "I am the

Lord's angel."

A hawk-faced emigrant yelled at the preacher. "Let her speak her piece."

"We'll know the devil when we hear him," said another man.

Steve and Cynthia Wellman had pressed forward through the crowd. They now stood only a few feet from Hattie Gill. Her plain features were reddened by light from the bonfire. The girl was agitated, a grim tightness to her lips, a glint of blazing intensity in her eyes.

"Truth!" cried the preacher. "Speak God's truth and I'll be quiet."

The crowd hushed. Hattie Gill looked around. Her face became charged with deep emotion.

"You are all doomed to a fiery lake in hell," she cried. "God will puke you up for the devil to devour. Satan is walking in this camp. I've seen his ugly face peeking from behind trees. The people are listening to the devil. I saw a man playing a fiddle last night. Men are drinking whiskey and playing cards. There is lust in everyone's eyes for their neighbor's wives. Woe unto you, sayeth the Lord. I will smite you with a rod. I will chastise you. Your children shall be killed. The water between here and Oregon will be poisoned to the unbelievers. I will not be merciful to those who sin against my word. I will—"

"Tell 'em, sister Hattie," shouted a follower.

"Hallejulah!" yelled a woman. "Praise his name."

"My enemies are here tonight," Hattie went on. "There are sinners sowing the devil's word. This man—" she pointed to the Methodist preacher—"is the devil walking among us. We have allowed Papists into our campground. But the great God has chosen to spare anyone who becomes a True Christian. They will be shown a trail through the wilderness. They—"

Abruptly, without making a conscious decision to do so, Steve Wellman shouted up at the girl.

"You're mad!" Wellman cried.

A hulking man with eyes burning from spite rushed through the crowd. His face was set in fearful yet resolute fury. He grabbed Wellman by the shoulder.

"Be quiet!" he commanded. "Hattie is speaking the word of God."

"Get your hands off me," said Wellman angrily.

The man trembled. He released his grip. He urged, "Be quiet."

Ignoring the man, Wellman turned back to Hattie. The girl paced the top of the planking.

"We are forming our own train of True Christians," she announced. "This wagon train will have God's blessing. He will show the way to Oregon. God will be our guide. Those who are True Christians can join our train. The devil will destroy the unbelievers! The Holy Ghost will strangle their children whilst they sleep. The angels will chastise them because of their false beliefs. The sinners will be delivered into slavery amongst the Indian tribes."

"Praise the lord," shouted a woman. She brought her arms high above her head, clapping loudly. She began to shuffle around the clearing.

"Shout for the Lord," cried Hattie.

Steve Wellman took Cynthia's arm.

"Come on," he said. "Let's get away from here. I've heard too much of this madness."

They walked back to their wagon. While Cynthia prepared for bed, Wellman walked over to Mike Gorman's wagon. He spoke briefly with the young Irishman.

"I'd watch those people who think that girl is a prophet," Wellman advised.

Mike asked, "Something afoot?"

"She was comparing Catholics with the devil."

"That's just more of the same old prejudice."

"The girl is crazy," said Wellman.

"What about the people who're following her?"

"Crazy as bedbugs."

Mike said, "Surely they're not dangerous."

"I've seen the look of madness."

Gorman looked puzzled.

"Saw it back home," Wellman explained. "A homesteader and his wife settled way back on the prairie. Too far out to get into town much. Just the two of them lived out there. One morning the husband brought his wife to town. She'd been trying to kill him. I saw her after they tied her up. She had this strange sort of glaze in her eyes. Like she really didn't belong to the human race. She was talking about a ghost ordering her to kill her man. She would talk like that for a while, then go quiet. Like she was listening to a voice inside her head or something. I figured she was someplace far off. I get a cold chill up my back when I see that look in people's eyes."

Mike sounded alarmed. "Hattie got that look?"

"I almost froze to death at her meeting."

Mike crossed himself. "I'll kinda watch for them."

"Maybe I'm imagining things," Wellman went on. "She's got that look in her eyes. I spoke out against her while she was preaching. A man came over. He was ready to fight. He believed in Hattie and that same look was on him." He told Gorman about the True Christians forming their own wagon train.

Mike smiled, "Don't they know better than to have her

71

lead them?"

"Remember they're wound up tight."

"Sounds like they're brainless as well."

"Yes," said Wellman. "Maybe that's the right way to look at them. Mad people led by a mad girl. If you know people are crazy, you don't get surprised."

Gorman glanced around the camp. "When are they leaving with their train?"

"I suppose when enough people join them."

"Hope we're way ahead of that bunch."

They said good night and went back to their wagons.

Molly Gorman pretended to be asleep when Mike crawled into their wagon. She did not make a sound as he undressed. Even in the dimness of the wagon, she could see the compact muscular strength of her husband's body. He pulled up the covers and lay down beside her. Slowly, sleepily, she turned to him. Her round, firm satiny breasts pressed heavily against his chest. His response was warm and fierce, his mouth widening and coming down upon her lips.

Molly moved back for a moment. She took off her nightgown and dropped down nude beside him. They adjusted their bodies to fit each other. Mike moaned far back in his throat. His hands caressed the round, firm, smooth silkiness of her breasts. She pressed her mouth tighter against him, tongue darting out in tiny teasing probes. She felt his breath quicken, become heavier. His hand moved gently over her stomach, down her abdomen and cupped her firm hips.

Molly felt a fieriness growing inside her, a pounding intensity that demanded to be fed. She drew her mouth away from his, showered tiny little kisses on his face. Her fingers moved rapidly, twisting through Mike's curly hair. Her desire was a primitive appetite that cried out for release.

Molly's hand moved across Mike's hairy chest, fingers lingering there for a moment to tug at his body hair. Then, they traced a gentle path over his stomach, his abdomen. She was excited by that special hardness. A touch here, fingers moving like feathers. A gentle little pressure there. Now a squeeze in this spot, a light caress at that point.

"Lay back," Molly whispered.

She felt his hardness as her leg went over his body. She smiled down at her husband. He did not see the joy on her face. His eyes were closed tight, his face contorted by a mounting pleasure.

Afterward, Molly lay beside Mike. His arms were entwined around her neck. Enjoying a warm glow throughout her very being, Molly prayed fervently that this would be the time. She wanted desperately to be pregnant again, to feel the movement of life inside her.

"I'm wondering," Mike whispered.

"Yes, husband mine?"

"You being on top is pretty racy."

Molly giggled.

Mike asked, "What makes a proper Irish lady suddenly take up those wild positions?"

"You know I want to be pregnant."

"We both want that."

"I've been talking to some of the women." Molly kissed his nose. "Some of them say it helps if the woman is on top. The man's seed goes into her a lot further."

"That's a fact?"

"Lady two wagons down said she didn't get pregnant

for a couple years after they were married."

"That long?"

"Said she went to see a midwife. Some old woman who was older than anyone else in the area. The midwife said the best way of getting pregnant was for a woman to mount her husband. Swore it couldn't fail."

"Did she get with a baby?"

Molly giggled. "Twins. Two of the cutest little girls you'll ever see."

"Lord help us," Mike said with mock alarm.

"Something wrong?" Molly giggled.

"The way you perform, Molly, we ought to have triplets at least. Maybe a dozen or two."

"I want to get pregnant."

"Now I have found your motive," Mike said in a lilting Irish brogue, his accent exaggerated. "All this time I thought I was something special. Maybe had found some sort of magic that drove you wild. You've been an insatiable wench the past few months. Absolutely divine. Ready to tumble anytime a man had the hankering. Lately, I get the feeling that you're tumbling me. I step into the wagon and this wife of mine tears my clothes off. I look up from my work and here comes Molly with a gleam in her eye. All this while I figured it was that special thing I had." He chuckled.

Molly giggled and snuggled close to him.

SIX

Jim "Ole Gabe" Bridger was eating breakfast in the rear of the tavern the next morning. Bridger was a lean, middle-aged man with long salt-and-pepper hair. His face was absent of fat. Although Wellman expected to find a brutish quality in Bridger's eye, he discovered a glint of good humor and amusement. His face was darkened by a deep tan. The mountain man's skin was the consistency of parchment paper. This was due to many years of exposure to the elements in the wilderness. Bridger had prominent, thin ears that stuck out from the sides of his head. He was dressed in the traditional buckskin outfit of the Rocky Mountain trappers. His movements were fluid. Bridger wore a holstered Green River skinning knife on his hip. A beaded Indian necklace hung around his scrawny neck.

Wellman and Mike Gorman waited outside the tavern until Bridger finished his meal. After a few minutes the mountain man came out of the tavern. He wiped his lips with the back of his hand.

He asked, "You fellows want to see this chile?"

"Heard you were heading back to your fort," Wellman said. "Figured we'd like to go that far with you. The bartender told us you were the best man for that."

"I'm only going as far as my fort."

Gorman nodded. "Figured you might help us find a guide for the rest of the way."

Wellman told the mountain man about his meeting with Sam Lawson and Paul Spurlock.

"Spurlock's already gone," Bridger said. "Hooked on as guide to a train yesterday. Lawson's still in town."

"Is he good?" asked Gorman.

"Better than most," Bridger replied. "He drinks a mite too much sometimes. Likes his liquor when it's available. But even drunk he's better than most guides hiring out. He also has some funny ideas on how to set up a train."

"Like what?" asked Gorman.

"Won't take a big train out. Not more'n around twenty wagons. Says anything bigger and you get to fighting amongst yourselves." Bridger grinned. "I've found that to be true with most pilgrims. Everyone maneuvers about to head up the column. Sometimes they bicker a lot about whose wagon is in the lead. 'Nother thing he won't allow is women handling their own wagons. He took a train across a couple years back that had a wagon with four schoolmarms. Rest of the wives got jealous. Couple of the single men started fighting over one of the women. Whole trip was a fight from Independence to Oregon City."

"Those sound like sensible rules," Wellman admitted.

"He's firm on them."

Wellman asked, "When are you leaving?"

"Steamboat is late now getting to Westport Landing,"

said Bridger. "When it hits the dock, we'll load my wagons and take off. I want to get back to my fort. Plenty of people are going to need help this summer. Going to Oregon isn't a picnic."

"How bad is it?" asked Gorman.

"Worse than you can imagine." Bridger grinned. "Two thousand miles of hard country slapped down by the devil. A man traveling alone can make the trip without too many problems. He can walk to Oregon if need be. Add a bunch of wagons, women, children and livestock and you're responsible for a lot of lives."

"Can we hire Lawson and go with you?" Wellman looked directly at Bridger.

Bridger reflected for a few moments. "Maybe. What are you boys using for animals to pull your wagons?"

"Oxen," Wellman replied.

"Mules," said Gorman.

Bridger looked at the Irishman. "Get rid of your mules. They'll get you there, but Indians like them too much. They'll sneak into camp and go for the horses and mules first. They won't bother trying to steal oxen."

Gorman protested. "I got a lot of money in my team."

"Sell 'em and buy oxen," Bridger said firmly. "I won't go west with mules. They tempt the Indians too much. Son, you're standing right now on the edge of the law 'tween here and Oregon City. Indians ain't bad people if you understand them. Got me an Indian wife tending my fort back home. Nice woman. A whole sight better than most women. But most Indians don't like pilgrims of any kind. They don't understand that someone can own land. An Indian figures the Great Spirit put the land here for everyone to use. They're different because their whole code of life is opposite ours. Ain't nobody ever going to fully understand an Indian if he's a white man. Not even this chile and I've lived with the tribes for a few years. Ever since I was a tadpole. Most pilgrims speak of the tribes as if they're all the same. Indians are Indians. That ain't true. There's a whole lot of difference between a Digger and a Blackfoot, a Dakota and a Pawnee. Some tribes hate each other worse than we'll ever hate them. Never make the mistake of figuring they're all alike."

Wellman asked, "Where do we find Lawson this morning?"

Bridger grinned. "Already told that chile to be ready to go. My old buddy in there"—he jerked his thumb toward the tavern—"said you boys sounded sensible. We got the matter of setting a fee for everything. Figure your bunch can help me with my wagons. That takes care of anything you'd owe me. Sam's a different story. You pay him about $10 per day and he'll keep you roaming around 'til snow's ready to fall. Give him $600 for the trip and he'll get you to Oregon before you wink your eye. He won't dally along the trail. That sound fair?"

"With twenty wagons that'd be $30 a man," said Mike Gorman.

"We can manage it." Wellman sounded pleased.

"That settles it." Bridger extended his hand. "You got anyone in mind for the train?"

"Nope."

"Haven't talked to anyone," Wellman admitted.

"Then you better start lining up a few wagons," Bridger said urgently. "The steamboat hits Westport Landing and I'm gone. The grass is starting to green up. Some trains have left already. But they're taking a chance the grass won't be up on the Nebraska coast. 'Course, you don't want to get a late start. Snow starts flying in the Blue Mountains awful early some years."

Wellman asked, "Is there much grass along the way?"

Bridger frowned. "You taking cattle?"

"No sir."

"Just as well because Indians love cattle."

Gorman appraised the mountain man. "Any suggestions on how to pick the people for our train?"

"Mosey around the town and look over the pilgrims," advised Bridger. "Don't be in any hurry. Pick out people who look as if they use their heads for something besides a hatrack. You're traveling a long ways over rough country. Pick your fellow travelers for their brains. You'll have some brave men and a few cowards. No way of knowing who'll be which one until you get out on the trail. Ever' man has a weakness of one kind or another. I wouldn't fret about that. Watch for men with good judgment. They're the people who should travel with you. Like, maybe, you're camped out in Blackfoot country some night and a brave decides to steal himself a horse or two. He slips into camp while you're guarding the livestock and, before you know it, that chile has slipped up and put a knife at your throat. Now a pilgrim comes along and sees the predicament you're in. Pick your folks so's you know the pilgrim coming to your aid is the right kind of man."

Wellman asked, "You mean a good shot?"

"That's helpful," Bridger agreed. "Maybe, though, if he shoots that Indian the chile will still cut your throat. The horses and oxen might stampede. A shot can spook 'em late at night. Look for a man who will slip up behind the Indian and do him in silently."

"How much food should we carry with us?" Gorman inquired.

"Lawson will make up a list. He won't allow a train to go out without enough food."

Mike Gorman stood thoughtfully for a moment. "Do you suppose Lawson might change his mind—maybe just this one time I grant you—but do you suppose he would let me keep my mules? I mean, they're the best mules I've ever seen. Trained and sure footed. Best animals I've ever owned and I'd hate to part with them for a bunch of ugly oxen."

"I wouldn't go from here to Scott's Bluff with mules," Bridger said abruptly.

"I've seen folks heading out with mules," Gorman persisted.

"But they ain't traveling with me," Bridger explained. "They don't have Sam Lawson for a guide. What another chile does is his business. I don't poke my nose into any man's affairs. You want to travel with us, you'll pull your wagon with oxen."

"No chance, huh?" Gorman looked sour.

"Sorry."

"We'll lose a lot more than mules before we get to Oregon," Wellman said heartily.

"You're lucky," said Bridger. He looked directly at Gorman.

"How's that?"

"You're just giving up mules."

"Best animals I'll ever own."

"Fellow come through last year on the steamboat. I was over there when they unloaded his rig and horses," Bridger explained. "Finest horses a man could buy in Kentucky. Sleek and trim. Beautiful animals. Had those tiny ankles they breed into horses down there. He had to trade those beauties off for oxen. An even swap cause the traders had too many horses last season. One horse for one dumb ox. He didn't like doing that, just as this sticks in your craw. But he wanted to get to Oregon and those horses wouldn't have pulled his rig to the Blue River. The legs were too fragile. They'd have all been down within a week. Too many prairie dog villages and gopher holes in the plains."

"I'll trade," Gorman said firmly.

"Go out to the edge of town." Bridger pointed south. "Do some dickering with the traders out there. Season's about over. You won't get skinned too much. I'm heading over to Westport and see if the boat's come upriver with my stuff."

Wellman inquired, "You know an honest trader?"

Bridger laughed. "Honesty and horse trading don't fit together too good."

"Maybe there's someone who ain't as bad as the rest."

"That'd be Andy Adkins," Bridger replied.

Andy Adkins was a florid-faced man in a beaver top hat, dirty white waistcoat and dust-covered pantaloons and boots. His eyes appraised the two men as they approached the trader's corral. He smiled broadly when Gorman and Wellman came up.

"We're looking for oxen," said Gorman.

Adkins waved toward the corral. "Take your pick, gents. Probably the best bunch in town."

"I got mules to trade."

"Ain't worth much," said Adkins. "Everybody has mules to trade."

"Good gentle mules from Kentucky," Gorman went on.

"Still not worth much." Adkins shook his head.

"We'd want a hundred apiece for them," said Wellman.

"Too high." The trader looked at Gorman. "They broke good?"

"Best animals I'll ever own," Gorman said with some impatience. "I'd like to take them to Oregon. Jim Bridger says oxen are best."

"Of course," said Adkins. "Indians like mules. They won't bother oxen. You say these are good ones?"

"Pulled me all the way from Kentucky."

Adkins grinned. "You wouldn't mislead an ole trader with a soft heart?"

"Come out to the camp. Judge them for yourself."

"Naw, too much bother," said Adkins. "I believe you. Just trying to mess up your mind a bit. Makes trading a lot easier if a man gets unsettled."

Wellman approached the corral. He looked over the herd.

"How much you asking?" he inquired.

"Twenty-five a head."

Gorman whistled. "That seems high."

"It is high," admitted the trader. "You go on down the road and you'll find oxen selling for five or ten dollars a head. But those aren't hearty animals. Those traders won't buy mules. My animals are young, strong and they're well fed. I don't skimp on grain and fill the poor things up with water. Some traders do that. I won't. I ain't a Christian but I believe in treating a man square and making a profit for myself."

Gorman grinned. "A horse trader with a heart of gold."

Adkins laughed. "That does sound kind of noble. Reason I won't jack-leg my customers is because of where we're at. A man buys a team from me and heads out for Oregon. I wouldn't sleep right knowing I sold him a bad animal. I won't skin a man and put him in danger. Let's get down to business. Look my oxen over. They're good ones. Now, how many mules you got? Eight?"

"Ten," Gorman replied. "I've been carrying two for extras."

"Good idea but ten mules is a lot to handle." Andy Adkins looked dubious. He paced to and fro for a moment. "Make you a deal, pilgrim. Take your mules—and they better be what you say—and give you ten oxen."

Gorman looked incredulous. "You ain't offering any boot?"

Adkins smiled. "I'm coming to that."

"How much?"

"A hundred cash."

"I was thinking more like a hundred a mule," said Gorman. "Paid a hundred and a half for each one back home."

"Two hundred then."

"Eight."

Adkins winced visibly. "Too high."

"This is the first place I've looked," Gorman warned him. "There are other traders I can visit."

Wellman left the two men bickering over the trade. He walked into the corral and appraised the oxen. Andy Adkins was correct. His animals were fat and sleek. Backs and shoulders were free from harness marks. The oxen looked healthy and alert. He crawled through the log corral and rejoined the men.

"Oxen look pretty good close up," Wellman told Gorman.

Andy Adkins knew the deal had reached a decisive point. "Ten oxen for ten mules," the trader said, "with four hundred boot. Cash money."

Wellman and the trader waited with interest as Gorman pondered the deal. The Irishman was soured at giving up his mules. Wellman wondered if his friend might not join another train. That moment Gorman glanced across the corral and saw two milk cows tied to the edge of a fence.

"Those cows belong to you?" Gorman asked the trader.

"Best milkers in the state."

"Throw them in and we got a deal."

Andy Adkins laughed. He thrust his hand toward the Irishman.

"Pilgrim, you got a deal."

SEVEN

That afternoon, Steve Wellman found Sam Lawson sleeping in the loft of a livery stable. The mountain man grumbled when he awoke, but his temperament changed when told he was hired as a guide. Lawson rubbed the sleep from his eyes. He held up his hand for silence, walked to a horse tank and ducked his head under the water. Wellman waited patiently. Lawson combed his hair, wiped his face on a feed bag, and suddenly let loose with a blood-chilling whoop. After that, he grinned at Wellman, grabbed the emigrant's arm and headed for the nearest food tent. Within a few minutes, Lawson was pouring coffee from a large iron pot. A Chinese cook prepared a thick slab of ham, four eggs and a heaping plate of fried potatoes.

Wellman watched in awe as Lawson devoured the food. Wellman waited until Lawson's appetite had been sated, then got to the point. "Bridger says you're a heavy drinker."

"No more than most," Lawson said, without offense.

"I'm out in the wilderness for a long time. A spree in town doesn't hurt anyone. You won't have any trouble with me because of liquor."

"Fair enough."

Lawson pointed his fork at Wellman. "Old Gabe has poured down a few barrels of Taos lightning himself."

"He didn't mean it unkindly," Wellman said.

"I know Ole Gabe better than you. Figure he told you so you'd watch me."

"What about outfitting the wagons?"

Lawson speared a large chunk of ham, wolfed the meat down. "I won't take anything across except oxen. Got my—"

"That's understood."

"Every wagon should have four yokes of oxen. Eight animals," said Lawson. "Each wagon carries plenty of feed for the oxen. They'll eat regularly and work it down before we hit the mountains. Everything in the wagon should be lightweight. No pianos. No heavy furniture. I'll inspect every wagon with you or the captain of the train. Absolutely nothing useless will be taken. Every family going out should have a few milk cows. They bring a good price in Oregon and provide milk along the way. Each wagon must have a good camp stove with a boiler. I'll show you how to rig it on the hind end of the wagon. Everyone has to carry a good tent, plenty of tenting cord and big needles for fixing holes in the canvas.

"Cooking pots and pans are best made from iron. Everyone should carry a dutch oven, a skillet, plenty of metal plates and cups. Two churns, a one-gallon keg for carrying water, an axe, shovel, two or three augers, a crosscut saw and a plow mold. Carry plenty of rope for tying animals. Plus, we'll need rope to get the wagons down a steep incline."

"The mountains are that bad?"

Lawson chuckled. "You don't have to wait for the mountains. You'll hit Windlass Hill in Nebraska. That's a real booger. Now, every man should have at least one rifle and shotgun. Up in the mountains a .56-caliber gun works best. Down on the plains I prefer a .60- to .80-caliber because buffalo have the toughest hides, the hardest heads, in God's kingdom. People can take what provisions they want for food. But nobody sets out without having 200 pounds of flour, 300 pounds of pilot bread, 100 pounds of salted bacon, 20 to 30 pounds of dried rice, five pounds of coffee, two pounds of tea. A bushel of dried beans and the same amount of dried fruit. Ten pounds of salt will be about right. At least a bushel of cornmeal. Every family should have two pounds of saleratus. I—"

"What's that?"

"Baking soda's what they call it back east," said Lawson. "Every family should take a bushel of parched corn. If we can't stop and fix a meal, that'll keep our bellies from growling. Each wagon should also carry a gallon tin of vinegar. We'll be on the trail for four or five months. Four months if we're lucky and have a good crossing. Five if we run into hardships. The wagons will be pretty much emptied of food when we get to Oregon. I'll supply the train with fresh meat. Plenty of wild game along the way. But greenhorns gets the runs from eating too much meat. So every family should have some medicine for that. A person with the shits gets weak and is a fit subject for disease. All pilgrims would be smart to carry all the medicine they'll need. Don't ask me what kind. Ain't seen much of it work worth a damn. They'll be subject to a lot of insect bites, gnats, ticks and fleas. Chiggers are bad but rubbing salt on those boogers is as good as anything I've found. Any family with children should take along schoolbooks. There's plenty of time for book learning on the trail. A man should take the tools of his trade and a farmer better take plenty of tools for growing his crops."

"Is there a chance of cholera?" Wellman inquired.

"Not if we boil the water." Lawson speared the last of his fried potatoes. He sat back with a satisfied expression on his face. "Fever can be bad. The best thing is to boil the water, that's a fact. You best do that by making coffee. The ladies'll get squeamish about drinking water with polliwogs swimming around."

"Polliwogs?"

"Tiny little tadpoles," Lawson went on. "Easiest way to handle those suckers is to boil water into coffee. You don't even know they're in there."

"What about Indians?"

Lawson shook his head. "They haven't given too much trouble. 'Course, the tribes are getting upset. They see the wagons going across and don't like it. Most are a bunch of beggars. They like whiskey and tobacco so we'll carry some of both. Plus, whiskey's a good remedy for snakebite. Almost forgot that each wagon has to carry a bucket of tar. Just stick in a hook and carry the stuff swinging under the wagon."

Wellman looked perplexed. "What's that for?"

"Well, the Indians have a bad habit of setting fire to prairie grass. They do that to draw wild game into an ambush." Lawson explained. "This leaves a lot of short, sharp stubs of grass to cut up an ox's hoof. Grass and dirt gets drawn into these cuts and festers. Best remedy for that is to wash the animal's foot with water and strong soap. After that, you cut away any part of the hoof that's diseased. Finally, you dress the hoof with hot tar. Works every time I've seen it done."

"Never heard of that."

Lawson chuckled. "Everyone likes it except the oxen. They get right upset for a while."

Wellman's respect for Sam Lawson increased geometrically as the mountain man continued to talk. Nobody could listen to the man without detecting the authority of his words, the undercurrent of experience behind his statements. Without a doubt, the choice of Sam Lawson as guide for the train had been a good move. For his part, Sam Lawson's grin was wider than it had been for several weeks. Paul Spurlock had gone ahead with another train, a group from Illinois. Lawson feared being stuck in Independence for the summer. He could make about $10 each day taking Wellman and his pilgrims to Oregon. The misery was starting in his bones when he awoke each morning. Sleeping outdoors, or in a drafty stable, gambling and wenching, drinking away your money on a wild spree was a young man's game. Lawson grinned inwardly. It was the only life he knew. Maybe the miseries could be abated by a young Shoshone girl in his tent. Or maybe after getting this train to Oregon he'd slip down to California. The sun was warm there. Maybe drop down into Mexico with those pretty dark-eyed girls with long black hair falling over their shoulders. Don't give up yet, Sam. There's still plenty of land, plenty of time, to live free and enjoy life.

Lawson heard Wellman talking about organizing a train. The emigrant was asking about the number of wagons in the organization.

"The important part is picking the right people," Lawson answered. "Twenty wagons full of bickering women, cowardly men and wild kids is a score too many. Seventy wagons of good folks wouldn't be too many. Depends on your people."

Wellman hesitated. "Not sure I'm qualified to select who'll go."

Lawson slapped him on the back.

"Don't worry, partner." The mountain man laughed heartily. "You'll find your mettle out here."

Wellman left Lawson in the restaurant tent. He walked over to the tavern, thanked the bartender for his advice. He explained Lawson would be guiding the train to Oregon, that any emigrants judged worthy by the bartender could be given a place in the column.

"Got just the man for you," said the bartender. He winked conspiratorially and jerked his thumb toward a solitary man sitting at a back table. "He's a doctor."

"Going to Oregon?" Wellman sounded incredulous.

"That's what he says. Figure any train can use a doctor." The bartender grinned craftily. "I've already convinced him to go with you. Still, you might mosey back and work things out."

Steve Wellman walked back and introduced himself to Dr. Josh McDonald, who stood up and shook hands in a formal manner. The doctor was of medium height with a slight tendency toward overweight. He had a kind, open face and a pair of penetrating blue eyes. Josh McDonald looked to be about thirty, Wellman gauged, and he looked like a physician. His hands were uncallused, fingers long and thin. Those were the hands of a gambler—or a surgeon.

Wellman asked, "You want to join our train?"

"Sure."

"How many in your family?"

Josh McDonald smiled. "I'm alone."

"You running from any debts?"

McDonald grinned, although his eyes were bitter. "Nothing financial. A few moral obligations maybe. Mostly patients I left. Do debts really matter out here on the frontier?"

"Not to me. I'm just going through the motions."

"When do we leave?"

"As soon as Jim Bridger gets some supplies coming up by boat."

Josh McDonald poured another tin cup of whiskey. "I'll be right here when you're ready to leave. Barkeep's going to let me sleep here nights. Better'n sleeping outside in a tent."

Wellman asked, "What about your livestock?"

"Over at the livery stable. I bought a wagon and oxen in St. Louis and came up by boat." McDonald's words indicated the matter was settled.

Wellman was perplexed by the physician. "Costs $600 to hire a good guide. We'll prorate that between the number of wagons we have."

"Fair enough." McDonald looked down into the murky liquid in his cup.

"I'll see you when we get things organized."

After Wellman had gone, Dr. Josh McDonald tried not to think. He found the state of mindlessness a difficult goal. It was hard to fuzz the edges of reality, blunt memory, dim the cold light of rationality. He believed in responsibility: first to himself, next to his patients and then to all of humanity. Do your duty—even if that axiom entailed driving yourself ruthlessly. For the first time in his life he was running away. *Damn the woman!* He closed his eyes and thought back to that afternoon. He had come home early to be with his wife. Unable to find her in their home, he walked around their property on the edge of Oneida, New York. He went down toward the creek, saw the strange horse tethered near the old cabin on the back of their property. Approaching the ramshackle structure, he heard a man's laughter. That sound was followed by his wife's nervous giggle. He came up to the wall of the cabin, pressed his eye against a chinkhole in the aging mortar.

She was naked!

Marie was inside the cabin with a strange man. She smiled wantonly as his hands roamed over her exposed breasts. The pink tip of her tongue came forward to caress the stranger's lips. Josh McDonald watched as his wife unbuttoned the stranger's trousers, kneeling down in front of the man. She moistened her lips.

It couldn't be!

Dr. Josiah Eugene McDonald trembled with rage. Blindly, he moved away from the wall of the cabin. He turned and ran through the stubbled field toward their home.

Not Marie!

They had been married for two years; she had never undressed before him. It wasn't proper, she declared coyly, for a husband to see his wife's bare body. She always turned out the light before coming to bed. When she came to his side in the midst of that soft featherbed, Marie was dressed in a long flannel nightgown.

He had spoken often of his love. She must have felt his desire to feel her strong firm body, to enjoy the satiny smoothness of her skin.

The slut!

He stumbled through the backyard, past the well and up onto the porch. He opened the door and caught a glimpse of the lead crystal pitcher sitting on the table. His present for their second anniversary which had been celebrated last month. He slammed the pitcher against the oak floor. The glass shattered. Numbly, he walked into the parlor and threw himself down on the pale blue horsehide sofa.

He cried.

Tears were still coming when Marie walked through the front door. She gave the impression of small town respectability: ankle-length velvet dress, high patent leather black shoes, a wool shawl to ward off the wind. Her long wheat-colored hair was slightly mussed. She carried the thick beaver coat he had given her last Christmas.

She saw the anguish on his face. "What's wrong?"

"I saw you."

Her blue eyes were warm and open. "Saw me? I don't understand."

"In the cabin with that man."

She laughed nervously and backed toward the front door. He grabbed her arm and pulled her back into the room.

"Let me loose!" Marie screamed.

"Naked before him."

"I'm going to visit my mother. I'll be there when you've calmed down."

"Not until I get done with you," he snarled.

"Sweetheart . . ." Her voice was husky, seductive. "It won't work anymore."

"Baby," she pouted.

"I saw you doing those things with him."

She tried to jerk away, but his grip held fast. Her eyes narrowed with animal cunning. Without warning, she grabbed a parasol out of the umbrella stand. The pointed tip came flying toward his eyes. She screamed, "Bastard!"

He leaped away. The tip missed his face, plunged deep into a plaster wall. He saw the crazed fury in her eyes, realizing instantly that she hated him. He slapped Marie on the face, a solid blow that knocked her sprawling onto the sofa. She cried loudly, then shrieked her murderous rage. A trickle of blood leaked out of the side of her mouth. Instantly, he was upon her. He ripped at her dress, pulled the garment from her limbs. He tore away her petticoat.

"Don't touch me!" She spat in his face.

Snarling like a wild animal, he tore off the remainder of her clothing. Her large breasts, smooth and globular, fell free. Excitement skipped along his nerves. She rolled off the sofa, tried to crawl away. He went after her and grabbed one of her long slender legs. Forcing her legs apart, he thrust at her with fierce intensity. She raised her head. Her teeth sank deep into his shoulder. He squalled with pain as the blood came. He slapped her again and all the fight went out of his wife. She accepted him without fight, without protest, with a detached indifference that was infuriating. At the end, he slumped over her, heart pounding.

Her voice was icy. "Are you finished?"

He was startled by the puffiness of her face. The reddening skin would soon be dark and bruised. He got up and started for the door.

He turned, asking: "Why did you do it?"

Hate flared in her face.

"He wasn't the first," she shrieked with spite.

"But why?"

"There's been lots more. Would've liked to had someone on our wedding night. I couldn't get away from you mooning all over me."

"Haven't I been a decent husband?"

"You're a dumb doctor," she said with venom. "You've always been the big shot in town. You lived like a swell. While I was down there in that shack with paw dying of drink. Maw working night and day taking in washing. Think I liked washing and ironing your clothes? I've always hated you. But I played my cards right. Married you for your money. Just for the money, you—"

"You're mad."

"Figured you would find out about me someday," Marie went on. "Somebody must have slipped the word to you."

"I come home early this afternoon," he explained. "Wanted to spend some time with you."

She laughed mirthlessly. "And you just happened to walk out in back to that old cabin?"

"I saw the man's horse back there. Wondered about it."

She smirked. "Well now you know about your wife. Ain't nothing you can do about it. Rich doctor Josh wouldn't want his patients to know about his wife. Because, dear husband, I make love my way to anything in pants."

"I won't live with you." He stared at the nude woman in front of him. She was like a stranger.

"There'll be just one change." Marie smiled. "I don't

like sleeping with you. So you move into the other bedroom."

Josh McDonald realized his knowledge of women was limited. He was a romantic where women were concerned. They were beautiful goddesses, innocent beings sent as a special gift by the Creator. This narrow concept of love had allowed Marie's deception. The thought of being cuckolded by a promiscuous wife would never enter Josh McDonald's mind. He realized now that the naked woman standing before him was a stranger. He had never known who she really was. His love had allowed her greed to be seen as girlish delight. Hate had been divined as maidenly innocence. Marie's frequent display of sullen resentment had been interpreted as preoccupation with feminine temperament. Her lack of passion had been viewed as proper respectability. On those frequent occasions when her rage was expressed, he had assumed the outburst was due to some mysterious feminine malady. Now he faced a woman of hank, hair, flesh and bone. A promiscuous female with carnal appetites—a stranger.

"I'll be traveling most of the time," Marie was saying with a superior attitude. "You can stay here and care for your patients. I'm going to see the world. Visit Paris, New York, London, and all the places they talk about in the lady's magazines. Buy some nice clothes. Meet some fun-loving people. You were my ticket out of that hellhole called home, a chance to get away from never having a dime."

He gave an anguished cry. Marie shrank back, realizing her words had triggered a murderous rage in her husband.

"Please . . ." she begged. "Don't hit me again!"

Josh grabbed a handful of her long hair. He was surprised to find those long tresses as soft and fine as ever. Marie screamed.

His voice was cold. "Do me like you did him."

"No!"

"Like out there!"

"I don't do that to people I hate."

"You're going to do me."

She snapped, "I'll bite!"

"Exactly like you did that guy."

Her eyes narrowed with cunning. "If I do will you forget everything?"

"What do you mean?"

"We stay here and I'm still your wife."

"I'll never ask you again for anything," he promised.

Marie smiled and dropped to her knees before him. Her soft fingers came up and touched him, expertly manipulating him. She glanced up for an instant with a fiery look of hatred. There was no need to moisten her lips this time. The blood trickling from her mouth had done that. Her lips touched him. They were soft, intense, demanding.

Not a bad deal, Marie thought. He was responding like all men did. A quick, urgent series of tiny shuddering motions flexed through his body. No need to worry, Marie dearest. You'll get everything you need from now on. Stay home a few days until the bruises go away. Start thinking about a trip to New York City when you look good enough to travel. Leave Josh here to earn the money.

He shuddered.

Afterward, he walked into the bedroom and packed a few clothes in a leather valise. Marie was lying on the couch when he came out into the parlor.

"Where you going?" she demanded.

"Damned if I know."

She bolted upright, her large breasts jiggling. "You can't leave me."

"It could have really been great, Marie," he said with sincerity. "I really loved you with all my heart."

A shocked look of comprehension came over Marie's face.

"What'll I do for money?" she whined.

His hand closed over the doorknob. "That should be relatively simple for someone like you. Entertain strangers as you've been doing. I'm sure they're willing to pay a reasonable fee for your expert services."

"Bastard!" She grabbed a clock, threw the instrument at him.

Closing the door behind him, he heard the clock strike the wall. He walked downtown to the livery stable and picked up his carriage and horse. Although the bank had closed a few moments before, he rapped on the outside window and Henry Railton opened the door. The two men had been childhood friends, gone to school together, been involved in recent years with affairs of the community. Josh said he wished to withdraw all of his money.

Railton was startled. "We done something to offend you?"

"Got a real estate deal," lied Josh. "Need the money to bind the deal."

The banker sighed. He went back in the vault and returned with $1157. He counted out the money. Josh started to place the funds in his valise, then hesitated for a moment. Impulsively he laid a hundred dollars back on the counter.

"Put that in an account for my wife," he said.

The banker made an entry in an account book.

"You'd better notify her that it's here," added Josh.

"Then you're not buying land?" Railton looked speculatively at his friend.

"I'm leaving town."

"Trouble with Marie?" An expression of relief appeared on the banker's face. He laid down his quill pen and sighed.

"Everyone must have known except me."

"Just about," agreed Railton.

"Why didn't you tell me?"

Railton shrugged. He smiled slightly, nervously. "I've thought about telling you. So have a lot of your other friends. There's just no way to say that to a friend. I kept hoping Marie would change." The banker inclined his head toward Josh. "I hope to God you didn't kill her."

"I thought about it."

"At least you're not running from murder," Railton said thoughtfully. "Any idea where you're going?"

"West. I don't know how far. Right now I'm shook up too much to think."

A wistfulness crept into Railton's voice. "I'm thirty-two years old. That makes you thirty-one. Maybe things happen for the best. Going west sounds like a good idea. New land. New adventures. New people."

Josh picked up his suitcase. "You're welcome to ride along."

"I got a wife and family. Responsibilities with the kids." Railton's voice trailed off.

Josh hesitated. "Help Marie if she needs it. She doesn't have much of a head for business. The house is paid for, free and clear. She can always sell that. I also own that piece of land outside town. See that's sold and she gets the money. I'm taking all my medical books, instruments and stuff with me. Sell the office furniture and give her the money."

"Whatever you say." Henry Railton's voice was choked with emotion. He came from behind the counter. His eyes blinked behind his spectacles. He extended his hand to McDonald. As they shook hands, Railton said something about Josh being sure to write.

"I'll do that when I get settled. Don't let Marie know."

"Have a good trip." Railton put his arm around Josh McDonald and gave his friend a quick hug. The banker stepped back, an embarrassed look on his face. He looked down at the floor.

At the livery stable, Josh found his black mare hitched to his buggy. He drove the rig over to his office, went inside the small frame building. Half an hour was consumed in loading his medical bag, instruments, books and several large boxes of medicine. He took his rifle from the office wall, his pistol from a desk drawer and placed the weapons in the buggy. The sun was barely visible when he headed west out of town. The night wind was cold so he buttoned his greatcoat. It would be another two hours before he reached the western pike. Darkness descended and added to his depression. He felt totally alone in the world, unloved by anyone. He was bewildered by Marie's infidelity and puzzled at his inability to feel her hatred until that afternoon.

His head fell forward on his chest.

He cried.

EIGHT

When Hattie Gill first heard the voices inside her
head, she was overjoyed to have company. An only child,
she lived with her mother and father on the edge of New
Madrid, Missouri. Hattie had always been a bit "queer,"
as her mother phrased it, and seldom played with other
children. Her parents were engaged in a brutal struggle to
survive on the Missouri frontier; they seldom had time
for Hattie. Therefore, she welcomed the voices when
they manifested themselves one morning while she
played alone at home. Maw and Paw were out back,
hoeing weeds out of the cornpatch. The voices started
with a buzzing gibberish. That noisy din could be
dispelled when Hattie gave her head a series of vigorous
shakes. After that, the voices were nice. They told
stories. A woman's voice sang. A little girl about her own
age whispered sly, obscene words. Sometimes the voices
made her afraid, especially when they chastised Hattie
for her misconduct. Then she would run to the big
walnut tree beyond the garden and beat her head against

the trunk. When she pounded her head with enough force, bringing on a rush of pain, the mean voices stopped abusing her.

As she grew older, Hattie Gill wondered about the voices. It seemed odd for a voice to exist without a body. Were there tiny little people who lived in her head? How did they get food and water? Heavens! Did they go doo-doo in there? Surely not in her head! Maybe they were the voices of ghosts. Her paw said a lot of Indians had been killed just down the hollow. Maybe Indian ghosts were haunting her head.

The voices were with Hattie that one summer when she went to the big meeting. Hattie liked it when she went with maw and paw to the place where the preachers stood outdoors and shouted. She liked the preachers because they told stories about people like Moses, Abraham, the prophets and multitudes going into the wilderness. Hattie listened especially careful when the preachers talked about a lake of fire at someplace called hell. Mr. Devil would poke sinners with his sharp pitchfork, burn those rascals forevermore. Sinners were the bad ones! The preachers said they didn't listen to the voice of god.

The voice of god!

Hattie decided that was who did the talking in her head. She asked Maw if preachers ever lied. Maw said they were men of the cloth, always told the truth. Maw said God would strike a lying preacher dead with a lightning bolt. He might cut out their tongues with a razor-sharp knife. Send down an angel to cut their throats because, according to Maw, God didn't like liars. When God talked to somebody, Hattie decided, they had better listen.

After the camp meeting, another voice began to speak

102

to Hattie. This was a thundering sound: firm, unyielding, never to be questioned. This voice discussed sinners, spoke on the glories of heaven, the reward that awaited each True Christian departing from this vale of tears.

Hattie never told anyone about the voices. Not until that morning in the wagon camp east of Independence. She hadn't slept well that night because Paw came back from town in a drunken stupor. He had snorted, coughed and snored all through the night.

After breakfast, Hattie decided that Paw was a sinner. He was heading for that lake of fire. He'd be gouged and poked by the devil's pitchfork. The voice of God spoke: *"Unless your Paw mends his ways he will surely die like the sinner he is."*

Hattie asked, "Is there nothing I can do?"

"Lead my children through the wilderness."

"I'm just a little girl barely sixteen."

"The multitudes will perish unless they are led by a True Christian."

"I don't know how to begin," Hattie complained audibly.

Gladys Gill came around the side of their covered wagon. Hattie's mother asked, "Begin what, child?"

Hattie looked sullen. "I shouldn't tell you."

"I'm your mother."

"God's been talking to me."

Gladys Gill looked around. "I don't see him any-wheres."

"He talks in my head, Maw. A lot of voices are in there."

"You always were a little funny."

Hattie glared spitefully. "I'm telling the truth. I'm a True Christian."

Her mother looked doubtful. "Is God talking to you right this minute?"

"He is."

"What's he saying?" Gladys Gill wiped her hands on her apron. She sat down beside Hattie.

"Just talking about me leading the mutitudes through the wilderness."

"What's that mean?"

"I don't know."

Gladys wearily shook her head. "Ask God to explain it to you."

Hattie intoned: "I am the Creator, the alpha and omega of all time. I am the true god who now declares this child to be a prophet of the lord of Israel . . . pick-a-ninnie . . . coming down the road with silly syrup . . . redblack . . . bluegreen . . . greenrednedbickback . . . Hattie . . . Bluejays in hell . . . Screamcracks! . . . Flammerjams with smidgets . . . Sixteen buffox on a squigwam . . . Worms . . . Oought Suzanna and why not? . . . Wave your hangydang! . . . Bring out the fleaflats . . . Listen to the word, Children of Israel, which will destroy the sinners!"

Gladys stared at her daughter. She said, "That don't sound like God. More like when you had the fever last winter."

"It is God."

"Nothing more than gibberish."

"Paw's going to burn for drinking. He'll be fried to a crisp."

"God said that?"

"'Pon my honor."

"Now, Hattie, you're just funning your Maw."

Hattie glared spitefully. "God says you're just a dumb

old woman who—"

Gladys slapped Hattie's face. The girl stumbled back against a wagon wheel. She tottered for an instant, a wounded expression on her face, and slid to the ground. Staring down at the unconscious girl, Gladys Gill was impressed by the peaceful appearance of her face. Hattie looked almost like a sleeping angel. Gladys panicked. Wild thoughts flashed through her consciousness. Prophets were born through the womb and, after all, Hattie'd been touched in the head since birth.

Gladys bent down and shook Hattie's shoulders. The girl opened her eyes and smiled weakly.

"I'm sorry, baby," Gladys said. "I didn't mean to hit you."

"Do you believe me, Maw?"

"You're one of God's prophets."

"Just like in the Bible."

"A very special person."

"Like the people the preachers talk about."

Hattie smiled. "We got to tell the others, Maw. I'm supposed to lead the lost tribes through the wilderness."

Gladys beamed. "I got to tell your Paw he's to quit drinking."

"He'll be burnt if he don't."

"Oh God, honey!" Gladys hugged her daughter. "Nothing like this ever happened to me. You're a prophet! That means I'm somebody. People got to respect me now. I'm more than just a drunken farmer's wife. I'm the mother of God's new messenger. Why, Hattie, you're just like the Christ child."

Hattie snuggled close to her mother. She felt warm and secure for the first time in her life.

"We got to tell the others," Hattie said again.

"We will, baby, we will." Gladys Gill was surprised to find she loved her daughter.

There was opposition, of course, and much laughter. A prophetess was expected to be more imposing, not a silly slip of a girl who fainted away into trances and mouthed gibberish. Even the father of the prophetess, Clay Gill, was dubious. His skepticism turned to downright hostility when Clay learned of God's plans. Giving up whiskey was not Clay's idea of divine guidance. He argued with his wife, then went off to Independence and stayed drunk for two days.

The men in the camp laughed at Hattie's claims. Besides, they were too busy to get involved in religion. Even the Archangel Michael would need a few dramatic miracles to get attention in Independence that spring. "Forget that talk about heaven," drawled an emigrant from Mississippi. "Oregon will be our paradise."

A handful of people blindly accepted Hattie's claims for being God's messenger. They were convinced she was a true prophetess. Her followers suffered from boredom, anxiety about the trip to Oregon, and sexual repression. They longed to become a part of some great cause, some gigantic undertaking to overcome their personal short-comings. The first True Christians were a man and woman from Indiana. They were baptized by Hattie in a creek near the campgrounds. Next came a couple from Kentucky who were soured on life. They liked the parts in Hattie's sermons about chastising the sinners. A shy young man and his withdrawn wife, just in from Pennsylvania, nervously embraced Hattie as the Anointed One. When Clay Gill sobered up from his drunk, he met the new converts and decided religion might be better than farming.

"Have each person go forth and spread the word," he told his wife and daughter. "Each member brings another person into the church. Hattie's flock will grow faster that way."

At the next meeting, Hattie received a revelation that echoed her father's advice. The True Christians went forth as zealots to spread the word through the camp. The young man from Pennsylvania miraculously lost his shy nature; he was surprised to find himself talking easily to strangers about Hattie's church. The True Christians became an obnoxious group in the camp, forever talking about Hattie, religion, the revealed path to heaven. Their efforts were rewarded. Within a matter of days, the flock included eleven families. They were identified by large crosses painted on the sides of their canvas-topped wagons.

"That way God will know who's who when judgment comes," Clay Gill had told his daughter. It was also a way for Clay Gill to remember who was in the church. He couldn't remember the converts' names or faces. None of them knew enough, he figured, to keep their powder dry. He figured they were a senseless bunch who needed a good drunk, a few tumbles in the old haystack, to get straightened out. But he figured there was money to be made going along with Hattie's nonsense.

Clay Gill was seven years old—really just a tadpole!— when his parents moved from Vincennes, Indiana, to establish a general store at New Madrid, Missouri territory. They opened their business on April 10, 1810, six years after the Spanish ended their rule along the upper Mississippi River. By then, hundreds of families had settled in eastern Missouri. They were attracted by the rich farm land.

Land speculators, and the inevitable town boosters, figured New Madrid would be the metropolis of the western frontier in a couple of years. The gangs of murderous river pirates was not mentioned. No one talked about the river fever, ague, that turned a man's skin to a yellow color. Nor of the fever that accompanied ague, so high that some victims thought their brains were being boiled in its juices. They never talked about the Indian tales of great earth upheavals around New Madrid. That was all in the past and, besides, those savages didn't know anything.

The earthquakes did them in. Shortly after two o'clock on the morning of December 16, 1811, Clay was tossed from his bed. Rising groggily from the dirt floor of his parents' log cabin, Clay heard a groaning and squeaking in the cabin's structure. A loud rumble seemed to come from the earth itself. The cabin danced up and down on the foundation. The chimney fell away from the house.

Clay remembered being bundled up against the cold winds of that winter night. He was led out of the house by his parents, both talking in hushed tones. Outside, the land heaved and fell, buckled and jumped. They reached the middle of town and stood, with other frightened families, in the center of the streets until morning.

Daylight brought a horrible sight to the survivors. Great cracks had formed in the earth. A seemingly bottomless chasm could be seen in the earth down by the levee. Giant landslides had destroyed the banks of the river. The Mississippi seemed to be flowing north— instead of proceeding south as usual. A keelboat had been tied up at the town's levee. The vessel was picked up by churning waves. It had been carried inland for half a mile. The boat stood that morning atop a small hill outside town. The crew of rivermen were never seen again. Great trees were bent asunder. Their limbs were twisted violently. Clay and his friends found the roof of a home sticking out of the earth. The adults decided the earth had opened at that point, swallowed most of the house, then snapped shut. A man, his wife and their four children had been sleeping when their doom came. Some parts of New Madrid had dropped twenty-five feet during the night. At other points, the land had thrust up forty-five feet or more. The survivors were viewing the results of the greatest earthquake in American history. A few years later, Clay learned that Reelfoot Lake in Tennessee had been created by the earthquake that night.

Despite their fears, the townsmen began to rebuild that same morning. True, the ground rumbled fiercely and many people wanted to leave. Most had their savings invested in homes and businesses; flight was out of their options. The succession of earth shocks continued for two years. A man could repair the chimney on his cabin in the morning, see a tremor destroy the structure in the afternoon. A farmwife walking to her barn was swallowed up by a deep chasm.

The settlers clung precariously to the trembling land. Their woes were multiplied when a fiery-eyed visionary led a band of religious fanatics upriver. They were searching for the site of a New Jerusalem. They landed at New Madrid, at least what was left of the town, a few weeks after the first quake. The leader of the sect was a bearded old crackpot, Amos Milner. He claimed the quake resulted from God's anger at the sinners in the town. What Jehovah had smitten, Amos Milner and his group set out to convert. The group quickly became known as the Fanatical Pilgrims. They were a gaunt, ragged band of zealots. Their doctrine, as outlined by Amos Milner, forbade a member from washing. God made the earth, hence dirt was a blessing from on high. Work was the devil's trick to prevent the full time worship of God. Ownership of property was another of wily old Satan's tricks. Lusting for land meant less time to prepare for the next life. Funerals and burial of the dead were forbidden. Let the dead remain where they dropped, declared Amos Milner. Folderol over an empty vessel, a dead body, didn't help to convert the heathens.

The townspeople were shocked by the Fanatical Pilgrim's dietary practices. A true pilgrim, said Milner, ate a single meal after the evening prayer each day. Lunch and breakfast were heathen practices. The pilgrims prepared a large kettle of cornmeal mush and milk. This gruel was poured into a large wooden trough that sat on thick legs. Shouting words of praise to the sky, the pilgrims gathered around the trough. Each member of the sect carried a long hollow cornstalk. When Amos Milner gave the command, everyone dipped their stalks into the gruel. They noisily sucked up nourishment.

Day and night, the pilgrims roamed through New Madrid seeking converts. When people shunned their meetings, Amos Milner adopted another plan. New Madrid was sinful; forceful ways of conversion were required. The sect began to gather in front of a business or cabin, crying to the heavens about the sinful folk inside the dwelling. If a settler and his family remained inside their home, the sect knocked down the door, crawled through windows, once even coming down a large chimney. Once inside, they ran about like demented creatures.

110

"Repent!" cried Amos Milner.

"Praise the Lord!" answered a pilgrim.

"Repent now or we'll stay here until you do!" Milner claimed.

The pilgrims were the final plague to descend on the Gill family. Sorrowfully, they packed their belongings in a small cart. They bought a mule and headed back to Vincennes. All of their savings had been lost setting up the store in New Madrid. They lived precariously in Indiana until Clay's father found work supplying timber to a wagon factory. Clay's father snorted indignantly when religion was brought up.

"Craziness! That's what it is," the old man said angrily. "Those Fanatical Pilgrims were nothing but a pack of troublemakers. Drove people almost mad with their tactics. Always underfoot in my store. Bothered the customers. Converted my hired man, the best clerk I ever knew. Wouldn't even let a man rest in his bed at night. Woke up one night with a whole passel of those nuts gathered around my bed. The wife and me were scared half to death. I jumped up to get my pants. That's when the galoots started chanting. Repent! Always repent! I picked up a big stick of firewood and chased them out into the yard. The boogers mooned around like ghouls, finally camped out on my front porch. Swore they'd stay there until I gave in and repented. I took their shenanigans for a couple days. Didn't want to hurt anybody, that's been my view on life. But those yahoos shouted and hollered all night. Picked and poked at my wife when she came outside the house. Even tried to slip my little boy, Clay, out the back door. Planned on taking him into their group, I expect. Finally I put the dogs on the whole bunch. Should've seen them yelp when the hounds took after them. They cleared out fast, they did. Headed right over to my neighbor's house and started in on him. Yessiree! I might have stuck out there in New Madrid except for those yahoos. I hear tell that most've died. Don't doubt it. Mush and milk ain't much of a meal."

Remembering the Fanatical Pilgrims, Clay Gill stayed in camp most days. On the afternoon that Steve Wellman was talking to Dr. Josh McDonald, Clay fussed over Hattie and Gladys until the two women positively beamed. The number of Hattie's followers was growing. Eleven families had paid $100 to Clay Gill as a tithe, so to speak. A fee to have Hattie guide their wagons through the wilderness. Although the brethren trusted Hattie, some were getting restless. They wanted to leave for Oregon. The grass was up, other trains were headed out. They didn't want to wait and gather more families into the fold.

Clay sensed that the flock thrived on excitement. Movement, action, pageantry nourished the true believers. Preaching was all that Hattie practiced and, being honest with himself, Clay realized that was done better by the Methodists and Presbyterians. He forbade the brethren to speak in tongues. While that would occupy their time, it was risky. The whole babbling bunch might decide everyone was a messenger from God.

Clay walked around the camp, musing on these private thoughts. A few more days in camp, a few more converts, a few more $100 fees and he would head for Oregon. Prophesying sure as hell beat farming for profits. Although he was preoccupied, Clay's attention was drawn to a shapely young woman standing by a wagon. She was currying the back of a nice-looking mule. Suddenly, the animal kicked out. The hoof flew through the air, almost striking the woman's leg. Clay saw Molly Gorman swear at the animal. He was surprised to see the woman pause and cross her bosom.

"A Papist," he exclaimed. He recalled the recent accounts in newspapers of the anti-Catholic riots in Philadelphia and New York City. Mobs of Protestants stormed through the streets, roared into the Irish slums, beating anyone suspected of being Catholic.

Clay continued on his walk until, on the edge of the rendezvous, he saw two men arguing heatedly. He came closer and saw an emigrant in homespun shirt and trousers shouting at a man in a dark woolen suit.

"We are filled up. We don't have room in the train," the emigrant was saying.

"I'll pay to go along," said the man in the suit. "I have funds."

"The folks wouldn't want you along."

"I can handle my share of the work."

"That's not what I meant."

The man in the suit pondered that for a moment. "Maybe you'd better spell it out for me."

"You're a Jew."

"That bothers you?"

"Damn right," the emigrant said vigorously. "My train don't carry any Christ killers to Oregon."

For an instant, Clay thought the Jew would strike the wagon captain. The Jew's face darkened to the color of burnt stone. His mouth trembled for an instant, then the moment passed.

"I thought this was a free country," said the Jew.

"Reckon you're free to go to Oregon. Same as anyone else," drawled the wagon captain. "You just aren't traveling with my train."

The Jew asked, "What about the other trains?"

"Don't know of any that would take a Jew."

"I'll pay double the usual fee," said the Jew.

"Nope."

"I come all the way from Philadelphia. I can't go back."

"You'd be trouble in my train," said the emigrant. "We're Protestants. Most ain't very religious. Religion really ain't an issue. I let a Jew join the column and we'll be squabbling all the way to Oregon. Nope, my folks wouldn't cotton to a Jew tagging along."

Clay saw the Jew turn away without another word. He walked proudly away from the wagon captain.

Clay knew he had an issue that would occupy the brethren. Hattie's revelations had been the same old garbage the past couple of days. He would plant the suggestion and let his daughter's addled mind handle the rest. Yessiree! It was time to chastise the Jews to avenge Christ's death.

NINE

Hattie listened attentively during supper to her father's rantings about the Jews. He was distressed because one of the Christ-killers was in the wagon camp. Perhaps, he suggested, the True Christians should chastise this Hebrew assassin. Hattie was surprised by her father's grave concern. She did not wish to lose his new devotion. She prayed that her voices would provide heavenly guidance in the matter. She was waiting for a message when the time arrived to give her nightly sermon.

On their way to the meeting, Clay asked: "Is God mad at the Jews?"

"He doesn't say anything, Paw."

"Maybe I'd better give the sermon tonight."

Hattie protested. "God wouldn't like that."

"Maybe I can give a little talk after you finish."

Which is the way things happened. Hattie provided her usual revelatory sermon. Clay noted that the faithful seemed restless. A large portion of Hattie's talk was

115

gibberish about treating animals like humans. It didn't make sense to anyone, not even Hattie. After the girl stepped down, Clay got up on the platform and discussed a Christian's duty to do away with God's enemies. He pointed out that the Jews killed Christ, that Hebrews were rumored to be in the camp that very night. They were undoubtedly plotting against the True Christians. Maybe the Jews were plotting with the Papists to destroy God-fearing people. He'd seen a gang of Papists walking through the camp that very afternoon. They were out to destroy Hattie and God's chosen people. The rendezvous itself might be in danger.

A rational man would have stopped there. The seeds of bigotry were planted and, in time, would bring forth a bitter harvest. But this was the first time Clay Gill had addressed any group of people. Without conscious knowledge, he crossed the line of prudence.

"I've seen Satan walking around the camp at night," Clay cried.

"The witches are here," cried a man. "Saw one flying across my wagon last night. They're here to kill us all."

"Jews are poisoning the water!"

"I'll bet the Catholics lamed my best ox."

Within a few moments, the twenty-two people had been turned into a howling mob. They were ready to chastise the Lord's enemies. Prepared to beat Christianity into the heart and mind of those who wavered. They roared for action, howled for blood. Struck suddenly by the ferocious nature of the mob, Clay Gill stood speechless on the platform.

Wild, angry words shot up from the crowd.

"String 'em up!" cried a zealot.

"Drive 'em into the wilderness!"

116

"Tar and feather the whole bunch!"

"Burn the witches!"

"Show 'em no mercy!" yelled a thin-faced woman with stringy hair. Her eyes blazed with zeal.

Clay thought: These yahoos are getting out of control. They're acting crazier than a hound with the fits. He stepped down from the platform, walking through the crowd to pacify them. The mob was a lustful beast searching for a victim. They surged away from the platform, paying no heed to Hattie, Clay or Gladys. The time for prophecy was past; the moment of action was at hand.

A woman was walking past with a pail of water in her hand. The mob howled and grabbed her like a wild beast. Cries of witchcraft and curses floated through the twilight. A score of hands grabbed the woman's body, forced her to the ground. Fingers tightened on her throat. She was stripped naked by a woman who claimed that each witch was marked. Someone slapped her into insensibility. The woman's husband came running to her aid. He was knocked down. Two men grabbed his feet and dragged him away from the mob. Another man came running up. He carried a piece of firewood, slamming True Christians in the head. They fell back, regrouped and surrounded him. He went down under the weight of a dozen men. Women's hands clawed at his face, scratched at his eyes.

Clay Gill pressed into the mob, demanding full attention. Someone spat in his face. A fist came out and knocked him down. A woman started to choke Clay, then loosen her grip on his throat. She saw her victim was the father of the True Christian's prophetess. Looking around, the mob headed across the encampment to where

117

the Jews were gathered. Someone cried that a hundred Jews, armed with pistols, were in the camp.

"We'll stuff their weapons in their craws!" screamed the formerly shy man from Pennsylvania.

They came to the wagon occupied by the Jew. He was repairing a box on the back of his rig when he heard the noise of the mob. The group came forward yelling like wild men. One man had picked up an axe. He began to chop and maul the Jew's wagon.

"Just a minute!" Jay Samuels exploded.

"Lynch 'em," cried a voice.

"Get some tar. Cover 'im with pitch and feathers!"

A hand reached out and grabbed the frightened man. He was thrust back against the side of his wagon. A fist slammed into his chest. Two men were up in his wagon, throwing down plunder. The man with the axe chopped at the wagon.

"Wait a minute!" cried the shy man from Pennsylvania. His name was Abner Hager.

"Why wait?"

"Give him a choice," Abner shouted above the noise. "Accept the Bible and become a True Christian or die!"

"Don't kill him," argued a woman. "Tar and feathers are enough."

"Shut up! Kill the Jew!"

Jay Samuels was terrified. He stared at the unruly group and wondered what insanity had seized their senses. On the fringes of the crowd, several small children were screaming shrilly.

"Question him before he goes to Satan's home," yelled Abner Hager.

The crowd fell silent.

"Do you believe in Jesus Christ as your savior?"

Abner demanded.

Samuels looked from face to face. All expressed a murderous anger. "I believe in the Lord," he said.

"Is Jesus the Messiah?"

"If you say so."

"What do you say?"

"I'm willing to abide by that," Samuels replied. "Look, I—"

"Speak when you're spoken to." Abner slammed his fist into the young man's face.

A man came running up with a rope.

"Hang him," shrilled a woman. She pressed forward and clawed at Jay Samuels's face. Two women came running up to the fringe of the mob. They carried a bucket of steaming black tar. Another True Christian, a middle-aged man with glazed eyes, came into the crowd with a featherbed on his back. The mob began to tear at the seams to obtain feathers for their grisly action.

A dark figure came up to the edge of the mob. The man carried a shotgun cradled in his arms. He pointed the weapon to the night sky, pulled the trigger. Flame belched from the barrel. The mob was frozen by the deafening blast of gunfire. They saw a curly-headed man standing a few feet away. The man's eyes were hard, firm, angry. He held the shotgun low on his hip, pointed upward slightly toward the belly of the mob.

"What the hell's going on?" demanded Mike Gorman.

Abner Hager jerked his hand toward Jay Samuels.

"This man is a Jew," Hager said shrilly.

"What business is it to you?"

"His kind killed Christ."

Mike Gorman sighed audibly.

"Not his kind," growled the Irishman. "It was a

senseless mob like yours that caused Christ to be crucified. Now back away from him."

"Listen to him!" roared the man holding the featherbed. "We need to kill this bastard too!"

Gorman cocked his shotgun.

"Come ahead," he said.

"God almighty!" yelled Abner Hager. "Who are you to stop us from chastising the Jews?"

"I'm the man holding the gun."

A man edged away from the fringe of the crowd. He slipped almost into darkness, planning to circle around and come in behind Gorman.

"Stop right there," Gorman ordered, "or I'll blow your belly off."

The man whined an inaudible curse, then rejoined the mob.

Abnew Hager said lamely, "We were just going to tar and feather him."

A crowd of curious onlookers was gathering. People stared at the True Christians, wondered who the man with the shotgun might be. Clay and Gladys Gill came through the ring of bystanders. Clay's face was scratched across the forehead. Hattie tagged along behind her father.

Hattie glared at the Irishman. "God will punish—"

"Shut up!" Clay Gill snarled. He turned to Gorman. "Things got out of hand at the meeting and . . ."

"Get 'em back to their wagons," said the Irishman. "I'm going to be standing guard tonight in camp. I see one of your paddies tiptoeing around tonight and I'll blast him to kingdom come. That goes for your harpies, too."

"Let's go to bed," suggested Clay to the True

Christians.

A few members of the sect protested. Hattie chimed in and ordered the group to disperse. Reluctantly, the mob fell back. They wandered off into the darkness. Some left with a feeling of shame. Most felt disappointment that the Jew had not been punished. Gorman saw a tall, red-faced man standing among the onlookers. The emigrant was head of the camp council, an elected governing body to uphold law and order in the rendezvous. After a brief discussion with the council member, Gorman asked for volunteer guards for the night. He called for a meeting of the council after breakfast. The emigrants went back to their wagons. The camp settled back into quietness.

Jay Samuels surveyed the damage to his wagon. He walked around the rig with a lantern in his hand.

"Not too bad," said Mike Gorman. "You'll have to replace a couple of sideboards."

Samuels felt nauseous. He had purchased the wagon upon arrival in Independence, a large Conestoga with eight oxen. The hardwood used by the Pennsylvania wagonmakers had withstood the mob's axes fairly well. Behind the wagon a pile of merchandise was thrown out onto the grass. Samuels hung his lantern on a hook attached to the back of the wagon. He went down on his knees and began to salvage the supplies.

"Going to Oregon?" asked Gorman.

"If I find a train."

"What's the problem?"

"No one wants to take a Jew."

Gorman laughed. "They feel the same way about Catholics. We're getting a train together. I'll talk to Steve Wellman who's been looking for people to join us. Maybe you can join us."

"You think there's a chance I can go along?"

"I don't see why not." Gorman released the hammer on his shotgun. He walked off toward his wagon.

After getting his supplies in order. Jay Samuels unrolled his bedpack and turned in. He didn't feel like setting up his one-man tent. He slipped the bedroll under the wagon, crawled under the covers. The camp was quiet. The air was chilly, almost cold now, and hundreds of stars winked back from the clear night sky. He was grateful to the man with the shotgun. Said his name was Gorman—an Irishman. Samuels thought: I know where it started. He wondered where his journey would end.

His trip had started when he walked to the front of *Davidson's Emporium—General Merchandise and Clothing* on Broad Street in Philadelphia. Beyond the glass doors, people hurried through the gloomy winter dusk toward home. Jay Samuels snapped the locks, checked their security and felt a sense of security. A few weeks past his seventeenth birthday, Jay Samuels had been clerking at the store for three years, four months. He had been promoted to the position of chief clerk. He welcomed the responsibility and treasured the keys to the front door carried in his pocket.

Jay Samuels was the last employee to leave the store at night. He remained late to balance the day's books and make a night deposit at the bank on the corner. That was the drudgery connected with his work. The extras that came with his new position—in addition to a raise in his salary—was a chance to have dinner with the drummers. These were the salesmen who hoped to sell their wares to

Davidson's store. Drummers were jovial, intense men with an outgoing temperament. They stayed at the best hotels, ate in the most fashionable restaurants. Each man had a racy joke or two that excited Jay's sense of humor. Even more important, they traveled widely on their sales trips. By careful questioning, Jay frequently obtained information on new sales methods.

"Yard goods are going awful good at Miller's in Chester."

"Guy in Lancaster set a barrelful of brooms on the sidewalk. Sold twenty-five the first day."

"Manny over in Pittsburgh has a new department to supply hardware to farmers. He's selling a ton of horseshoes each month."

Jay Samuels walked through the store turning off the lights. He went to the big desk in the center of the store. An hour later he had gone through the sales slips, recorded credit entries, and balanced the books. The new line of women's blouses was moving better than expected. He'd have to suggest an immediate reorder. He had frowned at another return slip from Mrs. Potter: she had brought back four gowns in as many months. He made a mental note to bring the matter to the attention of Sol or Walter Davidson, owners of the store.

Sales were still off in the hardware and harness department, having gone down since the day Ralph Davidson took charge of that section. Ralph was the store owner's nephew. He had been moved to harness and hardware when Jay Samuels was promoted to chief clerk. At first, the nephew was sullen and uncooperative. He accepted orders with a sullen air. In the past week, Jay reflected, their relationship had improved. Ralph had been friendlier, more open to Jay's suggestions on managing the department. Jay decided the nephew realized that the Davidson brothers were nearing retirement age. A good chief clerk would be needed when they left the store.

Being chief clerk offered other pleasing opportunities to Jay Samuels. He lived in a small boarding house near the downtown section. This arrangement offered scant opportunity to entertain a girl. Although there were thousands of attractive young women in Philadelphia, none would venture into a man's boarding house. His landlady, a doughy-faced Dutch woman with puritanical views, would never stand for such visitations from females.

The keys to the store were his salvation. He developed a vigorous love life with several shop girls who worked in stores near Davidson Brothers. He settled down eventually to a steady liasion with Mary Grell, a pert dark-haired German girl who worked in the linen department. Twice each week, on Tuesday and Thursday nights, Mary returned to Davidson Brothers store at seven in the evening. They had been sparking now for two months. Although Mary had been hinting about marriage, Jay Samuels was content with their present arrangement. Mary was an agreeable companion, bright and intelligent, and her sexual appetite seemed limitless. Each time they met the girl suggested a new position, a new technique, something different from the ordinary.

Jay Samuels made up the store's deposit. Wednesday was a slow day. The year's business had been less than he anticipated; sales had to increase or a number of clerks would be laid off. He laid the bank deposit on the edge of the desk, pulled out the payroll book. He decided to play a game: if the store was his alone to manage, which clerks would be let go. He pored over the list of names. Deliveries could not be cut back. Clerks were needed to staff each department yet, he considered, ladies ready-to-wear was overstaffed. So was the department containing household supplies. He picked up another book, checked the sales figures for household goods. It would be a step forward to close out the section, add a candy department.

The clock had finished chiming nine o'clock when a sharp pounding sounded on the front door. Jay's thoughts went to Mary Grell, but he recalled this was Wednesday night. He opened a drawer and pulled out a small pistol, shoving the weapon into his belt. He walked uneasily through the dim store and pulled back the shade on the door. Ralph Davidson stood in the entryway pounding vigorously on the glass door.

Jay unsnapped the lock.

Ralph came rushing inside. He had a wild, hunted expression on his face.

"Thank God! Thank God! You're here!" said Davidson.

"What's wrong?"

"I was afraid you might have gone home. It would have been too late."

"What's wrong?" Jay Samuels stared at the store owner's nephew.

"They're after you."

"Who?"

"Mary Grell's father and her brothers."

Alarm bells went off in Jay Samuels's mind. He swallowed hard. "Start from the beginning," he said to Davidson.

"Maybe I didn't mention it," Ralph Davidson said. "I moved a few weeks ago. Wanted to get away from home, find a place I could entertain girls. I got a nice place over in the German section. A big apartment for reasonable rent. I was going out tonight to a new dance hall that just opened up. I bumped into Mary Grell. The poor child was running down the street like a madwoman. Her eyes were red from crying. There was a bruise on her left cheek, like someone had really popped her there. She was nervous, really crying, and it took several minutes to find out what happened. Finally I managed to get the story. Her family found out that Mary has been meeting you here at the store. She had to tell them about those Tuesday and Thursday nights. You have been meeting her, haven't you?"

Jay Samuels reddened with embarrassment.

"Once or twice," he mumbled.

"Mary said you met every week," Ralph went on. "But women often lie about those things. Anyway, when the Grell family found out, her Paw went berserk. He's a laborer down on the docks, you know. Unloads the ships. Has muscles like a piece of iron. He started slapping Mary around, swearing she was probably pregnant and going to disgrace their family name. She slipped away somehow and was headed down here to warn you."

"About what?" Jay's eyebrows shot up.

"Her Paw and brothers are coming to beat you."

"Beat me?" echoed Jay.

"You know how these German families are," Ralph continued. "Mess with their daughters and the whole clan goes insane. They'll kick and stomp a man until he's crippled for life."

Jay asked quickly, "Have you seen them?"

Ralph gave him a look of concern. "They probably stopped off to fortify themselves with some liquid courage. They like to brawl in those bloody bucket saloons. A tough bunch. I ran as fast as possible to warn you."

"Where's Mary?" Jay inquired.

"I convinced her to go back home."

Ralph walked quickly to the front door. He made certain the green shade covered the glass portion of the door.

Jay asked, "You think they're coming here?"

Ralph cast a look of consternation in Jay's direction.

"That's what I've been trying to tell you," he explained. "The whole bunch of thugs may be here any minute. They'll beat you into a bloody mess. Knock out your teeth. Break your arms and legs. Smash your jaw. Pound in your ribs. They're vicious fighters who don't gave a man a chance."

"But what about Mary—" Jay blurted out.

"Take care of yourself. Get out of town." Ralph spoke with concern. "Lay low outside the city for a couple of weeks. I can keep my uncles happy. Tell them you had to leave suddenly to attend your mother's funeral."

"They know I'm an orphan."

Ralph glowered. "I'll think of something. The main thing is to get away before that bunch of hoodlums finds you."

Jay Samuels looked about wildly. "Where can I hide?"

"Not here in the store. Get out of town."

"I can't get my money out of the bank."

"Hell, man, this is an emergency. Take the store's deposit there."

"That's thievery." Jay was adamant.

"I'll tell my uncles you needed an advance on your pay," Ralph said quickly. "Take today's deposit. Grab whatever you need here in the store. Pack a bag and head out the back way."

"No," Jay countered. "I'll stay and face them."

"Suit yourself. Your funeral, you know."

Both men jumped when a loud pounding sounded on the front door. A loud voice, thick with a guttural German accent, roared.

"Ye be there, Jay Samuels," growled the knocker. "Ye dirty cur! Messing with a young girl's life. I got something for the likes of you. Open this door, you mountebank, or I'll break it down."

"Get moving," Ralph hissed.

"I—I—" Jay stammered.

"Get moving," Ralph cried.

"Open up," yelled the man outside. He pounded the door.

"One moment," Ralph yelled toward the door. "This is Ralph Davidson. What do you want?"

The German yelled, "We want Jay Samuels."

"He's not here." Ralph grinned at Jay.

"Open up or we'll kick in the door."

"Grab what you need off the counters. Pack a bag." Ralph Samuels looked panic-stricken. "Get out the back. I'll try to keep them occupied while you escape. Run, man, while there is still time."

The fist began to pound heavily against the front door. Jay's mind reeled with indecision. He came to life suddenly, grabbing a large carpetbag off a shelf. He crammed a suit, two shirts, some toiletries into the bag. Ralph was stuffing jewelry, expensive broaches and silk undergarments into the bag.

The voice thundered through the door.

"Open up! We want to talk with Jay Samuels!"

"Grab the money," Ralph whispered. He ran to the desk, grabbed the bank bag and shoved it into the carpetbag. "Good luck!" He shook Jay's hand. "I'll let you know when things cool down. Cut out the alley and you can get to the stage depot. Don't worry! I'll tell my uncles you will be back in a couple of weeks."

Jay allowed Ralph to push him toward the back door. The nephew fumbled for a moment with the bar and bolt, then threw open the entry into the alley. Jay took a deep breath and hurried out into the night. He heard the door slam shut behind him.

Jay was rushing toward the stage terminal when Ralph Davidson walked to the front of the door. He slipped the lock. A red-nosed German with an unsteady gait walked into the store. The man was old, unshaven and his eyes were rheumy. His breath stank with the stale odor of cheap beer.

The old man grinned. "Did I do it right?"

Ralph Davidson smiled.

"Perfect!" he exclaimed. "Absolutely perfect."

"We agreed on two dollars."

Davidson pulled a handful of coins from his pocket. "Plus an additional bonus for your theatrics, my friend."

The old man accepted the coins. He expressed his gratitude. "If you ever need me again . . . I can use the money."

Ralph laughed. "I'll keep you in mind. You're a convincing actor, my friend. That bastard won't stop until he's a hundred miles from here."

"Whatever you say, governor." The old man clutched the coins. He said good night and headed for the closest tavern.

Davidson locked the door. He grinned expansively and

danced around the counters. "Set up for life! The bastard won't know what hit him. My uncles can get a warrant for his arrest tomorrow!" He chortled. "I get the store."

Jay Samuels was a passenger on a coach headed for Pittsburgh. The rig rolled through the night, wheels clattering on the pike road. Gradually, a rational attitude returned. He went over the night's events. He clutched the carpetbag that rested on his lap. He giggled suddenly and, for a moment, wanted to laugh hysterically. What a set-up! That bastard Ralph had tricked him! It was probably the best performance of the poor incompetent idiot's life. Jay Samuels had left town with the store's money, a bagful of expensive merchandise. Like a fool, he had gone for the whole story like a fish after a fat worm. The high sheriff would soon be after him.

Later, he counted the money and found two thousand and eleven dollars in the bag. That matched what he remembered from the deposit figures. More than enough to take a man west. With plenty left over to set up a business of his own. He decided to write an anonymous letter someday to Ralph Davidson and thank him for his efforts.

TEN

When the council met the next morning, the camp was in an uproar. Opinion was divided among the emigrants as to whether camp laws protected Jews. The meeting was delayed because several of the council members had left for Oregon. After much confusion, and the election of two new board members, the group listened to Mike Gorman's complaints against the True Christians. Jay Samuels was not allowed to attend; some council members felt his presence would enrage the sect. Hattie and Gladys Gill accused the council of being in bed with the devil. They denounced everyone in sight, including dogs and children, and swore their vengeance. Some of their followers, insane with frustration and rage, stomped out of the meeting. In the end, after much bickering, the True Christians were expelled from camp. Shouting "Praise the Lord!" and "Kill the heathen!" the sect loaded up their wagons and moved out. Clay Gill rode at the head of the column of eleven wagons containing that same number of couples and sixteen children.

"Good riddance!" exclaimed Mike Gorman, watching the wagons roll west.

He went over to see Steve Wellman who was painfully writing out a list of the families in their wagon train. Gorman mentioned that Jay Samuels needed to join a train.

"Will you vouch for him?" asked Wellman.

"Don't know him," admitted Gorman. "He seems like a nice person. He's only eighteen years old. I talked with him a few minutes this morning and he sounds sensible."

"Why's he going to Oregon?"

"He's got a wagon filled with goods. Plans to open a store."

"You figure he might turn sour?"

Gorman shrugged. "Hell, Steve, I don't know what we'll be facing. I can't say that I might not be a problem."

"Exactly how I feel," Wellman agreed. "Tell him we'll take him on the same terms as everyone else."

Gorman grinned. "The Irish and the Jews salute you."

"Not me," protested Wellman. "We hold an election for wagon captain after the train is organized. He'll have to deal with the people we elect."

Wellman added Jay Samuels's name to the growing list of people in the train. Both men were absorbed in studying the list when a woman walked up. Steve saw her standing near his wagon, her feet planted firmly and squarely, head lifted, jaw jutting out, hands planted on her hips. He looked up into a face that was soft and composed. There was a slight hint of power, or perhaps stubbornness, in the set of her mouth.

"I'm Agnes Miller." The woman stepped forward and extended her hand.

Wellman shook her hands and looked into her soft

brown eyes. He judged Agnes Miller to be about forty years old. She was youthful in appearance, although tiny crow's lines were etched around her eyes. Her nose was patrician, slightly larger than needed for her oval face. She would not have been judged the winner in a beauty contest, yet her expression was that of spiritual purity. This added a charming dimension to her personality. Her long brown hair was tied at the back of her head in a severe knot.

Wellman stood up. He judged that Agnes Miller was at least two inches taller than he was. She wore a severely cut wool dress, devoid of any jewelry or decoration. The fullness of her breasts and the suppleness of her slender body added to the impression of youth. At a distance Wellman felt she would look no more than twenty-five years old.

Agnes Miller spoke in a soft, gentle voice.

"I understand you're forming a caravan," she said.

"That's right."

"I'd like to join it."

Wellman looked down at his boots. "You got a husband?"

"What's that got to do with it?"

"Our guide won't accept single women."

"Pshaw!" Agnes Miller laughed musically. "I don't need a worthless man to slow me down. There's my two girls—they're seventeen and eighteen—and myself. We brought our wagon all the way from Natchez, Mississippi. We can manage by ourselves."

Wellman appraised the woman. "I'm sure you can. I don't have any say in the matter. Those were the rules our guide laid down. We'd be going against his judgment if I accepted you."

The woman's eyes narrowed. "Is the guide here?"

"In town." Wellman mentioned Sam Lawson's name. "Sam feels women without men are trouble on the trail."

Agnes Miller sniffed. "He sounds like an old mossback to me."

"Begging your pardon, ma'am," interjected Mike Gorman. "What happened to your man?"

"That's none of your business!"

Mike Gorman stepped back as if he had been slapped. "Sorry for asking. I apologize."

"The apology should come from me," said Agnes Miller. "My tongue gets a bit sharp at times when men tell me I can't do something. Mister—"

"Mike Gorman."

"Well, Mr. Gorman," Agnes went on. "I'm what everyone calls a spinster. I've never been married. I've been busy doing the Lord's work. Never found the time for marriage."

"But your two girls..." Mike's voice trailed off.

"I'm not that wicked," said Agnes. "They're orphan girls. Homeless when I found them. Took them in and I've been their guardian ever since."

"Wish we could help you, ma'am."

Agnes Miller stared directly into Steve Wellman's face. "You know I have to get to Oregon. That's part of the Lord's plan."

Mike smiled. "Maybe you could hurry up and catch the train of True Christians."

"Don't be ridiculous!" Agnes Miller cast a scornful look in the Irishman's direction. "I wouldn't go across the campground with those lunatics. They're headed for trouble. That girl is mentally deranged. Hattie whatever they call her. The Anointed One; indeed!" She snorted.

134

"The whole pack probably won't make it to the Nebraska coast."

Mike Gorman looked sheepish. "I was just trying to help."

"Then talk sense. I don't have time for anything else."

"I wish we could help you, ma'am," Wellman said. "I'll talk with Sam Lawson. He makes the rules."

Agnes Miller brightened. "You think there's a chance?"

"I'll hunt him up and find out."

Agnes Miller went along with Wellman. They rode into town and, after hunting through the saloons, found Sam Lawson drinking whiskey at a table in back of Blackwell's Tavern. Agnes Miller stood back while Wellman approached the inebriated guide. Lawson had trouble focusing on Wellman's form. When his gaze connected, the mountain man blinked several times. He let out a bloodcurdling whoop of delight that made Agnes Miller jump with alarm.

"Dang gone!" said Lawson, slapping Wellman over the shoulder. "You ready to head for Oregon."

"Got eleven wagons."

"About time to go," said Lawson. "Get another five or six and we're ready to roll. Better think about leaving within another couple days."

Wellman nodded. "Looks like you've been celebrating."

"Last dang drunk from now until we reach Oregon City."

"I hope so," Wellman said anxiously.

"Oh, don't worry none about me," said the mountain man. "I like my liquor about as well as any man. But

135

when I'm guiding I know that's serious business."

"Got a question to ask."

"No," grinned Lawson. "I ain't tumbling ten young girls at the same time."

"There's a woman and her two guardian girls headed for Oregon."

"Fair enough."

"She ain't married."

"Told you my thoughts on that," Lawson replied. "Single women in a train gets every man acting frisky. They start showing off. Next thing you know the wives are madder than hornets. Single women are nothing but TNT—time and trouble. Nosiree. Sam Lawson won't allow no unmarried women in his caravan."

Steve persisted. "She's a Christian lady. A nice, gentle person."

Lawson belched. "They all say that, but it ain't always a fact."

Agnes Miller came to life with a quickening fury. She strode over to the table, slammed her hand down. "Why you drunken old dog!" she roared at Sam Lawson. "Sitting here swilling down the devil's whiskey and making judgment on who goes to Oregon. You're the poorest excuse for a man I've ever seen."

Sam Lawson stared speechlessly at Agnes Miller. He noted the firmness of her stance, the determination in her eyes.

"Are you talking to me?" Lawson asked suspiciously.

"You're the only drunken fool around here," snapped Agnes.

"Ma'am, if I was going to Ore—" began Steve.

"I won't appease this whiskey sopping neer-do-well," Agnes said firmly. "Why this man hasn't bathed in years.

You should have told me I had to stand downwind or be suffocated."

Lawson looked over at Wellman. He swallowed hard and tried to control his anger. His whole body was seized with a desperate trembling. Then the anger passed and an amused smile appeared on his face.

"Son," Lawson said in a strangled voice. "I figure this must be your gentle Christian lady."

"This is Agnes Miller," Steve said grimly.

Lawson nodded gravely. "She has a bit of a temper."

Agnes slapped her palm down on the table. "Look at me, you miserable excuse for a human being!" she yelled at Lawson. "It is the Lord's wish that I go to Oregon and spread the gospel. I need to join a caravan. This man"— she jerked her thumb in Steve's direction—"seems to be a capable and competent individual. I saw Mr. Gorman come to a poor man's aid last night. I want to go west with this train."

Lawson belched. "That's all right with me."

"You mean I can join?" Agnes asked in a surprised voice.

Lawson smiled slyly.

"Just as soon as you get married, lady," he said with finality. "Find yourself a husband and you're welcome."

"I don't want to get married."

"Then," Lawson said in a voice filled with amusement, "you won't go to Oregon with our train."

Agnes had a pleading look on her face when she turned to Wellman. "Can't you make him take us?" she begged.

"Sam makes the rules."

Agnes cast a contemptuous glance at the guide. "His brain is probably rotted by strong drink."

"Probably is," smiled Lawson. "Strong drink did part

137

of the job. The rest was chewed up by a sharp-tongued woman."

"Mr. Lawson," the woman said softly, "Would it help if I offer an apology?"

"It might help my feelings a bit," Lawson agreed.

"Then I offer my apology," Agnes said gravely.

"Thank you, ma'am."

"Now can I join the train?"

Sam shook his head. "Not unless you get married."

Agnes exploded. A surge of hot fury raced through her body and mind. She looked at Lawson and hated the man for his patronizing attitude. Her hand came up and her finger shook under Lawson's nose. "You're nothing but a washed-up old drunk," she shrilled. "Sitting there destroying your mind and body with rotgut booze. Playing God with honest, God-fearing people who need to go to Oregon. Well, you stinking old man, I warn you. I am a determined woman and I always get what I start for. I'm not going to allow you to stop me from joining this train."

Lawson grinned. "That's swell, ma'am. Give my regards to the groom."

Agnes turned and stalked away. Wellman looked apologetically at the guide.

"I didn't know she would be like that," Wellman said.

Lawson took another sip from his cup. He spat. "She's right about one thing. It is rotgut."

"I'd better get her back to camp." Wellman stood up.

"Watch yourself," advised Lawson. "Don't get close to her tongue. You'd get cut to pieces."

Agnes Miller was silent during their walk back to the camp. At first, Steve tried to strike up a conversation. When she refused to answer his questions, he faltered.

138

As they came up to the rendezvous, Agnes wiped her eyes with a lace handkerchief. She sniffed several times and then turned to Wellman. He was surprised to find her expression was peaceful and contented.

"Save me a place on the train," Agnes said.

Wellman looked aghast. "You're not really getting married?"

"If that's what it takes to get to Oregon." A distasteful expression crossed her face.

Wellman felt a rush of pity for the woman. "I wish there was something I could do," he said lamely. "Sam made the rules. We agreed to abide by them."

The woman smiled. "I lost my temper back there," she said. "You're sure Mr. Lawson will let me join if I'm married."

"You were pretty hard on him," Steve admitted.

"We'll see." Agnes grinned as if she held a secret. "He doesn't know what hard luck is all about."

As she walked to her wagon, Agnes Miller thought back to that afternoon at Natchez-under-the-Hill. She could remember the very moment when the decision was made to go to Oregon. She had been sitting on the creaky front porch of the clapboard house on Front Street. She squinted down the thoroughfare toward the riverfront. The scene was enough to squelch the missionary zeal of any Christian lady. Burly keelboatsmen, Indians, a couple of Spanish dandies, soldiers, gamblers, planters, ne'er-do-wells, black slaves and plain ordinary white trash were out in force that afternoon. They drank, gambled, yelled, whored and roared like the devil himself was in their midst. Satan probably walked every night in Natchez-under-the-Hill, Agnes decided.

139

The sinfulness of the town had attracted her because, where the sinners were, she took the Lord's word. Although she was not officially associated with an organized church, both the Presbyterians and Methodists supported her work. Churches in Natchez frequently took up a special collection for her mission. Several concerned merchants in the town donated money, food or supplies. The contributors were not deluded about converting the rabble on the river. Few people expected Agnes to lead many sinners into a temperate, moral life. They did feel she might be a civilizing influence on the degenerates in Natchez-under-the-Hill.

Agnes operated her small mission in a rickety frame house donated rent-free by a wealthy cotton broker. The place was sparsely furnished. Visitors were given strong black coffee, a chance to talk, a few words of encouragement and a pallet to sleep on. A keelboatsman could sleep off a spree at "Miz Miller's place." A gambler with a streak of bad luck could obtain a sandwich, a cup of coffee and a pallet. A prostitute trying to mend her ways could find help and guidance, perhaps a few dollars in cash, from Agnes. She took in the unwashed, the unwanted, the unruly and, without judgment, provided love and self-respect. She never ranted or raved about their deeds. She did not condemn and seldom preached. What she did provide was something few of the river people had ever experienced—loving acceptance.

In time, Agnes earned a grudging respect from the whores, gamblers, river men, brothel keepers, and blind pig operators. The owner of the town's most notorious blind pig—a tavern serving whiskey so bad that customers sometimes went blind—made the ultimate compliment. Dressed in his best shirt, shoes shined, carrying a handful of daisies, the man called on Agnes one Sunday morning. He stammered, thrust the flowers at her and made a formal proposal of marriage. Mistaking the confusion in her eyes for anger, the suitor almost bolted and ran. Agnes trembled visibly in pushing down her temper. She wanted to tongue-lash the stupid little man, but her common sense prevailed. She thanked the man, mentioned her commitment to her missionary work. The man nodded his understanding. He suggested that if she ever changed her mind, well . . . she knew where to find him.

For her part, Agnes learned the city's "sporting people" were not total degenerates. Each was a unique person. None had made a conscious decision to live lawlessly. Chance, circumstances and ignorance had brought them to Natchez-under-the-Hill. She served coffee, gave her attention fully to her visitors. She listened.

". . . Never set out to be a whore, Miz Miller. Paw and Maw died and I didn't have any place to go. Didn't know how to earn a dollar. Almost starved to death before finding out I made a good whore. That's the only thing I ever been good at."

". . . Lord, I been a keelboatsman for twenty years. Since I was a tadpole about twelve. Always planned to save my money and get married. Always blow my pay in a couple nights after a trip. But a man has to do something."

". . . I been whorin' for thirty years and, Missus Miller, I bet you wouldn't know I'm only forty-two. Usta live back in the Kentucky hills with Maw and Paw. She died and Paw kept trying to get my virginhead. Kept rutting me all the time. I didn't mind that too much, you understand, 'cause an old man can't spend more'n thirty minutes a day messin' round. Not even that most days 'cause they bodies can't keep up with they minds. But Paw was downright mean. Always pinching and hurtin' me. Bite me something fierce down there onct . . . drew blood and I hurt for a week. So I got the old geezer drunk 'n I run away. Only thing I knowed how to do was fry 'taters and pleasure a man. Ain't much call for 'tater cooks, so I been workin' on my back ever since."

". . . I'm a mechanic. Not on machinery, understand, but with a deck of cards. Watch this: see, here's the ace of spades. You shuffle the deck. Mix 'em up good. That's it. Now, I deal you the king of hearts. Ah! Here's the old ace of spades for myself."

". . . Wanted to marry the girl. She wouldn't do it. I couldn't stand to see her walking around the village, hanging on to that other man's arm. He had more money then me. He owned most of the stores in town. A fat little toad with snake-ugly eyes. I went crazy just thinking about them being together. I had to leave town or kill them."

". . . My folks was killed by bandits on the Natchez trace. I ain't been right in the head since then."

". . . Paw usta beat me with a stick!"

". . . Maw would pour liquid down his gullet 'til Daddy was dead drunk, then slip out and see other men."

". . . My first recollection is of my crazy uncle chasing me with a butcher knife."

". . . My oldest brother did things to me. Bad things. I complained to Maw. She tole me it helped keep the family together. Said I shouldn't whine 'cause my brother loved me."

". . . I tried living with the goody-goodies. They got a

142

different blood. Thin and cold. I left everything and I've just been roaming since then. One place to another, but always where folks have fun. Wouldn't trade my life for anything. I like it. Truly do."

". . . I used to be a schoolmarm before I took up whoring. Believe me, Miss Miller, a bunch of horny men ain't near the trouble you find wet-nursing a gang of wild kids."

". . . I got the French pox. Do you know of a cure?"

The first major change in life for Agnes Miller occurred one spring when the Mississippi river was at flood stage. A boat coming down river struck a snag, overturned, and most of the occupants were drowned. The only survivors were two teen-age girls—now orphaned—without a known relative. The rescue workers brought the two grieving and frightened girls to the mission. They lived with Agnes at the mission for several weeks. Although she worried about exposing the girls to the raw life of a river town, Melissa and Jane appeared to be model young ladies. They attended an academy set up by a man in Natchez, sharpened their educational skills. They helped her with the chores around the mission, cleaned house, helped make coffee and prepare meals. Nevertheless, Agnes was concerned about their environment in Natchez-under-the-Hill. She began to question her selfless devotion to help others. At what point, she wondered, did sacrifice turn into stupidity? Could she be expected to right all the moral wrongs of the world? What was wrong with living for yourself, forgetting the needs of others? If the rabble wished to run hog-wild through life, did they have the right to ask her to pick up the pieces? Was devotion to a cause—religion, philosophy, politics—more important than caring for one's self? Who is the victim and who is victimized?

The break came one day in autumn when the trees were turning color. The girls had been sent on an errand to purchase a slab of bacon at the store. They left on the errand in early morning and, by mid-afternoon, Agnes paced the rough boarded front porch. The girls should have returned hours ago. She was still pacing when the racuous laughter of men sounded down the street.

She saw that Melissa and Jane were staggering along the sidewalk, hair falling over their faces, bemused and drunken smiles on their lips. Agnes hurried to their side. The girls weaved unsteadily as she guided them toward the mission house.

She turned on the gang of amused men.

"Who got these girls drunk?" she demanded.

A stout man with a soft belly grinned wolfishly. "They just had a glass of wine with us."

"More like a bottle each," added a riverman.

"We didn't mean any harm, Miss Miller." This from a gambler in a silk frock coat. "The girls were walking by the saloon. We enticed them in for a drink."

"Dirty dogs!" Agnes stormed.

"We didn't mean anything by it," the gambler said lamely.

Jane giggled and waved toward the nearest man. "You're handsome," she giggled.

Agnes took a firm grip on each girl's arm. She marched them up the street toward the mission. The crowd of men followed at a discreet distance. Agnes was partially leading, partially dragging the girls up the steps to the porch. Melissa missed her step, tumbled backward onto the lawn. She lay on her back, giggling maniacally. Her dress was up around her knees, exposing her limbs to the men.

"Let me help you up," Agnes bent down and offered her hand.

The girl whooped with drunken laughter. Suddenly, her mirth stopped and a bemused expression crossed her face.

"Oh shit!" Melissa said gravely. "Now I've gone and done it."

"Done what?"

Melissa slurred her words. "Done pissed all over myself."

That night, while the girls slept off their stupor, Agnes Miller prayed for guidance. She beseeched the Lord to provide a sign to lead her. She cried out for guidance from on high to be revealed. From time to time, she rose from her kneeling position and wandered out on the porch. The sound of revelers could be heard in the nearest saloons.

She was standing there when two men walked past. They were unaware of her observation.

"Anybody who's looking for a good life should go to Oregon," one man said.

"Plenty of opportunity there," agreed his companion. "Wish I had the money. I'd go in a minute."

"Would you go by boat or land?"

"Land," said the man, now almost out of earshot. "Much cheaper that way."

Agnes wondered if the two passersby were her sign from the Lord. She dismissed this as being too irrational. They were a couple of drunks walking to their lodgings. Nevertheless, her mind begin to ponder the problems of getting the money, outfitting a wagon, getting her and the two girls to Oregon.

ELEVEN

Agnes appeared casual, even optimistic, when she returned to her wagon. Inwardly, she was seething with outraged frustration. She didn't want the girls to know they might not get to Oregon. She hated herself when her temper was turned loose on some poor soul like Sam Lawson. Fortunately, the guide had reacted with humorous detachment. Lately, her tempestuous outbursts had been directed at people who blocked her personal progress. These obstructionists were everywhere, chained to the illusion that life was a mystery, that fate ruled and a person's destiny could not be controlled. According to their view, all things were impossible. Go to Oregon? Land 'o goshen, lady. You don't have the wherewithal. That's man's work. With that attitude, humanity was powerless to reach great goals. Individuals were buffeted on a sea of causeless events. Man's destiny could not be determined by his own efforts, but was left to the providence of a cast of dice.

During her time spent as a student in one of the nation's first female seminaries, Agnes had observed the actions of the faculty and administration. These were selfless men and women who gave of themselves, sacrificing their personal goals, giving up their ideals to the needs of their students. Their pay was minimal; their rewards were certainly not the accumulation of material wealth. They talked dreamily of opening other schools, cutting across prejudice and apathy, building an educational system to educate hundreds, perhaps thousands, of girls each year. The plans, financial backing and energy were available to transform the dream into reality.

Instead, the faculty and administration became a political animal. Their strength was dissipated through endless bickering. Factions sprang up. Sides had to be taken on obscure, third-rate issues. Cliques developed. Those rational teachers who tried to rebel, attempting to bring the organization back to the original purpose, were destroyed by the politicians. Agnes judged that half of the organization's energy went into political maneuvering.

We fight with all our strength against success, she thought. At that moment, she resolved to reach Oregon regardless of the obstacles. She made a firm commitment to travel there in the caravan guided by Sam Lawson. Slowly, a smile tugged at her lips. As she helped the girls cook supper on the small camp stove, Agnes Miller mentally composed her plans.

After the meal had been eaten, Agnes sent Jane down to the creek to wash their plates and utensils. When the girl had gone out of earshot, Agnes told Melissa of their problems. She explained the rule of not allowing unmarried women in a caravan.

Melissa asked sadly, "What're we going to do?"

"I've got a plan. Don't worry."

Melissa was doubtful. "I don't see how we'll overcome that. I sure don't want to marry someone just so's we get to Oregon."

"Sit down for a minute." Agnes patted the seat across from her. "You and I are going to do something about it."

"When?"

"Tonight. And you're not to say anything to Jane. She gets upset too easily."

Over the next few minutes, Agnes Miller outlined her plan. It was a devious, underhanded and thoroughly terrible plot. Such intrigue would have been applauded in a medieval kingdom. Summing up, Agnes asked, "Can you pull off your part?"

"Lord, I don't know," Melissa admitted. "I never tried to seduce someone."

"Try is all you do," Agnes said firmly.

"I'll try."

"Good, we'll do it tonight." Agnes stood up. "We'll leave Jane with the folks in the next wagon. She'll be safe there. Get dressed out in your best finery. We got a big job of selling."

Sam Lawson was leaning against the bar in the dram shop. He sipped his cup of whiskey and listened to the murmur of conversation around him. He decided fuzzily that no one ever talked about anything except Oregon. Looked like someone would think about something else for a minute or two. He took another sip of whiskey, wiped his mouth with his buckskin sleeve. Gradually, he became aware that conversation had stopped in the room. He turned around, saw that everyone was staring toward the door.

Sam focused his eyes. His mouth opened in surprise. A young woman of extraordinary beauty stood just inside the doorway. She was not more than eighteen or nineteen, of obvious vitality, wearing a tight velvet gown which failed to hide her curvaceous figure. The gown was cut low, as if someone had cut away a portion of the material. Behind a lacy shawl were the girl's white shoulders, her slender neck, bejeweled with a small silver brooch. Her face was soft and open, glowing with the dewiness of youth. Her lips, although obviously unrouged, were pinked with a soft color. Her eyes were uncommonly large, shimmering blue beneath her dark long lashes. Her long brown hair was worn long over her shoulders. She came forward into the dram shop and every man eyed her with desire.

Melissa ignored the staring men. She walked down the line and spoke softly to the bartender.

"I'm looking for a man named Sam Lawson."

"That's him over there." The barkeep pointed to where the mountain man stood.

Lawson gulped hard, scarcely able to believe his luck. He watched the girl raise her skirt above the dirt on the floor, move toward him with small, fluid steps.

"Are you Mr. Lawson?" Melissa asked breathlessly.

"A pleasure, ma'am," Lawson beamed.

"I'm Abigail Patterson," Melissa lied." I'm looking for my brother. He's been out in the wilderness trapping for beaver. Did you ever meet a Raymond Patterson during your travels?"

Lawson licked his lips. "Don't recall the name."

"Then I'd better thank you and leave," Melissa said delicately. She lowered her long lashes. "A girl shouldn't

149

be seen in a place like this."

"Just a minute!" Lawson spoke hastily. "Maybe I'll remember his name. Takes me a little time to function sometimes."

"Do you have a table we could share?"

Lawson jumped. He moved quickly to a scarred table near the end of the room. He dusted off a chair as Melissa came up. "Care for a drink?" he asked.

"Something soft," Melissa said breathlessly in a seductive tone. "Perhaps a small glass of wine if it's available."

"Mind if I have a snort?"

"Go right ahead." Melissa blinked her lashes, looked directly into Sam Lawson's eyes. "My Daddy was a great bourbon fan. He was the biggest cotton broker in Natchez, Mississippi, and I learned to love sitting on the veranda of our plantation in the evening. Daddy would smoke a long cheroot, sip his bourbon and talk to me. That's how I learned to appreciate what whiskey can do for a man."

Sam looked at the girl with an incredulous expression. He thought of walking over to the bar for a refill, decided he shouldn't risk leaving her alone for a single moment. He waved for the barkeep to bring another cup.

"Daddy always said that whiskey calmed a man down," Melissa was saying. "Changed the temperament from downright mean to calmness. He also said that bourbon allowed a man to view life from a different perspective."

"Your Daddy must have been a great man."

Melissa pushed her lace shawl back. Her white shoulders and delicate throat were exposed to Lawson's gaze. Without appearing to do so, he fixed his eyes on the slight rise of flesh just above the top of her gown. He decided the velvet hid one helluva set of breasts.

"Back to my brother," giggled Melissa. "You think you might have seen him?"

"Describe him," said Lawson, fascinated by the girl's intense vitality.

Hours later, Sam Lawson and Melissa were the only customers in the dram shop. They sat at the table or rather Sam tried to sit. His mind was fuzzed by too many cups of whiskey. His eyes were bloodshot, bleary. His head lolled on the back of his chair, pushing forward on his chest.

"You're such a strong man," Melissa said. "I'll bet you have the biggest chest in the whole world."

Sam hiccuped drunkenly. "This chile has plensh hairsh on itsh, too."

Melissa tilted her head. She flickered her eyes wickedly at the mountain man.

"Oh, I can't do it," she said heatedly. "You'd think I was a bad girl."

"Nothish of the kind."

"I'd like . . . oh Mr. Lawson . . . you're such a powerful man."

"Thash me."

"I've never . . . you see . . ."

Lawson forced his mind into a moment of sobriety. "You can tell me, little lady . . . I'm your friend."

Melissa's lashes dropped demurely.

"Mr. Lawson," she said huskily. "Would you walk me back to my wagon?"

"Glad to."

"You won't take advantage of me, will you?"

"Ish jush like yore uncle."

"Bless you." Melissa stood up and let her hip move against Lawson's shoulder. "I'm going to trust you. It's just that I get so excited when I'm around a strong man like you. I'd love to feel your arms around me—but a girl must remain proper. Mustn't she?"

Sam stood up. He lurched drunkenly. His arm slid around the girl's waist. His nostrils felt the musky scent of her perfume. "Damn! this chile is sure lucky!" he said without slurring his words.

Together, they walked out into the dark night. Sam was barely able to stand after consuming so much whiskey. Fuzzily, he recalled something about going into a house. People were standing around. A pinch-faced man came up to meet him. Somebody had screamed about someone vomiting on their good rug. He looked around for Melissa, couldn't find her and everything went blank.

Blackness. An absence of consciousness. A tongue dry and thickened. Then the first glimmer of wakefulness penetrated the pathways of Sam Lawson's brain. He rolled over and opened his eyes. The onrushing light almost blinded him. He closed his lids tight and prayed for death. The heavy throbbing around his temples was like the blow of a hundred hammers. He wanted to crawl off into cave, snuggle up to a she-bear, sleep through the winter.

"Time to rise and shine!" A woman's voice spoke near him.

Sam groaned.

"Get up and have some breakfast." The woman again.

Sam made a feeble attempt to sit up. He fell back and hit his head on the ground. He moaned.

"Get up, you big ox."

Sam opened his eyes. "Am I alive?"

The woman looked down at him with disgust. Sam thought she looked familiar.

"You're alive, you drunken old bum."

Sam licked his lips. "Water," he croaked dryly. "Get me a dipper of water."

The woman left and returned in a few moments with a dipper of drinking water. Sam drank thirstily. He glanced around and saw he was sitting beside a wagon. He saw other wagons and decided he was somewhere near the rendezvous. "Where am I?" he asked.

"Home."

Sam was puzzled. "What's that mean?"

"Pshaw!" said the woman. "Don't tell me you don't remember what happened. Your words just swept me off my feet. I didn't realize a man could be so romantic. You were just magnificent."

Sunlight flashed on the whiteness of the woman's face. With a start, Sam Lawson remembered her. Whatshername? Wait a minute. Evelyn . . . no, Agnes Miller. He wondered what he was doing with her.

"Mr. Lawson, we have a great deal to discuss," Agnes was saying. "We have to make plans for our future. I'm going to need your help in getting this wagon ready for the trip to Oregon. I'm sure you're hungry so I'll have the girls fry you some eggs and a couple of pork chops."

Sam shook his head vigorously. He sat up. "'Member you now," he mumbled. "You're the unmarried lady. Did you find yourself a husband?"

"Sure did."

Sam growled. "I pity the poor soul."

"I'm married now," Agnes said somewhat gleefully. "Can I join your train?"

"Have to talk to your husband first. Make sure he's a

153

good man."

Agnes smirked. "You know him."

"I do?"

Agnes said in the prettiest voice, "I'm now Mrs. Sam Lawson. We were married last night in town."

Sam Lawson was thunderstruck. Time and space ceased to exist as he stared speechlessly at Agnes Miller's face. His mind made an attempt to function, to digest this new information. The blood drained from his face. His nerves pulsed, quickened, slowed and dropped into a comatose state. He opened his mouth to speak, but was unable to form the words.

"You'll get used to it," Agnes smiled.

"I—I—"

"Don't worry, Sam darling," Agnes said with sarcasm. "Everything is legal. We're truly man and wife. The minister was an ordained Presbyterian. His wife and another lady witnessed the ceremony. I've got the marriage certificate put away. I believe folks call this getting hitched up."

Sam sighed and considered her. "Think you're a smart woman, don't you?"

Agnes grinned. "Smart enough to fool you!"

Sam swore.

"From now on watch your language," Agnes declared. "We have two young daughters. They're not accustomed to profane language."

A stunned look appeared on the mountain man's face. His body slumped. "Children?"

"Two nice girls."

"Oh my God!" Lawson began to pound his head against a wagon wheel.

"If you're wondering," said Agnes, "you've probably

done a lot of things in the past to deserve this."

Sam stood up. He glared down at the woman.

"'Nuff of this foolishness," he said gruffly. "You probably tricked me. Assuming we did get married last night. That don't mean I'm stuck with you. Nosiree, baby. Sam Lawson travels light and fast. He ain't going to get hunkered down with a sharp-tongued wife and a couple scraggly children. Before you ask—you ain't going to Oregon with my caravan. Smoke that in your peace pipe."

"I will. But I got something for you to consider."

"Like what?" Sam asked sullenly. He asked the question fearfully, not knowing what new horrors would assault his mind.

"Debtors aren't allowed with trains. Am I right?"

"That's true."

"You'll have to pay your debts before you leave."

Sam felt as if a tight belt was going around his limbs. He shook his head in a deliberate manner.

"I ain't even going to ask about that."

"You borrowed a lot of money last night," Agnes told him.

"Why'd I borrow the money?"

Agnes smiled. "You wanted to buy me a wedding present."

"Who'd I borrow from?"

"Bought a brooch off one of the witnesses. Signed a note for five hundred dollars. Made your X with witnesses right there." Agnes fingered a familiar brooch. Sam tried to remember where he had seen the bauble.

Sam tilted his head. "You think I'm stuck, huh?"

"Like a pig at killing time."

"I don't have to go to Oregon."

She smiled. "You committed your word to Steve Wellman."

"Drastic times require emergency steps."

"Now you sit down for a minute and let's talk sense." A serious look formed in Agnes's eyes.

"I don't even want to talk with you."

"Sit down. We can work this out," Agnes said.

Sam dropped down on the ground. Agnes sat down on a camp stool. She looked down at the mountain man, felt a tinge of pity for him.

"I'm not proud of what I've done to you," Agnes said with sincerity. "You can check it out. We are married and you did mark your X on a note to the minister's wife. I sent Melissa out to get you drunk. We tricked you into the marriage. But—and you understand this, Sam Lawson—I'll never admit that to anyone. If another person asks, you were eager to marry me. You swept me off my feet.

"Now, the girls and I want to get to Oregon. We want to go along in your train. We'll do our best to keep up, not cause any trouble. If you don't let us go, I'll use every weapon I can find to prevent you from leaving Independence. Do you understand?"

"Yes ma'am," Sam said.

"Get us to Oregon and I'll give you a divorce."

"You promise?"

"I'm not interested in you as a husband."

Sam looked hurt. "I ain't that bad."

"There isn't time in one life to train you."

Sam considered her. He winked knowingly. "Man and wife, eh? What privileges go with that?"

"None to speak of," snapped Agnes.

"Lord, you're a sassy wench."

"Actually, I'm a pretty nice person. It's just that you got my dander up yesterday. Saying I had to get married to join your train."

"You know how to cook?"

"The girls and I are excellent cooks."

"Will you feed me along the way?"

Agnes smiled. "I'd consider that an honor, sir."

"You mean that, don't you?" Sam was incredulous.

"I don't mean to hurt you," Agnes explained. "You're probably a good man out in the wilderness. You've got the brawn, strength and experience to get us across the trail to Oregon. Maybe you don't have good manners—we'll teach them to you. We'll show you how to keep clean, take a bath and act like a civilized person in mixed company of ladies and gentlemen. You just need a little help to knock off the rough edges."

"Oh Lord!" Sam glowered.

Melissa came around the corner of the wagon. She carried a plate of eggs and fried pork chops. She approached the mountain man cautiously, setting the plate down without a word. Sam asked the girl, "You one of my daughters?"

Melissa nodded. "I'm the oldest." She told him her name.

Sam appraised the simple gingham dress worn by the girl. The garment was cut high, severe, and the collar rode high on the neck. He said dryly, "Dressed a little different this morning, ain't you?"

"This is my normal clothing."

"Ever find that brother of yours?"

"I don't have a brother."

Sam smiled faintly. "Must've been some other gal I met." He turned his attention to breakfast.

157

CHAPTER TWELVE

The emigrants at the campground were in high spirits. The True Christians had dampened the natural gaiety of the camp. After the sect had left for Oregon, the camp relaxed. Following breakfast, an elderly man with a long white beard and twinkling eyes took up his fiddle and bow. He stood under a maple tree, tapping his booted feet, playing a lively tune. Within minutes, a crowd of men and women collected to dance the Virginia reel. Children jigged and laughed wildly.

Three trains had pulled out that morning. One was a long forty-seven wagon caravan guided by Kit Carson, mountain man and scout. This column of canvas-topped wagons stretched across the landscape like a white serpent. The Liberty caravan, composed of twenty-seven settlers from Illinois, rolled out before noon. After lunch, sixteen families from Providence, Rhode Island, hitched up their teams and left. The easterners had pulled their wagons all the way to Independence. The oxen and horses were sore-footed. Their shoulders were rubbed raw by harness. Few guides gave the Rhode Islanders much of a chance to reach Oregon.

After breakfast that day, when Cynthia was down at the creek washing their dishes, Steve Wellman made a last minute check of his wagon. He was inspecting the wheels and axles when Jim Bridger rode up. The mountain man looked sheepish. He got off his horse and walked over.

"I'm looking for Sam Lawson," Bridger said.

"Should be in Independence."

"Left a tavern last night with a young girl," Bridger related. "I haven't been able to find him this morning."

Wellman grinned. "Maybe he doesn't want to be found."

Bridger's eyes twinkled. "That thought has occurred to me. You satisfied with that chile as a guide?"

"He seems to be a good man."

"When are you pulling out?"

"Probably tomorrow morning."

Bridger frowned. "My goods come up river by boat. Loaded the wagons yesterday. I promised to let you come along with me. Would you mind if I left this morning?"

Wellman looked at him sharply. Bridger's face was grave. A man's word on the frontier was his bond.

"We can catch up with you," Wellman answered.

"Good!" Bridger appeared relieved.

Wellman asked, "What's your hurry?"

"Got my craw full of town life. My wife's back at the fort. The trains are running ahead of me. A lot of pilgrims will need blacksmith work when they get to my place. Figure I'd better be there to help them." He got back onto his horse. "I'll see you at the fort. Follow Sam's advice. He's a good man."

*   *   *

Less than fifty wagons remained at the rendezvous. The emigrants rushed about frantically to connect with a train. That morning, Steve Wellman was besieged by applicants. He walked over to Mike Gorman's wagon. The two men talked with the remaining emigrants. Mike spotted Sam Lawson walking dourly around the camp. He hailed the guide and asked him to interview some of the settlers. Lawson judged every man suitable for their wagon train. The mountain man appeared sullen, depressed.

"Hell, take anyone who wants to go," Lawson said with annoyance. "We can't leave anyone stuck here in Independence."

Wellman was surprised. "You're sure?"

"They'll either make it or they won't," Lawson said with finality. He jerked his head toward a tree behind Gorman's wagon. "I'm going over there and sleep for a spell. This chile had a hard night. Don't wake me unless you've seen a Pawnee war party coming down the road."

After Lawson left, Mike gave Wellman a puzzled look.

"What's wrong with Sam?" he asked.

"Needs some sleep."

"Do you suppose he's hung over?"

"I did consider that," Steve replied with a straight face. "Sam's been living in saloons for the past week."

Mike chuckled. "The first week out should be great. Sam'll be sweating out the whiskey. He should be meaner than a she-bear giving breech birth."

A fairly competent judge of human nature, Steve Wellman felt he understood the guide's dour outlook. The rendezvous was ending. The good times were over. Sam Lawson would have to assume his duties, assert his authority, when the train left Independence. He was responsible for human lives. His decisions could well be a matter of life or death. Next, he would have to supply fresh meat to the caravan. At first, this would be small game and birds. When they reached the western plains, Lawson would kill buffalo for their daily fare. He would be expected to know the location of water holes. All matters involving Indians would fall under his jurisdiction. In another day, Sam Lawson would have to go to work.

Steve returned his attention to the emigrants. Their tight-set faces revealed the dreadful fear of being left behind. Most of the men were farmers. Plows and farming tools were stowed in their wagons. Energetic, these men exuded a quiet vitality. The campground was alive with their coming and going. They would be the backbone of the caravan. Their knowledge of livestock, nature, and hazards of the outdoors was considerable.

A few applicants were beaten men with downcast eyes. Their hangdog expressions indicated they were running from something—or someone. Debtors at home might wonder where they had gone. A sheriff could have a warrant in his pocket. Or, perhaps, they were attempting to outrun their personal demons. An invisible mark of shame seemed to be stamped on their personalities.

Sam Lawson was right. No one should be left behind. Poor devils . . .

"My name is Dan Pitzen. I want to go to Oregon."

Steve wrote his name on the emigrants' list. "Fair enough, Mr. Pitzen. We leave in the morning. Our guide is Sam Lawson. His fee is $600. We split that between the families in the train. What line of work do you do?"

"I've been working on a riverboat."

"A pilot?" Wellman noticed the softness of the

man's hands.

Pitzen gave him a forthright look. "I was a gambler."

"We won't allow games of chance on the trail."

"I understand. Gambling brings out the worst in people."

"You going to open a gambling hall in Oregon?"

Pitzen shook his head. "I won a fairly good stake last week in St. Louis. I married my girl friend. We're heading to Oregon for a new life."

"I hope you find it."

A short, squat man of about fifty with a jowly face stepped forward. "Elmer J. Johnson," he said. "I'll be ready to leave in the morning."

"You have all of your supplies?"

"Got a few things to pick up in town this afternoon."

"We'll leave at sunrise."

Elmer J. Johnson nodded. "I'll be ready."

A tall, gangly man with a large, tobacco-stained mustache approached Wellman. "I'm Bruce Middleton," he said. "You're my last chance for a caravan."

"You ready to go in the morning?"

Middleton nodded. "I'm taking two wagons. One for our personal effects. The other to carry my equipment."

Wellman frowned. "You got extra help?"

"My wife can handle the second rig."

"Is she capable?"

"She drove it here from St. Louis."

"All right." Wellman wrote their names on his list. He explained the details about the train's organization. Bruce Middleton listened politely and left.

Steve Wellman looked up and saw an old man standing before him. His bent body was resting on his cane. His double chin rested on his chest. His eyelids drooped down until, at first glance, he appeared to be asleep. The man aroused himself at Wellman's greeting.

"Good morning, young man," he said in a deep voice. "I do not have a wagon. I am too poor to buy oxen. I have no home. I want to go to Oregon."

"That's a tall order."

"Admittedly." The old man adjusted his hat to a jaunty angle.

"What line of work do you do?"

The old man drew a pipe from his coat pocket, tamped in tobacco. He sucked hard and the pipe gurgled.

"Line of work?" mused the man. "Anything from stock handler to running a manufacturing firm. I know a bit about bookkeeping, beekeeping, raising flax, indigo, wheat, corn, vegetables or any cash crop you can name. I understand the contrary nature of mules, the best time of the moon for planting, and how to find a bee tree for wild honey. I have slept outdoors because I had no money for a bed. I have lived in one of the largest mansions in Chicago, and owned several firms there. I have been wandering about in my declining years because of the Panic of 1837. I was a bit overextended and the financial wolves sold me out."

Steve asked, "Don't you have a home?"

The old man puffed on his pipe. "Wherever I lay my head."

"No money for a wagon or supplies?"

"Not a single cent. I am dependent upon your charity."

"What do you intend to do in Oregon?"

The man coughed, a deep hollow sound coming from far inside his chest. "Young man, I may never make it to Oregon. There is always that distinct possibility. I am

163

three score and ten years of age. A time when most men should be enjoying the fruits of their life's labor. Unfortunately, other men are warm and comfortable on my efforts. I live from day to day, like the sparrow which the Lord watches over. I will worry about survival in Oregon when I arrive there."

Wellman said, "I'll speak to our guide. What's your name?"

"Uncle Durg. Uncle Durgeon Adkins."

"Well, uncle, are you certain you want to go?"

The old man raised and pointed his cane at two boys standing at a distance. "Not only myself, sir, but those two able-bodied boys have received the call. While I might be a small liability, they have the strength and willingness to work for their keep along the route."

Wellman recalled Bruce Middleton's two wagons. He liked the old man. Uncle Durg Adkins sounded like a character, a man whose experience might enliven the trip to Oregon. "See me in a couple of hours," he told the old man. "I'll see what can be worked out."

The last emigrant had been signed up. Wellman was studying the list of the train's members. A shadow fell across the sheet. He looked up to see a well-built man in a dark wool suit. He was about twenty-nine, although his hair was thinning on the front and sides. His face was peeling from sunburn. His oval face contained a drooping mustache that was heavily waxed. His teeth were surprisingly white and even; their incandescence was enhanced by the tanned darkness of his skin. He said his name was Brad Payne.

He spoke with a New England accent and came from a socially prominent family in Boston. After a couple of nerve-wracking escapades running away from home, the youngster was sent to a boarding school. He won special attention from the instructors at school. He could compose an understandable sentence and, according to the headmaster, this was an unusual talent. Brad was advanced to a special composition class. The teacher, a slight, bespectacled fellow who liked to lay his hand on Brad's knee, spent many hours tutoring the young boy. The teacher suggested that his talent should be that of an author. After weeks of writing with pen and quill, Brad became acquainted with the drudgery of writing, revision and the hard discipline of literary creation. He decided the work was much too demanding, that composing poems and short stories was a dull routine. With a charming smile, and a disarming manner, he succeeded in graduating from the academy. His father made arrangements to enroll the boy in Harvard. Without saying good-bye to his parents, Brad Payne left home. He carried a few dollars saved from his allowance, a knowledge of the English language, and a sense of history. He also had a desperate desire to experience life, to visit the farthest regions of the emerging nation.

His first job was on *The New York Tribune*. The new daily newspaper had been established in New York City by Horace Greeley, who was rapidly gaining a reputation as dean of American editors. Brad started to work in the newspaper's advertising department, handling several small businesses as his accounts. He wrote copy for his accounts, ran proofs of the advertisements back to their premises, and performed his duties in a competent manner. Within a few weeks, Greeley moved him into the editorial department where he worked as a police reporter. Attentive and dependable, Brad quickly became one of Greeley's favorite reporters. As Greeley often said, the fourth estate was not endowed with an abundance of dedicated journalists.

Greeley encouraged him to read classical literature. Brad continued to read everything he could find on history. Each night, after the *Tribune* went to press, the newsroom became Greeley's lecture hall. He dazzled his editors and reporters with impromptu lectures on the true meaning of current events. Greeley preached the doctrine that a reporter must know the historical perspective of his subject.

At twenty-two, Brad Payne was one of the *Tribune*'s most promising reporters. He had mastered his craft. His writing was clear and precise, requiring little editing. Instinctively, he had acquired a certain skill at interviewing: knowing the subtle physical signals that told when a man or woman was lying. He had created a valuable network of sources. These people could be depended upon to tip Brad Payne when a story was available. His tipsters ranged from draymen to politicans, from maids to clerks, from policemen to members of the city's toughest street gangs.

With the mastery of his work came dissatisfaction. There was nothing more to learn.

He was capable of being the teacher—rather than the student.

He lost interest in his work.

Greeley, always sensitive, quickly caught the loss of quality in Brad's work. He waited for a week and then called the reporter into his office for a conference. Brad blurted out his honest feelings about his job, fully expecting to be fired.

"Once I learn something," he said, "I lose interest."

Greeley pondered. "Maybe you're one of the lucky

ones. Some people need a challenge to keep their interest high. Do you want to remain in the newspaper business?"

"I love it," Brad admitted. "I just don't want to be a reporter anymore."

"Want to go back into the advertising department?"

"No."

Greeley fell silent for a moment. "How about a transfer to the composing room?" he inquired. "There's plenty to learn back there."

Brad Payne reported to the composing room the next day. The foreman, a harried man with spectacles, gave him a composing stick. He led Brad to a corner of the shop, pointed to a type case. "Looks difficult," the foreman said gruffly. "Just a matter of memorizing where every letter is."

When the foreman left, Brad looked helplessly at the small partitioned sections of the type case. Each held a pile of lead type. He read the inscription on the front of the case: *18 point Gothic Condensed.* By mid-afternoon he was placing the lead characters in the composing stick, filling in spaces with various types of lead and brass quads. When he went home that evening he felt as if every cell in his body was in tune with some universal law. He felt wonderful.

Within six months, Brad Payne was one of the fastest compositors in the shop. He learned the tricks of picking lead characters out of the case, his hands a blurring movement. He could set as many strings of type as any man in the composing room, although Mr. Compton, an older printer with years of experience, was more accurate. Compton could set type for a week and never make an error.

Brad Payne introduced himself to Steve Wellman and Mike Gorman.

"I'd like to go to Oregon with you," he said.

Mike Gorman provided the details on the train.

"That suits me," Payne replied. He pulled a sheet of paper from his pocket. "I'm sending some copy back to *The New York Tribune.* I used to work there. Would you mind telling me about yourselves, how you got interested in Oregon, why you're going out there?"

Mike brightened. "This is for a newspaper?"

"My former boss is Horace Greeley," Payne explained. "He thinks the future of this country is in the West."

Steve grinned. "Sounds like a smart man. You going to be a reporter on this trip?"

"Sort of."

"Either you are or aren't."

Payne explained, "I used to work for Greeley. I've decided to go west and start my own newspaper. Got the type, presses, ink and everything I need in my wagon."

During the next hour, Payne interviewed Wellman and Gorman. Both men were honest, open and reflective in their replies to his questions. They were pleased to be the object of his attention, asking when the stories would be published, how they could obtain copies. They were surprised when Brad Payne asked a number of questions about oxen.

Gorman recounted his experience in trading his mules for oxen.

"I didn't like it, but I did it," he said.

"You were given good advice," said Payne. "This is probably the last great migration. Everyone considers oxen to be dumb beasts of burden. Even tempered, slow, sure footed, stolid, dependable, low headed, indomitable animals. However, if we look at oxen from a historical perspective, we find they have played a unique role in humanity's past. They have been pulling humans from one place to another for thousands of years. Alexander the Great used them to transport supplies during his world conquest. The great migration of the Israelites was powered by oxen. They're the same locomotive power that brought the great hordes out of Asia into eastern Europe.

"In those times, the mongol warriors carried all of their possessions into a campaign. The warrior's entire family, his wife, children and relatives, were camp followers. They even took their livestock with them— just as we emigrants are taking cattle to Oregon. Everything they owned was packed into their oxcarts.

"Whenever people start migrating, they turn to the ox for power. Oxen brought the hordes of Genghis Khan out of Asia steppes. They carried Marco Polo's silk and spices back to Venice. The Bible tells how the jawbone of an ass was used to slay enemies. Europe, Asia or America—the ox is king when people pick up and head to another region. Horses are great, mules are a compromise, but oxen are adaptable to the bleak terrain. A horse or mule needs a thick, high stand of grass for grazing. An ox has a different conformation of teeth, jaws and mouth. They can graze on grass that is barely visible to the naked eye. Nature made the ox capable of surviving where a horse or mule would starve."

"I wonder," said Mike Gorman, "if Sam Lawson knows that."

"He knows enough not to take mules out on the trail," remarked Steve.

"A smart man," said Brad Payne. "Now I had best get

back to my wagon and get ready to leave."

When they were alone, Mike Gorman was silent. His fingers drummed the wood table. He shuffled the sheets of paper listing members of the caravan. Wellman detected the Irishman's nervousness.

"What's wrong?" Steve inquired.

"Just thinking about tomorrow."

"You should be cheerful."

Mike agreed. "Except I figure maybe half of us are going to make it to Oregon. You figure those odds are right?"

"I'd say three out of four."

Gorman didn't argue the point. "We got twenty-one wagons. That means at least twenty-five percent of the people are going to die on the trail."

"We'll make it."

"Maybe we will," said Mike, "and maybe we won't."

Wellman stood up. "At least we'll give it the best we've got."

THIRTEEN

The spring night was filled with fog. The thickening mist had crept in after midnight to cover the campground. It twisted around, over, under and through the wagons. Heavy dew had also fallen on the white canvas tops; the wagons were covered with moisture. At half-past four, a rooster noted the thin light before dawn and crowed. A coyote howled from his distant kingdom in the woods. A blue tick hound shook his head, then bayed loudly. An emigrant stirred in his bedroll. He slipped on his clothes and left his tent. He stood stationary for a moment, yawning widely, stretching sleepily. He padded quietly to the edge of the campground and placed a bugle to his lips.

The horn trumpeted the start of the day.

Those who were eager to leave leaped from their bed, eyes wide and bright. They dressed quickly and made plans for the day. Those who were lazy opened their eyes for an instant, groaned audibly, and turned over into the warmth of their bedrolls. The realists grumbled. They wondered if the grass was truly up, whether the train would actually leave that morning, if a man could prevail in this vale of tears. And those who were frightened wondered if Oregon actually existed. Perhaps the ancients were right: the earth was flat. The whole kaboodle was headed toward the edge of the world. The fearful ones were scarcely able to contain their anxiety. Their nerves were stretched to a screaming tightness, pressing against the breaking point. They felt like actors in some grotesque nightmare, barely conscious, scarcely able to function, at the mercy of some dreadful peril.

The camp came to life. Emigrants moved hurriedly through the camp. They ate a quick breakfast, stuffing their mouths like gluttons, hardly taking the time to chew. The women packed the wagons. They stowed the tents, bedrolls, pans, dishes and food. They emptied ashes from their campstoves, poured water on the metal for quicker cooling, loaded the heavy device on board. They checked the ground around the wagon once, twice, a half dozen times; they could not risk leaving something behind. Children squalled, ran about or lay sleepily atop a box or crate in the wagons.

The men fed and watered their oxen. They brought out the great wooden yokes, attached the leather harness, and made up their teams. The reluctant oxen moved slowly, if at all. The sound of muffled curses drifted across the campground. An ox bellowed. A dog barked. Two families in another train decided during the night to return home to Pennsylvania. The two bearded Amish men were sour-faced and angry. Their wives were red-eyed from crying. They pulled their wagons to the side, standing quietly and watched the confusion.

His wagon loaded, oxen quiet but alert, Steve Wellman pulled his wagon into line. He had made plans to get the first spot in the column. The rule was that each wagon occupied the same position in line all the way to Oregon. The handsome black Spanish horse was tied to the back of the wagon.

Mike Gorman pulled up behind Wellman's rig. His oxen were frisky, unsure of what was happening, scared of the noise in the camp.

Mike called, "You get everything?"

"Positively."

Other wagons began to pull into the column.

Loud Hebrew curses could be heard somewhere behind them. Wellman walked back and saw Jay Samuels struggling with his oxen. The boy looked up, a plaintive expression on his face.

"You've got them harnessed too tight," Wellman said. He loosened the leather around the animals' shoulders. "Don't tighten too much. Harness will rub the hide right off their shoulders and backs if you do."

Samuels grinned sheepishly.

"I was afraid they might run away."

Wellman put a softness in his tone. "You'll learn. Everyone tightens harness too tight the first few times."

The sound of a woman's quiet firm voice halted Wellman. He walked back and caught sight of Agnes Miller, Jane and Melissa pulling their wagon into the line.

"You talk to Sam?" he asked.

Agnes crawled up on the wagon seat. "He hitched up the team this morning. We're going along."

Wellman pondered. "You got him to change his mind, huh?"

"You can rest assured that we're going along."

Wellman saluted. "You're a better woman than I thought."

He continued walking along the line of wagons. Near the rear, he found Bruce Middleton screaming violently at a fallen ox. The man held a whip in his hand and, with each frustrated cry, brought the last down on the animal's back.

Wellman went over, grabbed the whip.

"Don't ever beat your oxen," he growled.

Middleton looked around with a startled expression. "They're my animals. I'll whip them if I please."

"Then you won't go in this train. Those animals have to get you to Oregon. They're the only chance you have. Start mistreating them and you won't make it halfway there."

A woman jumped down from Middleton's wagon. She was in her mid-forties, slender and athletic in appearance, hair cropped short.

"I told him to quit beating that poor thing," the woman said.

Middleton grinned nervously. "This is my wife, Vivian. If Jesus was walking across the Missouri River this morning, she would tell him how to do it."

Wellman grimaced. He shook hands with the woman. "I'll help your husband get the ox up," he said curtly.

The beast was in the front yoke, lying on its side.

"Check the hooves," Wellman said.

"Looks more like broken bones to me," Mrs. Middleton asserted. "Bruce, check the legs first."

"Never thought of something in the hoof," said Middleton. He bent to pick up the oxen's leg.

"Any fool knows it can't be a hoof," said Vivian Middleton. She started to pick up the fallen animal's back leg. The animal reacted violently to being grabbed from behind. With a wild toss of its head, the ox began to stand

174

up. Bruce Middleton was thrown down onto the ground. The hooves of the ox barely missed stomping onto his hand.

Middleton got up and brushed off his clothes.

"At least we got him up," he said, shortly.

"And almost got injured in the process," added Wellman.

"No harm done," Vivian said lightly. "I knew it wasn't a hoof."

"I'd check just the same," Wellman said with a firm intonation. "You sure don't want to lame an animal the first day out." He bent down and checked the animal's feet. The left front hoof contained a sharp granite stone. He spoke in parting, "Put some pitch on that hoof tonight."

Going back to the head of the column, Wellman stopped when he caught a glimpse of Dr. Josh McDonald on his wagon.

"Ready, doc?" he inquired.

The physician nodded easily. "My future is an open ledger. Fate may write whatever she wishes for my life ahead."

Sam Lawson was waiting when Wellman got back to his wagon. The guide had shaved off his beard. He was dressed in clean buckskin garments. His boots had been stowed away and Lawson wore Indian moccasins. His rifle was in the scabbard beside his saddle, bedroll tied behind. He wore a holster low on his hip containing a Colt repeating pistol. The gun was identical to the one worn by Wellman.

"Where'd you find the pistol?" Wellman inquired.

"Dude in town was selling them."

"They're good ones."

"It better be for what I paid," Lawson remarked. "You think this caravan is about ready to high-tail to Oregon?"

"Some of the oxen aren't up to go two miles."

Lawson's eyes were expressionless. "Don't fret about it. Happens for the first couple days. Last year we barely got through Independence. Twelve hours of running and didn't make more'n a couple miles. Takes a while to get the teams worked in."

"How far we going today?"

"Like to make the campground out at Elm Grove."

"It'll take some doing," Wellman replied.

"Let me check them out." Lawson spurred his horse and rode back along the line. Steve and Cynthia sat on the seat of their wagon, watching the sun rise in the east. Cynthia had pulled on a wool sweater to ward off the morning chill. Nevertheless, she shivered from some inner emotion rather than from the morning's temperature. Cynthia Wellman understood herself fairly well. She recognized her personal assets and shortcomings better than most people. She freely admitted to herself that her vivid imagination was overly optimistic, that she viewed the world, and most people, with a divine acceptance. That morning, however, her rose-colored spectacles had been pushed aside. Her inner calm was disturbed by visions of unknown hazards: cholera, fever, diarrhea, accidents, Indian attacks, floods, predatory animals and the natural consequences of a two-thousand-mile overland journey through wilderness. She recognized her husband's strength, but wondered if the weakness in other men might pull him down. Yet, at the same time, she knew that even the most spineless men sometimes rose to a majestic grandeur. They could call upon their reserves of courage at critical moments in their lives. She hoped that everyone in the train would be heroic, responsible to their duties. Before the trip ended, she knew they would all—every man, woman and child—need to call upon the mysterious power within themselves.

Cynthia's thoughts were interrupted when Sam Lawson came riding up.

"Who's the old man back there?" the guide asked gruffly.

"He's driving Middleton's second wagon. Name's Uncle Durgeon Adkins."

Sam licked his lips. "Kind of old isn't he?"

"You said to take whoever wanted to go."

"I didn't mean dig them up out of the graveyard."

"Middleton needed a driver."

"Glad he's stuck in the middle," Sam said indulgently. "If he was leading the column we'd probably end up in Philadelphia. I don't think he can see. Now I think these children are ready to roll back there. You want to call them out?"

Steve smiled with delight. He stood up on the seat of his wagon, turned around. Mike and Molly Gorman were waiting expectantly.

"Wagons ho!" Steve yelled.

Mike passed the cry along to the wagons behind him. With each man crying to the wagon behind, the caravan moved out.

As the prairie schooners rolled out of the campground, onto the road, the emigrants continued to shout with happiness.

". . . Westward ho!"

". . . Wagons West!"

". . . On to Oregon!"

". . . Oregon or bust!"

". . . Oregon City, here I come!"

In the middle of the column, Uncle Durgeon Adkins hunched his aged body over the reins. His tired eyes glistened brightly when the wagon moved forward. He was finally getting his wish: heading to Oregon. He shifted his weight to relax the ache in his left shoulder. That was from a Wynadotte arrow taken when he crossed the mountains with Daniel Boone and Simon Kenyon. The dull throb in his back was from old age, weak kidneys and a tired liver. The pain in his leg was from that free-for-all in Chicago with those sculpin off the lake boats.

A tear formed in his bleary eyes, rolled past his graying lashes and onto his leathery cheek.

Finally going to Oregon.

A fine and noble land.

El Dorado!

A land of myrrh, sandalwood and precious jewels!

A place of majestic mountains, cascading waterfalls, and cool streams glistening in the sun!

Oregon would be a fitting place to die.

The wagon train passed through Independence. The town was quiet, sedate in the morning mist. It was only half-past six and most of the stores were closed. The town had a look of abandonment, the emigrants having headed west from this year's rendezvous. A few men were stirring sleepily, muttering loudly, as they loaded a large freight wagon for the Santa Fe trail. A Spanish *vaquero*, rigid and emotionless, smiled broadly as the train passed. He removed his large Texican sombrero and waved in a salute. Sam Lawson halted his horse at the front of a tavern, dashed inside and quickly downed a cup of whiskey. He came back out a few moments later, grinning widely, wiping his mouth on the sleeve of his buckskin shirt.

They had gone four miles when Sam halted the caravan for the noon meal. While Cynthia fixed sandwiches, the guide and Steve Wellman walked down the line of wagons. Lawson's advice was given quickly and gruffly to the members of the train.

". . . Watch that wheel. Better grease your axle tonight!"

". . . Don't worry about the Indians. Nothing but Kaws around here. They're beggars. Save your worries for when we reach Pawnee country."

". . . Check your harness. Don't cut the shoulders!"

". . . You're loaded too high!" This with a shake of his head. "You'll have to dump some of this stuff before you cross the mountains."

". . . Ma'am, I suggest you start fixing sandwiches in the morning. We can't take the time to build a fire for the noon meal. If we don't make twelve miles a day, we'll freeze to death, or—" an immense grin—"have to eat each other like the Donner train."

". . . Foodstuffs look a little light. Sure you got enough? Oughta throw away some of that fancy furniture and pack more beans."

They walked back to Wellman's wagon. Sam chewed noisily on his bacon and cold egg sandwich, surveying the wagon train, checking the trail ahead. His sardonic eyes viewed the emigrants with a certain glint of detached amusement. "They'll shape up," he said curtly. "Have to. Ain't nobody getting to Oregon except those that deserve it. A lot of these folks think we're out on a picnic. They will shape up."

179

The emigrants ate their noon meal, munching on ham, cold egg, bacon, and pork chop sandwiches. They stared at the bleak prairie and wondered about their future. They were now beyond the rule of law. Organized government had been left behind in Independence. Their next entry into a structured, law-abiding society would come when they rolled into Oregon City. They would depend on the train's captain for justice.

There was little bickering about their choice. Steve Wellman was the favorite. The emigrants recognized that a captain should be resourceful, even-tempered, intelligent, courageous and able to make a good decision quickly. They knew that Steve Wellman's wagon was well organized, his equipment maintained, his animals sleek and fat. His demeanor was one of fairness. A lesser man might have organized the train, then profited on the guide's fee.

Furthermore, Wellman ran his affairs smoothly, without panic or excitement. Some said this was due to his having been a wealthy farmer back east. Others claimed it was a result of a large bag of gold hidden in his wagon. Moreover—and this was important to emigrants from the northern states—Wellman appeared to be without bias or prejudice. He had allowed the young Jewish man—Jay Samuels—to join the caravan, along with Mike and Molly Gorman. That probably meant Wellman was not one of Calhoun's Secessionists, nor one of fiery Senator Thomas Hart Benton's Democrats. He acted like an anti-slavery, free-soil man. And the provisional constitution of the state of Oregon, a document devised by the diplomats and thinkers of two nations, had declared Oregon to be free soil forevermore.

"Listen, he's the best man for the job," Brad Payne

was telling a group of emigrants. "He judges people by what they do, not by the color of their skin, the religion of their parents or whether they worship at a camp meeting or a cathedral. Why, if the man was able-bodied, I bet Wellman would allow an Indian to go west with us."

A lanky man laughed darkly.

"I'm Wade Jackson," the emigrant said. "There won't be any Indians with this train."

Brad Payne turned to stare into dark, malevolent eyes.

"My point is that Wellman's a fair man," Payne explained.

"Maybe he is, maybe he isn't."

"He'd make a good captain."

Wade Jackson shifted uneasily. No more than thirty years old, he was sparse of frame, thin, bony. "That's the trouble with the world. We leave the law behind. Not a day has past and you people are yammering for someone to tell us what to do. Now I don't happen to be an Indian lover. They're lousy stinking savages that should be killed out. The only good one is dead."

"That's bad talk," Payne said. "We've got to pass through their land."

Jackson's eyes glinted with hatred.

His bony hand flashed into his pocket. Suddenly, his hand came up and forward. Payne saw the tip of a knife blade between the bony thumb and forefinger.

"Wait a minute!" Payne protested.

"Calling me a liar and crazy, huh?" Jackson licked his thin lips. He crouched and started to circle around Payne.

"Wade!" A woman stepped forward. Although she could not be more than twenty-five, she had an ageless look of defeat in her face, in her posture.

"Keep out of this," snarled Jackson. "I aim to teach this dude some manners."

Payne backed away. "You're overreacting, mister."

Jackson smiled condescendingly. He slipped the knife back into his pocket.

"Just a sissy boy from the city," he said sullenly. "Not worth the trouble to draw blood."

Payne stood quiet and looked grimly at the emigrant.

"I don't like Indians." Jackson spat out the words. "The main reason I'm going to Oregon is to get away from all the bastards back home. The second reason is because I want to kill a few Indians. I get an itchy trigger finger when I see a redskin. This country ain't gonna be worth a tinker's damn 'til the Indians are killed off. The government keeps mollycoddling the tribes. Shoot 'em. That's the answer. Savages don't deserve any better than that. There's going to be a lot of Indians die 'tween here and Oregon. You can bet your best pair of boots on that. Wade Jackson is going to take a few of them off their high horse."

Brad Payne did not comment. He turned abruptly and walked back to his wagon. From a distance, he gazed at Wade Jackson. The man had wandered over to a cottonwood tree. His thin arms flailed wildly as he talked heatedly with a woman. She was about Jackson's age with a look of desperate fear on her face. Payne decided the woman was probably Jackson's wife. He imagined what life would be living with a mean, bitter man.

Jackson appeared to be arguing with the woman. His hand came up to strike her. A fourteen-year-old boy, certainly no older than that, came running up. The boy moved protectively between the couple. Although his fear of his father's rage was evident, the young boy held his stance with trembling defiance. Wade Jackson hesitated for a moment, then spat and stomped away. The boy led the woman back to their wagon.

Josh McDonald came walking up. He cast a sidelong glance at Jackson's back.

"That one means trouble," McDonald remarked. "The woman is his wife. She's scared to death of him. She has a bad scar on her left arm. There's a bruise on her left eye. I figure he's the kind who enjoys knocking women around."

"He scared me with that knife," Payne admitted.

"That was a senseless move on his part."

"He's got a hair-spring trigger on his temper."

"You going to report it?"

"Who to?"

"Lawson or Wellman should know."

Payne reflected. "No need to stir up trouble. We're hardly out of sight of Independence."

"Jackson may not be dependable. They should know."

Payne shrugged. "Let's give him the benefit of our doubt."

Darkness was falling when the caravan pulled into the campground. The emigrants were informed the wagons should be pulled into a circle. Sam Lawson directed these tricky maneuvers. He was enthusiastic about the wagon train, pleased with their progress on the first day.

"You chil'ren are simply fan-dam-tastic!" boomed Sam. He roared like a wild animal, whooping joyously, when the last wagon completed the circle. "You-all are sure 'nuff wagon handlers! I never seen a how-de-dee circle any better than this one. Every dang man must've spent ten years bullwhacking on the Santa Fe trail. You drive them oxen like they was high-bred horses!"

The men were delighted to receive Sam's compliments. They laughed and joked as Sam went about the camp, shouting instructions, helping an emigrant unfamiliar with a chore. He explained how a corral would be set up inside the circle of wagons. A bit smelly, he admitted, but the livestock couldn't wander away during the night. Lord, man, don't hobble that horse, Sam cautioned. Animals can move twenty miles in a night, hobbles and all. Put that chile on a long rope and stake him out.

During this hubbub of confusion, the women began to prepare the evening meal. Camp stoves were hauled down from the wagons. Pots and pans—neatly packed in a single box—were set out. Sharp knives cut off generous chunks of smoked ham, a thick slab of bacon or fatback. Rabbits and squirrels, shot during the day, were skinned and tossed into a pot. Bowls were brought out. Cornbread, biscuits, johnnycake or fried bread were mixed and cooked. The pungent smell of strong black coffee assailed every nostril in the camp.

Within a short time, the men had fed and watered their animals. They dropped down on the ground beside their wagons, bone weary and tired. The women served up steaming tin cups of coffee. The men sipped the brew gratefully.

While the families ate, Sam Lawson moved through the camp.

"Get your bellies full," he announced. "Get a good feeling in your minds and bodies. After supper we're going to elect captain of the train. While we're all together, I'm also going to explain a few rules. They ain't debatable. You go on this train you follow my

184

regulations. If you think I'm too tough, then you got time to head back to Independence. Or, if you're a mind to, move ahead and hook up with another train."

FOURTEEN

Vivian Middleton listened to Sam Lawson's announcement with silent resentment. A woman of medium height in her late thirties, Vivian Middleton had a thin and fleshless face. The determined tilt of her chin, the rigid set of her lips, created a firm tightness in her expression. Her nose was long and thin, nearly fleshless. Her brown eyes glittered with arrogant determination. Their direct gaze signaled that Vivian Middleton was a woman who seldom compromised on any matter. Her mass of black hair, lightening to gray at the roots, was tied tightly in the back. This fashion heightened the severity of her appearance.

The manner in which she walked, the entire thrust of her body moving forward, was without feminine grace. A neighbor in Galena, Illinois, had once remarked when Vivian went past: "There goes an argument looking for a fight." People seemed to realize, without Vivian ever speaking a single word, that she wanted to run things. They pitied her husband, Bruce Middleton, and wondered how he'd let her get so bossy. Vivian had always had difficulty with store clerks, maids, anyone in a position she considered inferior to her own. She wanted her commands to be obeyed instantly, without question. She was capable of violently ridiculing a person holding opposing views. A single burning glance from her prideful eyes withered her husband's opposition to Vivian's plans. Not once had Bruce Middleton ever won an argument with his wife. One way or another, by wiles or ridicule, Vivian prevailed. Bruce Middleton was a quiet, docile man with a mousy appearance. To avoid trouble, he frequently accepted his wife's views with sullen resentment.

After Sam Lawson had gone down the line, Vivian Middleton chewed heavily on her last bite of bacon and beans.

"That man irriates me," she announced regally.

Bruce looked up. "Who, dear?"

"That Sam Lawson. This is supposed to be a free country. His rules. His regulations. His way of doing things. You'd think he's the only intelligent person in the whole wagon train."

Middleton eyed his wife cautiously.

"He's our guide, dear." Middleton speared the last bit of meat on his tin plate. "Sam's made the trip before. He knows what we have to do. We're lucky to have him."

"Lucky, indeed!" Vivian snorted.

"They say he's the best guide around."

"Who's this they you're quoting?"

"Steve Wellman and Mike Gorman."

"They're probably going free because they set up the train."

Bruce shook his head. "They're paying the same share

as everyone else."

"I'll bet." Vivian stood up and began to wash her dish. "I know that type. Always looking honest and forthright. Butter wouldn't melt in their mouth. Yesiree. Except you look behind those pretty smiles. Start checking things out. They're crookeder than a banker loaning money on a widow's farm. I want to be at their funerals."

"Don't say that." Bruce was horrified at the thought.

"Just want to see them crooked mugs screwed into the ground." Vivian was pleased with her remark. She continued to elaborate. "That'll be the only way they get buried. Screwed in head first."

"Be quiet! Someone might hear you!"

"Open up their minds a bit," Vivian replied. "Now, have you made any arrangements to get your name put in for captain?"

The thought had never occurred to Bruce Middleton and, should such an idea have intruded into his conscious, he would have pushed it aside.

"Vivian, Vivian," he implored. "I'm not qualified to be captain. I'm a bookkeeper and clerk. This first day out has worn me to a frazzle. I can't follow this train to Oregon, let alone lead it. I'd still be back at the bank in Galena if you hadn't argued with Mr. Springbrook. I liked that job."

"Springbrook may have owned the bank. He's still a fool!"

"I figure Wellman's the man for the job."

"We'll see about that at the meeting."

Bruce coughed. "Women aren't allowed. Only the men get to vote."

"That's another thing about this whole setup," Vivian declared. "Women and children face the same dangers as everyone else. We got to do the cooking, drive the wagons. Do this. Fix that. Jump down and get supper. Sit on a wagon seat and watch the tailend of an ox all the way to Oregon. I can accept most of that—but, doggone it, I got a right to vote. I got—"

Bruce interrupted. "I've heard this a hundred times already, Vivian. Maybe even a thousand."

Vivian glared. She stammered.

"You . . . you . . . you pervert!" she whined.

Bruce blushed.

Bruce stood up when the first group of men gathered at the far end of the circle. Vivian followed her husband, standing unobtrusively to the side. Mike Gorman called the meeting to order. He explained the purpose of the gathering. "Sam has a few words to say," the Irishman explained, "and then we'll elect a captain."

Sam Lawson explained the rules had been tested during previous trips to Oregon. He felt they insured that the majority of families would get there.

"Starting tonight, we're posting guards around the camp," Sam declared. "Every man, and any boy over fourteen, will be expected to stand duty. The only way you can miss is by being sick. I won't stand for any malingering. If you can walk, you can stand as guard. Also, there won't be any substitutions allowed."

Elmer J. Johnson raised his hand. He asked, "Why can't we trade off?"

"Good question. Things get confused. You're supposed to be on guard. 'Cept you thought someone else was taking your place. He didn't. That means the whole convoy is not protected."

"Makes sense," a man agreed.

Lawson explained that the caravan consisted of

twenty-five wagons and twenty-one families. "Some of them are single men without families," he went on. "We're a small train. We will elect a captain. He'll have the right to appoint a couple of lieutenants."

Brad Payne asked, "Why not elect the lieutenants? That's the democratic way."

"They got to work with the captain," Sam answered. "They should be able to work smooth. Now, we're going to elect the captain tonight. I hope the whole kit and kaboodle of you has given it some thought. We need good men to lead us. We're heading into dangerous country. Women and children are along. We made good time for the first day. I got no complaints on that. But the whole bunch of you better remember that we're the last train out of Independence. The trains ahead are chewing up the grass. Their livestock is trimming it down to the bare earth. That's one of the problems we face. Another is that the Mormons have a couple thousand wagons crossing to Salt Lake City. They're grazing their herds and livestock on the trail. If need be, we'll have to set up a detail to forage for grass away from the trail. Maybe go a mile or so out to find it. We can't depend on what the early trains have left us. The whole shebang of getting to Oregon amounts to two things: keep traveling and see that the ox and animals get their grass."

"What about Indians?" a man asked.

"Be ready at any minute to fight," Lawson advised. "The tribes around here are friendly. Not much to worry about from the Kaw, Osage or the Otos. Down south is the Cherokee, but they're civilized. They don't send out warparties. We don't run into much Indian trouble before Nebraska. When we hit the plains up there, we're in Pawnee territory. They're a bunch of nomads. Move

190

about except during the winter months. They follow the buffalo. Pawnee braves don't like wagons coming through. Claim we're ruining their best hunting land. They've been riled up for a couple years. I'm praying we don't run into a hornets' nest up there."

Wade Jackson stood up. "What about shooting a few redskins?"

"Main thing is to avoid a fight. Most Indians are beggars. Give those fellows a little bacon, some tobacco, a few trinkets and they're happy. We don't want fighting with any of the tribes. We got to keep traveling." Sam paused and looked around the assembled men. "Oh, yeah. I almost forgot. Some of you may be riding point. Or may be out getting grass. You'll see an Indian coming at you on his horse. That chile will be coming licketysplit. Like he's going to tear you apart. Just keep a cool head when that happens. That's their way of greeting a stranger. Don't shoot anyone out here. We don't want trouble. Fighting takes time. We don't have that to spare. Else, we end up like the Donner party from Illinois. Stuck in the mountains, locked in by the snow, and eating each other for breakfast."

Elmer J. Johnson inquired, "That happened?"

"Them chiles got shunted off on a bad trail. Didn't get to the mountains until winter. Too late to get through. The only thing they had to eat was each other." Sam surveyed the crowd. "Anybody got questions?"

A man stood up in the front.

He asked, "What kind of ground do we have to cover each day?"

"Ten or twelve miles."

"I'm a Christian."

"Christians got the good Lord helping them."

Vivian Middleton spoke up. "Do we have to travel on the Sabbath?"

"That's right," agreed the man. "We should rest on Sunday."

Two other men muttered their agreement. A man on the edge of the group declared that travel on the Sabbath went against Biblical teachings.

"Preaching won't get you there," growled Lawson. "Travel will. If the majority decides to stop on Sunday, I'll do the same. My advice is to keep moving every minute you can."

The guide turned and walked over to the nearest wagon. He leaned against the iron-rimmed wheel. Mike Gorman stepped forward. He asked for nominations for the position of captain.

Brad Payne stepped forward.

"I nominate Steve Wellman," he declared.

A man in back seconded the nomination.

Mike scanned the crowd. "Anyone else?"

Vivian Middleton smiled smugly as an emigrant to the side stood up. She had arranged for the man to place her husband's name in nomination.

The emigrant winked at Vivian Middleton. He said, "I nominate Bruce Middleton."

A shocked look came suddenly over Middleton's face. He stammered momentarily as if battling with himself. "I . . . well . . . that is . . . I appreciate being nominated for such an important post. I'm not fit to handle the job. Please withdraw my name."

"Don't be a fool!" Vivian cast a spiteful look in his direction. "You're as qualified as anyone. You might even win."

Bruce shook his head. "I withdraw."

Vivian seethed with rage.

"You got to have more than one candidate," she yelled at Mike Gorman. "Things should be done in a democratic way."

Gorman eyed the woman patiently. He considered asking her to withdraw from the meeting. Perhaps, he decided, she didn't realize that only men were allowed to participate in the assembly. He smiled.

"Mam," he said in his lilting Irish brogue, "I am open for nominations."

Elmer J. Jackson cleared his throat.

"I was talking with a fellow this afternoon," he announced. "He sounded like an all-round man. Not afraid of the devil hisself. So I'd like to enter his name for captain—Mr. Wade Jackson."

Mike located Jackson's thin face in the crowd.

"Will you serve?" Mike asked.

"If the people want me." Jackson smiled thinly, seemingly surprised his name had been entered.

A move to close the nominations was made, seconded. Wellman and Jackson stood at opposite ends of the circle. With Vivian Middleton muttering darkly about illegalities, the voting took place. Four men stood behind Wade Jackson, including Bruce Middleton. The remainder stood behind Steve Wellman. After his election, and congratulations from the emigrants, Wellman appointed Mike Gorman and Josh McDonald as his lieutenants. The meeting ended with appointment of guards for the night.

A half hour later, Vivian Middleton lay rigid beside her husband. Her breath came in short, rasping gasps. She had been enraged when Bruce pulled his name out of nomination. When she thought about the humiliation, her hands clenched tight. Her fingernails dug into her palms. At that moment, Vivian Middleton despised her husband. Her mind dredged up phrases and words. Lazy, shiftless, no-count idiot. Mouse. Worm. Worthless. Spineless. No good. Never amount to a hill of beans. She wanted to vent her rage, to shower curses down upon his worthless head. She trembled, checking her angry impulses. The other wagons were too close. Some of the families might not be asleep. If she started telling Bruce off, it might take the whole night.

Bruce stirred beside her.

"Don't be angry," he pleaded.

Vivian snapped, "You could have at least stood for election."

"Honey, I'm not able to handle the job."

"Don't honey me." She wanted to dig her nails into his face, claw away the skin. "You're better than Wellman or Jackson."

"At bookkeeping, maybe. But not running a wagon train."

"You might have won."

"I wouldn't know what to do if I had of." His hand slid across her stomach, then moved up to cup her breast.

"Don't start that. I'm not in the mood."

"We'll do it your way tonight."

"And every other night from here on out."

"Vivian, please . . ."

"Its like dogs licking around." Vivian felt her husband shrink back. "Nothing but a pervert's idea of love. Licking. Sucking. Like some animal."

"I think you enjoy it," Bruce protested. "I can sense the muscles in your body, the way you react. You can't mean that."

"I don't like that French stuff." Vivian pouted.

"Remember that night back in Galena?"

"Be specific. We lived there for nine years."

"The night of the bank's Christmas party."

"I was drunk."

"You were great that night. You should drink more."

"Drunks don't have good sense."

Vivian rolled away from her husband. "I won't talk about it. You're not a man. Mother's probably turning over in her grave. Looking down and seeing I married a pervert. Spinning in her cold grave."

Bruce sighed. He moved away from his wife.

He thought: Christ, it should be simple. Something brought people together. Maybe cupid, God, or some celestial matchmaking bureau. Men and women couldn't enter marriage by random chance. Love was too important, too sensitive, to be left to fate. Maybe there was a matchmaker in heaven. A bespectacled angel with the face and personality of a clerk. A good angel who matched reds with red, blue with blues, each according to his sexual tastes. Except the angel was getting old, not paying attention anymore. Or a demon was mixing up the cards. Blues were marrying reds, reds getting blues—things were getting confused. A woman who liked loving was doomed to marry an unresponsive man. A loving man was matched with a woman who blushed at the thought of nakedness.

A strange fluttering sounded in the night. For an instant, Bruce Middleton thought it was the rustle of angel wings. A man laughed. Christ, he thought the bastard angelic clerk is laughing at me.

He thought of angels, of sadistic clerks and files being mixed. His mind wandered to the beauty of a woman's body, the warmth of bare skin, the musky taste of a

195

woman's essence. And, thinking these thoughts and many others, he drifted off into a troubled sleep.

Molly Gorman raised her head, pushing back the bed covers. She kissed Mike on the cheek. She let her lips remain there. Her hot, pink tongue darted out to taste the saltiness of his skin.

"Love you," she whispered.

Mike Gorman groaned.

Molly rolled onto her side, facing him. Her hand went to that special place on his body, that warm spot that always excited him.

"Not tonight." Mike pushed her hand away.

Molly's fingers went back to that point, gently stroking with a feathery touch.

"I can't," Mike complained. "It's been a long day, Molly dear."

"We've got to make a baby," she whispered.

"Sleep is all I'm interested in."

"Lay back and relax. I'll do my tricks."

Instinctively, Molly knew she could soon have Mike aroused. Her fingers played a passionate melody on his flesh. They stroked, tightened, relaxed and pulsated until a warm, wonderful throbbing started deep inside him. Her desire rose swiftly at that point, a strange and terrifying desire for pleasure. Her mind vanished into limbo, replaced by a warming golden glow. Time and space vanished as if they now occupied a loving universe alone.

Mike's arms went around her waist, pulling powerfully. His mouth came against her lips, tongue darting and gliding like molten fire. His strong hand cupped her breasts, gently strumming her erect nipple. Under the pressure of his arms, her body responded with an undulating power. She thrust against him in a passionate manner. For an instant, she became aware of a wild, untamed passion that had never been present before. She went at him like a primitive woman.

Her hands glided over the hard flesh. Her fingers danced, stroked and flitted across his body. Her movements were delicate and gentle, then hard and demanding. He twisted and came moaning against her with renewed vigor. She felt his warm lips part, head dipping down against her breasts. His tongue left a warm trail wherever it touched.

Afterward, Molly was certain she would conceive that night.

"Marvelous . . ."

"You're the one who taught me, Mike."

He chuckled. "I didn't each you all of that. You're a good woman, Molly. You deserve more than I've given you."

She hugged him. "We've got all we want—except for a baby. I think we'll have that after tonight."

Mike slapped her fondly on the hip. "Not a baby. This was something special tonight, darling. I figure it will be at least five of the little boogers."

Molly closed her eyes.

"We'll make sure they all look like you," she whispered.

"Heaven forbid!" Mike kissed the tip of her nose. "Now I'd better get to sleep or I'll run our wagon in the river tomorrow."

"There's no rivers around here."

Mike turned onto his belly. "That's what I mean. Good night, Molly."

FIFTEEN

The caravan rolled north with a westerly course. The early days out were irritating. Everyone was being shaken down to their basic nature. Their true personalities were revealed in a thousand subtle ways. Men and women were stamped as weak, strong, gossipy, competent, whiners, complainers, grumblers, and happy-go-lucky. As a result, the wagon train carried an undercurrent of gloom. Seeking a new life, people also tried to shed old habits. Weak men tried to be leaders. Mean, bitter men and women tried to transform their temperament—to no avail. The hazards of the trail quickly destroyed their veneer of kindliness.

Steve Wellman and Mike Gorman believed the caravan was disintregating. They debated whether the train would reach the Platte River crossing. People moved about in a gloomy haze. Fear glittered in the eyes of weaker emigrants. People were soured by the natural discomfort of life in the wilderness. A plague of green-headed flies swarmed over the camp one morning, buzzing like hornets, biting everything and everyone in sight. Flying ants swarmed over the caravan that same afternoon. Camping in the open became an insufferable experience. Gnats, mosquitos, yellow jackets and other flying insects bit and stung. Oxen and horses bellowed all night from intolerable insect attacks. Women slapped and swore at the bugs while cooking supper. Children fretted without sleep each night. The bugs were everywhere, even during the day when tiny sting bees swarmed around their faces. Sam Lawson smeared his face with a thick layer of animal fat; he claimed the odorous substance stopped insect bites.

Although early in the season, the sun blazed with an intolerable intensity. Wherever a person looked, heat waves shimmered. When the heat did break, the caravan was struck by a savage thunderstorm. Menacing black clouds dipped low, seemingly touching the wagon tops. Massive bolts of lightning flashed ominously. The livestock bellowed, straining at their yokes and ropes. The trail was transformed within minutes into a mass of mud. Their third day out brought a vicious shower of hail. The pellets were the size of pullet eggs. Men, women and children huddled inside their hastily parked wagons. The din of hail on the canvas tops was frightful. After the storm, hail was two inches deep around the wagons. Animals were dazed and frightened. Canvas tops had to be mended.

That evening, Sam Lawson went from tent to tent offering encouragement.

"We're doing just fine," the guide drawled. "Circumstances ain't the best. Won't try and lie about that. Never seen nature get this bad starting out. Maybe this is a warning to them who feel fainthearted. Sort of a warning to turn back if a man's heart ain't in it. He can get back to Independence without having to go very far alone."

The rain and hail softened the ground. At one point the trail traveled along the banks of a creek for several miles. Two wagons became mired hub-deep in mud. Three hours and eleven men were required to free the vehicles. The storms had swollen the creeks and rivers. Fording any stream became a hazardous undertaking.

Despite these trials, the emigrants were impressed by the rich soil, the beautiful lay of the land. They passed through a series of alternating timbered valleys and gentle prairie ridges. Groves of elm, oak, hickory, walnut and ash trees lined the valleys. As they continued westward, the trees became poplar, cottonwood and willow stands. The white dogwood fell back, replaced by wild plum blossoms. Wild honeysuckle, sweetbriar, tulips and roses bloomed profusely.

Sam Lawson hunted daily to provision the emigrants. He reported that wild game was abundant. Every draw contained flocks of wild turkey; deer could be seen all around. Flocks of wild grouse nested in the hills. Vast flocks of snipe and plover, prairie hens, and green parakeets swarmed up before the train. Prairie gophers scampered away. On their fourth day out, a village of barking prairie dogs greeted their caravan. At night, the frightening howl of gray wolves kept people awake. Coyotes raised a howling chorus at the moon. Owls hooted and whippoorwills whistled.

Some men suggested Oregon should be forgotten. Why not stop here, where the land was so rich, the soil so good? Elmer J. Johnson, lately of Shawneetown, Illinois, swore the land was better on the plains than along the

Ohio River bottoms. "And you wouldn't have to worry about spring floods out here," he remarked.

Despite all that could be done, the train was strung out for four or five miles. The wagons broke formation right after the morning start. Some rushed ahead, others straggled behind. Sam Lawson cursed and swore the caravan would have to travel in a tight convoy. Men complained they were beset by problems. Oxen died. Weaker animals limped and jerked under the yoke.

The emigrants became afflicted with feelings of nostalgia. The loss of civilization was more troublesome than they chose to admit. Friends, relatives, acquaintances, all the substance of their memories, were being left behind. Women cried soundlessly at night. Men were surprised to find a sudden welling of tears in their eyes.

These factors strained their nerves to the breaking point. People became afflicted with a variety of mental and physical disorders. Arguments were triggered over the most trifling disagreements. Confused fear was transformed into sullen resentment, brooding anger. Intrigues developed. Cliques were formed to protect their members from incivility.

Women quickly tired of cooking under primitive conditions. They were tired, sleepy, short-tempered. Their days were spent with an endless list of chores: three meals to cook, kids to tend, animals to feed. Help drive the wagon. Keep the kids away from the mister. Don't forget anything in the camp. Watch out for animals preying at night. In some cases, men and women stopped speaking to each other. They communicated through their children.

Sam Lawson eavesdropped on one three-way conversation one evening. Elmer J. Johnson and his wife had stopped speaking to each other that morning. During their evening meal, they channeled their conversation through their twelve-year-old son.

Johnson stared distastefully down at a bowl of cornmeal mush.

"Son," he said gravely, "tell your Maw she's got to cook better'n this. A man needs three squares."

The boy said to his mother: "Paw says your food stinks."

"Tell him he can cook tomorrow."

"She says do it yourself, Paw."

"I got man's work to go."

"Maw, he says he's too busy."

Mrs. Johnson glared spitefully. "He got us in this mess."

"Paw, she says it's your fault."

Elmer J. Johnson's lower lip trembled for an instant.

"Tell your Maw I saw Sam Lawson hand her two rabbits just this afternoon. Why didn't she cook them?"

"You heard him, Maw."

"Tell that dumb old man of yours that I do the best I can," whined Mrs. Johnson. "I skinned those two rabbits. Laid them down on the stove and went to get my skillet and some grease to cook 'em in. While my back was turned, that hound dog belonging to Wade Jackson sneaked up. That dog grabbed the rabbits and took off."

"Paw," said the boy, "she's got problems."

Elmer J. Johnson seethed.

His words were spoken between clenched teeth. "Tell your mother that if it happens again, she is to tell me. I will get my gun and kill that damned dog. Then, we'll skin and eat him for supper."

The boy spoke with his mouth full of mush. "Maw,

sounds like Paw is fit to be tied."

Mid-morning of the sixth day, the caravan came to a fork in the trail. This was the point where the Oregon and Santa Fe Trails split. One road took a traveler into the southwest; the other into the northwest territories. The train turned north. Moments later, they topped the divide that led down into the great Kaw (or Kansas) River Valley.

The stream had been swollen by the spring rain. A frothing mass of swirling yellow water rushed downstream. The wagons pulled up before a rude ferry operated by Joseph and Lewis Papain, two half-breed brothers. Their usual and customary fee for taking a wagon across was one dollar. The ferry was a rough log raft supported by four canoes. The rude affair was held in place by a thick rope cable.

Sam Lawson had ridden ahead of the train. He was standing beside the ferry when Steve Wellman pulled up. Four Indians stood or sat on the raft. They were quiet and noncommittal.

"River's high," Sam remarked.

Wellman looked at the Indians. "How high is she?"

The Indians remained silent.

"Them bozos won't talk," Sam commented. "Cat's got their tongue."

A bearded man in a pair of black trousers and a filthy shirt came out of a rude log cabin. He approached Wellman as if all the time in the world existed. He stopped midway, picked up a rock and cast it in the swollen river.

"You the owner of this rig?" Steve called.

The bearded man looked in Wellman's direction. He

asked, "You want to get acrost?"

"I'm wondering if we could ford it ourselves."

"You'll have to make that decision."

Steve asked, "Anybody went across lately?"

"I wouldn't know about that," drawled the man. "I got a ferry for hire. I can put your people acrost without any trouble."

Sam Lawson looked at the angry yellow current. "How much you charging today?"

"How many wagons you got?"

"Twenty-one."

"That'd be $2 for each wagon, 50¢ a head for livestock and 10¢ for anything with two legs."

Sam cursed. "Mister, you're trying to gouge us. Your price last year was a dollar a wagon. The rest went over free."

The ferry operator's face assumed a cunning expression. "Figure you're about the last train this year. Ain't been a good season. Too many pilgrims setting out from Council Bluffs this spring. I got my help to pay. Plenty of cost to running a ferry like this."

"You Joseph or Lewis?" asked Sam.

"I'm Joe."

"Well Joe, I think you've been chewing loco weed. We ain't paying $2 per wagon."

"Suit yourself," smiled Joe Papain. "You're welcome to cross anywhere you wish. Just don't get your wagons upstream too close to my ferry. Don't want my raft damaged when your wagons come floating down."

Papain turned and walked over to the raft. He sat down beside two Indians. They remained silent, staring impassively at the wagons pulling up.

Wellman and Lawson walked to Mike Gorman's

wagon. The Irishman was sitting quietly on his wagon seat.

"We crossing?" he inquired.

"Fee's too high," snorted Lawson. "Half breed thinks he's got us by the short hairs."

Mike cast a glance at the river. "I'd hate to try fording that."

"Stick here for a spell," Lawson told them. "The Mormons run a ferry about five miles upriver. I'll go see what they're charging."

Lawson got on his horse and galloped away.

Steve Wellman walked to the river bank and surveyed the stream again. The current was swift. Yet, the water might be shallow. He went to the back of his wagon and untied his black Spanish horse. He dropped his gun belt. Riding bareback, he headed the stallion for the ferry. Joseph Papain's eyes popped when he saw the horse scramble onto the deck. The ferryman and his Indians rushed out of the animal's path. Hooves pounding on the rough timber, the horse raced across the wooden platform. Snorting wildly, the animal plunged into the river.

The horse sank out of sight. Wellman's head was barely visible above the swirling water. He swung off the animal's back and started swimming for the shore. Behind him, the horse surfaced and, kicking wildly, followed. Moments later, man and horse emerged from the street.

Wellman came back to Gorman. He was wet and dripping.

"Swift as hell and deeper than I thought," he said. "We don't dare risk fording it. We have to pay what Papain asks—or wait here until the water drops."

"That might take days," said Mike.

"Well, let's call a camp council and find out what they want to do."

Grumbling, complaining, the men of the caravan assembled. They complained mightily when informed of the ferry fee. Josh McDonald summed up their attitude.

"I don't like paying it," he said. "Corn's selling for practically nothing a bushel since the panic in 1837. In St. Louis, I heard a steamboat was burning bacon for firewood. Back home in New York State, a hired man will work hard all week for a dollar in wages. I figure this Papain is robbing us."

"I agree," interjected Mike. "There's nothing we can do except pay him or ford ourselves."

"Maybe the Mormons will be cheaper." This from Brad Payne.

Wellman pondered. "They're probably in cahoots with Papain."

Elmer J. Johnson stood up. "We'd better think of something. We can stay here until the flood runs out."

"Mr. Wellman?"

Steve saw Dan Pitzen leaning against a wagon wheel. The gambler was attired in a fashionable gray frock coat, finely pressed trousers and a low crowned, wide brim hat favored by riverboat gamblers. A black cheroot was held between his soft, uncallused fingers.

Pitzen smiled. "Maybe we could hornswoggle this fellow Papain."

"I don't get your meaning."

"You and me could walk over and talk with him."

Wellman was doubtful. "He's stuck with his price."

Pitzen took a deep puff on his cheroot. He blew a large smoke ring.

"It won't cost us anything to try," he explained.

"Anything's worth trying," Wellman agreed.

"I need a change of clothes," Pitzen announced. His manner was now efficient and direct. He looked over the assembled men, eyes affixed on Bruce Middleton. "You're about my size. You got any old clothes?"

"My regular wardrobe," Middleton replied.

Amid laughter, Pitzen explained he needed some worn clothes that a farmer might wear. Wade Jackson stood up. "Reckon I can outfit you, mister."

Jackson led the gambler down the line of wagons. The two men vanished in Jackson's wagon. Ten minutes passed. The emigrant's eyes widened in disbelief when Dan Pitzen jumped down and walked toward them. His hair was unruly now, slightly soiled, tucked uncombed under a farmer's hat. His boots were old, the leather cracked, scuffed at the toes, worn at the heels. The gambler now wore a threadbare pair of homespun trousers faded to a neutral gray color. His shirt had buttons missing in the front. A part of the left sleeve was missing. The gambler's springy, almost insolent, manner of walking was gone. His step was replaced by a hangdog shuffle. Pitzen looked like a tired, beaten farmer who had tilled the land for many unfruitful years.

Wade Jackson's thin lips parted with a smile. "Christ, you look just like my thievin' Uncle Caleb. Everything he touches turns to dust."

"That's what I want Papain to see," Pitzen said, not smiling. He was not totally devoted to business. He walked away from the wagons, followed by Wellman, and headed for the ferry.

Joe Papain complained when the two men walked up. He eyed Wellman with undisguised distaste. "Better give us a warning next time with that horse," Papain snapped. "I don't like people scaring my workers."

"I apologize," Steve said with humility.

"You pilgrims come to a decision?" Papain looked at Pitzen for the first time. His eyes roamed over the man, appraising his posture, dress and attitude.

"Seems high," Pitzen spoke in a strained, nervous voice.

"So's the river." Papain smiled.

"Our train's thinking about taking the gamble and fording 'er."

"Be fools to try it."

Pitzen whined. "Your price is just too high."

"No more'n any other ferry around here."

"Them Mormons charging the same?"

"You know Mormons," Papain said expansively. "They'd want at least $3 a wagon."

"Still awful high."

Papain grinned wolfishly. He wiped his mouth with the back of his hand. "Good luck on your fording."

Dan Pitzen looked down at his worn boots. He moved uneasily as if unsure of himself. He grinned shyly up at the ferry operator.

"Want to try something different?" Pitzen inquired.

"What you got on your mind?"

"Double or nothing," Pitzen said loudly.

Papain's eyes narrowed with suspicion. He stepped back two steps and his eyes appraised the two men. "You got some trick up your sleeve. True, you don't look like a gambler. More like a worn-out farmer. Seen a lot of them pass here. They all got a look of starvation 'bout them. You don't look as if there's $2 in your poke, let alone paying double for getting across."

The Indians, who had been sitting quietly on the back of the raft, moved forward. They listened attentively, black eyes darting over Joseph Papain and the two emigrants. Something was about to happen and, with luck, there would be something to talk about through the summer. They saw Joseph Papain put his hand up to his throat. He swallowed discreetly. Papain stepped back again and studied Wellman and Pitzen with all of his attention. The power of his cunning intellect was concentrated on the two emigrants. Outwardly, the two men exhibited no signs of chicanery. Neither had the appearance of a professional gambler.

"Wait a minute!" Steve Wellman's voice broke the silence. He cast a frowning look at Dan Pitzen. "I'm captain of the train. I can't commit us to paying double without a meeting."

Joseph Papain moved quickly between the two men. "I'll take your deal," he told Pitzen. "Double or nothing. How you want to do it?"

Pitzen fished a coin from his pocket. "We'll flip this coin."

The ferryman's hand shot out. His fingers clamped shut over the coin. He stepped back and inspected the gold piece. "Just as I thought," he crowed. "You were going to gull me with a two-headed coin. I knew there was something crooked going on. You intended to win by hook or crook."

Dan Pitzen shifted uneasily. He shuddered before the ferry man. He lifted his arms and spread his hands impotently. "I . . . I . . . you know . . . I didn't mean . . ." he stammered incoherently.

"The deal's still on," Papain said authoritatively. He handed the coin back to the gambler. "You'll probably *need* that, pilgrim. A lot of foolish men can be gulled with it."

"We can't do this," Wellman protested.

"Run up to the cabin," Papain boomed at an Indian worker. "Get that deck of cards laying on the window-sill."

"I can't go through with it," Dan Pitzen said in a choked voice. "I tried to rook you. It didn't work. You . . . you're too smart for me. I might lose cutting cards with you. That'd mean we'd have to pay double."

Joseph Papain threw back his head. He came forth with a high, barking laugh. "By God! You have made my day. I've seen every type of dag-nab emigrant come through here. A lot of them got all kinds of angles and gimmicks. Willing to pay anything 'cept good hard cash. One pilgrim was willing to loan me his wife for the night. All I had to do was ferry him over the next morning. She was uglier than a mud fence. Face looked like the buffalo had run over her—but she was right smart in bed. I seen 'em all—until you come along with that two-headed coin. I figure you tried to cheat me, mister, and a deal's a deal. Double or nothing and we draw the cards."

Pitzen asked, "Who shuffles them?"

"You sure as hell don't."

"I don't trust your deck."

"My deck or none, pilgrim," smiled Papain. "I'll send a couple boys up river to the Mormons, have them freeze you out. You either cut the cards or sit on this side of the river 'til dry rot moves in."

Steve Wellman bristled. He glared at the gambler. "This is a fine mess you've stirred up. Now we're in a real predicament."

The Indian returned with a deck of cards. He handed

them to Joseph Papain, then took a seat close to his employer. He watched the proceedings through hooded, impassive eyes.

"Maybe you got a marked bunch of cards," whined Dan Pitzen.

"That'd be more your fashion, pilgrim." The ferryman shuffled the cards. "I don't try and cheat people."

"Can I look over the deck?" Pitzen held out his hand and accepted the deck. He shuffled the cards clumsily. He turned the deck, fumbling, and slowly went through the cards. He remarked, "Looks like they're all here."

"It's a good deck." Papain grinned maliciously. "Draw one card for double my fee—or nothing."

Pitzen started to hand the cards back to the ferryman. He let loose of the deck too quickly and several cards fluttered to the deck of the platform. Apologizing profusely, Pitzen dropped to his knees and gathered up the cards. He laid the cards in the ferryman's hand. "Well, who shuffles them?" he asks.

"How about one of my workers?"

"He might set up the deck for you."

"Not likely," Papain commented sardonically. "If he was that smart, he wouldn't be working for me."

Against Wellman's protests, an Indian was called forward. The man made a fumbling attempt at shuffling the cards. Pitzen cut the deck. "We draw from anywhere in the deck," he said. "That way we know the deal isn't rigged. Go ahead and draw."

Joseph Papain approached the Indian, who held the cards in his upraised palm. The ferryman eyed the deck malevolently, reached down a third of the way in the deck. His face brightened triumphantly when he viewed his card.

"The king of hearts," he said with relish.

"Oh Jesus," Wellman's breath went out of his body. He could imagine the problems involved with forcing a double fee through the council. Every man would want a part of Dan Pitzen's hide. The fuss and turmoil would be beyond belief.

Pitzen was now inspecting the deck, moving cards in and out of the deck. He would begin to withdraw a card, think better of it, and push the deck back into position. He appeared hesitant, almost frightened of the consequences of drawing a card.

Papain smiled unpleasantly. "Quit fooling around! Draw your card!"

"I'm afraid to," Pitzen whined plaintively.

"Damn it! Draw a card or my men will whip the whole passel of you emigrants."

The Indian workers had moved forward. One man giggled nervously as Pitzen reached out, selected a card. He held the card face out toward Joseph Papain. The ferry man stared with numb incredulity. The Indians laughed and smiled. One man slapped his knee.

"You won?" Pitzen's voice was weak and thin.

Papain scrowled. "You drew the ace of spades. I got to ferry you damned pilgrims for nothing."

Steve breathed a sigh of sheer relief. Dan Pitzen smiled slightly and, pale-faced and shaking nervously, turned and walked back to the wagons.

"Get 'em down here," Papain snapped. "We'll start ferrying right now. Leastways, it ain't costing me anything. That crook with you sure has the luck."

"Indeeed he does," Wellman smiled. "Indeed he does!"

Two hours later, when Sam Lawson came riding back,

half of the caravan was ferried across the river. The remaining wagons presented few problems to the experienced ferrymen. By late afternoon, the entire caravan had been given a free crossing. Steve purposely withheld details of the free crossing from the emigrants. They camped that night four miles beyond the river, beside a small stream and deep in a grove of cottonwood trees. Dan Pitzen was back into his immaculate dress, looking as if he had just stepped out of the best and most expensive hotel in St. Louis. The gambler and his attractive wife were sitting at a small table beneath a tent fashioned of netting. Their food was on delicate china plates and, to his surprise, Wellman saw two crystal glasses and a bottle of wine on the table.

Wellman shook his head with admiration. "You know how to ease the problems of the trail."

The gambler smiled. "Have you met my wife?"

"Matter of fact, I haven't."

"Mr. Steve Wellman," the gambler said grandly with a flourish of his hand. "This is my wife, Erica. She's very adept at making do with whatever is available."

"But wine and crystal glasses and a tablecloth?"

"The fact that you're in the wilderness should not excuse a man from enjoying himself," said Pitzen in a cultured voice. "Perhaps we can have your lovely wife and you over to dine with us some evening."

"I make a lovely French stew," said Erica. Her long lashes dropped over her dark flashing eyes.

"Any time you want us, ma'am," said Wellman. He directed his attention on the gambler. "How much of that was luck this afternoon with that ferryman?"

"Why, it was all luck."

Erica Pitzen raised her wine glass. "Don't you believe

him, Mr. Wellman. My husband never does anything by luck."

"Well, whatever it was," said Steve, "you got us out of a tight spot."

"Any time. Any time you need me," Pitzen smiled.

SIXTEEN

Sam Lawson had long ago rejected civilization. He was at peace in the wilderness. Two things brought him back to town: a few essential supplies not supplied by nature and a good drinking spree. He lived unfettered in the outdoors and, during his years of roaming, became sensitive to the beauty of nature. He enjoyed traveling across the great land, seeing the lush spring growth, wild flowers, rushing creeks, wild game scampering over their unspoiled domain. The emigrants, however, were beginning to complain about the bleakness of the terrain. Lawson knew that any man with common sense could survive for years on this fertile prairie.

The Kaw River had been crossed easily. Gambler Dan Pitzen had proved his mettle in pulling the wool over Joe Papain's eyes. There would be many more rivers to cross before the caravan reached the Promised Land. Two days had been spent getting over the Wararusa River, now swollen by spring rain. They forded where the stream had widened. The ground was wet and mushy. Two wagons bogged down and the emigrants worked all morning to get them out of the mire.

The wilderness was getting close now. The Black and Red Vermilion, Big and Little Blue and, eventually, the Platte would have to be crossed. Trees were becoming scarce as the land flattened out. The wagons looked like schooners on a lush sea of green grass. Soon, in another day or two, the emigrants would be seized with dread. They would be fearful and anxious, unable to explain their panic. Sam knew their fears were the result of the American dependency on wood. When the first white man stepped on the Atlantic shore, he started chopping at the vast forest that stretched for a thousand miles inland. Wood was shaped, pounded, sawed, chopped, adzed, pegged and cut. Logs became warm cabins. Fences, boats, barns and bridges came out of the woodlands. Trees became the material for churns, rifle stocks, ox yokes, plows, saddle frames, furniture, wagons and a thousand other articles. The forest provided wood for fire. Hardwood trees were burned and leached for lye, which was needed to make soap. Walnut shells and flower blossoms were boiled to a dye for homespun clothes. Leather was cured with tannin, which came from chestnut trees. The paw-paw tree produced a delectable fruit. Maple trees could be tapped for syrup. Berries, leaves and bark were boiled down to make home remedies, medicine, and syrups for the table. Any settler with get-up-and-go stored nuts for winter.

Sam knew the settlers were attracted to Oregon by the forests. A man could put up a cabin, barn and corral shortly after arriving there. Logs would be pegged, carved and notched into furniture. The family fireplace would be fueled with wood. If a river was close by the homestead, wood rafts would float their crops to market. The guide figured that, while the plains were fertile, it would be many years before men dared to settle there. Sod huts and dugouts were not attractive. A plow with a cast-iron tip would break under the strength of prairie grass. A man needed more than dirt and grass to keep warm during a cold spell. Sam was struck by a sudden wave of sadness. He looked around with an agonized feeling. Someday this land would be settled. When that happened the wilderness was gone. The world would be surveyed, planted, fenced in. Roaming men—trappers, guides, scouts and hunters—would become aliens in a civilized nation.

Lawson wheeled his horse and rode back to the wagon train. The caravan had camped for the night in a low draw, close to a good spring. Women were struggling to prepare the evening meal. The jubilant laughter of children came from across the oblong encampment. Off to the side, a man was yelling loudly at an unruly ox. Agnes Miller cast a contemptuous look in Sam's direction as he walked up.

"How's my better half?" Sam chided cheerfully. He raised the lid of an iron kettle over the fire. The pungent smell of highly spiced rabbit stew wafted up to his nostrils. He grinned. "Aggie, marrying you was the best thing I ever did."

Her face turned crimson.

"Don't even mention that," she replied lowly. "I don't want other people to know."

"Face facts, Aggie. You're my wife."

"In name only."

Sam Lawson almost laughed. He grinned shyly as Agnes dished out a huge serving of stew on his plate.

"You're the one who went after me, Mrs. Miller. That's a fact. Can't dispute it. I was just hanging 'round Independence trying to drink the taverns dry. Wake up and find I'm hitched to you."

"I regret it. Especially after you decided to let any yahoo join the train."

"Honey, I'm a nice guy."

"Don't call me honey," Agnes said coldly.

"Common word of endearment."

"I'm warning you, Sam Lawson," Agnes said convincingly. "Just keep it up. Keep digging at me. Sniping and biting. Sitting there smelling like something out of the grave with that coyote fat all over you. A smelly mess. That's you. I've tried to get things done the best I can. Just keep it, up mister. You'll be eating cold mush from here to Oregon. Mush for breakfast, dinner and supper. Plain old mush and not even a drop of syrup to go on it."

Sam gave her a close scrutiny. He had not paid much attention to Agnes in the last few days. She looked tired, bone-weary. A hint of frantic nervousness could be detected in her expression. Her eyes, ordinarily warm and soft, glittered with a bitter hardness.

"I forgot," Sam said, "that you aren't a man. Guess I've been leaving you to handle all the work around the wagon. 'Course, it is your wagon."

"I'll manage," Agnes sniffed.

"Finding things tough?"

Agnes nodded. She did not speak.

"Want me to help you a bit?"

"Not if you think husbandly privileges go with it."

Sam lied. "Thought never crossed my mind. Honest."

"Well," Agnes said tentatively, "the wheel hubs are

218

starting to creak. I figure they need greasing. There's something wrong with one of the oxen. It's been limping all afternoon. A big tear showed up in the canvas last night. And I forgot to have the girls water the livestock before they left."

Sam looked around. Jane and Melissa were not about and, until then, he had not noticed their being gone. "Where they at?" he inquired.

"Over with that gambler and his wife." Agnes blew her nose gently. "They invited the girls over for supper. I don't know how Pitzen and his wife handle it. They served a nice dinner every night. Wine and china and crystal glasses. Act like they're living in the lap of luxury. Everybody else gets dusty and covered with dirt. Him and his wife look like they just stepped out of a parade back in St. Louis."

"The man knows what he's doing."

"A gambler? He probably isn't even a Christian."

"Maybe not," Sam commented. "But he sure knows the easy way to cover the distance between Independence and Oregon. The fellow has a bit of flair. Only fault I got against him is a personal grudge."

"A grudge?"

Sam stood up.

"They ain't invited me to dinner."

Agnes snorted. "Sam Lawson! Who'd want you for dinner? You eat like a pig. You got two inches of coyote fat smeared over your body. You smell like death warmed over. The perfect guest to be served dinner with fine china plates, a good wine in crystal goblets, and good conversation. The very idea!"

Sam snorted angrily. He got up and went off to do the chores.

* * *

As the train pulled toward Nebraska, men standing guard duty discovered another phenomenon of the prairie. Strange eyes glittered around the camp at night. Tiny circles of white, orange, pink and green light followed the sentry during his rounds. When they camped near Alcove Springs, one emigrant became unnerved pulling his first guard duty. He blasted away with his rifle. Sam Lawson came running up. The camp was in an uproar: men grabbing weapons, women hiding their children from a certain attack by the Indians. Sam came back inside the wagons and dispelled their fears. The guard had shot at a coyote.

Sam went on to tell of how firelight reflected back off an animal's eyes. Creatures were coming in from miles around to watch the wagon train. White was the color of firelight reflected off a rabbit's eyes. You knew when a curious wildcat or panther was around; their eyes were orange. A coyote was always pink. A yellowish-green reflection meant a deer or antelope was looking over the camp. "Critters are curious just like humans," Sam explained. "They've never seen anything like us. They sit back there in the darkness and stare at our wagons, our sentries, and wonder what's happening. Most of those creatures have probably never seen a human until now. The only thing you have to watch for is a pair of reddish eyes staring at you. That means there's a two-legged creature prowling about."

As he paced his rounds one night, Wade Jackson remembered the guide's instructions. He could understand the curiosity of the animals. Their homeland was being invaded. Critters couldn't live with humans around. Wade Jackson figured he had the same problem: something happened when he got close to people. His foul temper erupted even with his wife and kids. He spewed forth his bilious rage, screaming, striking out at anyone close to him. In Oregon, he planned to settle far back in the mountains away from other people.

As he paced guard duty each night, Wade Jackson prayed for an Indian attack. He wanted to see Indian blood on his knife blade. Indians had taken his mother from the living, transformed her into a demented vegetable. As a young girl, his mother had been taken captive during a raid on the farms around Boonesboro, Kentucky. She was held captive, treated like a slave, for two years. Wade's father was a frontiersman who married her after rescuing her from the Indians.

His first memories of his mother were of a gaunt, driven woman scarcely able to cope with life. Her night cries disturbed his childhood sleep. When he was seven, her mind shattered. She couldn't stand anyone's touch— including her husband and only child. When he was ten, his mother had been placed to a pallet in the cabin loft. She was clearly out of her mind. She lay childlike, uncaring, incapable of responding to the simplest conversation. While his father worked their hill farm, and hunted, Wade cared for his mother. He spooned gruel into her sucking mouth. He held his breath and cleaned her bed after an "accident," which was frequent. He had to lie downstairs in the darkness and listen to her body rolling to and fro over her pallet. She whirled incessantly at night, rolling from one side of the bed to the other. She screeched a single word as she rolled. One turn of her body equaled one syllable; some inner mechanism inside her kept count.

"In-juns!"

Thump . . . larump!

"In-juns!"

Larump . . . thump!

"In-juns!"

Thump . . . larump!

Wade gathered his courage one night, creeping up the ladder and peering into the moonlit loft. His mother rolled on the bed, spitting out the words through snarling lips. Her face held a feral expression. After that, he lay awake most of the night. He had figured his maw would someday get well. Now he knew she would never get better. She was like the kitten he'd played with two years ago. It had been playing in the yard, out back of the well, when a huge blacksnake came up. The snake coiled around the kitten, teasing the frightened animal. Reptilian eyes stared at the kitten with hypnotic horror. Hearing the kitten's pitiful cries, Wade rushed out into the yard. He killed the blacksnake with a hoe. He picked up the kitten, took it into the cabin for comfort. The poor thing was never any good after that. It lay on the floor and trembled. A few days later, the kitten started having "fits." Wade had to drown the kitten. He decided that night that his Maw was a lot like the kitten—the Indians had pestered her until her mind went off.

The next morning at breakfast he told his Paw: "I'm going to kill me a few Indians."

"Ain't likely," drawled the elder Jackson. "Ye got a right to hate 'em. I figger them skunks done in yer Maw. Fried her brain. I'd like t'cut every last one's throat. The gov'mint got 'em on a reservation. They b'long to 'em. We can't touch 'em. They got pertection."

"Ain't there Indians someplace to kill?"

"Out west. Plenty Injuns runnin' loose out there."

Without understanding the hatred boiling inside him,

Wade Jackson decided he would go west some day. He would kill a few Indians to avenge his Maw's condition. *Red-skinned bastards!* They didn't have any right to do that to Maw.

That night near Alcove Springs, Wade Jackson paced off the first guard duty. He carried his knife holstered on his hip. His Kentucky long-barreled rifle was cradled in his arms. A handful of beechnuts were in his pocket. Absently, from time to time, he took a few nuts, cracked the shells with his fingernails, and ate the meat.

He watched the eyes in the darkness. They were gone tonight except for a couple of reddish orbs moving close to the camp. He stiffened. Red meant a two-legged animal was out there. He hesitated for an instant, then resumed his pacing. His mouth took on a grim tightness. His senses sharpened with each step. He turned and started back along the line of wagons. He slipped the knife from his holster.

The eyes moved closer.

A twig snapped.

The eyes grew larger. They moved closer.

They were almost within touching distance when Wade Jackson whirled and shoved his knife blade before him. The eyes blinked shut as the steel struck a man's chest, deflected off a rib bone and drove deep into a fleshy substance. Wade moved by instinct now, slipping the knife out of the flesh and turning toward the second set of glowing orbs. He saw a shadowy form slipping across the prairie, rushing desperately through the tall grass.

The man he'd stabbed dropped onto the ground. Wade's knife came around and plunged deep into his belly. The man made a liquid, gurgling sound. He raised his arm in protest. Wade brought the sharp knife blade across the man's throat. He stood up and looked down on the dying Indian. The man's blood was seeping out on the ground. His eyes opened once, dark and filled with hate, and stared up at Wade Jackson. Then, heaving convulsively, the Indian died.

Wade Jackson looked down at the distorted face, the open but unseeing eyes. "That's one for Maw," he said, slipping the knife back into the holster.

Without fanfare, he went off and woke up Steve Wellman. He was shocked by Jackson's quiet, ordinary manner in describing the Indian's death. Wellman got Mike Gorman and Sam Lawson to come out and check the body. Lawson looked down at the slain brave while Gorman held a lantern. They talked in low, confidential tones.

Sam checked the wounds on the Indian's body.

"Right smart piece of fighting," he remarked to Jackson. "This chile's a Pawnee. Probably a young brave out trying to get a reputation. Sneak into camp, pick up a scalp and whatever horses he could steal."

"Other one got away," said Jackson.

This statement caused Lawson to become alarmed. "Which way did he go?" the guide demanded.

Wade Jackson pointed to the northeast. Moments later, Lawson was astride his saddleless horse riding hard out of the camp.

"What'll I do with this one?" Wade asked.

Wellman pondered. "Let's drag him far enough away so nobody sees him."

"Leave him for the animals?"

"I don't want to dig a grave. Do you?"

Wade shook his head. "I get the scalp."

Wellman looked at the Kentuckian's skin-tight face. "That's a pretty grisly thing to want."

"Hang it on my cabin wall when I get to Oregon."

Mike Gorman looked at Jackson with distaste. "Just the thing to perk up a drab room, eh?"

"I killed him. I get to scalp him."

Wellman reach down and took the dead Indian's arm. He began to drag the corpse away from the camp. Gorman stepped forward, took the other arm. Jackson followed them until, when they reached a sunken point in the earth about two hundred yards from the camp, they pushed the body into the ravine. Wade Jackson cursed, then jumped down and started knifing the scalp from the Indian's head. He came back to the wagon train a few minutes later, holding the dripping scalp.

"My first one," Jackson boasted, holding his grisly trophy up to the lantern light.

Steve Wellman turned away.

"You want to have me pull the rest of your guard duty?" he asked Jackson.

The Kentuckian grinned maliciously. "Not a chance! I want to collect a hundred scalps on this trip."

Jackson stood off to the side, the lantern light illuminating his features. His thin, fleshless face looked like a white skull. Sweat glistened on his forehead. He looked out into the darkness with cold determination. Both Wellman and Gorman felt the coldness of his personality. They turned and went back to their wagons.

Sam Lawson sat astride his horse. The animal raced through the night. Sam prayed the animal would avoid gopher holes and other prairie hazards. The night was quiet, dark, the moon hidden by a cloud. About a mile from the camp, Lawson reined in his steed. He waited quietly, muffling the animal's heavy breathing. The moon came from behind its cover. In the distance, a quarter mile off to the right, the guide's eyes caught sight of a running figure.

Sam leaped up on the horse. He kicked the animal's sides and felt powerful legs start pounding forward. The Indian heard the pounding hooves, stopped and stared back. By then, Sam was closing the distance between them at a fast clip. The Indian pulled an arrow and began to fit it onto his bow. Sam kicked his horse and the trained animal veered to the side. The arrow whizzed harmlessly away past. The Indian had decided to make a stand rather than try and outrun the horse. The second arrow plucked at the sleeve of Sam's deerskin shirt. He started to draw his pistol, then realized the noise might alert other Indians. He waited and rode forward. He tasted a coppery bile as he came closer to the lone Indian. The third arrow grazed his wrist.

He rode on and, as he came pounding up, he saw the look of fear in the Indian's face. He was nothing more than a boy, scarcely in his teens. The horse rode straight for the Indian, hooves pounding viciously on the earth. The boy wheeled and started to run. The horse veered at the last instant and Sam Lawson leaped off at an angle. He slammed hard against the Indian's back. Both men went rolling in the thick prairie grass. The Indian scrambled up, half running, half crawling. Sam caught up with him. The boy cried out in terror. Sam's fist slammed into the boy's body, deep into the mid-section. The Indian bent over with gasping pain. Sam's knee came rushing up. The sound of crunching bone came from the Indian's face. Blood gushed out of his mouth and nose.

The Indian whimpered.

Sam grabbed the Indian's head in a bear hug. His thumbs dug deep into the sockets of the eyes. Deftly, he popped both eyes out of their sockets. The Indian began to scream. Sam's fingers went around his throat. His thumb pressed viciously against the Indian's windpipe. The boy made a gurgling, pleading sound. His body went limp.

Sam dropped the dead Indian onto the ground. Breathing heavily, he listened to the night sounds. From a distance, over a small hill, he heard the neighing sound of Indian ponies. Sighing heavily, he loaded the corpse on his horse and went off in the opposite direction. Two miles past the camp, he dropped the corpse in a swampy area by a small stream. He covered the body with reeds and bulrushes. It would require a large scouting party to locate the boy's body. He came back to camp, picked up the scalpless corpse and hid it deeper in the swamp.

Sam's eyes were bleary and reddened when he spoke with Steve Wellman the next morning. Lawson smiled faintly when told that Jackson had scalped his corpse.

"He handled things real fine out there," Sam said. "Don't be too hard on the chile. Men who kills out here has a right to a trophy. Knew an old trapper who took little fingers. Another was sold on making a necklace out of Indian ears. I would congratulate Wade Jackson on a fine job. Let it go at that."

"What about the other one?" Steve asked.

"Just a boy." Lawson noticed Wellman wince. "There's a Pawnee hunting party down this way. Either that, or a war party out to pester the peaceful tribes further south. If they're hunting, we got problems. That means the wagons are destroying the hunting up in

Nebraska. Don't doubt it, either, for my part. That'll mean the Pawnees are madder'n hell. They'll be spoiling for a fight."

"I kept quiet about last night," said Wellman.

"Wait until Wade gets to talking," Lawson said with a slight smile. "The news will be all over the train. Best to be open about these things."

Wellman nodded and went off to talk with Wade Jackson. The Kentuckian was standing beside his oxen, surrounded by a group of admiring men. Jackson was holding up the bloody scalp. Wellman went back to yoke up his oxen. It was time to roll out.

SEVENTEEN

A feeling of numbness passed through the caravan. Minds were fogged by the monotony of the landscape. The lush, green flat land stretched endlessly in all directions. Without incident, the emigrants crossed the Blue River and headed up into Nebraska. The glare of the sun became intense. The wind blew relentlessly. Everything was covered with a thick layer of dust and dirt. Without trees to remind them of their homes, the emigrants became disagreeable. Husbands argued with their wives who, in turn, reprimanded their children. Arguments started over trifling matters. Each morning at four o'clock, the bugle sounded and people rolled out to start another day. The caravan covered eight, ten, sometimes fifteen miles before striking camp at night.

Eat breakfast!

Hitch the oxen!

Roll out!

Why won't those damned animals follow orders?

Elmer J. Johnson walked with a limp. An ox had

shifted weight, bringing a hoof down on Johnson's instep. Brad Payne was kicked in the shoulder by another ox. A mule, belonging to another emigrant, had bitten Uncle Durgeon Adkins when the old man dropped his guard.

Roll out!

"... *Lord! What I wouldn't give for the taste of fresh ice water!*"

Water was carried in barrels lashed to the sides or back of each wagon. By mid-morning, the temperature was tepid. By noon, water tasted almost as if it was boiling. As a result of their diet, and in some instances, water, the emigrants suffered from diarrhea. Children came down with painful stomach cramps. People grumbled about the train stopping so often. Sam Lawson allowed the caravan's line to be broken. Wagons could stop for a "nature call" without blocking the passage of other rigs. People averted their eyes when a suffering person leaped down from his wagon, dropped his clothes and passed a thin, yellow liquid.

Roll out!

"... *Push on! Man, we got to push on!*"

Sit rigid on that damned hard wagon seat. Stare off at the flat land. Feel every jolt come slamming up into your tail bone. Listen to the old woman and kids whine and complain. Swat away the flying insects. Wonder why you ever wanted to go to Oregon.

Roll out!

"... *I hope I never see another mosquito!*"

DEAR JOURNAL: It is not true that the mosquitos are the size of turkey buzzards. That appears to be an exaggeration. They are no more than the size of a large crow.

Roll out!

"*. . . Land of goshen! Keep those kids quiet! A man can't think!*"

Pull into camp at night, wondering if you can make it tomorrow. Feed the animals. Drag enough water in from the river to keep them through the night. Drop on your pallet after a quick supper. How far, O Lord, how far to Oregon?

Roll out!

"*. . . Them Kaw injuns seemed like children. Even ole Wade Jackson couldn't fault them boogers. Ain't that feller a prize? Getting that Pawnee scalp for hisself? Really something!*"

Worry about Indians until your mind chews on itself. Worry about whether the Pawnee might attack somewhere in Nebraska. Worry if you've got the courage to stand like a man during an Indian raid. What if you're all alone someplace when they come riding up hell-bent-for-election? Worry about the wife and kids getting hurt. Envision their bodies on the ground, arrows protruding from their breasts. Worry about the baby getting scalped, killed, because he is the best of the bunch. Hopes and dreams are riding on that little tow-headed kid.

Roll out!

"*. . . Damn! I didn't see that gopher hole. Twisted my ankle!*"

Roll out!

Don't stop for nothing!

Roll out!

The snow flies early in the mountains of eastern Oregon!

Roll out!

Chrissakes! The thing I hate most is that bugle

blowing in the morning. I'd love to stuff the horn down that gent's gullet.

Roll out!

Keep the wagons moving!

Roll out!

Oregon or bust!

Bruce Middleton lay beside his wife, Vivian, and listened to the night sounds outside their tent. The plaintive wail of a baby could be heard in a distant wagon. Someone was snoring in a nearby tent. Faintly, he could hear Vivian's muffled breathing. He tried to move from under a growing sense of dread, to dispel the oppressive loneliness that afflicted his psyche. With love he could withstand whatever lay ahead on the trail to Oregon. He would leave the girl waiting under the trees. Bruce sighed and moved closer to his wife. She endured his closeness for an instant, then growled with displeasure. To signal her growing irritation, she moved her arm quickly. Her elbow slammed against the bridge of his nose.

"Quit crawling me!" Vivian snarled.

"That hurt."

"I meant it to."

He whispered, "Talk with me a few minutes."

"I'm tired. I need my sleep."

Muttering lowly, Bruce picked up his clothes and boots. He slipped out of the tent, stood in the darkness and dressed quickly. His heart pounded with anticipation as he told the guard he was going for a walk. He hurried swiftly away from the wagon train to the grove of trees down by a small creek. He waited for Melissa to come to him.

His mind was feverish and confused. He had been

silently courting Melissa, the girl who traveled with Agnes Miller, for several days now. He was surprised when the girl's stare, bold and knowing, met his eyes one evening in camp. He held her gaze momentarily, then averted his glance. Next, she sweetly asked his help in putting up her tent. He was embarrassed around the girl. It seemed inconceivable that she would be interested in a tired, meek clerk, so many younger men were in the train.

The following day, Melissa came down to the creek when he was watering his oxen. She bent and dipped a pail in the fast flowing stream. She said, "I take walks at night. I heard you and your wife arguing the other night."

His heart skipped a beat. He tried to speak, but made a tight, strangled sound.

Melissa was direct.

"Your wife doesn't love you," she said.

"I don't know. We're married," he replied.

"She doesn't like you to do things to her."

"Oh, we get along pretty well."

"A real woman would keep her man wore out."

"I don't know about that."

"I do," Melissa looked up into his face. "I'm sure that the kind of love you want to give her isn't wicked. People did it all the time back in Natchez. Besides, a woman is supposed to surrender to her man."

He laughed. "Vivian wouldn't surrender to the devil himself."

She pulled her bucket out of the creek and stood up. "Maybe you ought to think about getting another woman."

"Leave Vivian?" The thought had never occurred to Bruce Middleton.

"Not that, silly." Melissa smiled. "Maybe someone on

233

the side. Somebody to cheer you up. Someone to talk to when you're feeling lonely."

He bristled. "How do you know how I feel?"

"Written all over your face. You're an unhappy man."

"That shows?"

"Sure does. You walk around with a hangdog look. Woe is me! The whole world is raining on my wagon train!"

He coughed. "You got anybody in mind for cheering me up?"

"Won't say for sure."

"You're talking awful brazen."

"Figure we might get acquainted a bit better. That's all."

His mind reeled. "How do we do that?"

"I'll meet you outside the camp some night."

"You'll . . . meet . . . me?" His words were slow and leaden.

"You can be my first beau."

"Let a married man spark you?"

"Great God in heaven!" Melissa said with exasperation. "I won't drag you out of your wife's bed, Bruce Middleton. I've gone much further than a proper girl would. The next step is up to you, fancy pants."

With a toss of her head, Melissa turned and walked angrily back to the camp. Bruce Middleton stood dumbfounded beside the small stream. He watched the sun glitter off the water pail onto the back of her dress. Beneath that fabric was a warm, firm young woman's body. His eyes locked on her hips, followed the undulation of her pelvic movements. Desire began to swell in his loins. Fearfully, he glanced around and sighed gratefully. No one had been close enough to overhear their conversation, to see the love growing in his eyes.

Two days later, he had whispered that Melissa should meet him under the trees that night. Purposely, he had sought warmth and affection from Vivian. The result was a painful jab against his nose. He thought about his marriage and, still fearful of breaking his vows, had gotten up and walked away from the camp.

He waited and wondered if Melissa would come. His mind became feverishly hot as he envisioned the face and body of the young woman. She had beautiful eyes, soft, deep, brown and liquid. The gaze of an innocent young girl intrigued by the mystery of love. Yet, with the erotic rationality peculiar to her species, Melissa would pick the man, time, and place of her deflowerment. Those eyes demanded a man with a strong sense of erotic pleasure, a man with romantic strength. A man who could listen to, and understand, the fears of a young girl. A man who could erase her doubts about life. A man who could gently guide her into maturing womanhood.

He felt that Melissa had the ability to love beyond what he had experienced. She could give of herself, surrender easily to another person. Yet, from the directness of her approach, she possibly realized that much of love was impersonal, physical intercourse between two lusting bodies. He hoped that, should Melissa join him, there would be a merging of body, mind and spirit.

During all of his years, Bruce Middleton had been puzzled by love. He believed the phenomenon was a mystery, a riddle beyond solution. He knew that the reason for human existence was related to the bonding chemistry between a man and woman. Yet, without that elusive quality known as love, sex became nothing more than a physical rote test. The act was memorized and repeated endlessly without feeling, without affection.

He waited. He paced under the cottonwood and willow trees. Love, he decided, was the essence of human existence—the greatest gift a person could bestow upon another individual. Yet, love had to be given without demands, qualifications or rules. The sheen of love became tarnished when boundaries were created. The satiny smoothness of a relationship became stained.

During the past few days, his every waking moment had been spent in thinking about Melissa. An incurable romantic who idealized women, Bruce Middleton felt Melissa had grown up under unusual circumstances. She was without inhibitions. Walls had not been erected around her emotions. She was free to receive or give love. Her affectionate nature could be fully expressed in a natural manner.

He stopped walking and glanced toward the camp. Melissa was walking across the grassy field. She appeared like a ghost in the moonlight. Moonbeams reflected off her white dress. His heart pounded frantically as the girl approached. She looked gravely toward him, a tight, nervous smile touching her lips. As she came up, he pushed a curl away from her forehead. They came together with a surprisingly natural embrace. Her small breasts pressed firmly against his chest. A hot wave of desire surged through him as their lips touched. He moaned softly, far back in his throat, when her tongue glided across his lips, pressing for entrance into his mouth. His hands left her shoulders and dropped to her hips. He pulled her close and, with a tiny liquid sound, she welcomed the thrust of his manhood. She shifted her legs slightly, opening and capturing his hardness within her limbs. Still kissing, she began to undulate against him.

"Oh God," he moaned.

"As good as I imagined."

"Better."

"You're so sweet!" Her soft warm lips brushed against his cheek.

"We shouldn't be doing this."

"But it feels so good."

"Oh God! Never like this before."

"Mmmmm. . ."

"Oooh! Do that again." A wave of passion swept through him.

"We have to be careful."

"Hmmm."

"I don't want to get pregnant."

"Honey, I've got to have you."

"We'll do it different—the way you like." Her lips pursed. She sucked his lower lip, gliding her tongue over the flesh. A wild and primitive feeling came over him. He wanted this woman, consequences be damned! A warm sensuality flooded his senses. He felt himself being pulled down into the grass, felt her hand tug at the buttons of his trousers.

Melissa smiled like a delighted child when he was exposed. She moistened her lips with her pink tongue, exclaiming, "Beautiful. Absolutely beautiful."

He was shocked when she pulled up her skirt. She wore no undergarments; her tight white flesh glistened in the moonlight.

"Oh my God," he whispered. His lips touched the mound of her hip, tasting, exploring. A warm and velvet smoothness of virginal flesh. His nostrils flared with the scent of her essence.

Lying there beneath the trees, they made love. The golden swirl of her mouth was more satisfying than he had imagined.

Afterward, they lay entwined and looked up into the sky.

She asked, "Was I good?"

"Tremendous!"

"Better than your wife?"

"Who?"

"Your wife."

"We never did it that way before."

"Cheer up!" she whispered, nibbling his ear. "You've got me."

He wanted to tell Melissa that this would be their only time together. "Melissa—" he began.

"Hmmm?"

"We'll have to be careful."

"We will, darling. Just think: like this all the way to Oregon. Maybe I can live close to you out there."

"Won't Agnes catch you sneaking out of camp?"

"I'll think of something. What about your wife?"

"Once she gets to sleep, the devil couldn't wake her."

She kissed him gently. "Then we've got nothing to worry about."

"Except getting past the guards each night."

She smiled. "We'll figure something out. This is too good to give up. You feel that way?"

"God, yes."

They made love again. After that, they waited until a high dark cloud obscured the moon. They walked back to the camp in the darkness. While Bruce diverted the guard's attention, Melissa slipped into her tent. Moments later, he removed his clothing and boots. He slipped into the tent and lay down beside his wife. Vivian was sleeping soundly, her lips making a rubbery sound when she exhaled. He felt exhilarated, truly alive for the first time in his life. Melissa was so damned beautiful, so lovely, so warm and eager to receive his touch. She was all that a man could want. Furthermore, he realized with a surprise that he did not feel unclean. Every part of his body tingled with a glowing energy. When Vivian rolled in her sleep, her back touching his arm, he moved away hastily.

EIGHTEEN

Trouble started the next morning when they were breaking camp. Steve Wellman was hitching up his oxen when a commotion started down by the creek. He dropped his harness and ran in that direction. Elmer J. Johnson and two young boys raced toward the camp across the grassy clearing. Their legs pumped fiercely and, within a few moments, they were safely inside the wagons.

"Indians!" Johnson blurted out.

"Where?" demanded Wellman.

Johnson pointed a trembling finger toward the creek. "We were getting ready to fill the water barrel. Heard a noise in the brush across the river. Looked over and Indians were staring directly at us. We dropped our buckets and run."

Sam Lawson came running up.

"How many did you see?" the guide inquired.

"Three—all with spears!"

Men scurried around the encampment, grabbing rifles

and pistols.

". . . Get ready for an attack!" yelled an emigrant.

". . . Women and children get behind the wagons!"

". . . Oh Lord, save us!" A woman's wailing voice was high-pitched and sharp.

Sam Lawson advanced into the middle of the crowd.

"Calm down," he ordered in an abrupt manner. "We don't know what they want. Johnson saw three Indians. That doesn't pose a threat."

"Maybe they're scouts," Johnson said, defensively. "Sent out by a big bunch."

"We don't know that."

"Don't get panicky," Steve Wellman added.

A woman shouted: "They're a-comin' in!"

The emigrants turned and saw three Braves advancing toward the camp. Two Indians rode ponies. They wore breechcloths; blankets were wrapped around their shoulders. Feather-tipped lances were held parallel to their bodies. Behind them walked a handsome brave of medium height. His skin was the color of copper, his hair worn in plaits on either side of his head. He wore a pair of homespun trousers, ragged at the knees, and a white shirt stained with dirt and blood. As they approached, it was evident that the Indian on foot had once suffered from smallpox. His face was marked with pox scars.

"Pawnee," said Lawson. "Hold your fire!"

"Maybe they're trying to trick us," snapped Wade Jackson. His face had a thin, wolfish look.

"Let's see what they want," Sam replied soberly.

Sam stepped outside the wagons and walked toward the advancing Indians. The braves raised their hands in the traditional sign of greeting. Sam raised his own hand in the same manner, speaking loudly in the language of the Pawnee. The guide conversed with the Indians for several minutes. The Indians pointed to horses and mules, speaking in a demanding tone.

Sam came back to the assembled emigrants.

"Most of that was bragging about their bravery," Sam said with a loud sigh.

"What do they want?" asked Dan Pitzen.

"Horses," Sam said with a thin smile.

"They've got ponies," Wade Jackson interjected.

"Old scarface out there lost his horse a couple days ago," Sam went on. He ignored the Kentuckian and spoke directly to Wellman and Mike Gorman. "His animal broke a leg in a gopher hole. Had to be killed. Indians are like anybody else. They'd rather ride than walk."

"Be damned!" Wade Jackson exploded. "Give him a bullet in the head. That'll stop him from bothering decent folks."

Sam gave no heed the Kentuckian had spoken. "There's just three of them," he drawled. "They ain't looking for a fight."

Mike Gorman asked, "What do you advise?"

"We'll do as you say," added Steve Wellman.

"They don't get my horse," Wade Jackson said angrily.

"For God's sake, Wade," Steve Wellman said with impatience. "We're not going to give away your horse."

"Better not," Jackson said sullenly.

"What should we do?" Gorman asked again.

"Palaver with the bunch," explained Lawson. "I'd figure they'll be happy with a few trinkets and a slab of bacon."

"Bribe Indians?" Wade Jackson cast a contemptuous look at the guide.

"Avoids trouble," Lawson related.

Jackson spoke quickly and firmly. "Not a dab of my bacon goes into an Indian belly. They want something? I say give them a bullet."

Elmer J. Johnson folded his arms in front of his chest. "Jackson is talking sense. We shouldn't start giving anything to a bunch of savages."

"Shoot 'em!" cried a boy on the edge of the crowd.

Sam Lawson sighed heavily. "These chiles are Pawnee. They're mean. Good fighters and sneakier than a drunken snake. We got to cross their land. We don't want to rile them up. I figure the best way of stirring up trouble is to shoot three defenseless Indians."

"They got spears," said an emigrant on the edge of the crowd.

"Yeah," added another man. "They act like they own this country."

"Not my bacon," said another man.

"Calm down!" Steve Wellman raised his hands. "We hired Sam to guide us. He knows Indians. If you're paying a man for what he knows, you should follow his advice."

"Then let Sam feed those redskins," snapped Wade Jackson. "He's the one who wants to mollycoddle them."

Sam gave the Kentuckian a cold, hostile look. "You want to take over as guide"—He paused, then added sarcastically—"Mister Jackson?"

Wade Jackson shrugged. "Figure I can do just as good. Don't take no talent to give everything away to the Indians. That's a coward's way."

The men gasped. Wade Jackson was the first man with courage—or foolhardiness—to test Sam Lawson's power. Suddenly mindful of the consequences, the Kentuckian's hand drifted toward the knife holstered on his belt.

Sam Lawson smiled cynically at Jackson. In a low, even voice he said, "I figured you for a troublemaker, Mister Jackson. You sure ain't proving me wrong."

Wade's hand rested on the handle of his knife. He looked around with a troubled expression. "Maybe I spoke a bit hastily," he began. "I—"

"Maybe you better take you hand off that knife," Sam interjected in a cold tone.

Jackson's hand rose quickly. He rubbed his nose. "Didn't mean nothing by it."

Brad Payne came pushing through the crown. He carried a slab of bacon in his hands. "I'm donating the bacon," said the printer. "No need to start a fracas if we can avoid it."

"Fair enough." Lawson appeared relieved.

"Will that satisfy them?" asked Mike Gorman.

"It might." Sam left the group and went outside the parked wagons. He started to talk with the Indians. They interrupted his statements with angry shouts. For an instant, one of the mounted Indians dropped his lance toward Sam's head. The burly guide swore loudly. He pushed the lance up, spoke angrily in Pawnee. The Indians laughed. The man with the scarred face stepped forward. He accepted the slab of bacon. Sam pulled a twist of chewing tobacco from his pocket. He cut off three portions, passed them to the Indians. The Indians grinned maliciously and popped the tobacco in their mouths. After that, they appeared less aggressive to the observing emigrants. Sam talked with them for several minutes, occasionally punctuating his conversation by slapping the pistol on his hip. After making the traditional Pawnee sign of farewell, the braves turned and moved away from the wagons.

Sam was quiet and serious when he came back inside the wagons.

"You handled that good," Steve Wellman said.

"Like a true mountain man," Wade Jackson added mockingly.

Sam sighed heavily. "They're headed back to their big camp. Somewhere up on the Platte River. The chiefs have called a big powwow up there. Sounds like we got trouble ahead."

"How's that?" asked Wellman.

"Wrong time of the year for a big gathering of the tribes," Sam went on. "Unless they're preparing to move against the trains. The one who was walking, the man with the scarred face, is the son of a chief. That chile was bragging the Pawnee had already done away with a couple of Mormon trains this year. Said he had a couple white women back in camp as prisoners. Said the Pawnee are going to dance on graves before we get through their land."

"Like hell he will!" Wade Jackson exploded. He left the group abruptly and walked away. Without warning, he leaned against a wagon, raised his rifle and took aim.

"Wade! Don't!" Sam Lawson lunged through the crowd of men.

The rifle exploded.

"Damn it! You fool!" Lawson was on top of the Kentuckian, grabbing his rifle. Jackson fell down on the ground.

Mike Gorman eyed the scene outside the camp. Across the field, the Indians had been moving away. The bullet tore into the back of the scar-faced Indian. The force of the shot knocked him to his knees. He rose unsteadily, turned to face the wagons. He stared through the thin morning air with a bewildered expression on his face. Tentatively, as if testing his strength, the Indian tried to take a step forward. An anguished expression came over his face. He crumpled to the ground. His two companions left him sprawled on the grassy earth. They kicked the sides of their ponies, gave an ear-splitting war cry and vanished into the trees.

Jackson's shot had raised a thundering echo in the camp. Men halted and glanced over their shoulders. Vivian Middleton grabbed the nearest child and hurried up inside her wagon. The other women did the same, expecting an Indian attack at any moment. The men ran to where Sam Lawson, his face fierce and dark, stood over Wade Jackson. The guide held the Kentuckian's rifle like a club, prepared to smash Jackson's skull.

"Sam," said Wellman, running up, "Don't kill him."

The guide turned to Steve, smiling slightly. Wade Jackson began to move away, crawling back on the ground. Sam's foot came down hard, imprisoning the Kentuckian's wrist.

"Stay right there, chile," snapped the guide.

"Leave me be," whined Jackson.

"I may do just that, you worthless piece of filth!" Sam stared malevolently at the emigrant. "I may just leave you right here in the middle of this prairie. You don't have the backbone to fight men to their faces. You sneak up behind their backs. Big man! Shot an Indian in the back!"

Steve said, "This is a matter for the council."

Sam smiled calmly. He stood menacingly over Jackson, who shrank back with fear. "I told you that Indian was scar-faced. He's the son of a chief."

"Doesn't matter," Steve said. "Leave Jackson be. The

Indian's already been shot."

Jackson's white and fearful face looked around for a sympathetic person.

"Just an Indian," he said defensively. "Nothing but an Indian."

Sam Lawson took a deep breath. He walked over to Wellman's side. The anger had left his face. "You had better understand what's happened," Lawson said calmly. "This idiot has shot a chief's son! Shot him in the back! Those other two braves are headed home right now. Riding as fast as they can go. When they get to camp, they'll spread the word. A war party will be after us about five minutes after those braves hit the camp. Wade Jackson has jeopardized everyone in this train!"

The other emigrants stood warily at a distance. They watched and listened to the proceedings with great interest. They saw Wade Jackson get to his feet, stare defiantly at Sam Lawson's back. The Kentuckian's hand rested on the handle of his knife. Sweat covered Jackson's strained face.

"We'll call a council and see what they say," Wellman said.

Sam nodded. "I'll go out and see if that Indian's alive."

As the guide walked out into the field, Wellman went among the men asking for an immediate council. Wade Jackson looked at them incredulously but remained silent. He fell back to the rear as the men gathered at one end of the oblong box of parked wagons. The men talked excitedly as they waited for the meeting to be called to order.

". . . Just a damn no count Indian. What's wrong with Lawson?"

". . . Should have shot the whole bunch right from

the start."

". . . Ole Wade knows how to handle Indians!"

". . . Shoot first, then hold a burying for 'em"

Mike Gorman crawled up on a wooden box. He stood self-consciously, a full head above the crowd. He was embarrassed to be in charge of the group.

"We all know why we're here," Mike said in a nervous, lilting voice. "Wade here went and shot an Indian. And—"

"Good for Wade!" A man grinned maliciously.

"Thank you," Wade said soberly.

"They were threatening the wagon." Elmer J. Johnson smiled.

Everyone started to talk.

"Silence!" demanded Mike Gorman. He faced the crowd. "How many of you approve of what Wade did? Raise your hands."

A majority of hands shot skyward. They yelled like demons and began to slap Wade Jackson on the back. Someone shouted that Jackson should be captain of the wagon train. Steve Wellman stepped up on the box with Gorman.

"Anybody want a new election?" he inquired.

There was a moment of confusion. Some of the men had not heard the suggestion for Jackson's leadership. But a man cried: "What do you mean treating Wade like he's a criminal?"

"He shot a man in the back. He went against Sam's orders!"

"That's his privilege."

"It's a free country," yelled Elmer J. Johnson.

Steve bristled. "Maybe you'd rather have him as captain."

"Wade would handle the Indians," Johnson said heatedly. "He wouldn't give an inch."

"No, by God!" shouted Brad Payne. "We elected Wellman and he's got a level head."

"This country don't have law 'n order. We got to make our own," countered Johnson.

Wade Jackson pushed through the crowd. A vicious grin covered his fleshless face. His eyes glittered with triumph.

"I'd like to say a few words," he announced firmly.

"We're in a meeting," Gorman answered.

"Let him speak," yelled Elmer J. Johnson.

"Yeah, it's a free country," another man agreed.

Mike Gorman stepped off the box. He looked exasperated as Wade Johnson stepped on the platform. Although Jackson had never addressed a group of men, he instinctively waited for quiet. Gradually, the men calmed down. They looked up expectantly.

"I appreciate your support," Wade Jackson said boldly. "I don't think this is the time, nor the place, to change captains. Steve Wellman's doing a good job. He listens to Sam Lawson and we've covered a lot of ground pretty fast. Lawson seems to like the Indians more'n he should. That's 'tween him and them. I figured that brave had to be shot this morning. A warning to the rest that this wagon train means business. We're not going to be bothered by beggars. The whole she-bang of tribes will recognize we're tougher than other trains. They'll leave us be. I got one scalp and, bedamned, before we finish I want a hundred hanging from my belt!"

"Give 'em hell, Wade," yelled Elmer J. Johnson.

"Now, we better get started to roll out," Jackson added. "We've already lost an hour."

"On to Oregon!" roared Johnson. He turned and ran back to his rig.

The other men drifted away.

"I guess," Mike said dryly, "we got problems."

"He's a cocky little bastard," Dan Pitzen agreed. "That kind always comes to a bad end—sooner or later."

"Bloodthirsty," said Brad Payne. "He didn't have to shoot that Indian."

Pitzen inquired, "What happens if he gets elected captain?"

"He can have the job," said Steve Wellman. "I'm tired of it."

"The train will split for sure." Mike Gorman spoke firmly and with conviction.

The emigrants were prepared to move out. They waited impatiently while Sam Lawson and Dr. Josh McDonald dug a grave for the Indian. There was another wait while the physician hitched up his team. When the train moved out, Sam Lawson got an extra supply of ammunition from Agnes Miller's wagon. Agnes greeted the guide warmly, now that he was performing most of her chores.

"What happened to the Indian?" she asked.

"Doc tried to save him. Didn't have a chance."

"He dead?" asked Melissa.

Sam saw the color in the young girl's cheeks. He wondered what had happened to add sparkle to her eyes.

"We buried him," said the guide.

"Well, that's that." Agnes spoke with a note of finality.

"Wish it was. We may have trouble up ahead."

Jane poked her small, mousy head out of the wagon. "Wade sure showed them Indians where to go."

"Fact is, he may have set us up for a bad Indian attack,"

Sam remarked. He wheeled his horse and rode along the line of wagons. He pulled up beside Steve Wellman, speaking respectfully to Cynthia. "Where's your husband ma'am?"

"Inside the wagon." Cynthia maintained a close vigil on the trail ahead.

"Tell him we got trouble a-brewing."

A moment later, Steve's head came out of the wagon. He tilted his face and told Lawson about the meeting.

"Fools never learn," remarked the guide. "Right now, they got a taste of blood. Wade could lead them straight to purgatory."

"He may be captain."

"Without a guide."

Cynthia looked at Lawson seriously. She said, "You wouldn't leave the train?"

"I wouldn't guide for Wade Jackson. He's too flighty. We're not out here to kill Indians. We don't have time for that kind of trouble."

Steve asked, "What's the worst that can happen?"

Sam considered. After a moment, he answered, "The dead one was a chief's son. Probably a pretty good warrior. He could have pulled rank when his horse went down. Made one of the other braves walk, while he rode. He didn't. Figure he was well liked by his tribe. That's just guessing, of course. But if it is true, them other two braves will high-tail it into camp. Figure we may have a party—with war on their minds—calling on us this afternoon. Maybe this evening if they're camped a long ways from here."

"An attack?" Cynthia asked in amazement.

"What would you do if some idiot shot your husband in the back?"

Cynthia looked frightened. "Try and kill him," she said lowly.

Lawson slapped his saddle horn. He roared: "That's what I'd do."

Sam Lawson galloped away. At forty yards, he wheeled and rode back to Wellman's wagon.

"Forgot to tell you," he said. "I'll be riding out more than usual today. No meat for the table tonight unless I spot something close up. I'm worried about getting a jump on any war parties coming this way."

He rode off again, leaving a trail of dust behind him.

NINETEEN

The caravan rolled on. The sun burnt the land. The emigrants slapped at sweat bees and mosquitos. They closed their eyes against the heat and dust as the wagons jolted over the trail. They stopped briefly at noon for a cold meal, then quickly resumed travel. Sam Lawson had not returned when they went on toward the next campground.

By mid-afternoon, Steve Wellman consulted his pocket watch for the twentieth time since noon. He frowned and looked up into the sunny sky. Although he had great faith in Sam's ability to survive, Wellman worried about the guide. A strong bond of affection was developing between the two men. Without Sam's presence and counsel, the emigrants did not know how far they must travel to reach that night's camp.

Rather than worry indecisively, Steve handed the wagon reins to Cynthia. He leaped down from the rig and saddled his horse.

Mike Gorman called out.

"Where's Sam?" asked the Irishman.

"I don't know."

"How far to the campground?"

"I'm riding ahead to find out."

"Watch out for Indians," Mike warned.

Wellman galloped off. The black Spanish stallion moved swiftly down the trail ahead of the wagons. Three miles beyond the column, the land dipped into a slight draw. Beyond the next rise was a littered campground with a small bubbling spring. Close by was a tiny creek that meandered through the rolling countryside. The greenery was thick and full, although many wagons had passed during the past few weeks. Wellman rode back to the caravan and passed the good news. With a sudden burst of energy, the emigrants quickly covered the distance to the campground. They pulled in and, under Wellman's direction, formed an oblong box. After their chores were done, the men came to Wellman's wagon. They wondered about Sam Lawson's whereabouts.

Wellman mollified their worries, not admitting his own concern for the guide.

"Sam can take care of himself," he said.

"Maybe he ran into Indian trouble," ventured Brad Payne.

"Bet they high-tailed it away from us," Wade Jackson smirked. He grinned with delight when an emigrant slapped him on the shoulder.

"Wade showed them Indians," said Elmer J. Johnson.

"Maybe he did," agreed Mike Gorman. "We'd still better set out double guards tonight."

The emigrants grumbled.

"A man needs his sleep," whined Wade Jackson. "I took care of those Indians. Those two that run away will pass the word. They won't mess with our caravan."

Over Jackson's protests, Wellman appointed more guards for the night.

While the men talked, the women worked at their chores. Agnes Miller and her two guardian girls, Melissa and Jane, had built a fire in their campstove. Agnes had trained the girls to run ahead when the wagons rendezvoused at the campsite each night. While the other emigrants remained on their wagons, Jane and Melissa quickly gathered up firewood and kindling. This enabled Agnes to get supper started early, while the other families were still hunting firewood.

This evening, Melissa was more attentive than usual about cooking the meal. She asked numerous questions about preparing the food. She offered to stir up a batch of biscuits.

"Thunderation!" Agnes said, happily. "You must be sparking some fellow."

Melissa smiled happily. "Be prepared is my motto. I might meet a nice fellow and not know how to cook."

"Well, you've got the right idea. Men are fools about good cooking.

"Sam says you're the best cook in the country," teased Melissa.

"That stinking old man! He'd eat anything."

"He smells a bit," Melissa admitted. "But he doesn't get bit by the bugs."

"A mosquito would gag near him."

"But you're his wife."

"Hush your mouth!" Agnes admonished.

Melissa grinned. "Don't you like Sam even a little bit?"

"Sam Lawson ain't the type to settle down."

Jane nodded in agreement. "Maybe you can tame him a

bit. Women have done that before."

Agnes was suddenly apprehensive about discussing her feelings toward the guide. Admittedly, her attitude toward Sam had softened in the last few days. Sam had been dutiful in helping with the chores; she was impressed with his knowledge of trail life, his ability to survive under adverse conditions.

She laughed inwardly at the thought of Sam Lawson dressed in a nice suit, stiff-collared shirt and a cravat. She envisioned the guide trying to look comfortable in a church pew. Yet, the gentlemen she knew back east would never lead a wagon train to Oregon. When a man or woman faced nature in its wildest form, Sam Lawson was a supreme guide. With a sudden rush of rationality, she realized how dependent she had become on his help. She had always fought to be independent throughout her life. Now, she needed Sam Lawson.

Leaving Melissa to watch the food cooking on the stove, Agnes and Jane checked out their oxen. The beasts were tired, raw-boned. Their bellies were rubbed sore by the harnesses. Their dull eyes blinked as they tried to find green grass. Agnes was dismayed to find that the grass around the campsite was deceptive. The area had been burned over the previous year, either sparked by the Indians or from an emigrant's campfire. This resulted in a thick matting of dry grass on top, holding back the new spring growth.

Jane volunteered to walk up on a hillock and pull some tall prairie grass.

"Stay close to camp," Agnes ordered. "Don't get out of sight of the wagons."

"The men say the Indians won't bother us," Jane replied.

"They don't know for sure."

"I'll stay in sight." Jane walked off toward a rolling ridge. She could see some greenery further up the slope. Always a quick learner, she was proud of her ability to handle chores competently. The grass was still smothered on the hill, entwined with the dead grass. She passed over the ridge, out of sight of the camp.

She found herself alone on the prairie, surrounded by a wild world untouched by human habitation. A warm breeze swept across the grassy slopes, undulating the silver-tipped surface of the grass. The prairie seemed to stretch endlessly. She looked up into the bright blue sky where a mass of dark-tipped clouds were gathering on the western horizon. She decided they didn't look like rain clouds.

She paused to observe the teeming bird life. Vast flocks of eskimo plovers circled above the fields seeking a nesting place. The cinnamon-tipped wings of the sickle-billed curlew flashed in the sunlight. They arced above her with their plaintive cry of "curlee! curlee! curlee!" The sweet yet mysterious notes of the nesting upland plovers came from some hidden place nearby.

A trio of deer bounded up the ridge. They wheeled quickly when they saw their first white woman. To her left, standing in a patch of berry bushes, stood a large, shaggy gray wolf. He stared speculatively at the young woman, then loped off. She wandered down the ridge to a small hollow. The draw was rich with yellow, gold, red and white wildflowers. She had never seen so many different blossoms and, forgetting the grass, picked a small bouquet.

Although she was seventeen years old, with the heat of womanhood surging through her veins, Jane lived in the shadow of Melissa. Men and boys alike found Melissa a desirable woman. They admired her charm, desired her beauty, courted her favor. Scant attention was paid to Jane, the plain younger sister with mousy gray hair, a receding chinline, and an undistinguished face.

Jane was too shy to look directly at a man. She became tongue-tied, unsure of herself, when a man spoke. In Natchez, she had looked on while men and boys courted Melissa. Jane longed to have Melissa's self-assurance, to be confident in handling men. Yet, deep down, deep down inside, Jane knew she could never be an aggressive woman. Some were bold; she would always remain shy.

Her reflections were interrupted by a vague feeling of unease. She stood up and looked around the countryside. Her first thought was of Indians. She looked fearfully around, saw no signs of their presence. A band of white-tailed deer came rushing past her. Their eyes bulged from the sockets. A large doe stopped. The animal trembled visibly looking back at the eastern horizon. Jane turned in that direction, seeing a faint dark line forming in the sky. Below, a reddening line appeared to be moving, rising, undulating toward her.

"Oh my God!" Jane blurted aloud. "The prairie's on fire!"

She had never seen a fire in the wilderness. Yet, she sensed the turmoil of the creatures running from the blaze. Prairie grouse were in full flight, sweeping past, unmindful of her presence. Rabbits and squirrels came hopping past. A heavy line of large, black birds came rushing up the ridge with their wings beating wildly. With incredible speed, wild turkeys were fleeing the fire.

Jane stood paralyzed. She realized dimly that the danger was worse than an Indian attack. The emigrants had no defense against fire. Even though the grass was greening up, the heavy layer of dry grass would be fiery tinder. People might manage to beat back the flames. Yet, the roiling mass of black smoke might suffocate everyone. The oxen would die from a lack of breathing air. Jane dimly envisioned what would happen when the fire swept through the camp.

A faint smell of smoke started her running toward the camp site. A band of plovers rose suddenly ahead of her, circling their nests, crying piteously. She stepped on something alive, heard a wild bleat. A squirrel darted from beneath her shoe and ran on. A group of rabbits came rushing past her like an ocean of gray bleating waves. At the crest of the hillock, with the wild animals racing past, she looked back. The sky was reddening and, above that, a dark cloud stretched high into the sky. Her nostrils were assailed by the odor of smoke.

Mike Gorman was the first emigrant to see the darkening smoke cloud. The Irishman was watering his oxen. By chance, he glanced east and saw the blackening sky. For a moment, the Irishman decided a thunderstorm was moving in. Then, like a ruby jewel, he saw the first flicker of flames. At that moment, his ox bellowed loudly. Mike ran and grabbed Steve Wellman's arm.

"Prairie fire!" Mike blurted out.

Wellman was stunned. "What do we do?"

Other men were now running up. They stared fearfully at the smoke-filled eastern sky.

"Run for the river," yelled Elmer J. Johnson.

"Never make it," cried Mike.

"That's at least ten miles," yelled Brad Payne.

Vivian Middleton tugged hard on Wellman's sleeve.

"You're the captain," she said shrilly. "Save us!"

The oxen in the camp began to bellow mournfully. Horses and mules jerked at their ropes.

"Hook up your plows," yelled Steve. "We'll plow a furrow around the camp."

Mike was doubtful. "Not in this thick grass."

Wellman was already running to hook up a team of oxen.

"It's our only hope!" he cried.

Agnes Miller came running up to the confused group. Her face was contorted with fear and doubt. She pointed a quavering finger toward the east. "Jane's out there," she yelled.

Jay Samuels stepped aside as an emigrant ran to harness his oxen team.

"I'll go get her!" he yelled. He looked around wildly for a horse.

"She went up the ridge," Agnes shouted.

The young Jew looked around in desperation. "I don't have a horse."

"Take the nearest one," Agnes said. She ran over and untied an animal belonging to Bruce Middleton. Samuels leaped on the mule's back and galloped up the ridge. Behind him, the emigrants frantically yoked their frightened oxen. Elmer J. Johnson was the first man to get a team harnessed. He ran up to Steve Wellman, wild-eyed and frightened.

"Where you want the furrow?" Johnson screamed.

"As far out as possible," Steve said, pulling his plow down from the wagon. "Wherever you can get a furrow started."

Johnson stopped a gang of running boys. He led his ox team while the youngsters carried the plow across the thick mat of dead grass. They dropped the plow about a hundred yards from camp. The iron-tipped implement was shoved deep into the heavy grass. Johnson cracked his whip. The oxen lurched forward. The plow skidded over the thick vegetation.

"Get up!" yelled Johnson. His whip slapped against the haunches of a straining ox.

Without warning, the plow popped out of the grass. Johnson looked around with bewilderment.

"We'll never get down to dirt!" he yelled.

Mike Gorman came rushing up, appraising the situation. The animals were getting skittish. They smelled smoke and wanted to run away from the blaze.

"Tear the grass away!" shouted the Irishman. "We got to get a hold for the plow."

Eager hands tore at the thick grassy covering. At last, black earth came into view. Mike maneuvered his plow around until the tip bit into the cleared ground. The oxen started forward. The tip of the plow cut into the earth. The forward thrust ended when the implement struck the thick root system beneath the surface. The Irishman yelled at his team. He cracked his whip over their straining haunches. Suddenly, the plow struck a weak point and moved forward. A thin furrow formed behind Gorman's plow. Men hurried up to pull grass and brush away from the plow's path. Behind Mike's plow, Elmer J. Johnson widened the original furrow. More emigrants fell in behind Johnson and, within a few minutes, the furrow was widened to a distance of seven feet. The teams were turned, coming back to widen the swath to about twelve feet.

Beyond the furrowed ground, men were setting fires. The grass leaped into flame and burned brightly. Oxen and horses were brought inside the wagon campment. Cynthia Wellman gathered up the young children in her wagon. She told an elaborate fairy tale to keep their minds off the onrushing fire.

Agnes Miller looked vainly for some sign of Jay Samuels or Jane. She was praying with desperate intensity when a wild cry sounded on the ridge. Hundreds of wild animals were running down the slope. They rushed toward the camp, then veered aside and raced past. The smoke blinded her view for a moment, then Agnes caught sight of Jay Samuels. The young man was clinging desperately to the back of the unsaddled animal. A small limp form clung tightly to Samuel's waist. Moments later, they came riding into the camp.

Samuels leaped down from the mule. Jane's limp body fell into his arms.

"Is she alive?" Agnes cried.

"She's sucked up a lot of smoke."

"Bring her to my tent."

Jane was laid out on a bed. Her face was blistered from heat. Agnes began to apply butter as Jay Samuels ran to find Dr. McDonald.

Outside, a hand-to-hand bucket brigade had been set up by the older boys and girls. It ran from the spring to inside the wagon corral. When a bucket reached camp, women began to wet down the canvas tops of the wagons. Wellman had realized that the tops were dry as tinder. A single spark might ignite a wagon. When the tops were thoroughly doused, the water barrels were filled in case of fire.

By now, the prairie fire raced down the ridge. It was met by the onrushing backfires. The flames merged there, a safe distance from the camp. The air in the camp

262

was hot and dry. Emigrants coughed, covered their mouths and waited for a sudden rush of clean air. The hot dry cloud swept over the camp. Then, as rapidly as it had arrived, the danger subsided. A wild cheering broke out among the emigrants. Husbands and wives hugged each other, grabbed their children and whooped with joy. Some people fell to their knees and gave thanks to the Creator for their deliverance. Children began to run around the camp, laughing hilariously, jumping and yelling.

Their joy was premature. Had Sam Lawson been in camp, the emigrants would have been told about another phenomenon on the prairie. Heat rising from the fire on the land created an atmospheric imbalance. A prairie fire was frequently followed by a raging thunderstorm. The heat had caused great masses of clouds to form in the west. Sheet lightning flashed across the sky. Ripping thunderbolts smashed out of the clouds. The emigrants heard this thunderous roar and stood silent, barely comprehending the danger of the storm moving toward their camp.

Children wailed with fright. Men hurried to tie their beasts securely. The atmosphere quickly became super-charged with electricity. Tiny blue fingers of twisting lightning flickered off metallic objects. Then the storm was upon the camp with a roaring fury. A curious green-gold pall was cast over the area. This was followed by ferocious thunderbolts. A huge ball of fire dropped out of the clouds, striking close to camp, detonating with a frightening blast. The animals bellowed mightily, strain-ing at their ropes.

The rain came with a hard wind. Articles not tied down were swept away from the camp. Buckets, blankets, and in one instance a campstove, were picked up and swept away. Small articles were sucked out of the interior of wagons. A woman saw a treasured shawl shoot out the back of her wagon. She made a desperate attempt to grab the garment, fell out of the wagon and was rolled across the ground by the powerful wind. Her face was bruised when the wind slammed her against a wagon wheel.

The camp was drenched with cold rain. Canvas tops were swept away from two wagons. Families huddled in the wagons' beds, desperately trying to hold onto their possessions. Suddenly, large hailstones began to fall with striking force. The animals roared in fright; some broke away and jumped wagon tongues. Outside the camp, their eyes dull and crazed, they ran wildly across the muddy, rain-soaked prairie. The hail tore holes in the canvas tops. A bellowing ox broke away inside the corral. The animal sought safety beneath a wagon. When a lightning bolt struck close by, the animal reared up with all of its strength. The two inside wheels of the wagon were raised up. The vehicle teetered precariously, then fell over on its side.

The storm was gone within five minutes. The camp was left in a shambles. Everyone was drenched; they shivered in the cold air. The animals moaned pitifully. Several had bloodied themselves trying to escape their ropes. People stepped down out of their wagons. They stared dully at the wreckage. Babies cried and refused to be comforted by their mothers.

The emigrants stood in utter confusion. Sodden, wretched, miserable, chilled, their self-reliance gone, they were overwhelmed with despair. The day had been enough to cause fright to the boldest man.

"To hell with Oregon," swore Cynthia Wellman. "I

want to go home."

"Try and get some rest," Steve suggested. He went off to try and find some dry firewood. His morale had vanished. Like Cynthia, he felt like turning back.

TWENTY

The emigrants spent a miserable night. The following morning, Steve Wellman called a general meeting. The men gathered quietly and looked at one another in silence. Their spirits had been sapped by the fire and storm.

"We're staying here for the day," Steve told them. "Everyone will have to pitch in, help his neighbors. We've got to have everyone in rolling condition by tomorrow morning."

"We're thinking of going back," said Elmer J. Johnson.

"My wife is in the wagon crying," said Mike Gorman.

Wade Jackson spoke up. "My wife's coming down with a fever."

"Get the doctor over to see her," Wellman said.

"I'll make the rounds this morning," Dr. McDonald shivered in his wet clothes. "Everyone should be checked out."

Steve Wellman reflected that the train would be lucky

not to be attacked by Indians that day. An additional danger was the threat of fever, maybe even cholera. He put two men on guard and urged every man to keep his gun close. Throughout the morning, he went through the camp urging the people to be cheerful. It was his calm attitude that brought hope back to the camp. People began to smile and joke about their trials and problems. "Make do with what we've got" was a phrase heard often that day.

Sam Lawson came riding in shortly before noon. The guide was bone-weary and tired. A dark patch of dried blood stained the front of his buckskin trousers. He dropped off his horse as several men rushed up.

Sam apologized for not getting back to the train. "Checking out the Indian situation," he explained. "Thunderation! That fire almost got me. The thing come up faster than a tornado. Figure the Pawnee set it. That's one of their weapons to get a wagon train."

"We survived," said Wellman.

Sam appraised the wreckage of the camp. "This is the most run-down train I've ever seen."

Later, Sam drew Wellman away from the other men. He spoke in a quiet, confidential tone.

"We got problems with the Indians," Sam said. "I killed one of those Pawnee braves yesterday. The other one got away. He's probably got them roused to a fever pitch by now. Coming in I saw a party of about seventy-five braves riding this way."

"A war party?"

"They ain't making a social call," the guide went on. "If that many warriors are headed this way, we're in for trouble. They're about twenty miles out. Figure they'll be here late this afternoon."

Steve looked bewildered. "Can we fight them off?"

"We ain't got a choice." Lawson's voice was calm. "We got maybe another two hours to get ready. Get the guns and ammunition out. Set up some defenses. Get ready."

During the next two hours, the emigrants prepared for battle. The people were called to a general meeting. They got information that left them serious. They went back to their wagons with instructions from Sam Lawson to prepare for an attack. The camp fell into a quietness.

The war party rode in from the north, a long column of Indians dressed in deerskin trousers or breechcloths. They were bronze-faced men astride small ponies. Their faces were painted with brilliant colors, a signal they were seeking scalps. Many of the warriors wore headdresses of buffalo horn. Their lances were also painted in brilliant colors, the shafts decorated with eagle feathers. Each brave carried a feathered shield made from cured buffalo hide. Some shields retained the thick, almost impenetrable buffalo hair. Others had been shaved clean, decorated with multicolored feathers. Each shield displayed the scalps taken by the warrior. At the head of the column rode Gray Wolf, whose feathered war bonnet fell down his back to signify his status as a chieftain.

A middle-aged man with a paint-daubed face, Gray Wolf raised his hand. The Indians stopped outside of gunshot range. Copper-skinned braves stared impassively at the wagon train. Several shook their tomahawks in a defiant gesture.

"Jesus Christ!" Brad Payne blurted out. "We'll never whip that many."

"Just remember," advised Lawson, "we've got guns.

They don't have over a half dozen rifles."

"Will they attack in daylight?" asked Jay Samuels.

"Gray Wolf isn't crazy." Lawson shook his head.

Across the way, Gray Wolf stood at the head of his war party. In his mid-forties, with twenty-two scalps hanging from his war shield, Gray Wolf was the most fierce warrior in his tribe. For most of his life, Gray Wolf had been content to lead his people, hunt, fish and enjoy the abundance of the great plains. So much had happened in the past few years; it was beyond Gray Wolf's understanding. The trappers and traders had arrived first, followed by the soldiers and the forts. Suddenly, an invasion of white eyes passed through his land. The wagon trains disturbed the tribal hunting grounds. The white men desecrated their sacred land. Squaws eyed the bright cloth and dazzling jewelry of white women, demanding such trinkets for themselves. Some of the best braves in the tribe invented excuses to leave camp, ride to Fort Kearney and beg for firewater. Meanwhile, the older men in the tribal council demanded war against the encroaching wagon trains. They claimed the wagons were the first signal of a settlement of the white eyes. Gray Wolf had resisted sending out war parties. He was a peaceful man who hoped the white men would go away. Although he had counted coup, he preferred to hunt buffalo and deer. News of his son's death had changed all that. His son had once been afflicted with the pock disease. Gray Wolf had thought his son would die from the illness. His life had been saved by an expensive ceremony performed by the tribe's most powerful medicine man. Now, his son was dead. Shot in the back by a treacherous white eye.

Gray Wolf made a sweeping gesture with his hand. A

brave rode forward from the rear of the column. He halted beside the chief and raised his lance to display a white flag. The banner was waved in the air.

"Thank God!" Sam Lawson said. "They want to talk."

Lawson tied a white handkerchief to the end of his rifle barrel. He rode out to meet with the Indians. The meeting continued for a quarter of an hour, then Sam rode back into the wagon camp. People flocked to the guide as he tied his horse and came inside the corral.

"Call a meeting," Sam said. "The Indians got a proposition."

"Are they going to attack?" demanded Wellman.

"Not yet."

"What do they have in mind?" Mike Gorman asked, excitedly.

"Tell you at the meeting," Lawson said. He took Gorman aside and asked the Irishman to stand close to Wade Jackson during the meeting.

The men and their families gathered at one end of the oblong corral. Sam stood on a wooden box and spoke quietly. "Gray Wolf is out there with maybe a hundred of his best men. He's mad. Make no mistake. They'll attack some time tonight. I figure we ain't got a chance against them. Too many. Gray Wolf has a pretty good military mind. He'll send in his braves first with flaming arrows. They'll set the wagons afire. While we're fighting the flames, the rest sneak up and do us in. Right now, Gray Wolf plans to kill every man, woman and child in this train. Wipe us out to the last breath as a warning to other trains. He also said he's a peaceable man. He doesn't like white eyes—that's us!—but by thunder he wants justice. He's willing to forget the attack if the man who killed his son is handed over."

The group milled around in confusion for an instant, then everyone looked at Wade Jackson.

"Wait a minute!" The Kentuckian exploded. "You're not handing me over!" Jackson's hand streaked toward his pistol.

Mike Gorman grabbed his arm. "Easy, Wade."

"Nobody better even think of that!" protested Jackson.

"Figure you-all are the ones to vote," Lawson went on. "If'en you don't want to fight the Indians, then you decide whether you're willing to hand over Wade to the Indians."

The magnitude of the proposition struck the emigrants. Every man began to talk at the same time. Sam shouted them down. He called for an orderly discussion.

Elmer J. Johnson asked, "What's our chance of whipping them?"

"None," Sam replied. "If we do beat them off, we'll have a lot of dead and wounded."

"It isn't Christian," Agnes Miller protested.

"Wade shot the chief's son," Sam replied. "In the back."

"Damn it!" roared Wade Jackson. "You're not handing me over to those savages!" He spun around wildly, looking for a friendly face. His heart sank when he saw the cold, impassive stares of his fellow emigrants.

Brad Payne asked, "Will the Indians keep their promise?"

"Maybe. Maybe not."

Wade Jackson screeched and tried to draw his pistol. Mike Gorman knocked the gun out of the Kentuckian's hand. Jackson went for the knife holstered on his belt. Steve Wellman imprisoned Jackson's hands behind his back.

"Take him away someplace 'til we've finished talking," advised Lawson.

"This is murder!" Jackson shouted, eyes glazed with terror.

Two emigrants rushed up with rope. They tied Jackson's arms against his body. He was led to the other end of the corral. He continued to scream until his mouth was gagged. He slumped back against a wagon, eyes glaring with hatred. His wife and children huddled near him.

Dr. Josh McDonald was speaking to the group. "There doesn't seem a fair way of deciding the issue," he said. "I sure ain't voting for sending Wade out to be killed by the Indians."

"Maybe," suggested Jay Samuels timidly, "we need to vote secretly."

"How's that?" asked Mike Gorman.

"Do it with beans," spoke up Uncle Durgeon Adkins. "Every man gets a white and brown bean. If he wants to fight the Indians, he drops one color in the box. Or the other way round."

Steve Wellman went off to get a supply of beans from his wagon. He returned with two pans filled with white and pinto beans. The emigrants were shamefaced when the beans were distributed.

"Do women get to vote?" Vivian Middleton inquired.

"Be quiet!" hissed her husband.

"I figure this is important enough for everyone to vote."

"Men only," Sam said.

Vivian stalked off. She joined Wade Jackson and his family.

The voting started. Each man walked away from the group. He deposited one of his beans in a bucket sitting on the ground. Tension hung over the camp. The two men guarding Wade Jackson were the last to vote. They came across the oblong area, took their beans and deposited one in the bucket.

When the balloting was finished, Steve Wellman began to make a count of the beans. He was still counting when one of the guards yelled. Wade Jackson was free from the ropes. He grabbed a rifle and ran toward a horse. He jumped astride the closest mule and, with a band of angry emigrants running behind him, dashed south from the camp. Several men started to saddle up and give chase. Sam Lawson stopped their attempt to chase down the departing man.

"Give him a half hour start," Sam suggested. "Then I'll ride out and tell Gray Wolf what happened."

"Can't we do better than that?" demanded Elmer J. Johnson.

"Damnation! There's a hundred Indians out there. You can't mess with a war party of that size."

Mrs. Jackson sobbed hysterically as Agnes led her to a wagon. The other women came over to comfort her. Agnes Miller then walked over to Sam Lawson. She put her hands on her spread hips.

"You ought to be ashamed of yourself," Agnes said angrily.

"I just made the proposition known," Sam drawled. "Don't get on a high horse with me. I didn't even vote."

Sam and Agnes were still arguing when Mike Gorman took the bucket and started to count the beans.

"Keep it to yourself," Wellman advised. "Every man voted to give Wade to the Indians."

273

Gorman nodded. "Thank God! He got away. At least we won't have to give him up. My conscience couldn't stand that."

"You voted to do it," Steve said.

"True, but I didn't like doing it."

Sam Lawson rode out under a white flag. He informed Chief Gray Wolf that Jackson had escaped. He did not inform the Indians in which direction Jackson had gone. Instantly, Gray Wolf ordered his warriors to spread out across the countryside. With ferocious war whoops, the braves took off in pursuit.

That night, the wagon camp was aroused by loud, agonized screams. The cries came from the direction of the creek. Steve Wellman and Sam Lawson slipped out of the camp. Knife in hand, they crept through the darkness to investigate the matter.

Wellman was shaken, face pale, when he returned to his wagon. He dropped down beside Cynthia with a heavy sigh.

"Who is it?" she inquired.

"Wade. They got him."

"My God! What are they doing?"

"They're skinning him alive!" Steve turned over and wept.

Wade Jackson stopped screaming an hour before dawn. No one in the camp had slept since his first scream of pain. His wife and children had been sedated by Dr. McDonald. They slept through the last two hours when Wade wailed pitifully, begging someone to come to his aid. The next morning, when they awakened the emigrants found a feathered lance standing in the midst of their corral. Tied to the end of the lance was a number of gourds. Each was decorated with dark, dull colors.

"A warning from Gray Wolf," Sam Lawson explained. "He probably sent a brave into camp last night. The guards must have been napping."

"What's it mean?" asked Agnes.

"We are to get out of Pawnee territory as quickly as possible."

"How can you tell that?" asked Mike Gorman.

"The gourds are an Indian warning when they're arranged this way," Lawson replied.

The men walked down by the creek before breakfast. The Indians had departed during the night. They found a sickening mass of flesh tied to a cottonwood tree. Wade Jackson's eyes were blank and unseeing. They stared out toward the rising sun. His eyelids had been cut off. He had been scalped. Every inch of skin had been stripped from his body; he looked like a piece of raw, red meat. Long strips of skin lay on the ground around the tree.

"Let's bury him quick," Wellman said, "then get out of here."

A quick grave marker was erected over Jackson's grave. In the years that followed, when other trains came along the trail, the stream was known as Rawhide Creek.

TWENTY-ONE

During the next week, the wagon train crossed the Little Blue River without difficulty, rolling northwesterly into what is now the state of Nebraska. Naomi Jackson, Wade's widow, appeared to recover rapidly from her ordeal. The Jackson children, eleven-year-old Mark and nine-year-old Betty began to run and play with the other children in the caravan. Josh McDonald remarked that Wade's absence appeared to be a blessing.

"He must have been a hellhound to live with," the physician explained. "With his bad temper, everyone was scared to death. They're probably better off without him."

The only person in the group to miss Wade Jackson was Elmer J. Johnson. Johnson had been impressed with Jackson's hair-trigger temper. He had been drawn to the Kentuckian's thinness. Although Johnson would have disputed the matter vigorously, he was unconsciously attracted to thin men. Less than a year before, Johnson had been a prominent merchant and gentleman farmer in

Shawneetown, Illinois. Leading citizens of the community, including the town's two bankers, frequently consulted Elmer J. Johnson before making an important decision.

Elmer and his family lived on a rich farm two miles from the Shawneetown city limits. They occupied a safe, quiet sandstone mansion staffed with servants. The farm was managed by an overseer who bossed the field hands and kept a sharp eye on Johnson's grist mill. As was customary on the third day of each month, Elmer set out for town in his buggy one evening in June. He went to *Johnson's General Store*, the largest general merchandise emporium in Shawneetown, to check the previous month's receipts. Elmer credited his success in business ventures to his attention to details. He trusted his store manager and clerks. He picked honest, Christian men to staff his store. Nevertheless, Elmer had seen good men turn bad. Some latent flaw in their character surfaced, without warning, and men turned sour. Elmer was fond of saying that no one really ever knew what a man really thought—not even his wife and family.

About eight thirty that evening, when the fire of setting sun reflected on the store windows, a knock sounded on the front door. Elmer rose from his chair, sighed heavily, and pulled a pistol from a desk drawer. A man couldn't be too careful living by the Ohio River. All sorts of scum, river pirates, counterfeiters, thieves and ne'er-do-wells, rode up and down the Ohio River. He placed the pistol in his belt, walked to the front and opened the door.

A slender youth of about twenty stood in the doorway. He was dressed in plain homespun garments that had seen considerable wear.

"Sorry, I'm closed," Elmer said.

"I just got into town," the stranger said. "I'm hungry."

"Go to the hotel."

The man smiled, his lips broadening into sensuous lines. "I don't have any money. I'll work for something to eat."

Against his better judgment, Elmer stepped back and allowed the young man to enter the store. The boy walked with a girlish, effeminate gait. His face was soft and beardless. Elmer looked away from the boy's penetrating eyes.

"I'll give you some cheese and crackers." Elmer walked back through the dimly lit aisles. The boy followed and stood close by as Elmer cut into the large cheddar cheese wheel on the counter.

The youth laughed. "Why are you afraid of me?"

"I'm not."

"You won't look at me."

"I'm busy. I have a lot of work to do." Elmer passed a generous slice of cheese to the boy. The youth's gestures were light, airy, as he accepted the food.

"You're one of us, you know."

"One of who?" demanded Elmer.

"You're thinking about it."

Elmer grabbed a handful of crackers from the barrel. "Take these and get out!"

The boy stepped closer. "Wouldn't you like to know what it is like to make love to me?"

"Get out!"

"Mightn't I be better than a woman."

The thought flashed through Elmer's mind that he was going crazy. The boy's hair was long and dark, his face tanned by the summer sun. His body was slim, without fat, and his legs were long and firm. The young man was silent as Elmer appraised his body. He walked over to Elmer and undid the buttons of his pants. He took Elmer's hand and laid it against his hardness. With a loud, uncontrollable moan, Elmer J. Johnson dropped to his knees in front of the stranger.

That night, as he lay against his wife's bulky form, Elmer J. Johnson prayed for deliverance from the demons inside his body. But the next night, and every night to follow during the next two months, were spent with the youth. His name was Richard. Elmer gave him money for his hotel room, paid for his meals and supplied a liberal weekly allowance. Richard teased Elmer unmercifully.

The young man wheedled large sums of money from Shawneetown's most influential citizen. Elmer's friends and associates noticed the change in his temperament. Preoccupied, he spoke abruptly, if at all, when he passed through the streets. Details concerning his business were neglected. He was sullen and short-tempered with his family and employees. Although his wife and children continued to attend church services each Sunday, and the prayer meeting on Wednesday night, Elmer stayed in the store. Elmer resented the power that Richard held over him; yet he was unable to end the relationship.

One evening one of Elmer's hired hands walked by the store. Staring past the display of lamps in the front window, the man's mouth dropped in shock. Richard leaned up against a back wall in the store. Elmer knelt before the boy, fondling his penis. Without thinking of the consequences, the hired hand ran to the nearest saloon and blurted out the news. Quietly, without speaking, several of the town's heaviest drinkers walked down the street. They stared through the window into the dim store room. Satisfied that the hired man had not been imbibing too freely, they retired to the saloon.

"Never thought—"

"Terrible. Terrible."

"Something should be done."

"Him so pious and church-going."

"Turned me down for credit last month, he did. Now he's down there on his knees mouthing that poor boy."

News of Elmer J. Johnson's transgression spread through Shawneetown with remarkable speed. A mob of men gathered in the saloon, drinking freely, shouting that something had to be done about the monster.

"By thunder!" yelled the hired hand, Tim Bannock. "Someone has to punish him!"

A man yelled that all sodomists should be destroyed.

"Drive 'im out of town!" cried another man.

Bannock roared and set out of the saloon leading the mob. Shouting like madmen, the mob advanced on Johnson's store. Using axes and clubs, they smashed in the front windows, kicked in the door. Elmer J. Johnson had been sitting quietly in his office talking with Richard. He rushed to the front when the mob burst into the building. At least thirty men were pushing to get into the room. Tim Bannock, who remembered his employer's low wages, slobbered with anger.

"You sissy!" Bannock screamed. "I saw you with that poor boy!"

Sensing the temper of the mob, Richard leaped up and ran out the back door. Johnson stood his ground, reasoning that every man in the mob was either his friend or an acquaintance. Johnson ran from man to man, pleading desperately, as they smashed his display cases. Men began to grab merchandise and carry goods outside.

Suddenly, a man came running in with a bucket of black tar. Hands grabbed Johnson, tore off his clothes. He screamed with horror as hot tar was poured over his bare body.

"We got lime in it," shouted another man, pushing through the mob. "That ought to burn his flesh!"

Two men, small farmers whose credit had been cut off at Johnson's store, came into the room. Each carried a feather mattress. Seams were torn open, feathers poured out onto the floor. Someone hit Johnson on the jaw. He was knocked down into the feathers. The mob rolled him across the floor. The feathers stuck to the tar. The lime burned his skin. Through the pain, now barely conscious, Elmer J. Johnson winced. The mob included one of the town's two bankers, Johnson's competitors, a deacon in his church and the local magistrate.

Johnson was booted and knocked past each man. Near the door, someone delivered a vicious kick to his rear. Covered with tar and feathers, he went sailing out into the night. He stumbled and sprawled in the street. The mob jeered loudly and turned to looting his store.

"Get out of town!" yelled Tim Bannock.

"Five minutes to get outside the city limits," roared a banker.

"Never come back!" This came from his competitor, who turned and went back inside the store to gather loot.

Darkness hid Johnson's escape from Shawneetown. Later, as he was running toward his farm, he heard the sound of riders coming fast along the road. Hiding in the bushes until they went past, he wept—not from pain, but from humiliation. As the horsemen rode by, one mentioned stopping at Johnson's farm to lynch him. He stayed out that night, desolate and cold. When morning came he crept across the fields toward home. His wife's face dropped with fear when he walked onto the back porch of their home.

"Polly, I'm sorry," he wept.

"Madmen! They must have been insane!"

Polly hid him in the cellar until the children could be taken to her mother's home in Shawneetown. She spent the rest of the day removing the tar and feathers from his body. She dug the black, sticky tar out of his ears and hair. She washed him in a tub of hot water, scraped him with a dull knife and bathed him again. By nightfall, most of the pitch had been removed. His body was raw and sore. He smelled like tar, but Polly's gentleness nurtured him.

"We can't stay here after this," Elmer said, his face pale and wan.

"I know. We'll sell the farm and go west."

"I'll have to leave as soon as possible."

"You can go ahead. I'll stay here until things are sold out."

"But—you're pregnant."

"That doesn't matter. I'll manage."

Three months later, Polly and the children joined him in St. Louis. Two weeks before they headed upriver by steamer to Independence, Polly gave birth to a healthy boy. They christened the infant in a small St. Louis church and left for Independence.

The caravan was nearing the Grand Island valley in Nebraska when tragedy struck the Johnson family. Polly, a bulky woman with a placid, bovine face, was riding on the wagon seat beside her husband. She cradled the baby in her arms. The trail dipped unexpectedly and, momentarily, the right rear wheel fell into a pothole. The wagon bounced under the strain. Both Elmer and Polly were jarred by the jolt. Polly reached out to brace herself. The baby slipped out of her arm and, with a sickening crunch, the front wagon wheel rolled over the infant's wailing face.

Elmer jerked the reins to halt the team. Polly leaped down and pulled her baby out of the path of the rear wheel. The child's head and face had been crushed. She picked up the limp body, crawling onto the side of the trail. Desperately, she tried to will the baby back to life.

Wagons halted behind them and, speechless at the sight, the emigrants looked on with dread. After half an hour, Steve Wellman led the weeping mother back to her wagon. She cradled the dead child in a blanket. The wagons rolled on until the night's campsite was reached.

Steve Wellman came up to Dr. McDonald after the wagons had been set into the oblong corral. "We got to get that baby buried," he said.

"They want a coffin."

"Hell, there's no wood around here for that."

"Mrs. Jackson has donated a small wooden box."

"I'll get someone to dig the grave."

A site was selected on a small knoll for the grave. Steve and Mike Gorman started to spade up the earth. Sam Lawson came walking up.

"Bad spot for a grave," said the guide.

"Seems all right to us," Mike said, tossing a spadeful of earth to the side.

"You putting up a marker?"

"The Johnsons will have to say about that."

"Indians will dig the chile up."

"They rob graves?" Steve was astonished.

"Sure do," drawled Sam. "First bunch comes along will dig the corpse up. They're looking for rings, clothing, jewelry and any kind of doo-dads. The Johnsons will want a marker put on the grave. That's like a flag to the Indians. But, you might as well keep digging. One place is about as good as the other. I'll ride back tomorrow morning and pull up the marker."

"Damn ghouls!" Mike Gorman swore. "How do you stop them?"

"Put the grave smack dab in the middle of the trail." Sam went back to the camp.

The funeral services were brief. Dr. McDonald walked with the Johnsons to their wagon, administering a powerful opium-based sleeping draught. Elmer and Polly moved slowly the next morning. The medicine had numbed their bodies and minds. When the train had rolled out of sight of the grave, Sam Lawson rode back and pulled up the marker.

TWENTY-TWO

The caravan rolled northwesterly through the flat-lands along the Little Blue River. Grime, dust and noise gnawed at the emigrants' nerves. The sound of their passage was unforgettable; Sam Lawson claimed their noise carried five miles in the thin prairie air. Pots, pans and loose articles banged against the interior of the wagon beds. Chickens squawked from their coops tied to the sides. Axle hubs noisily protested each turn of the wheel. Iron rims rumbled through ruts, chattered over rocks, howled over the tough prairie grass. Canvas tops vibrated wildly in the wind. Mules brayed; oxen bellowed. Men roared at their teams, dogs howled, babies cried. Night brought little relief from the uproar. Moaning animals, barking dogs and wailing children made a racket that lasted until dawn.

All of these hardships added to the discomfort of the emigrants. Tired beyond numbness, they grumbled their resentment to Steve Wellman. His waking hours were taken up by listening to complaints.

"Christ! I'm going crazy!" Steve lamented. "Every time I take a step through camp, someone bends my ear about something. Most of it isn't worth the breath to tell about."

In desperation, for his nerves were frayed raw, Steve asked for suggestions from the other emigrants. Mike Gorman came up with the best solution.

"Appoint someone to hear the complaints," the Irishman suggested. "Most people just want to talk out their tribulations."

"Good idea," agreed Brad Payne.

"Better than we realize," Dr. Josh McDonald added.

Steve looked directly at the group. "Who wants to do it?"

No one volunteered.

"You'll have to put a gun at my back before I'll do it," said Jay Samuels.

And so it came about, after much discussion, that Uncle Durgeon Adkins would listen to complaints. He had the patience to listen to people's troubles. His seventy years of living provided invaluable experience in settling arguments. Furthermore, the emigrants respected the man. Each morning and evening, Uncle Durgeon was available to the grumblers. To everyone's surprise, the old man's advice was generally accepted. He became the wise, gentle patriarch of the caravan. Nobody could resist his sage advice.

"We'll all die out here," a woman complained one morning. "I can feel it in my bones."

"We'll make it," said Uncle Durg.

"That old man of mine ain't treating me right."

"What's the trouble?"

"He ain't pestered me since we started west."

"He's for other things on his mind."

A man stepped forward. "There's too much racket in camp. A man can't sleep at night."

"You want to kill the mules and oxen?"

"Ought to be some way to keep them quiet."

"You think about it. We're open to any ideas that make sense."

A woman in a faded dress was angry.

"That Johnson woman was crying all night. Kept us awake."

"She just lost her baby."

"I'm going to lose my mind."

"Stitch it to your bonnet."

"Ain't there no way to quiet her down?"

"Give the poor woman a couple days. She's hurting real bad."

That evening a man drew Uncle Durg aside. "My beasts are shitting an awful lot."

"They got the runs?"

"Not yet. 'Pears, though, that they shouldn't go so much."

"Well, at least you don't have to shovel it."

"But my wife is complaining about the smell."

"Give her a clothespin for her nose."

Jay Samuels complained that someone was stealing merchandise out of his wagon.

"They taken much?"

"Two tins of hard candy."

"Probably kids. That's an awful temptation."

"What should I do?"

"Keep an eye on your stuff. There's all kinds of people in a wagon train. Some good, some bad. Don't blame kids if they snatch candy you leave laying around."

Molly Gorman had a complaint. "I want a baby and Mike ain't cooperating."

"What do you want me to do?"

"Tell him it takes two to make a baby."

"Thunderation, woman! Give the man his due. He's too tired for fun."

"But," Molly grumbled, "I want to get pregnant."

"Wait 'til you get to Oregon."

"That's too long. I could be quite a ways along by then."

"Leave your husband be, Molly. He's doing the best he can."

"Well, I never heard of a man turning away funning."

"I have," Uncle Durg replied. "Lots of times. Funning takes energy."

Dr. Josh McDonald came up to the old man one night. "I got a bad rim on my left rear wheel. I don't think it'll make it through tomorrow's trip."

"You bring any replacements?"

"Forgot to buy any."

"Then you'd better start praying someone will loan you one 'til we get to Fort Kearney. There's a blacksmith there, I'm told."

"How do I fix it?"

"Can't. You keep pouring water on the wheel. That'll keep the wood swoled up. Gets too bad we'll figure something out."

Betty Jackson, age nine, came up crying. "Mark pulled my hair."

"What made him do that?"

"I didn't do nothing. He just did it."

"Maybe you hit him."

"Not very hard."

"You children got to get along together and help your Maw." Uncle Durg's eyes sharpened. "What's that in your mouth?"

Betty hesitated. "Candy."

"Where'd you get it?"

"Found it beside the road yesterday."

"Indians must have left it there." Uncle Durg smiled. "People say they got lots of candy."

"Pawnees operate a big candy store just over the hill, eh?"

Betty look doubtful. "Maw said never to lie. Mark found a bag yesterday in that Jew's wagon."

"Tell Mark I want to talk to him."

Vivian Middleton grumbled about her husband's conduct. "He keeps getting up and wandering around at night."

"Maybe he's restless."

"I think he's sparking another woman."

Uncle Durg's eyes became slits. "You know that for a fact?"

"It would be something he'd do."

"That would be adultery. The punishment is death."

"If he's got another woman, he deserves it."

"I'll keep an eye cocked some night."

Mrs. Elmer J. Johnson registered a complaint against her neighbor. "That woman snores like a team of oxen. Told her to keep quiet."

"What did she do?"

"Told me to go to hell."

"My advice is not to go."

"Where?"

"To hell."

Mrs. Johnson walked off with a silly grin on her face.

She was pleasant for the rest of the day. By evening, she had made up with her neighbor.

Joe Halsey, a big man from Wisconsin, explained that his wife refused to do any work.

"She sick?" asked Durgeon.

"Says she is. Lays there and doesn't move a muscle."

"You jim-jawed numbskull. Why didn't you have the doctor see her?"

"She's always been a slacker."

"Maybe she's real sick this time. All sorts of things can happen out here on the trail. I'll have the doctor see her."

"What's he charge for that?"

"You know how to keep a wheel on a wagon?"

"I ain't no blacksmith."

"He don't charge nothing, but you ought to help him fix his wheel."

"Fair enough. I don't like to be beholden to anyone."

Later, Josh McDonald reported that Lydia Halsey had a bad case of dysentery. "She'll probably feel better in a couple days."

With Uncle Durg fielding complaints, Steve Wellman found time to ride out one afternoon with Sam Lawson. The caravan was approaching the Platte River, about twenty-five miles from the head of Grand Island. They had rolled through the flat country, a desolate terrain with few trees and little firewood. Earlier trains had picked the banks clean of timber. It became necessary for the emigrants to secure wood from the islands in the river. Far off across the prairie, the two men saw the first sign of sand hills. They had come to the "coast" of Nebraska as the emigrants termed this stretch of the trail.

When the wagons broke through the sand hills, a vast,

sweeping panorama came into view. The valley of the Platte stretched several miles across. The area was covered with thick green spring growth. A slender thread of timber grew along the river banks, outlining the course of the stream. The river, more than a mile wide in this spot, and not more than a foot deep, flowed through the undulating sandhills. The plain of the Platte Valley was as level as the surface of a table. For miles along the river, a number of campfires flared beside parked prairie schooners. In the distance, black specks signaled the presence of livestock.

"My God!" Sam roared. "There must be two hundred wagons out there."

"They're camped all over the place," Brad Payne shouted.

As the caravan rolled through a gap in the sandy "coast," Wellman and Lawson rode ahead. A mile beyond the wagons, they pulled up their horses and waited for an oncoming rider.

Jim Bridger came riding toward them, dressed in a deerskin shirt and leggings. He rode on an Indian pad saddle without stirrups. His feet were covered by beaded moccasins. Bridger came riding out at great speed, guiding his horse with a braided rope looped around the lower jaw.

"Christ!" said Wellman. "He looks exactly like an Indian."

Lawson laughed. "Old Gabe's more Indian than most of them."

Bridger pulled up beside them. They exchanged greetings without dismounting.

"Good to see you, Sam!" Bridger said heartily. "We got all kind of problems waiting for you."

"What's the trouble?"

"Damn True Christians," snorted Bridger. "Bunch of crazy people. We're right in between the Pawnee and the Sioux. They're out hunting buffalo not more'n ten miles from here. A lot of them, too. The whole Sioux nation is out right now for their spring hunt. Damn! Those True Christians have messed things up. That girl—what's her name—"

"Hattie Gill," Steve interjected.

"That's the one," Bridger drawled. "Having visions and claiming everyone's got a duty to convert the Indians. I been holding them in camp by near force. Told them fanatics that the first person to leave the camp would get a bullet right through the head. Damn the people! They won't listen. Right now, that girl and her mother are trying to convert the women and children in camp. Lord! I wonder if women really belong out here. We may be cutting our throats, Sam, by bringing them in. There ain't been much church talk this side of Independence. Now, every time a man does something there's a Bible-thumper watching every move."

Sam inquired, "How about the Indians?"

"Madder'n hell! The whole world busted loose this spring. Five thousand Mormons rolled through a couple weeks ago from Council Bluffs. They're headed for Brigham's promised land, praising the lord with every step and cutting the grass down to the roots. There's even a story out that those jack-legs are poisoning the wells on ahead. Might be some truth to that. Brigham's the toughest preacher I ever met. The Pawnee are real mad. I talked to a brave a couple days ago. He told me about your run-in with them. You're lucky to be alive."

"They took one of our people," Steve said.

"Skinned him alive, I hear."

"How'd you know?"

"Brave knew about it. Carried a real nice knife he must've taken off the man. Liked to have got it off that Indian, but there wasn't a chance to shoot him without raising a fuss."

"Why wait here?" Steve inquired.

Bridger looked dumbfounded. "Cause the dang Sioux are just west of us," he went on, patiently. "Not just a few hunters. The whole she-bang is down here. Braves, squaws, children. Carried all their lodges. They're hunting buffalo and claiming we're ruining their best hunting grounds. They got a right logical complaint."

"They made a move yet?" Sam asked.

"I've kept the tenderfeet piled up here. The Sioux's to the north of the Platte. All we had to do was ford and roll west on the south side. Nosiree. Captains are afraid of quicksand. They want to stick north of the river, go right through the Sioux hunting ground. That's bound to provoke the Indians. Good God almighty! Sam, there must be 10,000 Indians in the next twenty miles. We'll be lucky to make Fort Kearney. Mighty lucky."

"Got their dander up, eh?"

Bridger said: "Tribes are claiming there's too many women and children coming West. Yesiree. They figure we're moving onto their land. The damned Cayuses massacred most of the people at the Whitman mission last spring. The Shoshones are out doing war dances. The Crows is all pissed off, the Cheyenne is riding the war path and you never know what the Blackfoot tribe will do."

Sam agreed. "They're tough."

"Tough and mean. Never were very sociable critters—

even in the best of times."

"They acting worse than usual?"

"I reckon that may not be possible. They did grab a white woman this spring. A nun headed for the missions in California. Came down from the north with some French trappers. The Blackfeet took the poor woman back to camp. Tied her up and hauled her onto one of their lodge poles. Left her dangling there while they built a big bonfire beneath her. Kept the blaze roaring until they'd roasted the poor woman's feet and legs. She was still conscious when they cut her down. Next, they called in a pack of dogs and let the hounds fight over her feet and legs."

Steve shivered.

Sam asked, "What about the Bannocks?"

"East of the pass and looking for trouble."

"The Gros Verde?"

"Sharpening their tomahawks and making arrows."

"You figure the Sioux will attack us here?"

"Depends. I calculate they're about ready. They've been doing their war dances. Figure they'll hit us tonight or tomorrow night."

The caravan rolled into the encampment and pulled up into the oblong box. Oxen were quickly unyoked and outspanned. Picket ropes were staked out. Horses, mules and milk cows were led away from the camp for grazing. That night, a meeting of the entire camp was held after supper. Jim Bridger gave instructions that sobered everyone. The families returned to their wagons in a serious mood. A double guard was posted.

Bridger and Lawson came around to Wellman's wagon after dark.

"We're going out past the guards," said Bridger. "Sam

figures you're good enough to take along."

Steve grinned with pleasure. "Are the Indians out there?"

"Most likely not before dawn. But we can't be sure."

Sam added, "Some of the tribe may be spoiling for a fight. They'll come in around midnight if that's the case. That gives them a head start on the other braves. They'll come sneaking in to steal a few horses and stampede the livestock."

Steve picked up his rifle.

"Leave it," advised Bridger. "Knife and pistol's all you need. We'll be fighting hand-to-hand, man-to-man if we meet anyone out there."

"Be careful," Cynthia whispered.

"I'll watch out for him," Sam told her. "You'll be safe with Agnes and the girls."

The three men stepped across the wagon tongues. They vanished into the darkness.

Sam spoke briefly with the guards. "If trouble starts, don't start shooting until we're inside the corral. I don't want to get trapped between the Indians and our own guns."

Wellman followed the two mountain men across the sandy ground. They halted near the river, dropping down into a small indentation in the soil. They waited silently as the chilling numbness of the night came upon them.

TWENTY-THREE

The Sioux camp had been in an uproar all day. Many of the tribe's elders advised patience, but the young warriors had their anger up. Hundreds of white-topped wagons were rolling through their prized hunting grounds. The intrusion of these white invaders intensified each year. Their presence, even in passing along the trail to Oregon, angered the red men. The trappers and traders had been bad enough. Now, the white men were traveling with their squaws and children, proof they intended to settle permanently in the West.

A war council had been called that afternoon to discuss war against the whites.

"We must destroy them. Strike now!" declared White Bear, leader of the bear clan, a secret tribal society.

"They have said their intention is to settle in the West," countered Black Crow, a medicine man.

White Bear spat. "How long will they keep their promises?" he demanded. "Their words are like the wind. Will they build their wooden lodges here in our hunting ground in another season? Will we wait until they've killed off the buffalo?"

"They have many guns."

"Our warriors are brave."

"Bullets travel faster than arrows."

"We will surprise them in their sleep."

The argument continued for some time. Hoping to end the debate, a chief looked to He-Who-Walks-with-the-Wind for counsel. Bronzed and wrinkled, the old man stood up. His black eyes glittered as he looked around the gathering. The group waited expectantly because the elderly Indian was revered for his wisdom and courage.

"It is best to forget war and hunt the buffalo," said the old man. "We could do that before the white eyes came here. I was one of those who said we should welcome the white man. The trappers were our friends. They lived with us and traded firewater, salt, fishhooks for our furs. The things they brought made life easier for our people. They became like brothers, sharing our tepees and marrying into our nation. Now that has changed. The men in rolling tepees are not friends of the Indian. They care nothing for us. Their presence will cause the buffalo to disappear."

Each man at the meeting pondered his dependence upon the buffalo. Indian leaders had been discussing the demise of the bison herds for many years. Each man held his private theory on when the herds might vanish. Some felt the buffalo would last for many generations. Others believed the intrusion of white men on the plains had brought a time of tribulation. The last of the buffalo would be gone within their lifetime.

The buffalo—those lumbering shaggy beasts of the plains—were prey for men and animals. Packs of wolves followed the herds, attacking cows and devouring calves. White hunters killed indiscriminately to gain their hides. Indian hunters stampeded the herds, driving the great beasts into ravines. Every man in the council had seen buffalo piled eight, ten, twelve deep in a gully.

"White hunters are killing the buffalo every day," continued He-Who-Walks-with-the-Wind. "Buffalo hides are stacked higher than the top of a tepee at Fort Kearney. How long can the herds stand such slaughter?"

"Not long," agreed White Bear.

"Without the buffalo we are nothing," added the old Indian.

Hides were made into clothing, sleeping robes and covers for tepees. Horns were shaped into headdresses. Small bones were used as needles, knives, arrowheads and other useful implements. Large bones were used as clubs. Certain bones were shaped so that, with the marrow removed, they made excellent buckets and similar vessels. Shorn of hair, buffalo hides made excellent drum covers, saddles and rawhide. Every warrior prized shields covered with buffalo hide. Organs were dried, pulverized and prescribed by the medicine men. A man or woman suffering from disease might be cured through liberal doses of dried buffalo liver. Marrow was boiled into a tasty, nutritious pudding. And, of course, the buffalo supplied fresh meat during the summer hunting season. After gorging themselves on the most delectable parts of the animal, the Indians dried the remaining meat for their winter meals.

The old Indian continued to talk. "The Indians must forget their anger," declared He-Who-Walks-with-the-Wind. "We must stop killing each other. We must unite to fight off the white eyes who invade our land."

Warring against each other, the tribes had been unable to form an alliance against their enemies. The Pawnee preyed on the Oto, Omaha and Kaw. In turn, the Sioux despised the Pawnee. The Sioux were besieged by the Cheyenne and Arapahoe from the South, the Crow and Mandan from the North. Off in the West, the Blackfoot tribe hated everyone. Their top-knotted warriors raided any tribe's camp, killing the braves, carrying off women and children as slaves. The smaller nations like the Kiowa and Ute tried to remain aloof from the battle. They seldom succeeded.

He-Who-Walks-with-the-Wind spoke of these things. Finally, when his audience started to tire, he gave his opinion.

"We must kill the white eyes," declared the old Indian.

"Drive them from our hunting ground," yelled White Bear.

After more discussion, the chieftains decided to attack the wagon train. They declared that messengers must be sent to the tribes in the West. Emigrants who had gone by earlier in the season must be destroyed. Only then could the redman reclaim his rightful hunting grounds. When the whites were destroyed, the buffalo herds would increase in numbers.

White Bear, leader of the tribe's secret society, the bear clan, would make a daring raid against the wagon camp that night. The foray would test the white man's defenses. With this plan in mind, the bear clan slipped away from their encampment. They crept along the bank of the Platte River, waiting silently until the Big Dipper reached a prearranged point. Then they crawled from their hiding place and moved closer to the camp. They were approaching a small slough when the enemy rose up out of the darkness.

Guns boomed.

Four warriors fell dead.

Howling with anger, the bear clan chased the white men back to their camp of rolling tepees. The young braves launched a bold charge. Eight men were killed by the invader's bullets. The second group crawled toward the wagons, creeping through the reeds and bulrushes. On signal, they rose up with fierce war cries and made an assault on the wagons. Two more warriors were killed during the barrage of bullets. White Bear decided to use another tactic. Arrows had been prepared for this purpose. They were flinted into flames and shot into the canvas tops of the wagons. Men and women screamed in the wagons as the arrows soared toward their section of the camp. When the arrows struck home, canvas tops flared up into bright flames. Men shouted. Women screamed. Scores of people ran through the corral, carrying buckets of water to douse the fire.

When the fire arrows were depleted, the bear clan withdrew and returned to their camp. Casualties had been heavy. The white eyes had not turned coward and run away.

"We'll kill them tomorrow," boasted a young brave.

"Every man shall be there," promised He-Who-Walks-with-the-Wind.

In the wagon camp, Jim Bridger was satisfied with the night's fight. "We've beaten them off for now," he explained. "But we'd better keep an eye peeled for the rest of the night. They're spoiling for a fight. They're liable to try anything to get revenge."

At dawn, men from the wagon train went outside the corral to inspect the dead Indians. They returned with colorful shields, war bonnets and buffalo bows. The emigrants had not escaped damage during the night attack. Several wagon tops were burned away by fire. Two wagon boxes were charred. Eight oxen had been killed by arrows. Two horses had been hit; they had to be shot. The only emigrant to be wounded was Uncle Durgeon Adkins, struck by an arrow during the first charge. A shaft had come speeding from a powerful buffalo bow. The flint-tipped arrow had struck the iron rim of an outside wagon wheel, been deflected upward into the old man's shoulder. Dr. McDonald doused the shoulder with whiskey. The shaft was driven on through the shoulder, then ointment and bandage applied.

"Don't worry about that wound," Sam Lawson told Uncle Durgeon. "I caught an arrow up on the Yellowstone one season. Damned Indian hit me right in the leg. I drove it on through just like the doctor did with you. The whole thing was healed up inside of two weeks."

"Maybe so." Uncle Durgeon's rheumy eyes looked at the shaft. "I'm worried about the thing not healing. I'm not a spring chicken anymore. This old body has seen better days."

"Get some stuff tomorrow if I have a chance," Jim Bridger chimed in. "Indians got a special weed they rub on wounds. Works darn good in drawing away poisons."

"I'd be obliged," the old man said. "At least I picked up a real, honest-to-god Indian souvenir. I'm keeping the arrowhead. Make a nice watch fob when I get to Oregon."

"That's the spirit," Lawson agreed.

After a hasty breakfast, the people broke camp and started toward Fort Kearney. They did not stop for a noon meal, but continued to roll with great speed across the prairie. Bridger and Lawson scouted in the front of the column. They were looking for smoke signals or other signs of activity by the Indians.

Both men knew the Indians would be seeking revenge.

Lawson came galloping back to Wellman's wagon in mid-afternoon. He wore a worried expression on his face.

"Pass the word around," Lawson said hastily. "If they're going to hit us today, it'll come in the bend up ahead. The land dips down when we're coming out. They can come in from both sides before we know they're there."

"What'll we do?"

"Never outrun them," Lawson explained. "Oxen won't move that fast. We'll have to corral up and make a stand. Trouble is, we got to get through the bend before we can do that. Another complication is that there's a small creek feeding into the Platte up there. Not more than five feet across, but the wagons can pile up there if we don't watch things."

About thirty of the wagons passed unharmed through the bend. Suddenly, an outrider shouted an alarm. The emigrants looked in his direction and saw a hundred mounted Sioux braves roaring toward the train. Before this band reached them, another group of Indians, perhaps fifty warriors, came charging in from the opposite direction. Steve glanced toward the creek, catching sight of a third war party splashing down the stream.

"They're coming in from every direction," Steve shouted.

Cynthia bit her lower lip.

"Steve, I'm scared."

"So am I, honey." He handed the reins to Cynthia.

"You handle the team. I'm going to be busy with the guns."

Sam Lawson was standing near the creek. A wagon had started to cross the stream. The rig was bogged down in mud. A frightened emigrant, his wife and children looked fearfully at the riders coming down the creek.

"Leave your wagon there!" Sam yelled. "Get back here."

Sam jumped off his horse. He dropped to his knee, took aim with his rifle and pulled the trigger. A bonneted brave leading the war party cried with pain when the bullet smashed into his chest. He toppled from his horse and fell into the shallow water.

"Make a box!" Sam shouted. "Get into a corral!"

From the north and south, the two war parties came charging in on the train. Howling their anger, the braves came galloping up to close range beside the wagons. Feathered lances flashed in the sunlight. Arrows came speeding toward the emigrants on the drivers' seats. One Sioux leaped off his horse and gained a foothold on a speeding wagon. His tomahawk came flashing down on George Reynolds's head. The emigrant gave a tiny moan and dropped under the wheels of his wagon. The brave started back into the wagon. His eyes widened with horror when a tiny white woman with a wrinkled face raised a shotgun. The last thing the Indian saw was a spurt of fiery flame from the gun barrel. Frightened by the noise, the team bolted and raced out of the column. They ran across the countryside toward the creek. The rig struck the stream, then turned and ran toward the Platte River. A half dozen warriors clambered aboard, disappearing inside the canvas top. Gunfire sounded once, twice and then stopped. Moments later, an Indian leaped down from the rig. He held a woman's hair high above his head as proof of his invincibility as a warrior.

Two screaming children were pulled from the wagon, left standing in the middle of the stream. The braves rode off in pursuit of bigger coup.

Steve Wellman took aim, at close range, and shot a middle-aged Indian off his horse. Another brave came charging up, reaching out for the brake handle of Wellman's wagon. Steve clubbed the man from his mount with his rifle butt.

Cynthia screamed.

Steve turned instantly, saw a brave with a vividly painted face coming through the back of their wagon. He pulled his Colt revolver and shot the man in the groin. The Indian came on, pain wracking his features, tomahawk held high toward Cynthia's head. Steve shot the man a second time, the bullet entering his throat and traveling up into his mouth. Blood gushed from the Indian's nostrils as he pitched forward off the wagon.

"Make a corral!" Sam Lawson shouted. He stood on the ground, motioning for the wagons to pull into a box.

Cynthia pulled the wagon up beside the guide. Mike Gorman's team was out of control. They came smashing into the back of Wellman's wagon. The other wagons came up and, shooting at the Indians, Sam directed the emigrants into two parallel columns. Eight wagons were lined up on one side; the remainder pulled in about ten feet away. Although this did not create a tight box, the space between the wagons offered some sanctuary for the emigrants. Men, women and children leaped down into the space between the wagons. Several men stationed themselves at either end of the box. Firing at the Indians, they used their wagons as a partial shield.

Confusion reigned. Steve ran through the group. He yelled for the women to load guns, the men to keep firing. He was passing Brad Payne's wagon when an Indian pony leaped a wagon tongue. The brave's lance was held high. Steve took a quick shot at the man, missed, and then saw the Indian's mount crash into the side of Elmer J. Johnson's wagon. Both horse and rider were stunned for a moment. Before they recovered their faculties, Johnson grabbed an ax handle and clubbed the brave to the ground. Bleeding profusely from the forehead, the Indian scrambled under the wagon to safety.

Two Indians came running into the partial corral. Their horses picked up speed. Yelling like a banshee, one brave aimed his tomahawk for Molly Gorman's body. Moving swiftly, Mike threw out his arm to deflect the weapon. The hard, flinty surface cut deep into his arm, then fell to the ground. Mike fired at where the Indian had been, missing by several yards. He fell back against the wheel of his wagon, cursing loudly. When she saw the blood on her husband's arm, Molly's face paled. She started to leap down from the wagon seat.

"Later!" Mike yelled. "Keep behind me. It's just a scratch!"

Molly nodded grimly and bent to reload his rifle.

Sam Lawson worried about the open ends of their corral. He came running up to Elmer Johnson.

"Get some rope!" yelled the guide. "Tie it across that end!"

Johnson jumped up into his wagon, threw down a long strand of rawhide. He went off to tie the open end. Sam raced back through the box, yelled at another man. Moments later, the opposite end of the box had been tied with several strands of thick rope.

"Now they got to stay outside," Sam shouted.

Wellman came up and stationed a couple of men at either end of the corral. "Keep firing and loading if they try to jump over the rope," he ordered.

Grimly, the men took up their positions. It became necessary to start firing immediately as the Indians came charging against the ends. One brave, his face painted with brilliant hues, encouraged his pony to leap the rope. The mount failed to clear the rawhide barrier. Elmer J. Johnson's shotgun boomed and the Indian took the blast in his back.

Agnes Miller was shielded behind a wagon wheel. Jane and Melissa loaded her guns as quickly as Agnes fired. Although she was secure behind the wheel, Agnes found her sight limited. Indians came riding alongside the edge of the wagons. They rode close to the outside of the rigs. The Indians flashed by too quickly; Agnes had no time to aim. Although she was firing rapidly and consistently, her bullets were not finding a target.

Sam came running up.

"You're wasting powder!" He spoke with authority. "Wait until you're sure there's something to hit. Then aim carefully and fire fast."

Agnes yelled, "Stay here with us."

"Don't shoot until you got a target!" Sam hurried off, snapping off shots with his revolver.

Suddenly, Agnes was terrified by a scream near her. She wheeled and saw a young Indian, war bonnet hanging down his back, crawling from beneath her wagon. A buffalo bone tomahawk was in his left hand. His face was smeared with war paint. Agnes pointed her gun at the Indian. His eyes glittered with fear.

"Kill him!" Melissa shouted.

Agnes's finger tightened on the trigger. Suddenly, she stopped. The Indian looked so young, so vulnerable.

"Shoot him!" yelled Jane.

Agnes was paralyzed. The Indian was coming up from under the wagon. A cold, frigid glare replaced the fright on his face. He raised his tomahawk and, at the same instant, reached for Agnes's head. His hand was still coming toward her hair when she pulled the trigger. The gun roared, throwing Agnes back against the wheel. The brave stood for a moment, looking down at the gaping hole in his stomach. He started to speak. A rushing stream of blood came pouring from his mouth. Melissa kicked out against the young man's knee, knocked him down on the ground. Instantly, Jane brought a gun butt down on the Indian's head. A sharp cracking sound came from his skull. He rolled over and lay still.

"Oh God!" Agnes cried.

Dan Pitzen had stationed himself at the east end of the open box. He pumped lead over the rawhide barrier stretched between the two wagons. The Indians were riding down the outside line of wagons, wheeling across the open end and racing down the other side. As they passed the opening, Dan Pitzen had an unobstructed view of the riders. He took another shot, brought down a brave, and handed his gun back to Elmer J. Johnson.

"Keep loading 'em," Pitzen roared.

Wordlessly, Johnson handed a loaded gun to the gambler.

Pitzen raised the rifle, waited and took aim as a feathered Indian carrying a lance galloped into view. Eight-to-five he would miss. He pulled the trigger, saw the Indian ride away.

"You're shooting too high," Johnson told him. "Shoot

for the belly. You got a chance to hit either the Indian or his horse."

Pitzen took the loaded rifle from Johnson, aimed low and saw an Indian tumble off his horse.

"That's number four!" Johnson was jubilant.

At the opposite end of the box, Uncle Durgeon Adkins was loading for Bruce Middleton. Twice now, Indians had charged the rope stretched across the two lines of wagons. Both times, Middleton had stopped them dead with a charge from his shotgun. As the Indians fell, Bruce hoped that Melissa was watching his marksmanship.

Jay Samuels came up. He carried a large-bore buffalo gun. His coat was split in the shoulder, reddened with blood. Face pale and drawn, Samuels handed the gun to the two men.

"You can shoot," he told Johnson. "I'm getting weak. I can't see anything. I'll do the loading."

Johnson took the gun, waited for an open shot. "Christ!" he roared, "this thing weighs a ton!"

Suddenly, an eerie blast sounded on a horn. The emigrants froze as the strange notes drifted through the camp. Still yelling their war cries, the Indians withdrew from their attack. They grouped a quarter mile away from the wagons.

Sam Lawson came down the line.

"They're holding a powwow," he announced.

"They giving up?" someone asked.

"That's what they're deciding now," Sam replied. "Either they're massing for a big attack—or they've had enough. I think we'd better get ready for a real tough time."

TWENTY-FOUR

The wagon train was a shambles.

Steve Wellman went down the line to check on casualties. He found the body of Clarence Willmont, a thirty-eight-year-old farmer from Pennsylvania, lying on the outside of the wagons. He had made the error of jumping off his wagon to fight an Indian. He had been tomahawked to death. The weapon was still embedded in his skull. His wife, Janice, lay dead a few feet from her husband. She had rushed to her husband's aid. She lay impaled by a sharp, feathered lance.

"I tried to stop her," Vivian Middleton reported. "She was like a mad woman. I grabbed her arm but she tore away. Ran right out there to help him." She sobbed for a moment.

"I didn't know them very well," Steve said.

"They kept to themselves."

"Any children?"

"One little girl."

"Where's she at?"

"I'll go try and find her."

Jay Samuels had been hit by an arrow in the back of his shoulder. Josh McDonald was already bandaging the wound. Several emigrants were scarred with minor wounds. Sam Lawson's head was creased with a bloody bruise. The guide couldn't remember where or how he had been hit. Two oxen had been wounded, one belonging to Mrs. Wade Jackson, the other to Mike Gorman. They would have to be killed, butchered before the train moved out. Uncle Durgeon Adkins had broken open the wound in his shoulder.

"Damn! It hurts," the old man grimaced.

"Let me finish with Jay," McDonald told him. "Then I'll get you fixed up."

"Sam needs fixing first."

Agnes came up with a towel. She wiped the blood from Sam's face. "Better let me wash that."

"It'll have to wait." Sam looked around, spied Wellman down the line. He hurried off in that direction.

Wellman was pulling two wagons out of the line, placing the rigs at the end of the corral. He sent Mike Gorman to the opposite end to do the same. Wellman looked down as Sam came up.

"What're they doing over there?"

"Powwowing, like I said."

"They going to hit us again?"

Sam shrugged. "Who knows? You can't figure out how Indians will think. They were stupid to hit us in daylight."

Steve's hand was trembling. "Maybe not. They scared the shit out of me."

Sam extended his hand. "Help me up. I'll get a better view of what those yahoos are doing out there."

310

"Maybe they've had enough."

Sam stood up on the seat of the wagon. Across the prairie, the Indians were regrouping. In the midst of the war party, a medicine man danced about. He was decorated with a feathered bonnet that hung down from his buffalo headdress. His only attire was a breechcloth and, naked, his bronze skin shone coppery in the sunlight.

"Making medicine," Sam explained.

"That good or bad?"

"Depends," Sam grunted. "They're asking the great spirit what they should do. Things could go either way. At least we have time to rest and get organized before another attack. With luck, we may be able to move out and join up with Bridger and the rest."

Steve looked across the flat, grassy land. "Maybe they got wiped out."

"Not likely. Ole Gabe's too smart for that."

A horseman rode up alongside their wagon. "I'm Don Parks," the rider said breathlessly. "Captain of the Illinois Company. We're behind you folks. I come up to find out what's happening."

"We're still alive," Sam replied. "The Sioux are over there making medicine."

"You lose many?" asked Parks.

"Most of us are still alive."

"We lost three families." Parks shook his head. "Jesus! The damn fools wouldn't corral up. Tried to make a run across the country. Indians got them real quick."

Sam pointed to the wagon bogged down in the Platte River. "The team bolted. They didn't have a chance. George Reynolds and his wife were killed."

Parks turned and stared at the war party grouped

across the creek. "How long before they decide to run or fight?"

"Could be the next minute. Might be another week," Sam replied. "They're strange people. White men will never figure out the Indian. They're a chile from a different mold."

"Look!" Steve pointed at the Indians. "They're mounting up."

"Get ready for attack!" Sam growled.

The war party contained some of the bravest men in the Sioux nation. While the medicine man danced, chanting his entreaties to the great spirit, the braves discussed launching another attack. White Bear and the leaders of the other warrior clans urged caution. Their losses had been heavy during the raid. Perhaps, they reasoned, their medicine lacked strength. The shamen might have lost contact with the great spirit. Although the medicine man continued to dance and chant, they ordered their men to mount. The clan leaders led the howling braves toward the wagon camp.

"Get ready!" Wellman shouted.

The emigrants rushed to the barricades.

The Indians thundered wildly across the prairie. When the first wave of riders came to the far side of the creek, their ponies wheeled north.

"Thunderation!" Sam danced with glee. "They're riding out!"

"We whipped them!" screamed Mike Gorman.

"We're luckier than hogs with a new mud hole." Dan Pitzen rested his rifle on the ground.

"I'd better tell my group," said Don Parks. He rode swiftly back down the line of wagons.

During the next two hours, the emigrants dug graves

for their dead. Repairs were made on their wagons. The Reynolds vehicle was pulled from the muddy Platte River. When the Illinois Company pulled up, the caravan forded the creek. The long line of wagons moved out across the prairie. They camped that night near a small spring, some ten miles from Fort Kearney.

Shortly before dusk, a group of dragoon soldiers rode into camp. The lieutenant saluted Wellman and asked for a report on the casualties. The soldiers remained in camp that night, helping tend to the wounded, assisting in repairs to the wagons. Soldiers took the guard duties that night, relieving the men who had fought off the Indians. The camp rose early the next morning and, by mid-afternoon, rolled into Fort Kearney.

Fort Kearney, the only fort established on the trail for the protection of the emigrants, was a disappointment. Most of the buildings were still under construction. When the caravans pulled in, the lieutenant apologized for the rough, limited accommodations. Some emigrants had expected the fort to be an island of civilization in the wilderness. They were sorely disappointed.

Eight long adobe buildings with canvas roofs had been erected. A livery stable, blacksmith's and carpenter's shops were housed in sod dugouts. Near the headquarters building, a hospital tent had been erected. Two adobe corrals held the horses and mules used by the horse soldiers. These dragoons were backed up by two companies of infantrymen. A sutler had opened a store to supply provisions to the soldiers and emigrants. His prices were shockingly high.

West beyond the fort, a cluster of adobe buildings was being built. This was a private community named Dobytown. It was established to house the men and women camp followers who preyed on soldiers near any military installation. One small rude building, without windows and a canvas curtain for a door, housed the Dobytown saloon. While the caravan settled in at the fort, Sam Lawson headed straight for the saloon.

He was sorely disappointed.

"Ain't got any whiskey in yet." The saloonkeeper spread his hands in despair.

Sam licked his lips. "Not even a little bottle of your own in back?"

"I'd pay five in gold for a good bottle of bourbon."

"I should have brought a wagonload in from Independence."

"Even the soldiers are doing without," explained the saloonkeeper. "The fort went up so quick I didn't have time to order supplies. If you're coming back this way, I might have something by next month."

"A lot of good that'll do me," Sam complained. He turned and went back to the wagon camp.

The caravan had been on the trail for a month. They had traveled through to the sandy "coasts" of Nebraska, sandhills with the appearance of a coastal region. The wind blew constantly out on the prairie. The waist-high growth of prairie grass swayed under the breeze, giving the appearance of fleeting waves on the surface of an ocean. The emigrants had endured attacks from hostile Indians. They had surmounted the discomforts and inconveniences of life along the trail. Admittedly, they were afflicted with the inevitable anxiety of any group of people seeking a new land. Despite their apprehension, the majority of the people were determined to reach their destination, Oregon. They felt a home in Oregon was their God-given right—manifest destiny.

A small number doubted the wisdom of continuing their journey into an unknown region. Their memories were etched with the grisly sight of Wade Jackson's body, skinless, tied to a cottonwood tree. They fretted about the insects, the harshness of life on the trail. No one could ever adequately describe the horror they felt, the terror they had witnessed with their own eyes.

"Maybe we ought to go back," Vivian Middleton suggested to her husband.

Bruce disagreed. "You wanted to go to Oregon, that's where we're ending up."

"I didn't know it would be like this." Vivian sobbed.

"I don't care if you bawl 'til morning. We're not turning back."

"You would if you loved me."

Bruce shook his head angrily. "That has nothing to do with it."

"You've been taking an awful lot of walks most every night."

Ah! Bruce wondered, does she know about me and Melissa. No, he decided, she would blackmail him into going back if she had that information. The land might be wilderness, untamed and not worth settling, but it had brought him something he'd never known before. He tried to put his thoughts into words.

"I've found something out about myself out here," Bruce told his wife. "Back home, I was a meek little clerk. You ran my life. Do this, hop over and run that. Go here. Stay there. Somehow I accepted all that, Vivian, although I wasn't happy. I wasn't much of a man back in Galena. A man doesn't allow himself to become henpecked. Somehow you just wore me down, grinding away with your nagging, bitching and complaining. Rather than fight with you, I sort of meekly took everything."

Vivian protested. "It wasn't that bad."

"Maybe not for you," Bruce continued. "Back in Galena, I didn't even know I could feel like this. I'm a man, Vivian, and by God I'm going to stay one. You're not dragging me back to some town. I won't be a clerk anymore. I won't jump when your fingers are snapped."

"Look at the big man," Vivian sneered.

"Damn right! I can drive a team of oxen, grease an axle hub, chop wood, fight off Indians. And do you know something?"

Vivian sighed. "What don't I know."

"I do those things pretty well. I'm not as good as some of the men in the camp. Wellman, Gorman and Sam Lawson are better than me. But, by God! I'm above average as a man."

"We could go back to Independence. Start a store."

"I'm going to Oregon."

"St. Louis has lots of opportunity for a good man."

"I'm sure it does."

"We could settle down there."

"I'm not interested."

"You could get your job back at the bank in Galena."

Bruce laughed. "I don't want it. Maybe I'll start my own bank in Oregon."

"With what?" Vivian smiled with disgust.

"That's the funny thing about coming out here," Bruce explained. "I don't feel like my life's got boundaries. Back home, I was hog-tied and fettered. I couldn't see a single option. Just clerk for starvation wages. Accept whatever scraps they throw me. Let you run things. I'll admit something changed inside me. I feel alive for the first time in my life. We're going to Oregon. I'm going to do a lot of great things out there. Life is going to be fantastic."

"Big ideas take money."

"I'll get it."

"Pshaw! All you know is clerking."

Bruce Middleton's eyes took on a determined gleam. "I've always lived to what other people expected of me," he explained quietly. "First my parents, then my employers and, after our marriage, I tried to live to your expectations. I became someone who was like a stranger. Eventually, I built a shell around me. Don't think. Don't feel. Don't enjoy. Don't express an opinion. Don't act. Don't be myself. I built a fence around my feelings until it was like a stone wall. I wasn't alive back in Galena. I was being what everyone else wanted me to be, taking their expectations and chasing it down with a cup of bile."

"Was it that bad?"

"Probably worse," Bruce answered truthfully. "For the first time in my life, I realize there are options open for the remainder of my life. I can be the best damned farmer in Oregon. Banking? I can start the best bank in the whole territory. I can do anything I want. That's because I like myself."

"Everyone does that."

Bruce shook his head in disagreement. "Not the people I've observed. Most don't realize their potential. They don't grab life by the throat and take the whole loaf. They compromise—not for half a loaf—but for a few measly crumbs. Lord, woman! I'm not settling for the whole loaf. I want the whole dang feast on the banquet table. I'm a

317

nice person. I deserve it."

Vivian looked sour. "I don't understand what you're talking about."

"That's because I've learned to be honest with myself."

"What's that mean?"

"For one thing, I'm not a pervert."

Vivian's loathing increased. Bruce was talking about that Frenching again. Suddenly, with an instant rush of feminine intuition she realized that he was seeing another woman. Facts were not needed to confirm her suspicion. The transformation in his thinking, the spring in his step she'd noticed lately, verified her belief in his infidelity. She cast a suspicious look in his direction. A glimmer of fear came into his eyes.

Vivian said, "You've been seeing another woman."

"Don't be ridiculous!" Bruce lied.

"I'll bet that's why you take those walks at night. You're meeting someone outside the camp."

"That's absurd!" Bruce turned and started to walk away. He said over his shoulder, "I'd better check on the animals."

Sudden bitter rage swept over Vivian Middleton. She folded her hands, fingered her thin gold wedding band. She remembered her age: forty-two years old. Until the moment, she had been a wife enjoying the protection and security of matrimony, unthreatened by the terror of abandonment. The hideous fear of poverty had been erased from her life. Although Bruce had never been a great provider, his meager paycheck had been steady. Bruce had somehow eluded the bonds of their marital state, discovering that fortune was offering a second chance in life.

Trembling with anger and fear, Vivian went up into the wagon. She opened her trunk and pulled out a mirror. She looked at the face reflected back, realizing that she had very little to offer a man. The first hint of a sagging chin was evident. Wrinkles were etched deep into her forehead; crow's feet surrounded her eyes. Her cheeks sagged, lips drooped. Strands of gray dotted her hair. Her eyes had a dull glaze and, try as she might, they refused to sparkle.

She replaced the mirror in her trunk. Oh Christ! Her thoughts raced with feverish desperation. A woman needed something better than this kind of life. Exchanging your body and soul for a few scraps of food and a bed for the night was not an exact bargain. Wives never knew when another woman would entice their husbands away. Younger women, with firm bodies and a harlot's morals, could turn a husband's head.

The hussy!

Damned slut!

Adulterous bitch!

Vivian's heart pounded fiercely, leaping up into her breasts. She shook with rage. She wanted to destroy her husband, see him squirm knowing she had caused the pain. She decided to make a complaint to Steve Wellman, then realized that would mean defeat. Adultery on the trail carried the penalty of death. A dead husband couldn't provide for a wife. Ah, the other woman, she thought. I wonder who you are, you bitch! You'll regret the day you tried to steal my husband.

Vivian smiled. Destroy Bruce's paramour and he'd come to heel like a pup on a leash.

TWENTY-THREE

The wagon trains laid over at Fort Kearney for two days, making repairs, buying supplies, resting. A detachment of dragoons rode out and came back to report the Sioux had broken camp. The tribe had moved north to follow the buffalo herds. Travel west to Fort Laramie should be safe from attack. On their last evening at the fort, a meeting of all the emigrants was held. The commander of the fort announced that a group of soldiers would accompany ten supply wagons east to Independence. Families who wished to withdraw and return east were welcome to travel with the soldiers.

Two families in the True Christian company, weary of Hattie Gill's gibberish, left that caravan. A college professor in the Illinois Company, along with four families of farmers, realized the wilderness presented too many hazards. Frontier life had been rougher than expected; they pulled their rigs out of line and parked on the eastern edge of the fort. Despite her son's entreaties, Mrs. Wade Jackson made plans to return to her parents' home in Kentucky. Life in Oregon without a husband, she declared, would be unbearable. Two children orphaned in the Indian attack, their parents killed by arrow and tomahawk, would return to Independence with the detachment.

The air was crisp, the weather clear and bright, on the third morning. Rising at the first notes of the bugle's blast, Steve Wellman went down the line of wagons.

"Let's move out quick!" he said urgently. "We'll get a jump on the others. Let's go! Yoke 'em up! Let's get rolling!"

Despite his pleas, the emigrants were reluctant to leave Fort Kearney. They moved sluggishly, lingering at length over breakfast, hurrying to the sutler's store for a last purchase.

"Christ! They're like dead men!" Steve complained to Cynthia.

"This is the last civilized place we'll see for a while," she reminded him.

The sun was high when the caravan rolled westward. The other trains, including the True Christians, had gone out several hours earlier.

"We're still eating everyone's dust," Steve complained.

Creaking and groaning, the wagons moved across the plains. The trail was rutted now by hoof prints and wagon wheels. Vegetation on either side of the road was grazed to the roots. The land became flat, treeless, and covered with short grass. The emigrants were entering the eastern edge of the great herds of buffalo. Free, abundant meat would be available for several hundred miles. The Platte River valley was the center of these migrating herds. The plains were covered with their manure, which grumbling women and children now gathered for fuel. Buffalo wallows could be seen along the river, the animals crowded in to enjoy their ancient water holes. Buffalo tracks, chopped deep into the earth by millions of hooves, crisscrossed the trail.

Several days out of Fort Kearney, Sam Lawson halted the caravan early one afternoon. He had promised to take the men out for a buffalo hunt. Although most of the men were hunters, no one had ever shot one of the huge shaggy beasts.

For his weapon, Sam picked up a short buffalo bow taken off a Pawnee brave. Double-curved, sinew-backed, the resilient bow was made from *bois d'arc*. This was the treasured bow wood used by the Plains Indians. He slung a thick sheaf of arrows, sharpened and honed, in a beaver quill over his back.

"Bows are as good as anything for hunting buffalo," the guide explained. "No use wasting powder and lead."

They rode north from the trail for a half hour. Their nerves jumped when a ridge was topped. Below, stretching across the horizon, was a vast concourse of buffalo. Mike Gorman judged the herd was more than a mile wide. It stretched as far as he could see. It was a sight each man would always remember.

As they rode closer, dust clouds of combat rode here and there in the herd.

"The old bulls are tough," Sam remarked. "They get right fretful when the young bulls try to move in on their cows."

As they approached the outer rim of the herd, a hoarse bellowing sound came to them. Even at a distance, the spectacle of so many great animals was thrilling—and also terrifying. The herd moved slowly across the valley, grazing leisurely.

"We going right in them?" asked Elmer J. Johnson.
His voice was agitated.

"Got to get close to use a bow," Sam replied.

"What if they stampede?"

"Stick close to me and pray."

Straight ahead, a group of about one hundred cows and
bulls stood away from the main stream of buffalo. Several
of the animals heard the approach of the hunters. They
stood unafraid, staring stupidly at the men.

"Let's get 'em!" Sam whooped.

He kicked his horse. The animal charged forward
toward the herd. Snorting and weaving, the other men
followed the guide. Their horses closed the gap to the
plunging, suddenly terrified buffalo. Yelling like an
Indian, Sam braced himself on his racing mount. He
threw his strength into the bow. The feathered arrow
shot off when he loosened the sinew cord. The honed
arrow plunged deep into the flanks of the nearest cow.

Sam made one pass through the herd. He expended his
quiver of arrows. Most of the huge animals were running
toward the main herd. The wounded buffalo tried to
follow. Their steps faltered. They stood erect, mouths
flecked with a bloody foam. They began to kneel down
and die.

Pulling his buffalo gun, Sam wheeled his horse and
rode into the main herd. He was quickly engulfed by a sea
of buffalo humps. He shot at the front of the cows. His
bullets smashed into their lungs. He continued blasting
away until he was tired. Fifteen buffalo were dying on the
prairie. The other men were riding along the edge of the
herd. The sounds of their exploding guns were muffled
by the thunderous roar of hooves. Each man tried to

down at least one beast. Some succeeded, proving their mettle, while others misjudged their shots. Finally, they rode back to where Sam Lawson stood surrounded by dead animals.

"Plenty of meat," roared the guide.

Pulling his knife, Lawson demonstrated the proper way to butcher a buffalo. First, the carcass had to be lying on its belly. Then, the knife was shoved deep into the hide on the animal's back. When the seam was completed, cleanly through the shaggy hide, the cut was pulled open.

"This is your container for holding the meat," Sam told them. "Keeps the cuts off the ground, away from the bugs and worms."

Next, he went to the front of the beast, raised the shaggy, bearded head and shoved his blade deep into the lower jaw. Holding the horns, he continued to cut across the jaw and down into the throat. Once this opening was made, he severed the tongue and pulled it from the opening.

"This may be the best part of a buffalo," He said, displaying the enormous organ. "The meat's flavorful, rich and there's plenty of it. Tenderest part of the animal, although some men prefer hump meat."

He went back to butchering. "Keep the back fat, the hump and as many ribs as you want," he related. "There's nothing better than buffalo ribs roasted over an open fire."

The emigrants ate ravenously that night. When their appetites were sated, the remaining meat was thrown to the dogs.

"We can get plenty of buffalo tomorrow," Sam promised.

A camp meeting was held after the feast. The emigrants

decided to lay over for three days. They would hunt buffalo and make "jerky," a dried meat favored by trappers and mountain men. The first step was to construct a large platform a few feet off the ground. Fortunately, Sam Lawson had foreseen the need for wood. He had cut cottonwood trees on the Blue River, lashed them to the undersides of wagons. When these poles were erected, a series of rawhide strips were crisscrossed to form a platform. When the buffalo was killed, the meat was butchered out in long strips. These were laid across the platform to dry. Buffalo chips burned underneath to speed the process. Large chunks of meat, such as the hump, were smoked for the evening meal. When the jerky was dried, each emigrant received an equal portion.

"Stick it away!" Sam Lawson declared. "May not look like much now, but we'll need it before we reach Oregon."

During the layover, the merits of buffalo meat became an item of discussion. Jay Samuels leaned toward the hump as the most delicate part. Mike Gorman disagreed.

"That's because your taste has been ruined by Jewish food," teased the Irishman. "Anyone with taste at all knows the tongue is the best."

Dan Pitzen considered the flavor of both cuts and found them wanting.

"You're both strictly meat-and-potatoes men," he declared. "The tenderloin is the most flavorful cut. Erica cooked some last night in Burgundy and, my friends, it matched anything served at the finest restaurants in New Orleans. A man should round up a herd of these creatures, drive them east and sell the meat."

Steve Wellman looked dubious. "Maybe buffalo meat

isn't all that great. We've just been living off salt meat so long that anything tastes good."

Thirty buffalo were killed during their first day laying over. The jerky rack was covered with meaty strips. Women and children scoured the countryside for dried buffalo chips. Before they broke camp, Sam Lawson came in one night with a buffalo hide full of bones. He buried the bones in the flames beneath the jerky platform. A rich, mild and tantalizing scent began to spread through the camp. After an hour of intense cooking, Sam pulled a large bone from the fire. He cracked away the bone, dug into the marrow.

"Another rich meal from our friend, the buffalo," he told the emigrants. "Dig in and help yourself to the marrow."

Several emigrants were converted that evening.

"Best tasting I've had," admitted Jay Samuels.

"Delicious," agreed Mike Gorman.

"If it walks, you'd eat it," rejoined Molly.

The layover provided an opportunity to clean up. When rolling across the plains, the wagon train had the stench of a pest house. The oily smell of hot axle grease, the stench from crated chickens, the stink from lumbering oxen was overpowering. A person with sensitive nostrils learned to stand downwind from his friends. Clothing and bedrolls were saturated with human sweat. Foodstuffs spoiled and filled a wagon with odors. Corraling the animals each night added to the emigrants' distress. The dank smell of oxen, mules and horses filled the camp. The stench of manure was everywhere. So the layover provided time to wash clothes, scour the wagons, wipe down boxes, air beds and clean up.

The women worked hard each day to clean everything. Their efforts were doomed. When the train rolled out again, following the ambling course of the Platte River, the landscape changed. They rolled into a white, loamy alkali country. The white, powdery substance floated in like clouds of face powder. White dust lay in thick layers over the wagons and canvas tops. It covered the contents inside the wagons like freshly fallen snow. If a wind was blowing, a frequent occurrence on the plains, the emigrants and their animals took on an unearthly appearance. They became covered with white dust. One man said his team looked like ghosts plodding through a snowstorm.

Flesh exposed to the dust reddened to an itching rawness. If the skin peeled and cracked, the dust crept into the opening. Eyes smarted from contact with the tiny particles. People learned not to rub the dust deeper into their eye sockets. Those who could not withstand the irritation rubbed vigorously; they could barely see for several days. Adding to their discomfort, the dust clogged their nostrils and mouths.

A short distance east of the forks of the Platte River, Cottonwood Springs was a welcome sight when the caravan rolled in. The trees had been chopped down by earlier emigrants. The campground was littered with refuse. The ground around was littered with manure, garbage and, off to one side, the rotting carcass of a dead ox. Yet, Cottonwood Springs was the site of a bubbling spring of cool, sweet water. The caravan camped a quarter mile west, beyond the stench, and set about with their chores.

Steve Wellman cautioned them about the water. "Remember we have to boil it," he reminded the women. "Don't drink any until you've done that."

The women had been grumbling about boiling water since they left Independence. The men were not much better. After a long trek across the plains, a person needed to wipe the alkali taste away. Boiling water took away the fresh taste.

"Might as well drink pee," commented Charles Ordman. He was particularly irritated by the order. His wife, Nadine, was cut from the same mold. They complained about and to each other, gnawed about other people's behavior, and seldom found anything optimistic in any situation. Charles and Nadine came from northern Mississippi, near the new town of Holly Springs, and hoped to find something good in Oregon.

Ordman started his business career clerking for a cotton broker in New Orleans. The firm specialized in financing cotton planters throughout the south. In the fall of 1842, when he was thirty-three years old, Ordman was sent out to collect past due bills. Five years after the Panic of 1837, the South was still impoverished. Many small farms and plantations had been wiped out. The small farmers ranted and raved about bankers, paper money and New York financial wolves. They told Ordman it wasn't likely they'd be able to pay that year.

Ordman ran across an abandoned cotton farm in northern Mississippi one afternoon. He moved onto the place, bought a mule, plow, seed and other supplies. A hailstorm ruined his first year's crop. He fumed and swore, then set out to court a rich wife. The only woman answering that description was Nadine Morrison, the daughter of the richest planter in the mid-south. Her white-bearded father had come through the panic without being financially wounded; he believed in hard money buried in tin boxes on his plantation.

After five years of marriage, two children and bad crops, opportunity knocked for Charles Ordman. His father-in-law died. The family gathered to bury the old gentleman. While they remained in the great house, Ordman sneaked around the plantation looking for gold. He didn't find the whole hoard—that he was sure—but dug up enough gold coins to outfit a rig for Oregon.

When the caravan reached Cottonwood Springs, Charles Ordman suffered from a great thirst. After the wagons were corraled up, he grabbed a bucket and headed for the springs. He slipped his tin dipper into the cool water. He drank deeply. The water was sweet and tasty.

Nadine came up.

"You ain't supposed to drink 'til it's boiled," she cautioned.

"Take a taste." Charles refilled the dipper. "Best water I've had in weeks."

Nadine agreed. "Better'n that boiled stuff."

"Lawson don't know nothing."

"We ain't had no fever," Nadine pointed out.

"Water don't cause it."

"Some guide books say it does."

"What do they know?"

Nadine took another drink. "It sure is sweet tasting."

"We ain't boiling no more."

"Lawson won't like us doing that."

Charles Ordman smiled. "We won't tell him."

When the bugle blew the next morning, Charles Ordman was too weak to get up. Although she was light-headed and feverish, Nadine hurried through the camp to find Steve Wellman.

"My mister's feeling poorly this morning," she told him.

"What's wrong?"

"He's got the sweats."

"I'll send the doctor around."

"I ain't feeling good myself."

He asked, "You been boiling your water?"

Nadine lied. "All the time."

When Dr. Josh McDonald went into the Ordman tent, his eyes widened with alarm. Charles Ordman was covered with sweat. His bedroll was drenched with perspiration. The man shook with bone-jarring chills.

"Just the flu, ain't it doc?" Ordman's eyes were glittering from fever.

McDonald laid his hand on Ordman's forehead. "You're running an awful fever. How long you been like this?"

"Come on early this morning."

"Well, I'll give you something to sleep." McDonald dug into his bag, pulled out a bottle of opium-based medicine. He spooned two teaspoons of the pain-killing liquid into Ordman's mouth. He left the man lying weakly on the pallet. Outside, he gave the medicine to Nadine Ordman, sending her up into their wagon to rest.

The emigrants stood a safe distance from the Ordman wagon. Their faces were pinched with worry. They awaited the doctor's verdict because, on the plains, an epidemic of cholera could kill everyone in a wagon train.

Mike Gorman asked, "They bad?"

"Terrible. Looks like cholera."

"Oh God!" Cynthia Wellman wrung her hands in despair.

"We'll have to wait and see," McDonald said. "They

might pull through."

"Might be from fresh meat," suggested Uncle Durgeon Adkins. "I've heard tell of folks getting feverish from that. Specially if the animal was run a long ways before being killed."

McDonald looked surprised. "You sure of that?"

Sam Lawson agreed with the old man. "Indians call it buffalo sickness."

"Maybe there's a chance."

"Might be."

Around noon, Charles Ordman asked that the emigrants sing a hymn. Their voices were lifted in song when he died. An hour later, Nadine Ordman began to hallucinate. She cried out for forgiveness for her sins, pleaded with the women to care for her children. She swore the juices in her brain were bubbling to a boil. Praying fervently, she promised to boil her drinking water if she lived.

Nadine raised up on her elbows. Her eyes were glazed with fever.

"Where's little Nick?" she asked just before she died.

Her son, Nicholas Ordman, died a few minutes after his mother. The older boy lingered for another two hours, then expired. Graves were hastily dug in the trail, the bodies interred without coffins. Wellman asked Uncle Durgeon to drive the Ordman's wagon to Fort Laramie. The boy from New York City, Lonnie Thompson, would tend to Bruce Middleton's second wagon.

"We'll sell the Ordmans's rig at the fort," Wellman said. "The money can be sent back to their relatives."

The caravan pulled out late that afternoon, headed for the forks of the North and South Platte Rivers. From there, they headed west along the northern bank of the

North Platte, a route known as the Mormon Trail. The land took on a rugged, untamed appearance. Strange wildflowers bloomed in the meadows. The earth seemed silent and empty. Trees were non-existent and, in the clear air of the Platte Valley, distances became deceptive. The terrain took on a monotonous sameness.

People gumbled.

"We're not out sightseeing," Wellman told the complainers.

"But I hear Ash Hollow's the best camp grounds on the trail," complained Elmer J. Johnson.

"Better'n most. I have to admit that," Sam Lawson agreed. "Place has lush meadows. Plenty of trees. Lots of wildflowers. Good drinking water. But Ash Hollow is smack dab at the bottom of Windlass Hill. That's so steep a billy goat would get dizzy just looking at it. Going that way, we'll have to cross the Platte at least two times. Bound to lose a wagon. Maybe two in the crossing. At Windlass, we'll have to tie ropes on the wagons and ease 'em down the hill. If a rig gets going too fast, it'll break the ropes and break free. It'll turn over and be all busted up. If you want to visit Ash Hollow, you're welcome to do it. But the rest of us ain't waiting for you."

Johnson studied the guide's face. He moved away uncertainly, speaking from a distance.

"You don't have to get high horse about it." Johnson bristled.

"Just stating the facts."

"Folks may need a rest."

"That's true," agreed Lawson. "You got all the resting time you'll need when you reach Oregon City."

The caravan made good speed on the trail. Days, campgrounds and images blended into one fragmented memory. The trail seemed to stretch on forever. One bright spot was the imposing natural monument known as Courthouse Rock. Seen from a distance, the dome-capped sandstone structure resembled a county courthouse. The next landmark was Chimney Rock, a phallic shaft rising two hundred feet up from the empty earthen floor. Twenty miles west, the pink and ochre shades of Scott's Bluff came into view. The river lapped at the base of the huge limestone formation. The caravan turned inland and went through Mitchell's Pass, a gap in the rocks.

They stopped in Rabidoux Canyon where Antoine Rabidoux, a Frenchman, operated a blacksmith and tin shop. A sign *Tinware by A. Rabidoux* hung over the entrance of the small cabin. The train laid over for a day for repairs, then swung west toward Fort Laramie.

TWENTY-FOUR

The wagon train arrived at Fort Laramie on the Fourth of July. The white adobe walls of the fort were yellowed by the afternoon sun. A castlelike turret capped the top of the building, its whitewashed sides glistening in the light. The meadow around the fort was dotted with hundreds of colorful Indian tepees. Two hundred Cheyenne families had been camped there for two weeks. A larger number of Sioux tepees were set up at the other side of the field. The ground around the fort was littered with abandoned furniture, left there by wagon owners unwilling to carry the items further west. Empty boxes were stacked neatly against the stockade walls. Scores of wagon wheels rested nearby, their fellies ruined, spokes dried and cracking. The skeletons of a dozen wagons were scattered about, each symbolizing a broken dream. Outside the fort, spreading out from the gate were a hundred emigrant wagons drawn into a double column.

Their reception was tumultuous. Trappers, traders, buffalo hunters, emigrants and Indians were celebrating

Independence Day. After the silence of the plains, the noise was a welcome sound. Guns exploded, horns blared, drums roared and men, women and children raised their voices in cheerful greetings. The stockade, and the encampments outside, were a welter of confusion. People were running everywhere, laughing, singing, whooping. Children darted in and out of the clusters of celebrants. Jugs of liquor were passed from man to man while the women looked on without comment. A number of U.S. Army soldiers had gathered at the western edge of the fort, standing outside the walls, raising their voices lustily in song. They were quickly joined by an equal number of boisterous Cheyenne Indians who danced and whooped to the beat of a tribal drum. Hordes of Indian women, some scarcely clad, roamed through the crowd. A half hundred warriors were clustered around a fire, brewing an enormous drum of coffee.

Huge fires of buffalo chips flamed outside the stockade. Each bonfire was capped with large chunks of wild meat being roasted for the evening meal. Boisterous men gathered around a section of the meadow for hastily formed horse races. Indian and emigrant mounts alike participated in the contest, which was won by a young Sioux brave and his pony. And above the celebration waved the red, white and blue banner of the United States.

People had been celebrating the Fourth of July at Fort Laramie since 1818, when Jacques La Ramie, a Canadian fur trapper and trader, built a cabin at the junction of the North Platte and Laramie Rivers. Running his trap lines in the Laramie mountains, Jacques considered becoming a permanent settler in the region. The Indians helped him reach that goal by scalping him on the headwaters of the stream bearing his name. In 1836, the American Fur Company built a fort on a small slope upriver from La Ramie's original cabin. The stockade was a quadrangular structure, built from adobe after the fashion of dwellings in the southwest. The walls were fifteen feet high, capped with a wooden palisade. The walls surrounded a yard of about two hundred square feet. Gun holes looked out in every direction. To prevent possible Indian infiltration, the traders allowed only a few tribesmen inside the stockade at any time. However, the Indian wives of French and American trappers, buffalo hunters, emigrants, or the officials of fur companies were given free run of the fort.

While the caravan shaped up into a box encampment outside the stockade, Sam Lawson went through the gate to the trader's store. Against the dimness of the interior, he saw a dark form rise from a chair in back and walk forward. The immense room was cool and dry. The trader pulled a buffalo robe away from a window. Light streamed into the room.

"Howdy, Bordeaux," Sam greeted the trader. "How's trade?"

James Bordeaux waved his thick hands to the empty shelves running around the room. "Nothing left, Sam. Plumb out of everything. I tried to buy goods from Bridger when he came through last week. He wouldn't sell."

"He'll need the stuff at his place." Sam paused and eyed the trader. Although James Bordeaux was not as tall as the guide, there was a massiveness about his appearance. His long hair was worn over the nape of his neck, tied in the back with a rawhide strip. His wrinkled, tanned faced was clean shaven. Dressed in buckskin shirt and trousers, wearing Indian moccasins, the Frenchman gave the impression of being a hunter, certainly not a trader.

"You got anything to sell?"

"A wagon. Folks come down with fever."

"Can't use it."

"Ain't nobody headed back east?"

"More'n you want to count. But none of them need wagons."

Lawson looked out at the boisterous crowd. "Looks like your whiskey held out."

"Saved it for the celebration. Fourth of July is important."

"Bordeaux, you're a Frenchman."

The trader grinned. "Maybe so. I feel more American than most folks. We got Indians, Mexicans, a few Frenchmen and a half dozen Germans celebrating out there today."

Sam asked, "What's the news about the tribes?"

"Crows are down on the Sweetwater. Spoiling for trouble. They'll be waiting for you."

"How many Mormons gone by?"

"About eight thousand."

Sam whistled. "My God! The whole world's headed west."

"They sure don't buy much."

"Saints plan ahead."

Bordeaux looked down at his buckskin leggings. "Kit Carson come in last night from California. He's looking for you."

Sam thanked the trader and headed back out into the crowd. He stopped, drank and chatted with Jim Wilson, a gray-bearded "long-hair," down from the Wind River country. They discussed the passing of the west, as they knew it, and deplored the lack of beaver in the streams. Raoul Estobar, a Spanish trapper and trader from Santa Fe, had come in the week before with a mule train of supplies. He'd sold the whole load to a couple of trains headed west. Estobar said he was planning to stay drunk for a week, figuring he was an American since Mexico lost the war.

Hugo Lorton, Marty Canton and "Big Mike" Woodard whooped and hollered like drunken banshees when they spied Lawson coming through the crowd. Woodard threw his arms around Lawson's neck with a bear-hug grip.

"'Member the ole days on the Green River?" he roared.

"Best rendezvous in the world!"

"What you doing, Sam?"

"Guiding trains to Oregon."

Woodard tossed his jug to the guide. "Terrible, ain't it? Beaver's gone. Me and the boys are buffalo hunters. Awful work. Not clean and easy like beaver pelts. Got to kill 'em, skin 'em and haul those stinking hides up here to the fort. A man smells like something the dogs have played with for a week."

"You seen Kit?" Sam asked.

"Nope. That chile here?"

"Bordeaux said so."

Sam took a long swig from Woodard's jug. He went off to find Kit Carson.

Bruce Middleton unpinned the bow and pulled the yoke off his last ox. The docile animal plodded over and joined the other beasts in the corral. Bruce put the yoke away. He glanced down at his callused hands, his face tightening with pleasure. The palms and fingers were not soft and smooth like those of a clerk, a quill pusher who made tiny mathematical entries in a ledger book. They were the hardened hands of a man going across a continent.

Melissa had brought a sense of order into his life. For the first time in his memory, Bruce Middleton was free of the repressive anxiety about sex. Their relationship had brought a growing sense of masculine pride into Middleton's life. He vowed to retain his heightened feeling of self-acceptance. He had been cautious about slipping out to meet Melissa. Damn her soul! Vivian knew something was afoot! God only knew what she might do. The woman was a two-legged terror. Once spurned, she might strike out in any direction. He didn't put it past Vivian to pull him before the camp council on a charge of adultery.

Pressing back his fear, Bruce Middleton looked around the camp. Vivian was down the line, her back to him, talking with Erica Pitzen. He moved to the outside of the wagon, then went off to find Melissa. She was really something. A special girl. Her skin was cream colored, tight, soft and smooth. Her body was thrusts and valleys, warm mounds of pliant young flesh. Her mouth was warm, red, and incessant in the demand to engulf him.

Melissa was standing near her wagon, watching the crowd of celebrating Indians across the field. She smiled wickedly when he came up, her pink tongue darting out. She licked her lips and glided her tongue across her mouth.

"Tonight?" He could barely restrain an impulse to embrace her.

"How we going to work it?"

"Vivian's still suspicious."

"Well," Melissa pouted. "I can always find another sweetheart."

Bruce's face hardened. "Don't ever say that."

"You spend all your time with her."

"Wait 'til we get to Oregon."

"They won't do anything. Leave her here."

"You know the penalty for adultery."

"They won't kill us."

"Vivian would."

"I'll be some place around the camp," Melissa promised. Her hand darted out to touch the front of his trousers. She smiled wickedly.

"Oh baby," Bruce's voice cracked to a huskiness. "I love you."

"See you tonight."

Walking away, Melissa looked as innocent as a schoolgirl.

Jay Samuels looked into the shiny mirror in his hand. He sighed loudly and put his straight razor back into its leather case. He emptied the pan of cold water, touched the smoothness of his cheeks and neck. Next, he pulled his best shirt from a box inside the wagon, pulled the garment on and went down the line to the Miller wagon.

Agnes was mixing a bowl of cornbread.

"Mrs. Miller, I—I—" Jay stammered.

Agnes saw the glimmer of uncertainty in the young man's face.

"You sick?" she inquired.

"No, ma'am, I—well, that is—"

"You look pale around the gills."

"I feel fine."

"Sulphur and molasses will work wonders. You want me to fix you some?"

Jay Samuels spoke softly. "I'd like to court one of the girls. I—well—it seems proper to speak to you first. My intentions are honorable."

Agnes set the bowl down on a box. She studied the young man for a moment. He squirmed with embarrassment.

"Which girl?" she asked.

"Either one," said Samuels.

Agnes frowned. "Other words, you just want a girl."

"I don't know them well enough to choose."

"I have no objections to your seeing one of the girls," Agnes told him. "You'd best pick one right now. I don't want you to spark one for a while, then change your mind."

"Melissa is pretty."

"She's also full of the devil."

"Jane seems a little shy."

"She jumps at her shadow."

"Oh!—" cried the young Jew. "I don't know which to ask for."

Agnes shrugged. Annoyed, she stared at Jay Samuels with close scrutiny. "Tell you what," she said gently. "Why don't you come back in a few minutes. Tell me which of the girls you'd like to court."

Samuels shifted uneasily. "No, I woun't get the courage again."

"Then take Jane," Agnes advised him. "She's a little thing and you did save her from the prairie fire."

Samuels smiled. "I'll come courting this evening."

Agnes picked up her bowl of cornbread batter. "Come

for dinner, Jay. We need to get acquainted."

After a lengthy search, and much glad-handing with his friends from earlier days, Sam Lawson found Kit Carson, who had left the crowd to be alone. Carson was slumped back against the trunk of a cottonwood tree near the Sioux camp. Lawson looked at the shortness of Carson, barely five feet six inches in height, noted his slenderness. Men had judged his thinness as weakness, later regretting that error. The determination in Carson's features indicated he still retained his ability to lead men. The glint in his eyes showed he was still the most courageous man in the West. Carson smiled when Lawson ambled up. He raised a tin cup to his lips, took a brief sip of raw whiskey.

"How's the booze?" Sam asked.

"Don't spill any on your buckskins."

"Why's that?"

Carson grinned slyly. "It'll eat right trought in half a minute."

"You're heading for Leavenworth?"

Carson grinned slyly. "It'll eat right through in half a minute."

Sam eased himself down beside his friend. He took the cup extended by Carson and tentatively tasted the whiskey.

Sam coughed. "God Almighty! You weren't kidding."

"Told you it was poison," Carson laughed.

"What's they use to brew it—lye?"

"One more cup and I'll whip the whole Sioux nation."

Sam took another drink. He shuddered when he swallowed.

"Stuff must be aged for at least half a day."

"More like two hours," grinned Carson. "We'd better drink fast or it'll eat away the cup."

They sat under the tree for the next hour, drinking and recalling their days as fur trappers. Regret laced their conversation. Each man longed to find another unspoiled wilderness with beaver thick in the streams.

"We're just growing old," Sam said at last.

Carson shook his head. "Sam, you don't know how things are going to change. The old days are gone forever."

"Too many greenhorns here now."

"A lot more's coming next year. Something big is brewing."

"Quit playing, Kit. You got my curious nature all riled up."

Carson pulled a rock from his pocket, tossed the stone above his head and caught it.

"This is going to change everything," he said.

"That looks like a medicine man's charm."

"Much stronger."

"Real powerful medicine?"

Carson smiled. "Best there is."

Sam's face tightened. "You planning on telling me?"

"Thinking it over. Will you keep it secret?"

"You can trust me, Kit."

"You talk a lot when you're drinking."

Sam brimmed with curiosity. "I ain't begging."

Carson tossed the rock in Sam's direction. When his hand closed over the stone, Sam was surprised at the heaviness.

"Lead?" he asked.

"Heavy stuff," Carson grinned with delight. "What's that mean?"

"Gold!"

"Sam, that's gold all the way from California. We whipped the Mexicans. Chased their tails back across the Rio Grande. Took everything west of the river from them. They've been in California for a couple hundred years. Never did anything with the prettiest country God ever made. We get the land and find there's gold everywhere. They hit gold out there last winter."

Sam eyed the stone with feverish interest.

"How'd you get this nugget?"

"Part of a bunch I'm carrying east. Along with a lot of dispatches. Gold is everywhere out there, Sam. A man can walk around and pick nuggets up off the ground. One of the biggest gold strikes in history. I saw a man with a dishpan pull a pound of flakes out of a river in a few hours."

Sam whistled.

"You're sure about this?"

"You're holding the evidence. Saw it with my own eyes."

Carson reached inside his buckskin shirt, withdrew a poorly printed broadsheet. "I can't read," he said regretfully, "but this is supposed to tell about the find."

Lawson glanced over the meager sheet detailing news of the gold strike at Sutter's Mill.

"I'm taking dispatches and some of the nuggets to Fort Leavenworth," Carson explained. "Figured I'd spread the news along the way. Not to everybody, mind you, but to a few of the good old boys. Some of the trappers, traders and fellows who need to get ahead."

"You going?"

"Not sure," said Carson. "My wife's down at Taos. I'm heading down there after I finish this trip. Depends on how things work out. There's some talk of getting me a commission in the army. I'd like that."

Sam turned the stone in his hand, watching the sunlight glitter on the metal. "Christ! Who needs Oregon?"

"The country needs it," Carson replied. "Maybe you need to catch yourself a grubstake down in California, though. A man should make a good profit out there for a while. Stake himself a claim and start digging."

"You just pick it up off the ground?"

"Some places. Naturally, the whole territory isn't covered with nuggets."

A peculiar uneasiness came over Sam as he looked at the stone.

"Things will change," he said. "The wilderness will be gone. The Indians and buffalo don't have a chance."

"Progress," said Carson.

Sam tossed the nugget back into the air. "Can I keep it?"

"Sure," Carson replied. "I got a full sack."

"You think many will try for California?"

Carson spoke with mock seriousness. "Not many. Not more'n five or ten million, I figure."

"Not if the government keeps it secret."

"They won't. Human nature doesn't work that way."

"They can try."

Carson sighed. "Remember how it was when beaver was running out? We'd find a good stream with a few pelts left. Figured we were miles from anyone. Before the traps could be set, an army of trappers come running in on top of us."

Sam said, "So your report gets to Leavenworth. The general hears about it. Some of his clerks do, too. The whole she-bang down there will have gold fever inside of a day."

"And they'll pass the word to their friends and relatives back east," Carson added. "Within a month a couple thousand people are lusting for gold. The whole country's going wild in a few more months. The whole eastern half of the nation will be headed for the gold fields."

"A thousand wagons a day."

Carson poured more liquor into the tin cup. "That's why I'm sitting out here by myself, Sam. Sort of drinking a toast to the end of an era."

TWENTY-FIVE

A holiday feast had been held at Fort Laramie for several years. This Fourth of July was no exception as the meal was a tradition. A blast from a bugle signaled that the food was ready. A multitude of hungry people, whites and Indians, lined up to share buffalo, antelope, elk, moose, deer and bear roasted over great fires. Volunteers sliced tender, succulent chunks of meat from the carcasses. Several bushels of pinto beans simmered in iron kettles; they had been contributed by James Bordeaux, the trader. A washtub of deviled buffalo tongue was spooned out by Spanish traders from Taos. They grinned with delight at favorable comments about the spicy flavor of their dish.

"Mexico has lost the war. We're now *Americanos*," remarked a tall Spaniard in buckskins.

Women in the wagon trains had baked cornbread and biscuits. Fresh milk was served to the children, thick black coffee poured for the adults. The emigrants whooped with joy when several men wheeled up a wagon.

The box had been cleaned and washed down, the bed filled with wild mustard greens, green onions and parsley from the vegetable garden in back of the fort. Drippings from the meat had been retained, then mixed with vinegar, for a dressing.

The emigrants ate ravenously.

"Best food I've ever tasted, darling," Mike Gorman told his wife.

Molly wolfed down a mouthful of beans. "Delicious!"

Agnes Miller went back to the salad wagon four times. "Never thought wild greens would taste so good," she remarked.

Jay Samuels sat down beside Jane. They were silent during the meal. Jane was embarrassed to be seen sparking a boy. Samuels was engrossed in eating.

James Bordeaux went through the crowd, gracefully accepting hearty thanks from the diners.

"More to come," he told them. "Eat all you want. There's plenty for everyone. The trappers, hunters and tribes have worked hard the past couple days fixing things. Just don't eat too much. You'll need room to shake to leg at the dance tonight."

Sam Lawson joined Steve and Cynthia Wellman. The guide's tin plate was heaped with food.

"Like the good old days," Lawson said.

"Never thought we'd celebrate the Fourth like this," said Steve.

"Mountain men are patriotic." Lawson gobbled down a huge chunk of meat.

"But there's so much food." Cynthia Wellman rolled her eyes.

"Throwback to the days when the traders and trappers rendezvoused on the Green River," Sam Lawson explained. "The meadow there is one of the prettiest in the world. Traders brought in wagons from St. Louis. We'd hold a shindig there to keep a man for another year. Plenty of food, drinking and dancing with the loveliest Indian girls you'll ever see. Ole Bordeaux's nobody's fool, just a right smart trader. His Fourth of July celebration picked up when the rendezvous ended. Whether you're white or Indian, you find it hard to fault a man who feeds you and makes you feel important."

Steve Wellman glanced toward the west where the sun was falling behind the darkening mountains.

"Seems shameful to leave here," he remarked.

"Oregon's prettier," Lawson said, digging into his mound of pinto beans.

"What about the dance?" Cynthia asked. "What should I wear?"

"Finest dress you got," replied the guide. "Put on your best. Jewelry, too, if you got any. These yahoos have been out in the mountains all year. They're hungry to dance with a pretty woman." He pointed his fork at Steve. "A lot of these gents will want to dance with Cynthia. They don't mean nothing by it. Just want to enjoy themselves, have something to remember when they're out in the wilderness. They look mean and rough, and that they are, make no mistake. But they're sentimental about women and treat them with great courtesy."

A half hour after the dinner was finished, a group of men set up a large bonfire outside the gate of the fort. While women in the caravans dressed for the dance, a dozen or so fiddlers took up positions along the outside stockade wall. The notes of "Sweet Betsy From Pike" signaled the start of the festivities. Men and women came running up to the bare, grassless earth that served as a dance floor. A bold soul and his wife began to move across the dusty ground. They were quickly joined by other laughing couples.

The emigrants roared their approval at the end of each song. Everyone forgot the hazards of life in the wilderness. The emigrants forgot the dangers of the trail. Mountain men, buffalo hunters, and trappers forgot the loneliness of their life away from civilization. Indians and white men forgot the hostility existing between the tribes and the encroaching white invaders.

Unable to contain his excitement, a Sioux warrior ran off to his camp. He returned with a small drum decorated with feathers. Unsure of himself, the brave stood off to the side of the dance area, gently tapping the drumhead. He grinned widely when a musician invited him to join the fiddlers. He dropped cross-legged before the fiddlers, providing a gentle beat to the music.

With Bordeaux's approval, one of the Spanish traders wheeled a wagon to the edge of the dance arena. Behind the wagon, out of sight of the ladies the trader sold tin cups of Taos Lightning, a potent brew. As the word passed through the crowd, men slipped behind the rig to purchase the fiery drink.

Jane's pale blue dress, trimmed with white lace, revealed the soft contours of her youthful body. Jay Samuels found it difficult to keep his eyes off the girl. His glance roamed from her face, flushed with excitement, down to the budding firmness of her breasts. Neither of them had danced before, but by observing the other couples they picked up a few hesitant steps.

During their first foray, Jay felt her foot under

his boot.

"My fault," he apologized quickly.

"I'm too clumsy." Jane reddened.

"I'm like a dumb ox."

"You're not! I just never danced before."

He grinned. "You should be dancing every night."

Jane blushed, started to say something, when a huge form loomed up behind Jay Samuels. A large hand gently tapped the young man's shoulder. Jay turned around and saw a hugh man in buckskins. The man made a low, courteous bow.

"Beg yore pard'in," he said. "I'd sure 'preciate shakin' a leg with this purty woman."

"My pleasure."

Jay stood back, cursing inwardly, as the man danced away with Jane.

"So's we're comin' down't Windlass Hill," the emigrant told his new friend from another caravan. "Ten ropes tied to m'wagon, 'bout four men holdin' back on each rope. Figgered that was more'n enough. Dad gum! I sure judged 'er wrong. We was jest gettin' to the steepest part. Like a dumb fool, I figure we got 'er whupped. That's when a dang fool yelled: 'Rattlesnake!' Lordy, The whole dang bunch let loose the ropes 'bout the same instant. Wagon rolled over 'bout twenty times 'fore hittin' bottom. Wurst wreck I ever did see. Y'know, nothin' worth fixin'. Had to pile my plunder in a friend's rigs."

"Wot ye drivin' now?"

"'Nother wagon."

"What'd ye get hit?"

"Man in our train seed the el'phant. Started back to his

home in Ohio. A hunnerd in gold, it cost. Cheaper'n dirt."

"He walkin' back home?"

"Naw! I give up my bes' hoss as boot."

A mountain man stood outside the trader's whiskey wagon, holding a tin cup of Taos lightning in his hand. "Funniest thing. We was coming in from Fort Hall and our paths crost one of them Mormon trains. Heard about them yahoos having a lot of wives. My partner figured they's so busy shouting amens, they was neglecting the wimmin. We sneaked into their camp one night, started moseying around one of the tents used by the wives. Quicker'n a jackrabbit, we was staring downt the barrels of a big bunch of rifles. We was lucky to hightail it out of there. Nosiree, fellers, don't mess with the Mormons!"

He had been born in Bavaria, the youngest son of a titled nobleman. One woman had led to another until, one winter night, an angry husband and his friends forcefully expressed their displeasure. Fearful of additional revenge, and tired of buxom Teutonic lasses, he had traveled to France, England and eventually America. He was well educated, footloose, and looking for opportunity.

"This is the last frontier," he told an audience of emigrants. "If we don't catch a prize in Oregon, we're doomed. This land"—he waved his arms for emphasis—"is the last good soil in the world. This is the last great migration. When we're done out here, the whole world will have been surveyed, platted, fenced off and sold to the highest bidder."

"What about Mexico, *senor?*" asked a Taos trader.

"Too much desert, too arid."

"South America's got a lot of land," said an emigrant.

"Topsoil's not good."

"A lot of jungly land downt there."

The German paused. "It will stay jungle, my friend. The topsoil ain't more than a couple, three inches deep. You need plenty of good dirt for roots to take hold."

"That's true," agreed a farmer.

"This is the last?" asked the trader.

"Take a good look. God closes the store after this frontier is gone."

"Good Lord!" Agnes Miller struggled through the crowd. She found a cluster of women standing on the sidelines.

"You, too?" inquired an older woman in a linsey-woolsey dress.

"They danced me down to a nubbin." Agnes took a deep breath.

"They sure like to dance," agreed a middle-aged woman.

"Dance?" Agnes raised her eyebrows. "Dancing I can take. These fools don't dance. They're like a pack of addled grape stompers! Most of them are hitting the whiskey wagon. Then they start stomping my insteps!"

Vivian Middleton stood in the midst of a group of women. She was gilding the lily, speaking with pride about her life back home.

"We were doing so well back in Galena," Vivian told them. "Bruce was very successful back there. He was in charge of the bank, you know, second only to the owner himself. Bruce often had full control of the bank, especially when the owner went away on his business trips. It just got to be too much. Everyone in town depended on us for the craziest things. No one else seemed able to entertain. They depended on me to set the fashionable pace. We had so many friends, my word, that I was wore out giving dinners and parties. Everyone in town tried to stop us from leaving. Bruce was offered a partnership in the bank. Women swore I was the only person in town with taste and breeding. They were always asking my advice on fashions, home furnishings and other important matters."

The women in the caravan had become tolerant of Vivian's fantasies. They accepted her gloating lies without comment, seldom listening attentively to her rambling stories. The only woman listening intently that night was Molly Gorman. She stared at Vivian with intense concentration. When Vivian paused for breath, her glance fell on Molly's pert face. She shrank back under the Irish woman's direct and truthful appraisal. Molly's eyes carried a frank message: "You are a silly, pretentious woman without kindness or charity. You are a vulgar woman, a vicious bore without self-respect."

With jarring clarity, Vivian realized that Molly recognized the truth about her life. Beneath her blustering appearance, Vivian was a frightened, vindictive woman. Seeing this in Molly's eyes, Vivian paused for a moment. She trembled. Her eyes glimmered with anxiety, then gave way to a darker urge to lash out, claw at those dark and laughing Irish eyes. Strip the Catholic flesh from her bones! With her mind weighed down with hate, Vivian Middleton made a desperate leap to rationalize her anger.

She decided Molly Gorman was her husband's lover!

*   *   *

Bruce Middleton found Melissa dancing with a young man from another caravan. He had waited patiently before approaching the girl, although his loins ached for her touch. When he caught a glimpse of Vivian regaling the other women with her stories, he cut in on the dancing couple.

"My wagon," he whispered to Melissa. "Meet you there in a few minutes."

Her eyes flashed with excitement. "You're sure?"

"I got to have you, baby."

"Maybe I'd rather dance."

"Please . . ." He begged.

"Your wife's a pain in the ass!"

"Melissa!" Bruce was shocked. "Please, meet me after this song."

She gave him a tiny smile. The red tip of her small tongue darted out to glide sensuously across her red lips.

"Maybe," she said suggestively.

"You got to," he whispered as the music ended. "I'll see you at the wagon."

Bored by Vivian's monotonous lies, Molly Gorman left the women and went to find Mike. Her face brightened when she saw Steve Wellman standing alone on the edge of the dance area. He told her, confidentially, that Mike was testing the potency of Taos Lightning.

"He's over behind the wagon," he explained. "By the way, I haven't danced with you tonight."

"A pleasure," Molly said as the music started up again. "Where's your wife?"

"Dancing with every man except me."

"She's lucky. That darling man of mine is jealous."

"Not of me, I hope."

"Surely, that dark Irish temper won't mind you. I—"

Molly swore, bending down with a frown. She picked an object from the ground.

"My best shoes and I've just lost a heel. Wait here. I'll run to the wagon and change."

"I'll walk along," Steve said, taking her arm. "Too many strange men around for a pretty girl to walk alone tonight."

"Maybe you're right."

They walked away from the dancing couples, heading through the darkness to the wagons.

The subtle scent of Melissa's perfume drifted into his nostrils. They were standing at the end of the row of parked wagons and, as Melissa moved closer, Bruce shifted his body. She lifted her chin and looked into his eyes.

"You're pretty," Bruce whispered.

"You've said that before." Melissa sounded peeved.

"I love you."

"But you spend every night with your wife."

"I'll marry you when we get to Oregon."

Melissa's voice hardened. "You'd better. I'm not some girl you can drop when the funning is over."

"Baby, baby," he whispered. "You're the best thing that ever happened to me. I can't change the rules about adultery on the caravan. We just have to wait."

"That makes us sound like criminals."

"The rules say we are."

"Anything this good can't be bad!" Melissa's voice was edged with conviction. Her body relaxed as she moved closer. Bruce felt the hot pink tip of her tongue against his face. He opened his lips and her fiery tongue pressed

356

hard into his mouth. His arms encircled her waist. Gently, her fingers danced against the back of his neck. Her lips undulated against him and, fiercely, he began to swell. Suddenly she stepped back and raised her skirt up to her waist.

Bruce grasped with pleasure.

"I'm not wearing pants," Melissa smiled.

Then her hands were on his body, tugging at his hips, roaming over his swelling hardness. Fumbling, she unbuttoned the front of his trousers and, for one apprehensive moment, he felt as if his heart would burst from pleasure.

"You ready?" Melissa whispered deep down in her throat.

"Oh, baby!"

She was before him now, her white legs shining in the moonlight. His fingers entwined themselves in her hair. He drew her forward, feeling the searing wet touch of pleasure as her tongue traced a gentle pattern over his lips. He groaned deeply and moved down into the shadows as Melissa's legs opened wide.

Mike Gorman was frantic with anxiety. He had downed two cups of Taos Lightning at the trader's wagon. The fiery liquid had a potent kick. His head was light, his mind fuzzy. He had spent the last five minutes staggering about the dance area in search of his wife.

He came up to Cynthia Wellman.

"You seen Molly?"

Cynthia shook her head and danced away with a young man from another caravan.

Mike stumbled up to Vivian Middleton.

"Miss Middleton," he asked quietly. "You see Molly?"

"No!" spat Vivian.

She walked away to find her husband. That was his game, she thought with murderous hatred. Right now, Bruce was probably tumbling that Irish wench. There were few secrets in a wagon train and, like most people, Vivian knew about Molly's insatiable appetite for sex. Sounds traveled a long ways when the wagons were corraled up.

Mike circled the dancing couples again. Molly was not to be seen. Dreamily, he could see his darling Molly, the girl he had brought from the auld sod, lying in another man's arms. Lordy, any bucko knew he hadn't been much of a husband those past few weeks. But, his darling was asking too much. She was always pestering at a man. Never wanting to sleep, always thinking about tumbling. Boyo, he decided, you had better find your wife.

Vivian Middleton came back to his side.

"My husband's missing, too," she hinted darkly.

"Bruce?"

"Bruce isn't around."

"Molly wouldn't do that."

Vivian smiled maliciously. "Bruce might be a surprise to everyone. He's been slipping out of our tent at night."

"Guard duty. We all got to pull it."

"He's seeing another woman. We better check the wagons," Vivian replied urgently.

Mike took a step forward, lurched drunkenly.

"My own darling wife . . . crossed the ocean from the auld sod . . ."

Mike allowed the woman to lead him back to the wagons. Vivian paused at the edge of the column, took a lantern from a holder. Shoving Mike before her, she strode down to her wagon. She crawled noisily up into the rig.

Maudlin, his emotions blurred by the whiskey, Mike Gorman was relieved to find the wagon empty.

"We'd better check out your wagon," Vivian declared.

She marched resolutely up to the Irishman's wagon. Mike held the lantern while she started to crawl up into the rig.

"Who's there?" Molly cried out.

Vivian's cry was triumphant.

"I found them!" she yelled. "They're inside your wagon!"

Molly came to the front of the wagon. She leaped down to the ground. "What's wrong?"

"Huzzy!" Vivian's face was dark with hatred.

Mike stumbled and almost fell. "Don't talk like that to Molly."

"Slut! Tried to steal my husband."

"Are you mad?" asked Molly. She stared at the woman before her as if she was a stranger from another world.

A sound echoed inside the wagon.

"He's in there," Vivian gloated.

Steve Wellman's head appeared above them. Mike Gorman's mouth dropped open with disbelief.

"What's going on?" asked Steve.

"Caught you dead to rights!" shouted Vivian.

Steve leaped down to the ground. He started to speak with Vivian when a blurred motion appeared in the corner of his eyes. He wheeled around as Mike's fist crashed into his face. Molly screamed as Steve fell backward onto the ground. Vivian Middleton looked on with a malignant smile.

Bruce Middleton became alert. For an instant, he

359

wanted to remain entwined forever with Melissa. Instead, he pulled away from the girl.

"Get back to the dance," he hissed.

Eyes widened with fear, she took off in a run toward the gates of the fort.

After the dance, Agnes Miller and the girls went back to their wagon. The girls crawled into their tent while Agnes prepared for bed. After getting into her ankle-length nightgown, she entered her tent and knelt to say her prayers.

"Keep watch over everyone," she prayed, "and especially those who have been drinking. Watch over Sam Lawson, dear Lord, because he needs Your help. Bless those who have lost friends and relatives on our journey. Show me the way, Oh Lord, and I will follow Your directions."

Agnes gasped when a hand grabbed her foot. For an instant, she considered the touch a sign from the heavens. But only for a moment because her nostrils were suddenly soured by a foul odor. She turned and looked toward the door of her tent.

"Sam Lawson!" Agnes bellowed.

"Jesh stopped to saysh hello," he hiccuped.

"You drunken old fool!"

"Givsh Samsh a litish kiss." The guide's face moved closer.

"Get out!"

"Jush a . . ."

"You smell like death warmed over."

"Husbanlishly pri—got rights!"

Agnes tried to move past the guide. His arms shot out and encircled her waist. She twisted around, causing Sam

360

to lose his balance. He fell forward on a heap atop her bedroll.

"Jush a kish . . ." he mumbled, then fell asleep.

Snorting indignently, Agnes left the tent. She crawled up into her wagon, dug blankets out of a box and settled down under the canvas top. She lay quietly and listened to Sam's liquid snoring. She felt giddy and girlish. She smiled.

Molly Gorman was furious. Mike was passed out in their tent, barely conscious, his breath reeking of Taos Lightning.

"The very idea!" She told her moaning husband. "Bucko, you better apologize to Steve in the morning. Accusing me of sneaking away from the dance with him. Shows how much you think of my morals. When I figure I need someone besides the likes of you, pitiful as you are, I'll let you know. Steve's the best friend we've got. I won't let your drunken suspicions ruin our friendship. You'll beg his forgiveness in the morning."

Mike stirred. "Saw you with my own eyes, colleen. Coming out of the wagon with him. Terrible, Molly, terrible!"

"He was holding the lantern, he was, while I looked for my shoes."

"Hanky-pank, my girl. With my best friend."

"You dolt!" Molly jabbed her elbow into Mike's rib cage.

"Aye, beat up on the man you used to love," he said in a lilting brogue.

"You're proving that Irishmen are dumb."

"My own Molly," he said, rolling over away from her. He sobbed. "My own little Molly, the treasure of my life.

361

Up in the wagon hanky-panking with my dear friend."

"You'll ask his forgiveness tomorrow," Molly insisted.

"Never!"

Mike grumbled. He turned over and went to sleep.

Vivian Middleton lay awake beside her sleeping husband. Bruce had not pestered her in a month. He did not whine and plead for a tumble in bed. The trip west had changed his character. He was more forceful, refused her advice and ignored her commands. Vivian was disappointed that Steve Wellman hadn't started a real donnybrook with Mike Gorman. She expect more fight from the captain of a caravan. Besides, that snippy Molly Gorman needed taking down a peg or two. Vivian reasoned that Molly was probably a promiscuous wench hiding behind a prim and proper exterior. Some sluts were like that. Bruce's lover had to be Molly, she decided, because the other women in the caravan wouldn't look at another woman's husband. Agnes Miller was too much a Christian lady and Cynthia Wellman was too wrapped up in her husband. Bruce wouldn't stoop so low as to tumble with Polly Johnson, a huge buxom woman with a plain face. Jane and Melissa were too young and desirable to pick a dead fish like Bruce as a lover. Drowsily, she resolved to be more observant of Molly Gorman. Somehow, Vivian decided, she would put the Irish wench in her place.

TWENTY-SIX

The caravan pulled out of Fort Laramie early on the morning after the dance. Mike Gorman was hung over from consuming too much Taos Lightning. He could scarely open his eyes against the glaring sun. His head ached with throbbing intensity. Resentful and embittered, Mike ignored Molly's insistent demands for an apology.

"That boyo should beg for my forgiveness," Mike retorted. "He was up in the wagon with you. I wasn't hanky-panking with his wife."

"That nasty Irish temper!" snapped Molly. "The vile things that jealousy must cause you to think about me." She rummaged in the wagon and brought forth her heelless shoe as evidence for her innocence. Mike lapsed into a terse, brooding silence.

During the days that followed, Mike also ignored Steve's efforts to mend their friendship. He resigned as lieutenant of the caravan, sending word through Uncle Durgeon Adkins. Brad Payne was appointed to fill the post. Next, Mike pulled his wagon from second in the column, taking up a position at the end of the line. He also forbade Molly to talk with the emigrants or their wives.

For his part, Steve was uncertain on how to handle the matter. Everyone had dismissed the incident as the result of too much Taos Lightning. The Irishman was the only man to retain a grudge. Steve went about his duties, figuring Gorman would come to his senses in time. Vivian Middleton stoked Mike's fiery Gaelic temper, hinting slyly about unfaithful wives, cuckolded husbands and lustful philanderers masquerading in a best friends' garments.

The caravan progressed swiftly and smoothly into the Sweetwater River country. The trail rolled along the clear, cool stream at a rapid clip. They were nearing Independence Rock one afternoon when Steve Wellman saw a vast darkness spreading across the western sky. He galloped back along the column to find Sam Lawson driving Agnes Miller's wagon.

"Thunderstorm ahead!" Wellman shouted.

Sam looked up across the flat, sandy expanse of open land.

"Good God almighty!" yelled the guide. "That ain't no thunderstorm. We're in the path of a bad sandstorm! We got to corral up!"

Wellman raced to his lead wagon. He grabbed the halter of the lead oxen, pulling the animals off the trail. The emigrants behind his rig saw the darkening sky, quickly maneuvered their wagons into a corral. Men leaped down from the wagon seats. They began to unhitch their teams and guide the beasts into the corral. By now, the western sky was darkening with dirt, debris, alkali dust and sand. The oxen smelled the air, bellowing in fright as the dark mass bore down upon the encampment. Sensing the possibility of a stampede, Brad Payne went into the box corral. He forcefully pushed the scared animals down to the ground. The other families rushed about tying down their wagons and equipment.

The sky above the wagons filled with dirt as the front edge of the storm struck. Dust, dirt, sagebrush, and airborne objects came roaring toward them at tornado speed. Everyone scrambled for safety beneath the white-topped wagons. The animals roared angrily when sand and dirt were blasted into their eyes and nostrils.

Several crazed animals, roaring with fear, leaped up and stumbled around the corral. Men saw the start of a stampede, leaped down from their wagons and went out into the storm. They mustered their strength and pushed the frightened animals back to earth. Half blinded, their eyes smarting from the sand and dirt borne by the wind, the emigrants remained a few moments with the animals. When they felt the beasts were calmed, they stumbled back to cover.

Fifteen minutes passed before the full brunt of the storm hit the camp. The rigs trembled under the power of the onrushing wind. Flying sticks and small stones hammered against the wagon tops. Much of the debris bounced off, although many with sharp edges or ends embedded themselves into the straining canvas. Inside the wagons, children whimpered their distress. Women pulled out blankets, wrapped their children in the garments. Once those youngsters were protected, the mothers covered their heads for protection.

Outside, an ox went wild and charged up. The beast was clearly berserk, its mouth flecked with white foam, eyes glazed with torment. Roaring with displeasure, the ox ran blindly around the corral. Its hooves trampled other oxen who, in their anger and fright, began to rise and mill around. Hearing the noise, Steve Wellman glanced out into the herd. He leaped out into the turmoil as the ox lowered its head, prepared to charge, taking direct aim at Dan Pitzen's wagon. As he tried to reach the animal, Steve saw Sam Lawson push his way into the herd.

"He's gonna charge!" Steve yelled above the roar. He pulled his revolver and took aim at the beast's head.

Lawson crossed the corral swiftly. He grabbed Wellman's pistol.

"Shot'll cause a stampede," the guide yelled.

Drawing his trapper's knife, Lawson started after the crazed beast. His path was blocked by a bawling cow. Swiftly, Wellman moved toward the pawing ox. He grabbed Lawson's knife from the guide's hand, then slid the edge across the animal's throat. The arcing blade failed to penetrate the thick hide.

"Stab and pull!" screamed Lawson.

The ox was wheeling toward Wellman when he plunged the steel deep into the throat, stabbing upward with all of his strength. Blood spurted onto his arm. He quickly slid the blade across the throat as the horned head shook with rage. Bellowing with anguish, the animal lunged for Wellman. Sam Lawson had maneuvered around the cow and, coming up, delivered a vicious kick at the oxen's middle. The ox roared mightily, wheeling around in confusion. Lawson delivered another blow to the animal's side. The huge beast crashed to the ground. It fell on its side, moaning piteously, as blood foamed from its mouth.

Lawson went through the herd pushing animals down to the ground.

"You hurt?" he cried to Wellman.

Steve sheltered his eyes against the dust. "Let's get to cover."

The intensity of the storm lessened a few minutes later. Within another half hour, the sandstorm ended. The emigrants went out listlessly to inspect the damage to their rigs. Several wagon tops had been severely damaged. Others had merely been soiled by the flying debris. Listlessly, the women began to pull twigs and sharp pebbles from the canvas. Wellman intervened, suggesting the mending could wait until they reached camp that night. The oxen were dusted off, their eyes wiped, harnesses greased and the caravan continued westward. Sam Lawson, Lonnie Thompson and Uncle Durgeon remained behind to butcher out the ox.

That night the emigrants dined on roast beef. Although the meat was stringy and tough, the flavor was a treat. The animal had belonged to Mike Gorman and the Irishman accepted the loss philosophically. He became incensed only after learning the beast had been killed by Steve Wellman.

"That bucko is right handy with a blade," Mike complained that evening. "Especially when the ox belongs to someone else."

Sam Lawson intervened. "It had to be done."

"Maybe yes, maybe no."

"I'd have done the same as he did."

"That was my prime ox," Mike complained.

Sam snorted. "It was the worst of your bunch!"

"I'm the best judge of my animals."

"And the worst judge of who your friends are."

Mike had taken a step back. He stared angrily at the guide. "I'm thinking I ought to take it up with the council."

Sam spat. "Do that, Gorman. Every man has the right to act like a fool once in a while."

A few nights later they camped near Independence Rock. The wagons were parked a short distance from the Sweetwater River. The stream was a half mile wide, a few feet deep. The water was cool and fresh, flowing down from the Rocky Mountains. Ordinarily, the river would have received considerable attention from the emigrants. Instead, their thoughts were focused on Independence Rock, a massive structure that rose forty feet up out of the flat desert floor. The rock was almost a half mile long and, in the evening sun, resembled a scarred black turtle shell.

"Independence Rock's a register of the Oregon Trail," Lawson told the emigrants after supper. "Actually goes even further back than that. Most trappers, scouts and anyone coming this way have carved their names on it."

Dan Pitzen asked, "How did it get its name?"

"Back in 1832 Tom Fitzpatrick came loping through these parts," Sam explained. "He was part owner of the Rocky Mountain Fur Company down in St. Louis. He cached a big bunch of pelts near here on the Fourth of July. The name just stuck."

The emigrants feasted that night on venison stew. The sun was falling behind the mountains when they finished their meal. In the gloom before dark, the wagon tops glowed with a deep purple cast. Sam Lawson led a group of men from the camp, walking over to Independence Rock. Shortly, the sound of chisels hammered against stone could be heard.

Three men remained in the camp. Mike Gorman seethed inwardly, tending to his chores. He had refused to join the other men. Uncle Durgeon Adkins was too feeble to climb up the rock. He brightened when Sam promised to carve his name on the landmark. Bruce Middleton pretended to be watering his stock. He watched cautiously until Vivian walked to the river bank for a bucket of water. Quickly, Bruce hurried to find Melissa. She was using a large needle and thread to patch the canvas top of their wagon.

"Meet you outside tonight," Bruce whispered.

Melissa smiled. "What time?"

"Half hour after bedtime. We'll carve our names on the rock."

Bruce looked around for Vivian, then sauntered away.

Jane poked her head from beneath the wagon top. She watched Middleton walk toward his own wagon.

"What'd that old man want?" she asked Melissa.

"Just saying hello," was Melissa's reply.

"You made a date to spark him." Jane's voice was accusatory and suspicious. "Better be careful, Melissa. The penalty is death for a married man and girl messing around out here."

"He ain't married."

"He is, too."

"Name only," Melissa told her sister. "There's a lot more to marriage than standing before a preacher. Vivian Middleton is a pain in the ass."

"Just be careful," Jane warned. "Agnes finds you messing with a married man and she'll tan your hide."

Melissa smirked. "She ain't caught me yet."

"You were lucky in Natchez."

369

"Left a lot of fellows back home," Melissa said dreamily.

Jane blushed. "I got one now."

"That Jew boy's shy as you are."

"At least he's young."

"Jane, young men aren't the best," Melissa said with the authority of experience. "They're either tongue-tied or so eager a girl can't catch her breath. A big nothing or root-hog-or-die! I swear, give me an older man anytime because they like to please a young girl. Bruce treats me special and he knows how to do it. Most young boys don't realize what they're supposed to do. Why, right now, I could wind Bruce Middleton around my finger like a ribbon. Make him jump through a hoop. Make him leave that cold fish wife. He'd do anything for me."

"Just be careful," Jane grumbled.

"I'm always careful, Jane. I don't leave nothing to chance."

Molly Gorman waited until Mike was snoring. Then she slipped out of their tent, and dressed quickly in the darkness. She picked up a hammer and chisel and waited until the guard vanished around the corner of the wagons. Moving swiftly, she raced across the desert floor toward Independence Rock.

Breathlessly, Molly crawled to the top of the dark structure. The rock was larger than she expected, the incline steeper. When she reached the top, she paused for a series of deep breaths. She was surprised to find herself winded from the exertion. She sat down and glanced over at the wagon train parked far below beside the river. The nocturnal beauty of the country stretched out below her. To the west, the campfires of other camps wine-tinted the waters of the river. Beyond that, the dark and mysterious mountains rose up against the sky. Molly knew they would soon be in the mountains, passing into Green River country, rolling into Jim Bridger's fort for supplies. She wished, without anxiety, to be back on the farm with Mike, tending to her endless round of chores. She remembered cursing the river fever when their son died. She was sorry at having encouraged Mike to come West. Maybe Oregon was no better, equally as dangerous for children and women folk. While the West was beautiful, the scenery magnificent, it was difficult country. Molly heard a scraping sound. The noise came from near the base of the rock. A rush of panic-fear grew in her mind. Her imagination rushed forward into hideous possibilities. *Indians!* She recalled the stories of white women being captured, then tortured by the tribes. She pressed her body prone against the top of the rock. Visions of a thousand deadly fears babbled in her mind. Foolish lass, she thought, your stupidity has brought you to death's door. You've lost your bucko and probably your life.

She brightened when a man's voice carried through the darkness.

"We'll carve it over here," the man was saying. "Our initials inside a heart. Our names will stay here for a thousand years."

The chisel rang against the rock.

"Jesus, that's loud," a girl said. "We'll wake the whole damned camp."

"Melissa!" Bruce Middleton blurted out. "Your tongue . . ."

"I'm just so excited, darling."

Scarcely believing her ears, Molly moved across the top

371

of the rock. She crawled to the edge of the incline, looked down. Melissa's arm was wrapped around Bruce Middleton's neck. The girl's voice drifted up to Molly.

"Forget carving our names," Melissa was saying. "Let's make love."

Bruce chuckled. "That's what I like about you. First girl I ever met with her priorities right."

Molly stared with wonderment when Bruce dropped his hammer and chisel onto the ground. Melissa leaped toward him, arms flung out to grasp his body. They held an embrace for a long interval. With a tight passionate cry, Melissa stepped back. She whispered something to her lover. They started removing their clothes. Molly's eyes flickered over Bruce's muscular, hairy chest, down his flat stomach and to the point where his manhood stood erect. She gasped at his size, noting her husband was much smaller. She wondered how it would feel to receive such a large blunt instrument.

Bruce laughed. He spoke to Melissa. "Hurry up!"

"Keep cool!" The girl unbuttoned her dress. She tossed the garment in the sand. "Spread out the blanket."

Bruce rolled out a dun-colored blanket. He dropped down on the cloth.

"You worried about Vivian?" Melissa asked.

"I'm carving my name on Independence Rock."

Melissa eyed his growing manhood. "You have an interesting chisel, sir!"

"The better to cut you."

She removed her undergarments. Her white body glistened in the thin light cast down by a crescent moon.

"You're built like a dream!"

Melissa smiled. "The better to serve your needs!"

She dropped down beside him and grasped his manhood with her small hands. She placed her taut, small breasts against his mouth. Molly saw the girl's tongue dart out and press against her lover's ear.

"Do you . . ." Bruce began.

"Want me to?" she asked brightly.

"Do it!"

"I love the taste, smell and passion that you've got," Melissa said. She shifted positions. "I'll kiss you here!"

Molly's eyes widened, scarcely believing the tableau being enacted below her. My god! The girl was like a priestess at some ancient phallic shrine. Her moans of satisfaction drifed up through the night. Great Jehoshaphat! It was a wonder the girl didn't gag! Incredible! Molly stared with rapt fascination at the lovers below. They were doing things she'd never even considered in her most passionate moments. Then, Melissa dropped back on the blanket with a wild flurry of white flesh. Her white thighs glistened in the waning moonlight. Molly saw the girl's excitement, sensed her passion. Melissa's hips twisted like a frenzied snake. Her moans of pleasure sounded real, the passion of a young woman seeking fulfillment.

Molly suddenly became conscious of her own hips pressing against the rock. With a certain tinge of guilt, she realized her passions were aroused. Her fingers moved down her dress and pressed against her flesh. The movement was slow, light and fluid. She found herself becoming more passionate and, dismissing her Gaelic anxiety, she raised her dress. Her fingers slipped through the edges of her pantaloons. A wet stickiness was evident there. Her fingers glided gently over the small, erect clitoris. Her eyes remained fastened on the couple below.

Her hips began to move back and forth with a controlled frenzy.

Below, Melissa sounded a tight, orgiastic cry. The girl's arched body relaxed as her face contorted into a tight, twisted mask. With a trembling shudder, Bruce Middleton found that spot where time and space do not exist. He collapsed onto the girl's small body, breathing heavily. A second later, Molly bit her lip to prevent the outcry of her own exploding surge of passion.

Molly lay on the rock, watching the lovers get dressed. She waited until they had gone a discreet distance toward the camp. Then she slid down from her hiding place and followed their steps. The shadows of the huge rock masked their movement across the desert. The thin moon reappeared from behind a scudding cloud. Molly almost cried out when she caught sight of a dark form rising up behind Bruce and Melissa. Another menacing form appeared on the other side of the couple. Biting her lip in anxiety, Molly saw the feathered outlines of an Indian headdress. She was horror-stricken to see the shadowy outline of a tomahawk being raised above the couple's head.

TWENTY-SEVEN

Bruce Middleton came running breathlessly into camp. The night guard, Dan Pitzen, listened to the excited man's babbling. When the gambler heard the word "Indians," he went off to rouse Steve Wellman. The other emigrants were awakened by the commotion. Sleepy-eyed men hastily jerked on the trousers and ran to Wellman's wagon.

"What the hell happened?" Sam Lawson barked at Middleton.

"Indians got the women," Bruce answered quickly.

"Christ! That's all we need."

"What happened?" Steve asked.

"They jumped us coming back from the rock. We went out to carve our names. They got Melissa Miller and Molly Gorman."

"Damn fools!" Wellman snorted. "You're supposed to stay in camp at night."

Pitzen asked, "What about your wife?"

"My Vivian?" Middleton looked thunderstruck.

"She went out to the rock," explained the gambler. "Said her tomcat had strayed away."

Middleton looked incredulous. "We ain't got a cat."

Mike Gorman came running up. Without shame, he wept upon hearing the news.

"My poor darling," he sobbed.

"She saved our lives," Middleton told the weeping Irishman. "Melissa and I were walking back. Molly must've been behind us. A brave sneaked up behind me and Melissa. Molly popped his skull with a hammer. Then the rest of the war party rode up. The Indian Molly killed was probably an advance scout. They were all over us. I fought as hard as possible, but they knocked me out and took the women."

"Molly . . . gone," Mike mumbled.

"We'll get her back," Sam said with false cheer. "Indians probably grabbed them for ransom."

The other men added their equally false assurances. Steve Wellman added, "Tribes ain't much for hurting white women."

"I'm riding after her," Mike declared.

Sam told an emigrant to saddle two horses. He turned to the Irishman. "You're in no shape to do it. Middleton and I will go after them."

"Middleton got them in this mess."

"That's why he's been picked."

Ten minutes later, the horses had been saddled. A generous ration of feed was carried in saddlebags. Both men strapped on holstered revolvers. Repeating rifles rested in scabbards. Extra rounds of ammunition were tied to the saddle horns.

Sam addressed the emigrants. "Move out as usual in the morning. Don't wait for us. We'll get the women and catch up on down the trail."

Mike rushed forward. "We're not moving an inch 'til we find Molly."

Sam ignored the Irishman. He looked directly at Steve Wellman. "Keep moving," he advised.

Ignoring Mike's loud protests, the guide wheeled his horse and galloped out of camp. Bruce spurred his mount and followed. They paused at Independence Rock where Bruce pointed out the scene of the fight. While he waited apprehensively, Sam jumped off his horse and read the signs. He inspected the earth for a long interval, then climbed on his horse and headed in a northerly direction.

The last thing Molly Gorman remembered was hitting the Indian with her hammer. Dimly, she heard the pounding of hooves below her head. As her mind cleared, she found herself riding face down across the front of an Indian pony. Her hands and feet were bound with rawhide. She started to raise up, but rough hands pushed her down.

After two hours of relentless travel, the war party stopped beside a small brook to water their animals. When the Indians had drunk, Molly was lifted off the pony. She saw her captor was a young Indian wearing a buffalo headdress. He was dressed in deerskin leggings and shirt.

"Drink water," the Indian told her in broken English. He untied the thongs around her ankles. She hobbled to the water and drank greedily.

"Thank you," Molly said, raising up.

"Me Black Eagle." The Indian pointed a finger at his chest.

"I'm Molly."

"Pretty hair." The Indian caressed her long hair.

Molly shrank away from his touch. The Indian laughed heartily, then turned to his seven other tribesmen. He spoke in his language and, moments later, Melissa was pulled down from a pony. Her face was pale and thin. Her eyes glittered with fear. Molly stared dumbly as the frightened young girl drank from the stream. From the far side of the group, Molly heard a woman's angry voice. She turned and saw Vivian Middleton being pulled down off a mount.

"Damn it!" Vivian roared. "Keep your hands to yourself!"

Black Eagle chuckled. "Squaw mad."

Rolling their eyes foolishly, two young braves pretended to assist Vivian. Their hands cupped her breasts and hips suggestively. The older woman endured their indignities until her hands and feet were untied. Suddenly, she jabbed her elbow into the rib cage of the nearest Indian. He shrieked with mock pain, dropped to the ground and pretended to die.

"Damn savages!" Vivian roared.

"Squaw got big noise," said Black Eagle.

"That's true," Molly agreed.

Vivian smiled sweetly when she looked down at Melissa's body.

"Let me help you up, dear," Vivian told the girl.

She extended her hand and, after a moment's hesitation, Melissa accepted the offer. Vivian helped the girl to her feet, then glared malevolently into her face.

"Wanted to look a slut right in the eyes!" Vivian shouted. "A double-dealing, husband stealing bitch! Saw you with my own eyes out there doing whore's work with my husband!"

"Look, I . . . that is . . ." Melissa shrank back from the woman's rage.

"Damn your black soul!" Vivian roared with anger. "You'll die if we get back to camp. Saw it all. You laying there wiggling like a blacksnake in heat! Bruce has been sneaking around to see you. I'll see the both of you hang."

Molly started forward. "Vivian, don't start anything now."

"Oho! The Irish whore, I see," Vivian said brightly. "Who was tumbling you?"

Black Eagle walked up to Vivian. He raised a tomahawk above her head. "Big noise go," he declared.

Vivian stepped back with fright etched in her face. "I'll be quiet," she mumbled. She lay down and drank eagerly from the brook. When she stood up, the Indians mounted up to resume their journey. Two Indians retied their feet and hands. As the two men tied her feet, Vivian stared at Melissa with utter hatred, loathing the girl with every ounce of her energy. She drew strength from her anger, vowing to remain alive to get revenge on the two women. She lusted for the sight of her husband dangling from a gallow's rope—if the Indians hadn't killed him.

The women were tossed face down on the ponies. The war party rode on for another two hours without stopping. They were traveling at a fast pace and the women felt every bump and jolt. Melissa groggily slipped in and out of consciousness. Vivian forgot her hatred and prayed for death. Molly pleaded with Black Eagle and, after another rest stop, the Indian agreed to let them ride upright. As they set off again, the rushing glow of the morning sun rose behind them. The earth was tinted with a mellow yellow cast.

They arrived at the Indian camp late that afternoon. About fifty tepees were set up beside a stream flowing through a lush meadow. The presence of the white women electrified the camp. Bronze skinned men, women and children came rushing from the lodges. Dogs scampered about, yelping excitedly. Black eyes stared impassively at the pale faced women. Children giggled and peeked from behind the legs of their elders. The ranks of the braves parted when the elderly tribal chieftain strode forward. The chief wore a ceremonial feathered headdress, a beaded shirt, leggings and moccasins. He stood erect and delivered a brief monologue in his native tongue.

"Welcome," translated Black Eagle. "Indians not got enough women. You take Indian man. Stay here."

Vivian started to speak out. Molly hushed her with a warning glance.

"Don't be foolish," Molly warned. "We've got to stay alive until help gets here."

Vivian snorted. "That ain't likely."

"Living is better than dying foolishly."

"Be quiet," Black Eagle admonished Vivian.

Molly heard a chorus of laughter behind her. She wheeled around as an Indian girl tugged boldly at her sleeve. Suddenly, the rush was on! Indian women clustered around the white women, fingering the fabric of their garments, tugging at their shoes, plucking at their belts.

"Take off," Black Eagle demanded.

Vivian protested weakly. "Don't be ridiculous."

"I trade with them," Black Eagle said proudly, pointing to his tribesmen. "They want clothes. I trade."

Under the watchful eyes of the amused Indians, the

women were forced to disrobe. Molly stood shamefaced and naked while Black Eagle leisurely bartered her dress for an albino buffalo robe. Her undergarments were traded to a pock-faced Indian brave. The man grinned happily and strutted around the camp dressed in her pantaloons. Melissa's garments were given to the chief's youngest daughter, a beautiful copper-skinned young woman of slender build. Vivian's dress was exchanged for a trapper's knife.

Black Eagle eyed Molly's large breasts with an appreciative grin.

"Big," he commented.

Molly crossed her arms in front of her breasts. She looked away.

"I keep you," the Indian told her. "Chief will pick men for others. You stay. My lodge."

Molly did not protest when Black Eagle led her away. His tepee was one of the largest in the camp. It contained a pallet of cured buffalo robes, a few bows and a number of curious looking bone or wood tools and implements. The Indian dropped down on the robes. He pulled Molly down beside him. He stroked her nipples gently, nodding with satisfaction when they became erect. She tensed, expecting him to mount her.

Instead, he rolled over with a heavy sigh. "Black Eagle tired. We sleep 'til evening." He closed his eyes and was soon snoring peacefully.

Molly wondered about escaping from the camp. Although Black Eagle was sleeping, his arm was stretched across her mid-section. Assuming she could slip from the tepee, she might be unable to get out of the camp. She knew a nude woman would find difficulty in traveling cross country. Sighing heavily, and feeling deep despair,

Molly closed her eyes and slept.

She was roused some time later by Black Eagle, who handed her a worn garment made from deerskin. The dress was a poor fit, but was certainly better than none at all. She meekly followed the Indian out of the tepee to the end of the camp. A huge pit had been erected to contain a fire. A large animal carcass was roasting over the hot flames. Black Eagle knifed a large chunk of meat from the carcass. He inserted a sharp stick into the meat.

"Antelope," he said, handing the meat to Molly. "Good!"

Without comment, Molly ate ravenoulsy. She sank her teeth into the thick piece of meat, tearing off bite-sized chunks. Black Eagle sliced off his own dinner and, together, they strolled back through the camp. Forgetting her plight for the moment, Molly was impressed with the serenity of the landscape. The meadow around the camp was lush and green. A pool had been dammed in the stream; the surface shimmered with a hue of color from the falling sun. The high brows of distant mountains purpled darkly in the west.

Molly was surprised to find herself thinking about sex. For an instant, she wondered how Black Eagle would compare with her husband. Would he be gentle? Or would she be raped? She pushed the thoughts from her mind with fierce determination.

"You quiet," Black Eagle remarked.

"I want to go home."

He gestured around the camp. "This home."

"My home," she explained.

"No like Indian?" Black Eagle looked crestfallen.

"I have a man."

"With rolling tepees?"

"My husband."

"White eyes no good. Black Eagle big man." He paused before the entrance to his lodge. "Come. Me show."

Molly had in mind to protest so she drew back. She pleaded frantically until Black Eagle's strong fingers fastened around her wrist. He pulled her into the tepee. Still, she hesitated in removing her worn deerskin garment. The Indian grabbed the back of her hair with his hand, pulling cruelly. He pressed her face forward, pointing to a lance standing against the wall of the lodge.

"White eyes see coup," Black Eagle said.

Molly struggled to get away from his grip. Her face was pushed closer to the lance and, gradually, she recognized a dozen or more scalps attached to the weapon. She shrank back with horror. When she wheeled to move away from the dreadful display, Black Eagle ripped the seams of her dress. Then he tore the garment from her body. Molly stood before him, naked, trembling with fear. The Indian quickly pulled off his leggings and Molly gasped at the size of his erect member.

"Real man," Black Eagle said proudly. He walked around the tepee to exhibit his swollen manhood.

"Too big," Molly protested.

"Just right," Black Eagle grinned delightedly.

He dropped down on the pallet of buffalo robes. With a sense of despair, Molly lay down beside him.

"Like Black Eagle?" he asked, placing her hand on his hugeness.

"I don't want a baby," Molly replied. "Wait 'til my time is past."

"No worry. Papoose be good." Black Eagle motioned for her to move her hand up and down his thick shaft.

Molly complied with his orders. His hand glided gently

383

over her tense white thighs.

"No fight," he demanded.

Molly unclamped her legs. Black Eagle grunted with satisfaction. His hand danced upward to the apex of her legs. Molly lay rigid and unyielding. She resolved not to help the Indian in any way. Yet, as time passed and his gentle touch persisted, she felt a warm sensation spreading through her. With a deep guttural sigh, Black Eagle rolled onto his side. He drew Molly close, placing his enormous shaft between her legs. She rode the top of that huge protrusion as it lunged endlessly against her. Molly fought against his charging motion, but far down in her mind a tiny burning fuzziness glowed with white hot intensity. This tiny pinprick of passion blotted out her senses, drawing her into a mindless primeval passion. A searing wave of desire grew stronger until her back arced. She began to undulate across that powerful member. Black Eagle grunted with pleasure. His hand cupped and traveled with her grinding hips.

Molly drew back when his warm mouth came against her lips. She tried to turn away, but Black Eagle's hand cupped her chin in a strong grip. He pulled down until her mouth opened wide to receive his tongue. A hot gliding sensation passed her lips with the feel of molten fire. After that, Molly abandoned all pretense and, breathing heavily, rolled over and spread her legs apart. She felt a sharp pain when he entered her, then adjusted herself and made noisy, delightful love.

Afterward, Molly lay subdued and felt leprous. She felt guilty about her passion toward the young Indian brave. She also knew that however she might rationalize the fact, she had betrayed her husband. Women taken captive by Indians might expect to be raped. That was the system of rewards and punishment on the plains. The grotesque and unforgivable part was that she had enjoyed it!

"Molly think?" Black Eagle inquired.

She lay entwined in his arms under the thick buffalo robes.

"About you, me and the world."

"Me do that."

Black Eagle told her that he was twenty-seven years old, an incurable romantic who wanted to hunt and fish in peace. Yet, the world had become a dense, impenetrable pool. The answers had drifted to the muddy bottom. The wisest shamen was unable to define the present time. He worried about the future of his people, whether the rolling tepees would ruin the game, kill the fish. The natural balance of nature was being disturbed. Black Eagle wondered what the Indians had done to so displease the Great Spirit.

Twice more that night they made love. Molly threw herself into each session with guilt-ridden passion.

TWENTY-EIGHT

Sam Lawson and Bruce Middleton waited in an aspen grove on a hillside overlooking the Indian camp. Down below, the red, eye-like glow of campfires gleamed in the darkness. To their right, the mournful call of a wolf was answered by a distant howl across the valley. The trail to the camp had been surprisingly easy to follow. There was a tense moment when they ran into two Arapahoe braves tracking a killer grizzly bear. The animal had mauled an Indian child. Sam talked briefly with the two Indians, gave them tobacco and beads. When the braves doubled back on their trail, Sam reined into a rocky draw. He shot both men in the stomach as they rode past. Without emotion, he slit each of their throats. He made a lead line and Bruce followed with the two Indian ponies in tow. They arrived in the hills above the camp after dark.

"I'm going in for a look," Sam said curtly.

He slipped away through the trees without making a sound. Straining his eyes, Bruce was unable to follow the guide's progress into the camp. Half an hour passed. A dog yelped in the Indian camp, then went silent. Bruce tensed and his fingers gripped the butt of his holstered gun. He wondered what to do if Sam was captured or killed. The trail had been arduous and he'd paid little attention to directions. He made a vow to not rely so greatly on another man.

Another hour passed. Suddenly, Sam was standing beside him. Bruce started to cry out in alarm. The guide's hand slipped over his mouth.

"Sharpen your ears," Sam advised. "I might have been an Indian."

Bruce wondered how to hear sound that didn't exist.

"Camp's gone to bed for the night," Sam informed him. "Molly and Melissa must be in one of the tepees—if they're not dead. We could start a ruckus outside the camp tonight. Move in when they're confused. But they probably wouldn't leave the women without guards. Figure we can watch tomorrow and see which tepees they're in. Tomorrow night we'll slip in, grab them and take off. How's that sound to you?"

"Scary."

"We could ride in and try to bargain for them," Sam went on. "We've got the two ponies and a couple guns to trade. But that's a win-or-lose situation. If the Indians don't want to trade they might just kill us and take everything."

"I just want to get Melissa back to camp."

"You got something going with her?"

Bruce hesitated. "We went out to carve our name on the rock."

"Wouldn't blame you if you're cutting her. She's a pretty little thing. Nice and soft and pliable. A man can raise a girl like that to be the way he wants her."

"I've got a lot of problems. My wife's never going to let me forget this."

Sam dropped down and leaned back against a tree. "We'd better get some sleep. You take the first watch. Oh, by the way, I might mention that the guards have seen you and Melissa slipping away from camp at night. They agreed not to say anthing. Everyone knows that Vivian is a big cross for any man to bear."

"Jesus Christ!" Bruce bolted toward the guide.

"Relax," Sam chuckled. "Every man needs a little fun in his life. You probably deserve it more than most. Now keep your ears sharp. I don't want to get skinned alive in my sleep."

The morning dawned fresh and clear, the sun streaming through the aspen leaves. The two men breakfasted on tough strips of jerky and watched the awakening camp. They spotted Molly Gorman first; her flaming red hair stood out from the black-haired Indians. Melissa was eventually picked out of the crowd. She wore a ragged Indian dress; her escort around the camp was a middle-aged Indian brave.

About noon, Sam's mouth dropped open with shock. "There's another white woman down there," he asserted. "She complicates things."

They waited through the day and wondered about the third woman. During the late afternoon, the women gathered at the dammed pool for a communal bath. Sam slipped through the trees for a better view. He returned with a worried frown creasing his forehead.

"Get set for a shock," he told Bruce. "The third captive is your wife."

Bruce's face turned ashen. His voice squeaked.

"Vivian? Out here?"

"That's her down there."

"Oh my God! How'd they get her?"

"Maybe she followed you two out to the rock."

Bruce moaned. "Jesus! Is she ever going to cause trouble!"

"We can leave her out here."

Bruce looked incredulous. "With the Indians?"

"You ain't got much use for her anyways."

"But she's my wife."

"A third woman will create all kind of problems."

"No." Bruce's head shook adamantly. "She's still a human being. Maybe she ain't been much of a wife There's reasons for that."

"Always is," Sam agreed cheerfully.

"But we can't leave her out here to die with the Indians."

"We'll bring her out with the rest."

"That's the Christian way."

Vivian Middleton fumed about her captivity, stomping angrily around the camp. The chief had given her to a tough, muscular brave with foul breath and a putrid body odor. He rutted her without preliminaries, spreading her legs, mounting like a grunting animal. Despite her anger, Vivian was busily planning an escape across the mountains. At present the Indians watched too closely but, in a few days, their vigil would relax. Meanwhile, she plotted revenge against Melissa Miller.

For her part, Melissa walked through the warm summer air and trembled like a wounded bird. Her world was not fit for habitation; she flirted with madness. Sensing her despair, her brave reasoned that her mind was near the breaking point. He had not forced his passion upon her. That day, Melissa wandered tearfully through the camp with a listless shuffle.

Molly comforted Melissa whenever possible with soothing words of hope and encouragement. She avoided Vivian because the older woman did not conceal her hatred. Black Eagle had been pleased with their lovemaking, promising to keep Molly as his wife. He had gone off with the men to hunt, slapping her teasingly on the buttocks before leaving. She wondered about Mike and knew he was grieving. He would somehow rationalize that the blame for her abduction was his fault.

The tribe retired early that evening as camp would be broken the next day. The Indians planned to move east where game was more plentiful. Black Eagle gave Molly a gentle pinch on her nipple, then rolled over and went to sleep. During the night she awakened with the sound of barking dogs. Black Eagle stirred, grumbled and rose up from their pallet. He started out into the night. Suddenly, he grunted and fell back into the tepee. Molly's eyes widened in terror at the blood gushing from his stomach. Dimly, in the moonlight, she saw the dull pain of death in his eyes.

"Quick! Get dressed!" Sam Lawson was beside her.

Molly pulled a thin robe around her nude body. Black Eagle rolled over on his side. He looked directly up into her face. A thin shaft of moonlight revealed the anguish in his eyes. He started to speak but red foam poured from his mouth. Lawson slammed the butt of hs rifle down on the Indian's head. Molly whimpered at the sound of cracking bone. Black Eagle stared sightlessly up at her. Lawson was already across the tepee, slashing an opening in the covering. He handed a heavy pistol to her.

"Don't shoot unless you have to," he hissed lowly. "The horses are that way! I'll get the others and be right back!"

Molly ran through the night until she came to the horses waiting in the meadow.

Meanwhile, Sam slipped under the covering of the tepee where Vivian lay with her Indian husband. He waited until his eyes adjusted to the darkness. He could not discern her presence on the bed.

"Get up, Vivian!" He reached for the nearest body and shook vigorously.

"Who's 'at," she grumbled.

The Indian gave a loud cry. Sam slit the man's throat with a single stroke of his trapping knife.

"What's going on?" Vivian bellowed with fright.

"Get dressed. We're getting out!"

Close by, a gun exploded. An Indian shouted. Dogs barked. The camp began to rouse itself.

"Let's go!" Urgency laced the guide's voice.

"My dress . . ." Vivian felt around wildly in the darkness.

"No time. We'll have to go now!"

"I can't . . ."

Sam picked up a buffalo robe from the bed. "Either go now or I'm leaving you."

The sound of running men came from outside. Another gun roared down the line. Grabbing Vivian's wrist, Sam slashed an opening through the back wall of the tepee. Outside, he pulled her swiftly along the back of the lodges. Midway to the horses, an Indian brave with a tomahawk appeared in their path. Sam jerked his rifle up and shot the brave in the stomach. Moving around the wounded Indian, Sam cleared the distance to the horses

391

in record time. Without speaking, he helped Molly up on the nearest Indian pony, slapped the animal on the haunches and sent it running away from the camp. Bruce appeared out of the night with a wide-eyed and frightened Melissa Miller. The young girl trembled with fear.

"She's not going!" Vivian roared.

"Later!" Sam snapped. He shoved Melissa up on the pony.

Vivian rushed up and pulled the girl off the mount. "The slut stays here!"

The two women wrestled on the ground. Whimpering with fright, Melissa scrambled to her feet and ran back toward the camp. She heard cries ahead of her, realized her mistake and frantically turned around. She put forth an extra burst of speed and ran out into the meadow. An arrow whistled past her head. A tomahawk sailed by and landed on the ground before her. A feathered lance thudded into the grass.

"I've leaving!" Sam yelled. He kicked his horse and took off.

"I've got to get Melissa," Bruce shouted.

"Leave her!" Vivian hurriedly crawled up on the Indian pony.

Bruce kicked the pony's sides and raced across the meadow toward Melissa's running figure. In the tumult, he knew only that Vivian was shouting at him. The Indians were closing fast on the young girl. Vivian rode perilously close. Her fist struck his shoulder, almost knocking him from the saddle. He wheeled away and rode desperately toward the fleeing girl.

Melissa heard pounding hooves behind her. She put forth extra effort, crying out with alarm. The frightening staccato grew to a thundering roar. Melissa started to run in another direction when she was seized by the arms. She was pulled up on the horse. She found herself in Bruce Middleton's arms.

She hugged him with wild enthusiasm, raining kisses onto his face. Bruce spurred his horse and they galloped away from the turmoil. Melissa gazed back at the Indian camp. Vivian Middleton was being pulled off her Indian pony. When she gained her footing, her fist was shaken violently at the departing couple.

"I'll get you, Bruce Middleton!" Vivian roared. "I'll dance on your grave!"

Sam and Molly were waiting at the end of the meadow.

"We got to go back and get Vivian," Bruce told them.

"That's a hornets' nest back there," Sam replied. "She had her chance and didn't take it. Good riddance!"

"But she's my wife," Bruce protested.

"Then you go back and get her!" Sam wheeled his horse and started up the hill. Molly followed.

Bruce waited. From the camp came the sound of warriors preparing for pursuit. He kicked his horse and rode rapidly up the hill. Sam and Molly were waiting in a grove of aspens on top of the slope. From there, they rode swiftly across country toward the Oregon Trail. When they stopped to water their horses, Melissa asked, "Why haven't they caught up with us?"

"They're probably an hour behind," Sam answered. "We cut loose all the horses before we went after you."

"What'll happen to Vivian?" Bruce asked.

"She can live in the camp, more than likely, if she keeps her nose clean."

Melissa looked at the guide with despair. "She should have come with us."

"She almost got all of us killed," Molly interjected.

"She hates me so much," the girl said.

"Let's get moving." Sam crawled on his horse and moved out at a fast pace.

By evening they reached the Oregon Trail several miles west of Independence Rock. They stopped and let their horses water and graze. They rode on through the night, chewing jerky, watching the terrain for Indians. They halted around midnight to rest the horses and, an hour later, to hide from a small war party of Indians riding eastward. Near dawn, they caught sight of a line of campfires flickering on the horizon.

Sam held a meeting before they entered the camp.

"Figure we better get things straightened out," he explained tersely. He jerked his thumb toward Bruce and Melissa. "You two have been messing around. That's adultery and, according to the code of the trail, punishable by death. There may be talk when we ride in without Vivian. I figure we hold our tongues and stick together. That sound fair?"

"Tell them she couldn't get away," Molly suggested.

"Better to say we think she's dead."

Molly looked puzzled. "Why's that?"

"These two"—Sam jerked his head toward Bruce and Melissa—"can't get married if Vivian's known to be alive. Plus, a lot of people will want to stop the train, go back after her. She had a good chance at getting away. I don't aim to jeopardize the train—and my own life—by going back there again."

Molly looked at Bruce. "You planning to marry her?"

Bruce hesitated. Melissa looked apprehensive.

"I'm not making any promises right now," Bruce explained. "Things are mixed up in my mind. I've been happy for the first time in my life with Melissa. She's opened a whole new world for me. Made me feel like a man. I figure we'll get married—if she'll have me—after a decent interval."

Sam cleared his throat. "We'll say that Vivian was tomahawked when we tried to escape. I'll claim I saw an Indian get her. That way, nobody else has to lie. Fair enough?"

When the others agreed to the plan, Sam led the way to the wagon camp. The morning bugle sounded as they entered the box corral. The caravan started coming to life.

Black Eagle and two other warriors were slain during the rescue. Through the remainder of the night, an Indian shamen performed a solemn ritual over the bodies. In the yellow light of dawn, the bodies were carried up into the hills. They were placed on a platform constructed near the top of an aspen tree. As the mourners returned to camp, the medicine man chanted a liturgy of despair.

Black Eagle's mother was a raw-boned woman with a deep copper skin. She returned to camp and stood in the warm wind, glaring at Vivian Middleton. When the white woman glared back, the grieving mother spat in her face. Other women shouted ferociously, rushing to strike, claw and pound the captive. Vivian shrunk back from the onrushing horde. She stumbled and fell to her knees. A young girl raked her thick nails across Vivian's cheek. Two powerful women pounded her mid-section. An older squaw, screaming her anguish, slammed a large buffalo bone against the white woman's shoulder.

"Enough!" The tribe's chief waded through the crowd of angry women.

"She must die!" cried Black Eagle's mother.

"She did not kill your son."

"Her people did!"

The chief grunted. "Break camp. Get ready to leave. The curse of death is here."

The Indian mother pointed to Vivian. "What about her?"

"She is banished," replied the chief. "We will leave her here. The wolves will decide her fate. Go now and help the men round up the horses. They were scattered last night by the white eyes."

Three hours later, Vivian watched the Indians leave the valley. Fear, hatred and the terror of abandonment pounded her mind like battering fists. That awful slut, and Bruce's dreadful passion, had debased her to this terrible level. She wondered: How could this happen to a good Christian wife? She had been cast out by both her people and the Indians. Crying aloud, she lay in the littered campsite and moaned against such injustice.

In time, her body was nourished by racing thoughts of vengeance. This urge was so compelling that she trembled violently, hands clenching, eyes blazing with fury. She knew that Bruce and his hussy were confident she was dead, that they would soon share her marital bed. Such foulness was beyond belief. Another hour passed and cold reason returned. Vivian walked to the stream and bathed her face with cold water. She began to formulate a plan for survival.

First, she added more wood to the dying campfire. Next, she walked around the campsite to salvage anything of value. A dull flint rock lay where an Indian had dropped it. She clasped the stone and, tearfully, gave thanks to God. She found a plate formed from cottonwood bark, two bony slivers used as needles, a buffalo bone cup and the heavy thighbone used by the squaw to beat her. A decaying buffalo hide had been tossed outside the camp. Vivian scraped away the rancid fat, dragging the hide to the fire to dry.

During the afternoon, she scoured the grounds. A mangy gray wolf loped down the hill and started to cross the stream. Vivian threw stones at the animal, who snarled viciously and then retreated. She decided her travel would have to be restricted to daylight hours. A defensible shelter would be needed each night to fend off the wolves, mountain lions and bears.

She gathered more wood to keep the fire blazing through the night. Next, she went out into the meadow and picked a generous supply of gooseberries, wild onions and a handful of greens. The food was tasty, more filling then she expected. As darkness came over the land, she crawled under the stinking buffalo hide and fell asleep.

A raw wind came up during the night. She rose several times to add more wood to the fire. She was awakened before dawn by a sudden hard blow on her shoulder. She sprang to her feet, swinging the buffalo bone as a club. Her heart quickened at the sight of an Indian pony standing close by with a puzzled expression. She decided the animal had been missed when the Indians rounded up their herd. The pony remained close to the fire while she rigged a hobble from buffalo bone and pieces of rawhide. When the animal was caught and restrained, Vivian fell asleep with contentment on her face.

After breakfasting on berries, she went over the campground again. In the meadow, where she had pulled Melissa off the pony, she found a feathered lance with a sharp iron tip. She was buoyant about the find. She spoke aloud in a dry, hard voice: "Maybe you'll get out of this fix, Vivian. You've got a lance, a hide to sleep under and a pony. You'll have to watch yourself going across country. No question about that, old girl. There's danger all around and you don't understand the country. The world is tough out here. Remember that. Don't ever forget it or you'll be meat for some grizzly bear's dinner. But with some hard work and a lot of luck, you may survive. You may live to see that bastard and his little bitch hanging from a noose!"

She went back to the camp and rigged the lance and buffalo hide into a knapsack. This could be slung over her shoulder or hung over the pony's shoulders. She found the pony surprisingly gentle, not wild and untamed as she expected. When she mounted, and had the buffalo robe bundled in front of her, she looked around with cold despair. Her sense of direction was gone; she was without the faintest clue as to which way she should ride. The Indians had gone off in an easterly direction. She hesitated for some time and decided to head west toward the towering mountains. When this was decided, she dismissed all qualms and kicked the pony into motion. The beast stepped out with a steady gait.

TWENTY-NINE

A joyous reception swept the caravan when Molly and Melissa walked into camp. People yelled and hugged the women, whooped wildly, and showered teary affection on them. Mike Gorman hugged Molly so tightly that her ribcage was sore the next day. Bruce and Sam were besieged with questions. Everyone listened attentively as Sam told an exaggerated version of the rescue. His tale elaborated on the bravery of the other participants and, slyly, he claimed that Vivian Middleton was a courageous martyr.

"Never saw anyone with such courage," Sam lied. "You have to imagine our predicament out there surrounded by Indians. It looked like the end of everyone. I figured we didn't have a chance of getting back here. That's when that great woman, Vivian Middleton, quickly kissed Bruce on the cheek and said farewell. Before anyone could stop her, she grabbed a rifle and advanced against the redskins. She held off the whole tribe until we escaped. Believe me, I had to almost kill Bruce to make him leave. He cried all night long, weeping for that brave wife who sacrificed herself that we might live. Vivian gave up her life so that we might get back here. She was a great and glorious woman."

There wasn't a dry eye in camp when Sam completed his imaginative narration. Wiping her weepy eyes, Cynthia Wellman suggested a memorial service be held for the martyred woman. Dan Pitzen agreed to conduct the proceedings and, after the emigrants assembled, he read from the thirty-first chapter of Proverbs. This passage listed the virtues of a good wife. A hush passed over the crowd when Pitzen closed the Bible. Mrs. Elmer Johnson led the group in a short prayer. After the ceremony, people walked over to Bruce Middleton and expressed their sympathy.

". . . A great loss!"

". . . She was a jewel among women!"

". . . Her courage will never be forgotten."

". . . Our lives have been blessed by her presence."

Before the caravan pulled out that morning, Molly Gorman went over to where Sam was yoking up the Miller wagon.

"Bucko, I could not believe my ears," Molly said. "You're the biggest liar I've ever met. If lies were gold, you'd be worth more than King Midas."

"Now, Molly," protested the guide. "Don't badmouth the dead."

"The blarney stone must've dropped on you as a wee baby."

"I was just making sure the dearly departed had a nice sendoff."

Molly looked at him with wonderment. "You could make a fortune selling snake oil."

Sam attached the team of oxen to the wagon tongue.

"No harm done," he told the Irish woman. "First, Vivian was a troublesome woman. A few good words were said in her behalf. Second, the whole shebang stopped a lot of questions about why we left her out there. It also stopped people thinking about what you, Bruce, Melissa and Vivian were doing out by the rock that night. No need stirring up trouble. Mother Nature and the Indians give us enough problems."

"You think Vivian's dead?"

"Don't know. She may be crow bait. Mostly, though, the tribes treat captives fairly good. Vivian might just find a home with the tribe."

The emigrants were optimistic when the caravan pulled out that morning. Maybe, just maybe, they reasoned, things were not so tough. With a lot of luck, a family might get to Oregon without losing everything. Sensing these high spirits, Steve Wellman set a rapid pace for the caravan. They crossed the remainder of Wyoming at a rapid clip. Long stretches of the Sweetwater country were covered each day. Everyone was in a better mood. In camp each night, the emigrants forgot the sweating, swearing, bitching, groaning, backbreaking problems of the day. They joked and laughed about their misfortunes, however large or small. Their only worry was getting through the South Pass of the Rocky Mountains and these gnawing concerns proved unnecessary.

Brad Payne's entry in his journal described their passage through the mountains:

South Pass is supposed to have been discovered by Robert Stuart, a trapper and mountain man who traveled this way from

Astoria, Oregon, to St. Louis in 1812. He discovered this easy route through the mountains. We approached the area thinking the pass would be a narrow defile lined with rocky cliffs a few hundred, or a thousand or more, feet high. Instead, we rolled through an ascent so gentle that we had to watch closely to find the peak. Without any tiresome effort, we found ourselves in the beginning of the watershed flowing to the Pacific Ocean.

They camped at Pacific Springs, the first point on the trail where the western water started its long journey. It was here that an embarrassed Mike Gorman made a profuse apology to Steve Wellman.

"Forget it," Steve growled and the two men resumed their friendship.

The caravan was now in the high plains country. The trees had given way to sagebrush. The nights were chilled by winds blowing down from the snow-laden mountain peaks. The caravan continued to make good time each day, passing over the Big and Little Sandy Rivers and heading toward the fabled Green River. There was considerable debate about taking Sublette's Cutoff across country to the Bear River, then north to Fort Hall, located near the present community of Pocatello, Idaho.

Sam Lawson demanded that the caravan swing south and stop at Fort Bridger.

The guide's arguments were persuasive. "Our animals are footsore and tired, to say nothing of the people," Sam reminded the emigrants. "Old Gabe has a habit of trading oxen. He'll take in a few tired ones, let them graze until they're fat and healthy. We may be lucky to barter some of our tired teams at a reasonable price. Gabe is also a pretty fair blacksmith and everyone knows our equipment is falling apart. We also need supplies. Hell, this shows how hard up we are. I saw Dan Pitzen and his pretty wife eating cornbread and beans for dinner last night!"

"We're really in the pits," laughed the gambler.

Steve Wellman disagreed with the guide. "We can cut over on Sublette's Cutoff and save time getting to Fort Hall. We can rest and fix up there."

"That's an H.B.C. post," Sam remarked.

"What's that?"

"Here Before Christ or Hudson's Bay Company," Sam explained. "Take your pick. H.B.C. has been here a long time. They got an awful lot sticking in their craw right now. The treaty giving Oregon to the United States allows them nineteen years to close out their trading posts. The sutlers don't like seeing all these people pouring into Oregon. Means the king's flag won't be seen over the prettiest land in the nation. Last year, the sutler at Fort Hall was charging a king's ransom for food and supplies—and then doubling the price. Chances are, he'll be merciful and only triple prices this year. They got a blacksmith except he's a half-breed Indian who spends most of the summer fishing. When he does work the job isn't worth a whole lot. He'll fix a shoe and the horse will throw it inside of a day."

Although the emigrants fretted and fussed, they agreed to follow Lawson's suggestion. Several of the men were running dangerously low on funds. They were interested in buying their supplies at the cheapest price, although, as Sam quickly pointed out, he couldn't guarantee Bridger's prices. Ole Gabe was his own man.

The Green River was flowing high in the banks when they arrived at the Mormon ferry. After considerable dickering, the Saints agreed to ferry the caravan across for $3 for each wagon and team. That night they camped on the western banks of the Green before heading south to Fort Bridger. Sam was depressed and morose, seldom speaking during his evening meal with Agnes and the girls.

After checking out the livestock, he wandered out into the darkness. He sat on a large rock and watched the moon glitter on the rushing waters. It was a good place to organize his thoughts. His depression had been growing for a couple of days, ever since the wagon train came near the Green River. This area had been the stomping ground of the beaver men during the heyday of the fur trade. The lush meadows of the Green River country had been the site of several rip-snorting annual rendezvous for the trappers. Traders from Taos and St. Louis brought whiskey, knives, guns, cloth and all sorts of trade goods to these yearly pow-wows. Peltries were the medium of exchange and, chances were, a trapper blew his whole stack of hides during the rendezvous. The Indians came to trade—and to watch the crazy trappers get drunk and raise hell. Some years the meadow was covered with tepees. And it seemed like each one had one or more copper-skinned young maidens with dark eyes, firm bodies and a sweetness a man could hardly endure.

Everyone was dumb as sin in those days. They thought youth would last forever, that the flow of energy coursing through their veins would never ebb. The liquor was potent, the women were willing and everyone figured the beaver would last forever.

Agnes came up and sat down. "Penny for your thoughts," she said to Sam.

"They ain't worth it."

"You've been gnawing on something lately."

"Thinking about the past."

"That's always good for a cry."

"Ain't that the truth?" Sam grinned without mirth. "I was just a tadpole when I came to the Green River country. Lord, I never thought about getting old. That was for somebody else—not me. Nosiree! I was going to be young forever. And then one morning I woke up with some forty-odd years behind me. All I had to show for it was a fairly good gun, a pistol, a knife and the clothes on my back. Plus a whole lot of memories."

"That's more than most people get."

Sam looked puzzled. "Hell, I started out with a gun, pistol and knife."

"Most people don't have the memories, Sam."

"Maybe so." Sam was silent again. He looked up the river where he had heard so much boasting, so much yelling, so much freedom. He could hear the ghostly voices of those he had fought, wrestled, drunk with and loved through the years. It sure had been a good time. He couldn't remember the names of the women; there had been too many. There were now faceless and anonymous. Yet, he would never forget the warmth of their lips, the sweetness of their taste, the passionate movement of their hips.

Agnes was speaking. "Maybe you'd better think about settling down."

Sam protested. "Nothing I could do in town."

"You could maybe get a donor grant in Oregon."

Sam shook his head impatiently. "Starting at the rear end of a mule doesn't thrill me. I wasn't cut out to farm. First shout from an old buddy and I'd be high-tailing it to someplace looking for excitement."

"You could learn to like it."

•Sam dropped his eyes and watched the moonlight gleam on the surface of the river. "Old trappers never die with their feet in bed, Agnes. We got too big a dose of excitement when we were just tadpoles. Once a man gets that kind of thing pumping in his blood, he ain't fit for settling down. I was really alive when we was tracking Molly and Melissa into that Indian camp. Had to be sharp as the devil. One slip and we'd been food for the Indians' dogs. Seems like the only time I feel alive these days is when the whole shebang is riding on one turn of the cards."

Agnes nodded gloomily. "I'd thought you might be getting tired of moving around."

"Wished I was, Agnes. I'd start courting you."

She blushed. "Don't be ridiculous, Sam Lawson. We're too old for such foolishness."

"A man's never too old for a good woman's love."

Agnes smiled to herself. "I couldn't take this kind of life."

". . . And I ain't able to settle down," Sam added. "So maybe we'd better enjoy each other's company while we're together and forget the future."

"I don't understand."

"Well," drawled Sam. "We are legally man and wife."

"That was just a trick."

Sam put his arm around her shoulder. Instead of stiffening and moving away, as he expected, Agnes leaned toward him. She whispered, "Sam, I—"

A twig snapped behind them. Sam was up and whipping out his pistol when Mike Gorman came hurrying up.

"Don't shoot!" cried the Irishman. "It's just me!"

"Thunderation! You sure know when to interrupt

a man."

"Sorry, Sam," Mike said as Agnes giggled lightly.
"There's a rider just got into camp. Steve said you'd
better hear his story. He's a True Christian and they've
got problems out in the desert."

"Let them die," growled Sam. He turned and pulled
Agnes up off the rock. "We might as well go back to
camp. They sure ain't giving us any chance out here."

A tired, thirsty mule brought the rider into camp. The
man was about fifty, slender and somewhat regal in
bearing. He was dressed in a black frockcoat, trousers and
boots. A wide-brimmed black hat was perched rakishly
over his long locks of gray hair. His brown eyes darted
feverishly as he talked with the emigrants.

Sam walked up and asked abruptly, "Who are you?"

The man extended a pink hand. "Brother James
Henderson, formerly of Pittsburgh, Pennsylvania, and
now enroute to tend to the spiritual needs of the settlers
in Oregon. As an ordained minister of God, I expect my
services will be needed by the multitudes."

"You're a preacher," Sam said accusingly.

"A man of God," Henderson said, stepping back and
pursing his lips.

"What's the trouble."

"I joined a flock of people who planned to take
Sublette's Cutoff west to Fort Hall," Henderson related.
"Unfortunately, their preparations for crossing the
desert were—to say the least—very inadequate. They
reckoned that the Savior would tend to their needs. I
provided my counsel, suggesting that the Lord might be
too busy to supply new oxen, food and water during such
an arduous journey. They countered by claiming He

watched every sparrow in the sky, therefore He would provide what was needed to His followers. The Lord apparently looked down with disfavor on such foolishness. Many of the oxen died of thirst during the crossing. Several people perished for lack of water. Several went mad and ran screaming out into the wilderness. After much hardship and considerable loss of life, we almost reached the banks of the Green River. We are camped five miles out from the river now."

Sam growled, "Then your problems are over."

"The few who survived drank from some bad springs," Preacher Henderson went on. "The first to take down with fever died this afternoon. Many of the others are ailing. I set out to find help and ventured into your camp."

Steve Wellman interjected. "Would this company be the True Christians?"

Henderson's face stiffened. "One and the same."

Sam waved his hand in a gesture of dismissal. "Let them die! They're crazier than loons."

Henderson scrutinized the guide closely. "You are a hard man, sir. Have you no Christian compassion for sick people?"

"A great amount. But none for idiots."

Henderson's teeth flashed briefly in a tight smile. "I must admit that the young girl, Hattie Gill, is . . . well . . . shall we say . . . somewhat misguided?"

"Crazier than a bedbug," Sam snapped.

"We'll have to go help them." Steve Wellman looked around for volunteers.

"Don't risk it." Sam spoke with authority. "They've probably caught cholera. The whole camp's probably dead by now."

"They were quite ill," Henderson admitted. "As we know, the Lord works in mysterious ways."

"They'll need help." Dr. Josh McDonald spoke quietly, then walked off to get his physician's bag.

"We'll need you to guide us, Sam." Steve cast a pleading look in Sam's direction.

"Count this chile out!"

"But you're needed," Cynthia Wellman interjected.

"Just because someone needs me doesn't mean I'm dropping everything." Sam spoke with a hard defiance. "The True Christians sealed their fate when they took off with that loony girl leading their caravan. It doesn't make a never-mind to me if folks want to act crazy. That's their privilege in a free country. But if their craziness gets them in hot water, ole Sam don't have to come running to the rescue. I pick who I stick my neck out for."

Steve's mouth tightened. He regarded Lawson with a short silence, then asked, "You're sure you won't guide us there."

"Just follow the river. You'll find them."

Dr. Josh McDonald returned, carrying his black physician's bag. Steve looked around the group for volunteers, but the emigrants were already walking back to their wagons.

"We could use more help," McDonald said lamely.

"I'll go if Sam will look after our wagon," Cynthia Wellman stated.

The guide curtly refused the duty. He informed Cynthia that women should remain in camp. Cynthia flounced off and obtained Agnes Miller's promise to look after their things. Steve protested, stomping and cussing to no avail, while Cynthia saddled up a horse. Half an hour later they rode off along the river bank in search of the stricken wagon train.

As they galloped away, Sam eyed Reverend Henderson with disgust.

"You'd have better spoke the truth, preacher."

The minister stepped back, eyes blurred with fear.

"God is my witness," he said in a tight voice.

"Don't worry about God," Sam drawled. "Worry about what I'll do to you if they don't get back."

"Sir! I—"

Sam walked away, saying over his shoulder, "Have a good night's sleep, Parson."

THIRTY

Clay Gill was a man with a strong sense of survival. At the Independence rendezvous, he appraised the risks in starting to Oregon with a caravan of True Christians. Most of Hattie's followers were damned fools! She was also unpredictable, sometimes acting crazier than a hoot owl. Frequently, her sermons were little more than babbling gibberish. Yet her words, seldom clear, but always laced with hate, touched a dark part of a person's soul. Righteousness came over the audience until they wanted to smite the sinners, rip their evil hearts from their slimy bodies, stomp their blasphemous tongues into the earth.

Clay figured a blind man could lead a caravan to Oregon. Some places the wagons tracks were rutted a foot deep into the trail. So he had ramrodded the trip west. Most of the pilgrims treated the trip like a Sunday-meeting-with-dinner-on-the-ground gospel picnic. He'd heard enough Amens, Hallelujahs and Praise the Lords to last a lifetime.

Things had gone fine until Clay decided to take Sublette's Cutoff. The short cut, if indeed it was one, involved a thirty-five-mile race across waterless country to the banks of the Green River. They had camped at a gap near the Sandy River. Clay impressed on everyone that the country that lay ahead was totally without water. Bottles, kegs and barrels should be filled before they struck out on the cutoff. He suggested they lay over and make the run at night; only a damned fool rolled out in the scorching daylight hours. The True Christians swore night travel would interrupt their evening gospel meeting. Besides, they claimed the devil and his minions were prowling in the darkness.

When morning came, Clay filled every container he could find with water. He mounted his wagon and looked toward the vague outline of hills in the west. The shimmering witchery of heat waves obscured his vision. When the last of the group was ready to roll out, it was almost nine o'clock in the morning. The wagons rolled past Haystack Butte, crunching through dry beds of alkali lakes. Then the trail circled in and out of sandy valleys. The teams had trouble pulling through these depressions and, although the heat was fierce, everyone got out and walked.

The day got hotter and a hard wind came up. Dust was blown against their faces. People wrapped themselves in blankets, which increased their discomfort. Evening came and they were out in the sagebrush, miles from water, grumbling and ready to collapse. Several oxen had fallen during the day, been cut loose from their harnesses and left to die. A wheel fell off one wagon and the whole rig was abandoned.

Water was running low by now. The precious liquid

was rationed out to men and beasts alike, none receiving a large amount. The caravan pressed on through the night and, ten miles from the river, the country turned hard and dry. The sign of wagon tracks could not be discerned on the hard ground. Here, Clay had to give the reins of his team to Gladys, his wife, and mount his tired mule. Without his guidance, the whole wagon train would have wandered off in every direction. As they rolled over the next five miles, low prayers could be heard from every wagon.

The next problem was almost insurmountable. Five miles from the river, the caravan faced a steep three-hundred foot descent. Tired, thirsty, cursing the devil for their problems, the True Christians unyoked their teams. They let the wagons down the hill by ropes. Several of the oxen dashed off into the desert, outrunning their angry owners. A rope broke during one descent and a rig overturned, breaking up near the bottom.

They doubled up into the remaining wagons and started the final two-hour journey to the Green River. Suddenly, a woman screamed with delirious joy and pointed to a dead pool of water near the trail. Before Clay could intercede, the group halted their wagons and lapped up the dirty water. Although the taste was brackish and alkali, they watered their livestock from the hole. Clay was shouting to get the caravan moving when the True Christians gathered for a prayer of thanksgiving.

"The Lord has provided us with water," said a squat man in linsey-woolsey shirt and trousers. "He has seen the tribulation of His True Christians and created this pool to quench our thirst! Glory be Thy name, O Lord!"

Someone ran to a wagon, returned with a Bible.

"Time for a sermon from Sister Hattie," cried a woman. "Where is she?"

Hattie's face appeared from inside her father's wagon. Her face was pale, her eyes dull and lusterless. She started down out of the rig.

"Get inside!" hissed Clay. "We're rolling out! These fools will stay here until the sun comes up and bakes them."

"Daddy, they need me."

Gladys Gill came around the side of the wagon. She glared hatefully at her husband.

"Don't scream at Hattie," Gladys warned.

Brother James Henderson came strolling up. His face was creased with worry lines. The minister had joined the True Christians shortly before they approached South Pass. His wagon had overturned in a ravine and, while he remained to salvage whatever he could, his caravan had gone on. "We've got to get these people moving," the minister said. "That water's bad. We'd better get everyone to good water before they get sick."

"I'm trying," Clay lamented.

"They need you, darling," Gladys Gill told her daughter. "Let's go lead your flock in prayer. The Lord has given us a cool spring to slake our thirst."

Clay cursed and stomped off. Reverend Henderson and the two women joined the group of worshippers. Clay checked his team and fretted over their weakened condition. He had to pull out for the river soon, else his oxen would die of thirst. He looked over and saw the True Christians kneeling beside the waterhole. Hattie stood above them, arms outstretched like a crucified Christ. She was babbling something about Moses, forty years in the wilderness, Israelites and manna from heaven.

Christ, Clay thought, next she'll try to walk across the waters of the Green River. Or, perhaps, decide to part the waters.

Quickly, his mind raced with his chances for survival. He went down the line of wagons; all teams had been unyoked. Most of the beasts were lying beside the waterhole, but some had wandered off into the dessert. The sun was coming up, hot and high, in the east. Another hour and the heat would burn down on the camp. The men wouldn't have the strength to hunt their livestock. He decided it was every man for himself.

Methodically, while the group prayed and shouted, Clay plundered their wagons. He took money, guns, ammunition and food. While the whooping and hollering went on around the waterhole, he transferred equipment and supplies to his wagon. No one paid any heed to his activities. Hattie was madly talking as he emptied his keg of water and let his team drink.

The True Christians had been in worship for almost half an hour. Clay strode over, tapped Reverend Henderson on the shoulder. The minister opened his eyes, raised his head. Clay led the man to the edge of the group.

"I'm going for help," Clay told him. "We're in bad trouble out here."

"They are fanatics, sir! Your daughter—"

Clay interrupted. "There's supposed to be a ferry over the river. I'll head there and try to get back."

"Godspeed!"

"If you got any sense," Clay went on, "you'll high-tail out of here."

Henderson's face stiffened. "What about your wife and daughter?"

"I'm planning to take them with me."

"They may not go."

Clay nodded impassively. "That's their choice."

When Henderson bade him farewell, Clay walked over to his wife. He whispered in her ear and the minister saw Gladys shake her head adamantly. Clay shrugged and walked away. He got on his wagon and rolled westward toward the river. Henderson was the only person who watched his departure. The others were busy watching Hattie enter one of her visionary trances. Henderson got ready to ride out.

Two and a half hours later, Clay reached the river banks. His thirst-crazed oxen were near exhaustion. They raced the last mile to the river, having caught scent of the water. Clay was scarcely able to control the snorting animals until their harnesses could be removed. Once freed of these restraints, the beasts leaped into the cold, icy water and drank greedily. Clay drank his fill of water, then lay back on the thick grass along the bank. After a long rest, he pulled the oxen from the river, hobbled and turned them out to graze. He crawled under the wagon and went to sleep in the shade, thinking about a new life in Oregon. When the heat died down, he planned on crossing the river by ferry and heading through Sublette's Cutoff into the Bear River valley. There was danger in traveling alone, but if he pressed hard he might catch up with a caravan.

The foul odor of death soured the air. They smelled the True Christian camp a half mile across the arid ground. The vehicles were stretched in disarray along the trail by the waterhole. The bloated carcasses of dead oxen littered the area. A dead man lay sprawled by the edge of the waterhole. Through the thin yellow light of morning, Steve watched with horror as a flock of ravens pecked at the body. Off to the left, the swollen body of a woman lay face up, face blackened by the sun, eyes pecked out by carrion birds.

Cynthia retched when she stepped down from her horse. She held a handkerchief against her mouth and nose. "I . . . I . . . be all right in a minute!"

"Maybe you'd better wait out there," Steve said, pointing toward a small hill covered with sagebrush. "We'll have to bury them."

"Probably not," said Josh McDonald. "Animals will just dig them up." He went up into the first wagon, came back a few moments later with a dark look on his face. "Two dead ones in there."

"Fever?" Steve asked.

"Something like that."

They found a woman and a small infant in the third wagon. Both were dead.

Hattie Gill was lying under the fourth wagon. Her lips were swollen and cracked. She was unable to speak. Her lustless eyes looked pleadingly up to them as she stirred weakly. Steve placed the canteen to her lips, cautioning the girl to drink sparingly at first. Gladys Gill was found alive, just barely, in the last wagon. She had crawled into the rig to get shade from the sun. She was dehydrated, hungry and clawed desperately for the canteen Cynthia brought to her.

The rest of the True Christians were dead. While Cynthia nursed Gladys and Hattie, Steve and Josh stood outside in the shimmering heat and debated what could be done with the bodies. After much discussion, it was decided to leave the adults where they lay.

417

"We can find shovels in the wagons," said Steve.

"Graves would have to be deep. Otherwise, the wolves will dig them up."

"We could ride back to camp for help."

"Not likely," McDonald reminded him. "No one volunteered last night. Besides, they're probably pulled out for Bridger's place by now."

Steve was exasperated. "Damn it! At the least we can dig a grave for that baby."

While McDonald went off to treat the two women, Steve found a shovel and excavated a small grave for the infant. When the child's body had been covered, he turned aside and dug a shallow trench. The corpses were dumped into the grave and, once the dirt covered their remains, Steve piled rocks over the site. McDonald came out of the wagons where he had been treating the women. He said their condition had improved, that they felt strong enough to travel. Shortly after that, Hattie crawled on behind Cynthia; Gladys Gill was placed on Steve's Spanish stallion while he walked. They hurried out to catch up with the caravan.

They were approaching the Green River, moving along a parched draw between a series of hillocks. The land dipped into a ravine and, when they rode out, they faced a large party of Indians.

"Christ!" swore McDonald. "We're goners!"

"There's at least two hundred of them!" Steve's hand drifted to his holstered pistol.

A wild whoop went up when the Indians saw them. Yelling wildly, the boldest warriors galloped their ponies toward them. Bows were drawn and lances brought up into readiness.

*   *   *

Vivian Middleton reined in the pony, pulling on the rawhide harness she had rigged up. Just ahead, she could hear the roar of a river racing through the mountains. She sighed and slid down from the pony, got off and walked the rest of the way toward the stream. The mountain stream was about twenty yards wide, the water cool and clear. She knelt beside a moss-covered boulder, cupped her hands and drank eagerly. When the pony had slaked his thirst, she led the animal a short distance to a patch of thick grass. The pony stood quickly while she affixed the rawhide-and-buffalo bone hobble to his front legs.

"Now I'm off to find supper," she told the pony.

Carrying the lance, she walked out into the middle of the mountain brook. The water was icy cold on her bare feet and legs. The rocks were sharp and painful, although the soles of her feet were toughening. Vivian waited silently until the silvery flash of a large trout caught her eye. She followed the fish until it entered calm, shallow water near the edge of the stream. When the fish remained motionless, she jabbed with the lance. She brought the weapon out of the water with the fish impaled on the tip.

Another half hour passed before she flinted dry grass and twigs into a fire. When the blaze was going good, she took a small sliver of buffalo bone and jabbed an opening into the underside of the trout. Next, she pulled the body open and removed the innards. Another stick, longer and sharper, was jammed down the throat of the trout. She held this over the fire until the fish was thoroughly cooked. The firm flesh was tasty. Her appetite was quickly sated.

Next, she looked about for a safe refuge during the

night. After roaming up and down the stream, she found a rock hanging over the stream. One side was protected by a high cliff; the other was open but covered with small boulders and stones. Holding her lance in the crook of her elbow, she carried her buffalo robe to the rocky place. She pulled several armloads of grass, carried them to the spot and then led the pony to the shelter. She picked up firewood, used a torch from the fire to start a new blaze. Then she spread out the buffalo robe and wrapped herself into the furry folds.

She looked up at the pony and spoke aloud.

"Seems like we've been traveling for years," she told the animal. "I've been keeping track, though. Tie a knot in a rawhide cord every morning. This is the eighteenth day since we left the Indian camp. I just hope we're making good time 'cause the nights are getting colder this high up. Never knew there could be so many mountains so high up. Do you reckon we'll ever get out of here?"

The pony looked quizzically toward her.

"Too bad you can't talk," Vivian went on. "At least we could be better company for each other. I'd give anything to hear a human voice. Not Indian, mind you, 'cause I'm scared to death of them. Keep away at all costs from those savages. Never knew the sound of a person's voice could mean so much. But I figure we'll survive somehow. Take everything one mile at a time, one hour leads to another. We've managed pretty good so far, considering I don't have a knife or gun. I've even learned to ride pretty good on your bare back."

As the sun went down, Vivian fell into an exhausted sleep. She awakened once during the night, hearing the squall of a large mountain cat in the distance. When dawn arrived, she caught another fish for breakfast, loaded up her gear and rode westward, higher into the mountains.

THIRTY-ONE

Steve Wellman stiffened to rigidness, nerves taut. He cocked his pistol as the Indian braves galloped toward his group.

"Stay on the horses," he advised the others. He felt exposed and vulnerable on foot.

The first of the Indian braves roared directly toward them, veering their mounts at the last moment and racing in a circle around the frightened group. Grinning wildly, the riders whooped loudly and performed daring tricks of horsemanship. One stockily built young Indian stood up and balanced himself on his barebacked pony. Another brave did a backward flip off his pony, grabbed the animal's tail and ran along behind the running animal. Two others raced directly toward each other at a rapid clip, veering their mounts at the last possible moment.

Steve and the others were paralyzed with fear. Hattie Gill began to sob and pray in a piteous voice. Gladys Gill sat frozen and immobile on the Spanish stallion, her mind blank. Her lower lip trembled involuntarily and her legs shook violently. Suddenly, a hoarse shout was heard from the main group of Indians. Immediately, the ranks of the riders parted and an imposing, bronze-skinned man in a feathered headdress burst into view. He cast a blazing glance at the riders from his dark eyes. The braves were instantly silent; their faces were subdued as they rode back to rejoin their tribesmen. The Indian who had given the order advanced on foot. His dark eyes twinkled with amusement. He raised his hand in the traditional greeting, grinning broadly to reveal his brilliant white teeth.

He spoke with childish glee. "Me chief of Shoshone. I am Washanti, friend of white brothers!"

Steve returned the greeting. "You speak our tongue?" he inquired.

"Black robes show how," Washanti said with pride. "Man with cross come many moons ago. Tell of Christ brave nailed to tree. Me friend of white father."

Steve introduced himself. Washanti listened with smiling courtesy, bowing elaborately as the others were introduced. He complimented each person on their appearance, wished them good health, and told how happy he was to be in their presence. He came closer and continued to chatter with boyish enthusiasm, admiring Steve's black Spanish stallion, inspecting the silver-trimmed harness and saddle.

"You give?" Washanti inquired. He pointed to his chest.

Steve shook his head. "Never give horse away."

Washanti nodded with understanding and, ignoring Steve's presence, walked around to inspect the other animals. He came back and patted the stallion's head. "Best one," he said with an elaborate grin.

"No gift," Steve repeated.

"Where you go?" Washanti inquired.

"Fort Bridger."

"Old Gabe good man. We head there now. Get firewater." Saying this, Washanti gave a humorous impression of a drunken Indian, stumbling about, rolling his eyes, letting his tongue loll out the side of his mouth. Then he straightened himself up and looked dignified. "You travel with us?"

"Gladly," Steve agreed.

Washanti threw his arm around Steve's shoulders. "We are brothers," the chief said with delight. "We go see Gabe. He is my brother like you. Gabe and Washanti's sister good friends. She stay at fort. When Gabe goes on trip, she watches for drunk Indians. Chase them away."

As they traveled down the river toward Fort Bridger, Steve discovered the Shoshone tribe had never been hostile to emigrants. With great enthusiasm, the tribe had welcomed the first trappers and scouts, then extended this courtesy to the settlers. When the wagon trains came across the plains, some warriors in the tribe expressed their concern. A council was held and the matter debated for two weeks. The wise men and chieftains decided peaceful coexistence was the best policy. After all, they reasoned, the white men were superior in numbers and firepower. Their guns could shoot farther, and more accurately, than any bowman. Although disputes did arise from time to time, the Shoshone refused to send out war parties. The great Shoshone chief, Washanti, maintained peace between his people and the whites throughout the migration west, the Indian wars and the eventual resettlement of the tribes on reservations.

Washanti's entire group of southern Shoshone were heading for the fort. They were an affable, affectionate people who laughed often and easily. Copper-skinned warriors in rich robes of bearskins joked with their brothers decked out in panther skins trimmed with beads and feathers. They were accompanied by beautiful squaws wearing elegant mantles of bird skins and feathers. Lovely maidens with bold eyes and teasing mannerisms flirted with Steve Wellman and Josh McDonald, grinning innocently and longingly. Cynthia Wellman was enchanted by the dark-eyed papooses rolled in ornamental cradles on the backs of their mothers. Toddlers were given free reign, doing anything they wished, until their actions created a danger to themselves. Even then, the child received a gentle reprimand rather than harsh disciplinary measures.

The ponies were laden with thick packs of hides and pelts to be traded at the fort. As he became better acquainted with his guests, Washanti dropped the grunting, telegraphed sentences. "One must play a role," he told Wellman and McDonald. "Many white people become upset when an Indian talks as well as they do. Indians are not dumb. We exist in a different culture from your people. We could never be confined to living in cramped houses that cannot be moved. My people would sicken and die under such conditions. We must go where we please when the fancy strikes us. No, we are far from being ignorant savages. Take the loads of hides we are taking to Old Gabe. He will dicker with us, but give the highest possible price because our hides are tanned better than the best anyone else can offer. The secret has been handed down by my ancestors. To tan a hide into a soft texture you must rub the brains of the animal into the inside. Then the hide will remain soft and fresh for many years."

Packs of dogs traveled with the Indians. Each morning, the squaws attached a harness to the dogs. The rig fit over the animal's shoulder and held two poles on either side of the dog. Hides were stretched across the poles and the dog carried a family's belongings during the day's trek.

"Everything must be useful," explained Washanti, eyes twinkling. "My people like to laugh and play, to enjoy life, never working so hard that the joy of living is lost. Some tribes are nervous about their future. Their men hunt constantly; their squaws are always busy. They do not live off the land like the Shoshone. The land rules them. They are like your people"—he pointed to Steve and Josh—"always hurrying to be where they are not and, when they get there, run off to another place. They are so busy they forget their selves and their link with the great spirit."

"You know," said Josh after Washanti retired to his tepee, "I think the old boy has a good philosophy. Live easy. Don't worry. Enjoy things as they come. They're good at raising kids. I've never seen happier children."

Steve nodded. "Kids are given a lot of freedom."

"We could take a few lessons from the Shoshone." McDonald stood up, stretched and went to bed.

The group traveled down the Green River, hunting for prairie hens, rabbits and juicy berries. The landscape held an unreal beauty, a quick-changing landscape of sagebrush and small, gnarled trees that slowly grew on the emigrants. Snug in his bedroll, Josh McDonald listened to the ever-changing tempo of the night wind, looked up into a lowering cloud with silver-tipped edges.

426

They crossed into the valley of the Black Forks, staying close to the river lined with green willow trees. After considerable debate, Washanti declared the mosquitos were no larger than a blackbird, although he had seen one swarm that approached the eagle in size. They arrived at Bridger's fort in the late afternoon and found the caravan corraled up outside the gates.

Wellman reined in his stallion and looked at the fort with disappointment. "I sure expected more than this," he declared.

"Beggars can't choose," Cynthia told him.

Washanti laughed. "Old Gabe is not a master builder."

The trading post was built in the usual form of pickets. The office and living quarters opened onto a wide square. The fort was protected from attack by a heavy gate of wood. The walls of the buildings had been chinked with adobe mud. Spreading out from the establishment was the fertile Black Fork's valley, a verdant area watered by several icy streams flowing down out of the Uinta Mountains.

Sam Lawson came running through the crowd of Indians as Steve dismounted.

"Thunderation! You're going to be a scout better than the rest," the guide drawled, giving Steve a bear hug. He dropped Wellman and, with a broad smile, walked over and pulled Cynthia down from her horse. "Honey, you're a sight for tired old eyes!"

Cynthia giggled. "The greeting is worth the trip."

Sam jerked his thumb at Washanti and his tribe. "You traveling with this old fraud and his bunch of thieving Indians?"

"You know them?"

Sam cast a look of mock contempt toward Washanti.

"We shared a lodge one winter." He grinned at the chief. "We smoked loco weed and dreamed of spring."

Washanti came up and delivered a long ceremonial greeting in his native tongue. He smiled when the ritual was completed, laying his hand on Sam's shoulder.

Steve asked, "What did he say?"

Sam grinned. "He asked if I had any good whiskey."

Washanti chuckled and shook a rawhide bag attached to his belt. "The best loco weed, Sam. From the highest slopes of the tallest mountains. A few drags on the peace pipe tonight and you'll be talking to your ancestors."

"See you after a while," Sam told the Indian. He walked over and looked directly at Steve, listening to his brief report on the True Christian caravan. After Steve finished, Sam jerked his head in the direction of the women. "What do you figure on doing with them?"

"Leave them here. They can hitch a ride on a wagon headed east."

Sam looked dubious. "They might have to stay with Gabe all winter."

"At least they'll get home next spring."

"Steve, I don't think he'll take them."

"Why not?"

"They're crazy."

Steve's tone was stiff. "They haven't made a fuss."

"Damn it!" swore the guide. "Gladys and her crazy daughter are sick and tired right now. Wait until they get well. The hate and preaching will start up. Winter is coming on. Ole Gabe don't need a crazy couple of religious fanatics driving him loco. He may not take them in."

"We can take them to Oregon."

Sam cast a pained look in Wellman's direction. "Then

428

we'll have the problem. Let mad dogs die, I say."

"They're human."

Sam spat. "Right now we got more important news to gnaw on. Skip the vittles for now. We got to talk with Old Gabe."

Bridger was in his office, a small log structure inside the walls of the fort. The grizzled mountain man grinned affably when Steve walked through the door.

"Heard you come in with Washanti," said Bridger. "Brought two women with you."

Steve nodded. "That's correct."

Bridger's tone turned cold. "I ain't letting them women stay here. They caused trouble in Independence. They got the Indians riled up back there on the Platte. I don't want two harpies like that around here."

"Ain't there someone going east?"

"Not a dab-nabbed thing 'til spring. 'Pon my honor on that."

Steve shrugged. "We'll take them in the caravan."

Bridger looked remote and aloof. "See that you do that."

"That's settled," Sam said easily. "Let's get down to business, Gabe."

"Show the rock," said Bridger.

Sam tossed his gold nugget on Bridger's desk. He smiled at Wellman. "Know what that is?"

Steve examined the rock. "Sorry, I don't know much about rocks."

Sam smiled indulgently. "Gold! A gold nugget."

Steve's eyes widened. "From around here?"

"California."

"Where did you get it?"

"Doesn't matter," Sam drawled. "Thing is, me and Gabe have been powwowing most of the afternoon. A gold rush has started in California." He went on to repeat the news delivered by Kit Carson. He summed up, "Maybe folks in the caravan want to change their plans. California sounds appealing to me."

Confusion crept across Steve Wellman's face.

"I . . . well . . . that is . . . hell, I don't know," he stammered.

"Problem is," Bridger chimed in, "the news will soon be out."

Steve looked at Sam with a blank expression. He asked, "You planning on California?"

"I've been paid to guide you to Oregon."

"What if we decide on California?"

"I can get you there."

Bridger inquired, "What if just half the people vote for California?"

"A good point." Steve looked over at the guide.

"I'd still be bound to take the rest to Oregon," Sam shrugged.

Steve turned to Bridger. "You going?"

"Trading's better than digging for rocks—even gold nuggets."

"The greenhorns will be rolling in next year," Sam explained. "Several thousand will be heading for the gold fields. Gabe's going to need plenty of supplies and lots of help."

Bridger sounded doubtful. "They'll probably take Sublette's Cutoff."

"They'll hear what happened to the True Christians," Sam replied. "That should end talk about a short cut."

"People never learn," Bridger said with rancor.

The caravan lay over at Fort Bridger for two days for repairs and supplies. Wagons were blocked up, wheels slipped off the hubs, then taken to the blacksmith shop. A sour-faced Mexican pumped the forge while Bridger pounded the iron rims back onto the wheels. The men spent a considerable amount of their time greasing hubs, tightening boards and replacing worn parts on their wagons. Oxen could be traded at the fort on a two-for-one basis. Many of the animals in the caravan were tired. The shoulders of many beasts had been rubbed raw by harnesses, the wound infected by alkali dust. The emigrants looked over Bridger's animals. The corral was filled with healthy oxen. Trades were made and, if a man needed a complete team that was fresh, a fee of $20 per head was charged.

The women crowded into the cramped, dimly lit store. They purchased supplies, often grumbling about high prices at the fort. They also stood in small groups and watched as Washanti and the Shoshone celebrated their visit to the fort. The Indians were in a festive mood. Bridger had given the tribe a generous line of credit for their robes and pelts. Most of these funds were being spent on gaudy dresses, bright beads and whiskey.

Gladys and Hattie Gill remained at a distance from the other women. They watched the Indians with a contemptuous expression. Both mother and daughter were preoccupied with the future. Life seemed to have ended with their disaster along Sublette's Cutoff.

On the second morning, Hattie woke up trembling.

"Maw," she asked, "what's going to happen to us?"

Gladys patted her shoulder. "Don't worry. We'll survive."

"I had the strangest dream last night."

Gladys brightened. "Did you talk with God?"

"He ain't talked to me since we was—out there!" Hattie pointed toward the desert.

"Don't worry, baby. He'll be back."

"Maw, I'm scared."

Gladys Gill took her daughter's frail body in her arms. "I am, too, honey. Real scared. Your Paw ain't here no more. We ain't got nobody to tell us what to do."

Hattie loved the feel of her mother's hug. She brightened. "Maybe if I try really hard, God will take Paw's place."

Gladys squeezed the girl's bony shoulders.

"How you mean that, baby?" she inquired.

Hattie felt warm and dreamy. "Maybe God will take over where Paw left off. I can quit eating for a while. That always brings Him back. When I get a real empty feeling in my stomach, like my belly skin is about to touch my backbone, He comes back."

Gladys brushed a hair back from Hattie's forehead.

"That's too hard on you, child. Let's just wait and see what happens."

Hattie wailed lowly. "But, Maw, I'm scared."

"Don't worry. We'll figure something out."

The men in the caravan, of whatever age, were enthralled by the Shoshone women and their bold ways. Uncle Durgeon Adkins sat on a camp stool, resting his chin in his cupped hands and stared at the Indian camp.

"Never seen anything like it. Not in all my born days," he commented to anyone within earshot. "Beautiful grown women. Walking away with just a breechcloth to cover their lower parts. Lord Gawd almighty! I been east

432

and I been west. I been in sheep country. I been in cow country. I even been a passenger on a steamboat. Rode the Erie Canal both ways. And I never seen anything like it. Ever seen that many tits in all your life? Beats all! Tits all over the place. Bouncing and bobbing and flying here and going there! Makes a man wonder if being civilized is all that good. Maybe it ain't cracked up to be what the preachers say it is."

Mike Gorman walked past. "How you doing, bucko?" he inquired.

Uncle Durgeon chuckled lewdly. He jabbed his cane in the direction of a young Indian girl walking out of their encampment. "Hot damn! Ever seen anything like that pair? Not a droop in a wagon load. Standing out there and just waving in the breeze. Lordy! I can't see 'em but she must have some awful pretty nipples. Can you see that far, Mike?"

Mike pursed his lips. "Uncle, she's a beauty."

Uncle Durgeon cackled gleefully. "Knew it! Knew it!" He pounded his cane onto the ground. "Look at her wiggling when she walks!"

"Better than looking at the rear of an ox all day," Mike replied.

"You just don't have the taste," Uncle Durgeon said sourly. "You don't appreciate the beauty of a woman. Course, maybe that's to be expected. You got a wife and you're both young. Take an old worn-out bag of bones like me. I can sit here all day and dream away. God! If there's anything to that business about living more'n one life. That reinca—"

"Reincarnation."

"That's it, Mike," Uncle Durgeon said enthusiastically. "Maybe in my next life I'll be reborn as an Indian.

Won't be a warrior, either. Plan on just sitting in the doorway of my tepee and watching the pretty women walk by. My oh my! Look over there! See that slender one. A tall girl, ain't she? I'll bet she's pure living hell in bed. Wouldn't you love to have those long legs wrapped around you? Pulling you in, tight and warm? Wouldn't that be nice, Mike? Wouldn't it?"

Mike started to reply in the affirmative when fingers grabbed the edge of his ear. His head was pulled sharply to the side. Grinning sheepishly, he looked into the mock anger of Molly's eyes.

"Bucko! You are not getting the chores done," Molly said in a strident voice.

"My fault, Molly," Uncle Durgeon apologized, not looking anywhere except toward the Indian women. "We are discussing certain poetic qualities of life."

Molly tousled the old man's gray hair. "More like remembering the good old days."

Uncle Durgeon laughed. "Molly, they were never like this!" He slammed the lower tip of his cane into the ground for emphasis.

"Old men!" Molly said with a gentle glance. "Uncle, you can sit in the sun and dream. But my husband is supposed to be getting the rims tightened on our wagon wheels."

"Molly, I—" Mike blurted.

"—would rather watch tits bobbing in the breeze!"

Mike blushed. "I was just passing the time with Uncle Durg."

"A few more minutes of looking," Molly admonished, "then get over to the blacksmith shop."

As Molly walked away, Uncle Durgeon raised his cane. He pointed the tip in the direction of a bare-breasted

Indian woman.

"Now, Mike, that's a real pair," Uncle Durgeon remarked. "I could crawl between those big ones and nap the whole winter away."

Mike chuckled. "And hope the spring thaw never comes."

Uncle Durgeon blinked against the sun. His eyes sharpened as a firm-breasted Indian girl came into view.

"Think of it," the old man said. "My first wife was a farm girl from upstate Massachusetts. Real pretty woman. We were married for eleven years before the fever took her. In all that time I never had a glimpse of her breasts. Never saw the woman without her clothes. Yesiree! The Indians know how to live, Mike. They surely do!"

THIRTY-TWO

Reverend James Henderson had been sitting in a camp chair for most of the afternoon. He had observed the comings and goings around the fort with a sharp eye. Now, he gazed to the west as the blazing ball of sun fell behind the mountains. Soon, a hazy purple twilight fell over the landscape. Henderson continued to sit, rigid in posture, his lips pursed, desperately trying to push visions of the Indian women from his mind. The galleries of his consciousness were crowded with scantily garbed Indian maidens. They wandered through his mind with a wanton swing of their pneumatic hips. Their firm breasts were unfettered by garments. Their dark eyes twinkled with a glimmer of devilment.

The logical, God-fearing part of Henderson's mind branded the Indian women as brazen pagans. On another level, he was touched by the innocence of these female savages. Their bodies were exhibited without shame or guilt. They moved with a natural freedom, often smiling sweetly in a seductive manner.

Darkness began to fall. Campfires blazed around the fort and in the Indian encampment. From the middle of the Indian tepees came the steady booming of a drum. The beat was hard and sensuous, a melancholy rhythm that aroused Henderson's primitive instincts. Without knowing why, he became filled with a desperate loneliness.

Four years had passed since his wife perished on their way to church that Sunday morning. She had been following him up a dirt road to the church where he was to preach. Without warning, a large copperhead snake struck from a hidden place in the weeds. The fangs went through her thick cotton stockings, embedding themselves in her soft flesh. She expired as he carried her to the church house.

He had truly loved the plain hill girl who was his wife. Numbly, he wept as the congregation made a crude pine box for her coffin. An elder in the church preached a brief funeral service before the grave back of the church. The scent of dogwood blossoms perfumed the air. Two young girls placed bouquets of honeysuckles on the grave. Since that day of despair, Henderson had never been with another woman. His obsession for preaching the gospel neutralized the carnal stirrings of his manhood. As the months turned into years, and he preached and prayed his way along the frontier, Henderson forgot his sensuality.

Now, his blood was stirred by the incessant pounding of the drum. He closed his eyes, prayed for deliverance from his carnal thoughts. He halted abruptly when the cadence of his prayer picked up the beat of the tom-tom. Fearfully, and dreading the consequences, he stood up, brushed off his black frockcoat and walked in the direction of the Indian camp.

He hung back in the darkness and observed the ceremonial dancing. An Indian in a breechcloth sat near a campfire pounding the drum with his large hands. Chief Washanti and Sam Lawson sat on a tanned buffalo robe, exchanging puffs on a long-stemmed peace pipe, drinking whiskey from a stoneware jug. At least two score of Indian men and women danced, sang and drank around the campfire.

Henderson's eyes were riveted on the sensual movements of the dancing women. The gaiety of their laughter came floating through the night. One young maiden, a slender girl with large, globular breasts and long, finely shaped legs, was clad in a small rawhide breechcloth. She paused from time to time to take a drink of whiskey from a barrel sitting beyond the campfire. After several draughts, she came back into the light, stood rigid and swayed to the pounding beat. Henderson felt a stirring as the young woman smiled, revealing a set of even white teeth. The heat of the fire and the exertion of dancing created a thin layer of perspiration over her nubile body. Her skin glistened like burnished gold in the firelight.

Henderson was licking his lips when a growl sounded in the darkness behind. He turned and saw the face of a smiling Indian brave. The man spoke in his language, motioning the preacher toward the fire. Reluctantly, and blushing with embarrassment, Reverend James Henderson walked toward the celebrants.

"So the preacher is out spying," Sam Lawson said with sarcasm.

"Sit and join us!" Washanti patted the buffalo robe. "Do you drink whiskey?"

Henderson shook his head. "It's against my religion."

Washanti nodded with understanding. He picked up his peace pipe and tamped a finely ground mixture of weeds into the bowl. He grinned mischievously as the pipe was passed to the minister. "It is customary to smoke the pipe of peace with us."

Henderson cast a confused glance in Lawson's direction. "I don't use tobacco."

Sam shrugged. "Just a shot of loco weed in there. People always figure the Indians smoke tobacco in their peace pipe. That's foolish! The tribes don't have plantations to grow the stuff."

Henderson sniffed the bowl. "Will it hurt me?"

Sam grinned wickedly. "Preacher, it might do you a lot of good. Grab a twig from the fire. Light up the bowl. Take a couple of long, hard puffs. Hold the smoke in your lungs as long as you can. Enjoy! Enjoy!"

Henderson followed the guide's instructions. Ten minutes later, he sat listlessly on the buffalo robe. He giggled with happiness. Several times, he had tried to form a coherent sentence, only to lose his train of thought.

"How long we been here?" Sam asked the preacher.

Henderson chuckled. "A couple hundred years. Maybe a thousand."

Washanti took a small sip of whiskey. He handed the jug to Henderson. "A small sip will stop your mouth from being dry," the chief said.

Henderson tipped the jug up, let the fiery liquid flow down his throat. He giggled wildly, without control, and handed the container over to Lawson.

"Jesus!" Henderson blinked. "I feel strange. Never felt like this before. For the first time in years I'm at peace."

439

"That's why the tribes call this a peace pipe," Sam replied, laughing. "A few puffs and you can't hate anyone. You feel like a brother to everyone."

Washanti's face brightened with noble insight. "Someday I will take the peace pipe to the Great White Father in Washington place. We will sit on a blanket outside his tepee and smoke. When he is feeling like a brother to Washanti, we will resolve all questions between our people."

Henderson's eyes were fixed on the slender Indian girl. She had stopped dancing and sat across the fire from him. Washanti motioned to the girl and she smiled and came over to sit beside her chief.

Washanti looked into the girl's dark eyes. "Do you have a man?" he asked.

Long eyelashes fell demurely over her dark eyes.

"I have not chosen one," she replied.

"This man"—Washanti gestured to where Henderson sat—"is interested in you."

The girl smiled with evident approval. She moved to Henderson's side and her arm slipped around his shoulders. Her bare breasts pressed against the arm of his coat.

"Now really . . ." Henderson said without feeling.

Sam regarded the preacher with cold sarcasm. "Have another puff on the pipe, Reverend!"

"I can't . . ." protested Henderson. The scent of the young woman was sweet in his nostrils. The touch of her arm against the back of his neck was warm and agreeable. Her full red lips were set against the lobe of his ear. He wanted to protest when the girl unbuttoned his black frockcoat. Instead, his mind reeled frightfully with jagged fragments of thoughts. His starched white shirt

440

was unbuttoned and, like a warm and golden snake, the girl's arm slipped inside the open garment. Henderson moaned with happiness and fell back onto the buffalo robe.

"Helluva waste," Sam grumbled to Washanti. "She's too good for a sky pilot."

The chief smiled with good humor. "Washanti has many maidens in the tepees."

Sam jerked his thumb to where Henderson was stretched out. "Better tell the girl to get him inside a lodge. Things are getting a bit racy."

Washanti spoke to the girl in their language. Smiling with brazen delight, she pulled the minister to his feet. Grinning foolishly, and walking as if over a field of eggs, Henderson was partially carried, partially guided into a large tepee at the edge of the camp. He stretched out, giddy and unable to control his mind, onto a thick bear robe.

Humming sweetly, the girl joined him. She raised up on her elbow, her lips coming down on his mouth. Henderson was surprised and pleased by her ardor. Her mouth was a wet and warm place as her lips kissed his mouth, the tip of his nose, gently touched his forehead. Time was distorted and, unable to clock its passage, Henderson figured a year passed while the young woman removed his clothes. Once he was nude, his bare skin thrilled to the furry touch of the bear skin robe. He opened his eyes and saw a silver shaft of sunlight beaming into the tepee. The rays illuminated the contours of her firm bottom. She rolled toward him, breasts falling against his chest, her thick dark bush pressing against his leg. Her hands gently moved up and down his body, touching here, caressing there. She touched him with a

441

sudden urgency that brought desire scurrying through his body.

"Ummm!" She said something in her tribal language, then giggled.

Henderson groaned with satisfaction as he grew and swelled. During the past four years he had questioned his power as a male. Now, although his mind was drugged by the loco weed, he held a pleasant sense of satisfaction. The Lord God Jehovah was merciful! He was sure his swelling member was larger than the tallest pine tree in the forest. Here he was with a beautiful young woman. She was certainly no more than twenty-one years of age, physically beautiful, and willing to provide him with pleasure long believed lost.

"Dear girl, I love you," he whispered. He pulled her mouth down onto his lips. Her hands continued their marvelous performance and, dizzily, he made sounds of approval. Then she rolled onto her back, opening her legs and surrendering to him. He was amazed to find his mind clearing as he mounted her with eagerness.

Oh! Greatness is here again! She's so tight and warm! Such strength in her limbs! Like a warm place where a person can hide forever, safe from the dangers of life! A furry little beast moving up and down, to and fro, bringing joy beyond comprehension! Oh God! I'm getting there! Almost there! Another instant! One more thrust . . .

With an explosion of energy, he fell forward onto her warm breasts. He lay with his head pressed against one warm globe, lips sucking hard against her tumescent nipple.

The girl said something unintelligible, then got up and disappeared outside the tepee. Henderson lay quietly and, outside the lodge, heard the sound of water being splashed about. Moments later, she returned with a small bone vessel filled with water. She washed his limp genitals and then lay down on the pallet beside him. To his surprise, Reverend James Henderson discovered that a second, even more intense, arousal was possible.

Eventually, he fell asleep in the young woman's arms.

"Don't, Jay!"

Jane Miller stiffened as the young man's hand cupped her knee. They were lying in Jay Samuels's wagon and had been kissing for almost an hour. Now, Jay Samuels was aroused and eager to slip his hand up her dress.

"Baby," Jay said huskily. "It doesn't matter! We're going to be married."

"We can wait 'til our wedding night!"

"I'm dying for you."

Jane suppressed the desire inside her. "I'm a good girl." She threw her arms around his neck, nuzzled her face against his chest.

Jay's hand moved higher along her bare legs, passing the knees and caressing her firm thighs. Jane whimpered. She brought her legs tightly together, pushed gently against his hand.

"Just this once," he pleaded.

"I won't go all the way."

"Just let me feel you."

"Then you'll want more."

"I promise."

Jane's legs opened a fraction of an inch. He pressed his fingers down into the warm, pliant flesh. Slowly, ever so gently, his hand moved toward the apex of her femininity.

He kissed her with a loving gentleness.

"You're special."

Jane twisted with pleasure when his fingers reached the silkiness between her legs. Throbbing with passionate desire, she undulated under the light pressure of his touch. Her legs widened.

Jay stopped for a moment and fumbled with the buttons of his trousers.

"Honey—" Jane whispered huskily.

"I love you, Jane."

"Remember, you said we won't go all the way."

"Don't worry, darling." Jay's hand was feverishly stroking her pubic area.

"I trust you. I really do," Jane told him.

Jay Samuels sighed.

"Oh shit," he said sadly.

The bugle sounded early the next morning. The emigrants ate a quick breakfast, yoked up their teams and prepared to roll out. The wagons were forming a column when Uncle Durgeon Adkins hobbled up to Steve Wellman.

"Can you find someone to take my place?" the old man inquired.

"You sick? Better get over and have Josh look you over."

"I got old age. He can't cure that." Uncle Durgeon rested his weight on his cane. "Talked to Bridger and his partner last night. They could use an extra man around here. I can cipher with the best of them and it won't be like I'm living on their charity."

"Then," said Steve, "you don't plan on going on to Oregon."

Uncle Durgeon spoke in a dry voice. "Appreciate you

444

letting me come this far. It means a lot to me. The thing is I figure this is far as I need to go. A man can sit in the sun around here, watch the pretty Indian women and die gracefully. This old hoss"—he thumped his chest with a fist—"ain't got too many winters left. Here's where I'd like to end them."

Steve looked out over the terrain.

"You picked a fine spot, Uncle," he told the old man.

"Sure is," Uncle Durgeon agreed. His eyes blinked back his tears. "I'd better say good-bye to the others." He stared fixedly at Wellman for a moment. "Good luck on the trip, son."

Sam Lawson came up as the old man walked away. The guide's eyes were bloodshot; his gait was slow and unsteady.

"Damnation! I'll never understand women," Sam roared. "Agnes just spent the last half hour gnawing on me!"

"She got her dander up?"

"Higher'n a pine tree. She's claiming I'm a hellhound bound for a lake of fire. A four-square sinner of the lowest sort." Sam dropped his voice to a confidential tone. "All I did was lay out with an Indian gal last night."

"I wondered where you went."

"Smoked the peace pipe with Washanti and sipped a little whiskey," Sam said. "Got the sky pilot higher'n a drunken hoot owl. Incidentally, he won't be coming with us. Woke up this morning with a terrible hangover. He's planning on preaching the gospel to Washanti's tribe. The truth is he got involved with a sweet little Indian gal. She made him into a man last night. In another six weeks, Reverend Henderson will be a pipe-puffing, whiskey-drinking squaw man."

"Uncle Durg is staying here, too."

Sam looked startled. "Sight of all those tits got to him. Well, he's a good old man. I'll go over and tell Washanti to look after him."

"He plans on staying here 'til he dies."

"He does, does he?" Sam lifted his haggard face. "Old man's wiser than I figured."

He squared his shoulders and moved off toward the Indian camp.

The sun was high in the morning sky when the caravan set off with renewed energy. Gladys and Hattie Gill took over the reins of the wagon handled by Uncle Durgeon Adkins. As the white-topped rigs moved westward, Uncle Durgeon stood near the gate of the fort and watched their passage. His eyes were moist when Chief Washanti walked up and, with elaborate ceremony, invited the old man into the Indian camp.

"We will feast on bear meat," said Washanti, "and then smoke the peace pipe. A wise man is respected by my people. Besides, there are some widows who have lost their men. They would love to have a man to care for, someone they can fuss over."

Uncle Durgeon pulled in his stomach and smiled.

THIRTY-THREE

Vivian Middleton realized that she had to travel fast. She held no firm idea of when, or where, she might reach an outpost of civilization. She knew the odds were against her getting out of the wilderness. Yet she had moved swiftly across the Rocky Mountains and was now traveling due west. Vaguely, she recalled the guidebooks with their maps of the Oregon Trail. That highway for prairie schooners swung north after reaching Fort Bridger. So Vivian assumed that holding a westerly course would bring her to the trail.

She rode hard every day. She rose early each morning and traveled until near sundown, stopping when she reached a protected shelter for the night. Those defensible places had been easily found in the mountains. Boulders, caves and niches of overhanging rocks were plentiful. Now she was out in sparsely covered sagebrush country, a terrain almost desertlike in its barrenness. Protected areas were scarce in this God-forsaken land. Wolves prowled during the night and she slept lightly, rising often to throw wood on her fire.

Although she had cursed the difficulty of crossing rain-swollen rivers, she now longed for a plentiful supply of water. She traveled blindly from waterhole to dry creek bed, from small springs with murky water to swampy bogs inhabited by swarms of mosquitos. She entertained a faint hope each morning that she would stumble across the trail that day. By early afternoon, her optimism had sunk to dark despair. Depression weighed heavily on her mind as darkness fell. She longed for the sound of a friendly human voice, prayed for the sight of a white person. She had lost considerable weight, often going for two or three days without food when she crossed the desert land. Despite her problems, she maintained a steely resolve to survive the ordeal.

One afternoon she topped a grassy ridge and saw four cabins at the forks of a distant river. She slid down from the pony and stood looking down into the valley. She sobbed, her eyes brimming with tears, and fell to her knees. She prayed her thanks to her Creator, then wiped her face and rode toward the outpost.

The four cabins belonged to Pegleg Smith, a fabled mountain man. A round-faced man of about fifty-five with a portly figure, Smith had been living among the Shoshone Indians for twenty-five years. Smith explained that his nickname, Pegleg, came from his wooden leg. Years before, he had been wounded in the leg. When gangrene set in, it became necessary for the mountain man to take up a saw and knife to cut off his infected limb. The arteries were sealed with a hot bullet mold.

"Prob'ly deserved havin' to do that," Pegleg said truthfully. "I was stealin' little Injun babies and sellin' 'em in Mexico for slaves."

When the hospitable mountain man heard of Vivian's ordeal, he proposed marriage. "A white woman could hep around the place," he explained. "Injun wives are lazy. Won't do a lick of work after they bin in a man's bed."

Vivian accepted his food and shelter, but gracefully turned down his offer. "I want to get to Oregon," she said. "I got a big account to settle with that snake who's my husband."

Pegleg accepted her vision of vengeance. "Gettin' awful late in the year," he said. "Figure the last train went past here 'bout a week ago. Gettin' late in the year. Your bunch prob'ly went by last week."

"Can I catch up with them?"

Pegleg deliberated. "Depends on how fast they is runnin'. I figure your pony is wore out. You look wore down to a nubbin. Ain't an ounce of extra fat on your bones. Now, seein' how you're stranded out in the wilderness, I might be willin' to make you a deal."

Vivian chilled. "I got a husband."

"And a scoundrel he is, too," Pegleg added. "I ain't interested in beddin' down with you. Lots of Injun girls are willin' to share my blanket. Not that I'll mind if you set some stock in it. The thing is, ole Pegleg has a sweet tooth. I just love to sink my lips into something sweet and juicy. Ain't had a good pie since I visited Independence two years ago. I'll pick some berries in the morning. You bake me a pie. Rest a couple days. Get some meat back on your bones. When you're ready to leave I'll get a couple Shoshone braves to ride with you 'til you reach the wagon train. They'll take you to Fort Hall. Afore you say no, them braves might be helpful settlin' accounts with that no-count husband of your'n."

Vivian said, "Pegleg, you just made yourself a deal."

* * *

One thought was in Steve Wellman's mind as the caravan pulled away from Fort Bridger. *Keep the wagons rolling!* The nights were chilly, even for the high plains and mountains. In a short while, the cold wind would carry snow down from the peaks. Steve made arrangements for Sam Lawson to keep busy hunting game. The area contained plenty of bear, antelope, elk and deer. Each day, a volunteer from the train accompanied Sam on the hunting expedition. They rode ahead of the caravan and dropped the meat at the evening's campsite.

Steve watched everyone for signs of fever or dysentery. Although most epidemics ended when the wagons crossed the continental divide, he figured caution was in order. Tirelessly, he pushed the emigrants to keep the wagons rolling. They made ten miles every day, sometimes fifteen. A celebration was in order when they covered eighteen or twenty miles of trail. Everything had to be just right to cover these long stretches. Therefore, long days were rare occasions. The temperament of the people improved when they rolled into the valley along the Bear River. High mountains rose to lofty heights on the northern rim of this great horseshoe-shaped area. The bottomlands along the river's banks were hip-deep in grass. The streams were full of fat trout. Flowers bloomed everywhere. Ripening berries could be picked as the wagons moved along the trail. As a result of this splendor, the people forgot their worries, ate heartily and remained calm and optimistic.

Awake or asleep, Steve Wellman was driven by his secret vision. He wanted the caravan to reach Fort Hall in record time. Once there, he planned to drop out of the train. Although he had not shared this decision with his wife, Steve planned to take the California Trail to the gold fields. His vision of a small farm in a fertile valley in Oregon had lost its luster. Clearing the land, planting a crop, erecting a house and barn, now sounded like back-breaking labor. Gold fever clouded his mind. He was enthralled with a vision of sudden riches. He had purposely withheld news of the gold strike from his fellow travelers. First, he needed time to think about this remarkable opportunity. Secondly, the people would spend every minute talking about gold. He wanted them moving at a rapid clip toward Fort Hall, not standing around yammering about gold. The good Lord knew how much Steve was thinking about gold, great wealth and a chance to make his mark on the world.

The wagon train rolled past Pegleg Smith's settlement without stopping. Lawson felt the mountain man was a rascal, not to be trusted. Smith controlled the Shoshone tribes that lived along the Bear River. His domination was absolute. Smith feared outsiders coming through the region. A stranger might try to wrest control of the Indians from the one-legged dictator.

"The Indians around here breed the finest horses in the west," Sam told the emigrants. "Ain't better horseflesh anywhere in the world. But ole Pegleg won't allow them to sell or trade horses to white men. He's angry about the families coming west. Figures they'll likely mess up his little kingdom. He's nothing but a child-stealing papoose thief and isn't fit company for decent folks."

The caravan rolled north into what is now the state of Idaho. They camped early one night near Soda Springs. The emigrants took buckets and bottles and rushed off to sample the fabled waters from the various springs. The men sampled the water gushing out of Beer Springs. The water had the vaguely surprising taste of lager beer. Women and children were delighted with the bubbly water from Soda Springs, adding sugar or honey to sweeten the taste.

While the others were away at the springs, Steve Wellman remained in camp. He helped Brad Payne repair a broken spoke in a wagon wheel. Payne's wagon was in a sad state, creaking under the weight of lead type and the heavy printing press being carried west.

They had just finished the job, greased the hubs and went off to wash their hands. As they stepped out of the box corral of parked wagons, Steve saw Mike Gorman riding up with a stranger on a large gray horse. When the man dismounted, he moved with a precise military gait. His posture was stiff and erect. His bearing was that of a man who gave orders, expected them to be instantly executed. He was about Mike's age, certainly not more than thirty.

The stranger wore a navy blue jacket with polished brass buttons. The flaring collar of his stiff white shirt was open, although a blue cravat peeked out of his jacket pocket. The stranger followed Mike and waited patiently until Steve had been introduced as the wagon captain. Only then did he extend his hand and speak.

"I'm Lieutenant Raymond Blair of the U.S. Navy, sir!" The man stood stiffly. "I am on a mission for the U.S. government and would appreciate sharing your camp with you tonight."

"You're welcome," Steve said.

The man acknowledged Steve's hospitality. "I appreciate your kindness. I am riding to Washington, D.C., as quickly as possible. We have warships in San Francisco harbor that have been abandoned by the crews. The captains did the best they could, but the men went over the side. Conditions in San Francisco are desperate. The harbor is filled with ships. Merchantships and men-of-war alike have been left there while the crews head for the gold fields."

Brad Payne looked sharply at the navy man. "Gold fields?"

Lieutenant Blair looked surprised. "Haven't you heard the news back here? They've struck gold in California, man. The whole territory is in an uproar. Everyone who can walk and carry a shovel is digging for the blasted metal. Good U.S. seamen jump ship and take off. We've lost two entire crews of able-bodied seamen. A Russian warship was abandoned off the coast north of San Francisco. The crew heard about the gold strike. The whole bunch went overboard in a single night. Even the first mate vanished. All the officers left. The only man aboard the next morning was the ship's captain. He's been anchored there for the last month, trying desperately to get another crew together."

"Gold!" Mike Gorman whispered the word.

"A great opportunity for our country," Lieutenant Blair went on. "But we're going through a chaotic time in California. There must be a hundred unmanned ships in the harbor. No one wants to be a seaman when fortunes are being made in the gold fields. Lord, man, I saw a nugget displayed on my last night in San Francisco. Two men had gone into the mountains on Monday. They were back in San Francisco Thursday night with two mules packed with gold. That nugget was the size of a man's fist. It assayed out for $5,200 in value!"

"Gold!" Brad Payne spoke reverently.

"I figured the word got back here by now," said the lieutenant. "My captain sent me to Washington to bring back another crew. Even if I succeed, it won't help us get our ship out of San Francisco. That crew will go over the side like our regular one. I've never seen anything like it. The trail from California to Fort Hall is a solid column of covered wagons. They were headed for Oregon, but changed their minds when news of the gold strike reached them. Those Hudson Bay people at the fort aren't helping matters. They're diverting everyone to California, figuring the U.S. won't be able to hold Oregon without a lot of settlers. They may be right."

"I'm going," Mike said with enthusiasm. "Damn it! A gold strike looks good about now."

"You won't like things when you get there," Lieutenant Blair went on. "An egg for breakfast costs $5. Two eggs and a slab of ham will cost about $15. That's for breakfast. The rest of the day's meals will cost more than that. Everything's in short supply. Men are willing to kill for a shovel and pick. Saws, hammers, nails and stuff to build a sluice box are worth their weight in gold. A pan for sifting river sand will sell for a $100—if you can find one! A pair of boots will cost about $200. You can't find a room anywhere at any price. The hotels in San Francisco rent rooms by the hour. Sleep for four hours and then the next guest is ready to use the room."

"Doesn't matter!" Mike's voice assumed a high Irish lilt. "A man can get rich finding gold!"

Brad Payne ventured, "Businessmen must be making a fortune."

Lieutenant Blair shook his head negatively. "Nobody is willing to work—except on their own digging gold. All kinds of businesses have been abandoned. The owners take off for the gold fields. They don't even stop to lock the doors. Of course, they're sold out to the bare shelves. The whole business and economic fabric of the territory has been under tremendous strain. Once I get to Washington and report to the Secretary of the Navy, and hopefully get a new crew, I have dispatches for the president. When I left the area was starting to have shortages of everything. We'll have a serious problem with food this winter. Thousands of people are coming in needing food and supplies and shelter. There's no one working on those problems. Gold has swept through their minds until the whole place is a madhouse!"

Mike Gorman was fairly bursting with enthusiasm. His eyes took on a feverish glaze. His hands and arms moved in an agitated manner. He could barely contain the excitement welling up inside. Finally, he took off running toward Beer Springs. He stopped suddenly a few yards from camp and yelled back: "I'll tell the others! They'll need to know!"

When the men of the caravan returned, their faces were bright with anticipation. They bombarded the lieutenant with numerous questions, listened raptly to his answers. The women returned from Soda Springs and added to the tumult.

"Jehoshaphat!" Elmer J. Johnson danced a hopping jig around the corral. "Gold in California! Pick it up off the ground! River beds are full of it!"

"I'm going!" Mike Gorman smiled broadly. He grinned at Molly. "Ain't we, darling?"

"Maybe," his wife answered quietly.

"I figure a man can run a print shop in California as well as Oregon." Brad Payne was speaking to Jay Samuels. The young Jew nodded sagely.

Steve did not let the turmoil deter him. He appointed guards for the night, informed everyone they would pull out at the usual time the next morning.

"Might as well rest over," said Dan Pitzen. "The trail to California won't be snowbound."

"That's not true," admonished Lieutenant Blair. "You have to cross the Sierra Mountains. They get snow early every year."

"I want to hear more about California," said Mike Gorman. "We can sleep some other time."

"Faster we get to Fort Hall, the quicker we head to the land of gold," said Pitzen.

Jay Samuels tugged at Lieutenant Blair's sleeve. The Naval man turned as the young man inquired, "You're sure about the shortages of goods?"

"They're out of everything."

"What about spices?"

"They'll need them."

"Needle and thread?"

"All the clothes have been bought up. They'll have to start mending right soon." The lieutenant asked, "Are you a storekeeper?"

Jay nodded in agreement. "My wagon's full of spices, notions and things like that. Even got a few boxes of hard candy."

Lieutenant Blair ignored the other emigrants. He looked solemnly at Jay Samuels. "I never like to run another man's life," he said.

"I would appreciate your advice."

"If it was me with a wagon load of that stuff," said the lieutenant, "I'd head for California. Set your prices triple—maybe four times—what you think the item is worth. Then double it! Fact is, I'd just move around town

456

a day or two and see what the other merchants are asking for something similar. Assuming they have anything left in stock. I'd sell everything and try my hand in the gold fields. That way, I'd have some money from the profits of my load. I'd have a chance to dig gold! If I didn't make a strike in a few weeks I'd figure a way of supplying a service or product to the miners. That's what I would do."

Jay smiled. "Thank you. Good luck on your trip back east."

As Jay walked away, the other emigrants clustered around the Naval officer.

"Look! I'd like to talk!" Blair held up his hand. "But I've got to get some sleep. I've been riding all day and have to leave early in the morning."

"I can give you a tent for the night," Wellman said.

"I'll just slip my bedroll under one of the wagons." Blair walked to where his gear and saddle lay on the side of the corral. Coming back, he saw the expression of disappointment on the emigrants' faces. "I'll stay for breakfast if you'll have me. We can talk some more in the morning."

A chorus of excited cheers greeted his words.

Steve made an announcement. "I won't tell you not to talk about the news," he told the emigrants. "Yammer all you want. But do it outside the camp. A few of us are going to try and get some sleep."

Sam Lawson came strolling up to Wellman. "The secret is out!"

"Thank God, we're close to Fort Hall."

"You going to Oregon?"

"The gold fields are for me."

"Me too. But I signed on to get this caravan to Oregon."

"Looks like the whole bunch are bound for California."

Sam grimaced. "Never happen. A couple of spoil sports will go for Oregon. They'll demand I show the way. Damn it! I'd sure like to ease down to the gold fields and look things over for myself."

"Maybe we can work something out," Steve suggested.

"Never went back on my word. But there's always a first time." Sam fingered the nugget in his pocket.

Pegleg Smith's mouth was full of pie. He had savored a large gooseberry pie and was now tasting Vivian's skills with blackberries. Pegleg washed the pie down with a great dipper of milk. He smiled and patted his round stomach.

"Best I ever et," he said with satisfaction. Vivian thanked him.

"Glad you like them. Can I get started tomorrow morning?"

Pegleg frowned. "What's your hurry?"

"I want to get started. Time's being wasted."

Pegleg cut another slice of pie. "Cookin' like this isn't wasted on me! You're the best pie baker I've ever seen. Might think about stayin' here through the winter. I've et better since you've started cookin' than I ever have before."

"We made a deal."

"That's true." Pegleg savored the sweetness of the pie in his mouth. "Pegleg ain't the sort to forget. Never go back on my word."

"Then," Vivian told him, "I'd like to leave tomorrow."

"Them Injun braves ain't back from their huntin'

trip," lied Pegleg. He stood up from the rude wooden table, thumped his hickory leg across the floor of the cabin. He filled a tin dipper with cool milk and returned to his chair. "You know how no-count shiftless Injuns are."

Vivian glared. "When can I leave?"

Pegleg leaned back. "Whyn't you bake me 'bout a dozen pies in the mornin'? Leave ole Pegleg with a few extras. Fortified with all that eatin', I'll have the strength to hunt up those Injuns."

"You're sure about this?" Vivian looked fixedly at Pegleg's eyes.

The mountain man did not blink. He speared another bite of pie. "Cross my heart! Ole Pegleg never lies!"

TWENTY-FOUR

Fort Hall, a trading post on the Snake River, was operated by the Hudson Bay Company. It was similiar to the outposts previously visited by emigrants along the trail. The stockade walls were a bit thicker and higher; the buildings were a trifle larger, contained glass windows, and were constructed with a solid dash of British colonial permanence. Outwardly, the post served as the center of trade in a radius of several hundred square miles. The customers were Indians and mountain men who traded furs and hides for essential supplies, whiskey, guns and ammunition, knives and beads. The rate of exchange for hides to store bought goods provided a solid profit for the company.

On the side, Fort Hall also served as a source of information for British authorities. Englishmen in the New World bitterly opposed the treaty giving Oregon to the United States. These colonial zealots hoped that in some yet unknown way they could neutralize the treaty. Their activities were orchestrated by an official in a small bureau in London. "Why," the official wrote to one operative in the northwest, "the rebels are lusting for land. They won't stop until they've got all the land from the Atlantic to Pacific Oceans. Even then, they may cast an eye north toward Canada. Do what you can to discourage people from settling in Oregon. We must protect the interests of the Crown in the Northwest."

As a result, the staff at Fort Hall provided emigrants with a dour view of Oregon's opportunities. The weather was bad there, they explained, with too much rain. The land was boggy. Transportation was bad; a farmer couldn't get his crops to market. They asked: What good is corn or wheat if you can't sell it? The Indians were getting hostile, had wiped out the Whitman mission, and were on the warpath against outlying farms. War parties rampaged all over Oregon, they claimed, and settlers were being killed, scalped or driven out. Plus the winter snow came early in Oregon. Mind you, a man was foolish to settle there and risk losing everything. True, there was this thing about Manifest Destiny. But a man had to watch out for his pocketbook. California was the place for a real farmer. Yesiree! Black land, plenty of water and sunshine the year round. A true paradise, a land of milk and honey!

The Englishmen diverted a few settlers with these tactics. Surprisingly, the emigrants who accepted the advice prospered in California. They sent letters back to Fort Hall, thanking the clerks for their efforts as guides. Despite these efforts at sabotage, settlers continued rolling into Oregon. Then the gold strike took place at Sutter's Mill and the whole world was going mad. People talked about nothing except getting rich quick in California.

When Steve Wellman led the caravan up to the gates of Fort Hall, they had traveled twelve hundred and eighty miles from Independence. It was now mid-August and the nights were getting chilly. Fort Hall was the last settlement on the two-thousand-mile journey to Oregon. When they poured into the store, however, the emigrants needed everything. But the first question they asked the company clerks was "What's the news?"

News? The company clerks paused and reflected on the question.

"Well sir, a man named Abraham Lincoln just turned down a chance to be governor of Oregon territory," said a young clerk.

There was plenty of news after that. The staff at Fort Hall was regularly supplied with newspapers from England and Canada. They told the most lurid details about the Whitman massacre, emphasizing that a settler in Oregon was at the mercy of Indians. Yesiree, the southern states back home were whispering about secession. Just a whisper now but those things sometimes grew to a shout. A lot of people had their dander up on the question of fugitive slaves. Is a darkie still a slave if he escapes to free territory? The Mexicans were still yammering about losing the war, desperately trying to figure a way to regain their lost territory. A smart man might figure the Southern states and Mexico would link up and give the north a real fracas.

"Forget that stuff," Steve Wellman growled with finality. "We want to hear about California and the gold strike."

"Heard about that one, huh?" grinned the clerk, whose name was Martin Woodhull. "A lot of people are forgetting Oregon and heading down the California Trail. They're splitting off at the Raft River, going across the Humboldt Desert. Won't say the trail is easy. There's plenty of bones there, for sure! But a man has something

462

when he gets to California. Gold's laying right there on the ground to pick up."

"What about getting from here to Oregon?" asked Dan Pitzen.

"About sixty per cent of the families are still going up there," the clerk admitted truthfully. "The trail is horrible. The first crossing of the Snake River is like gambling with death. You may make it, maybe not. A lot of wagons have been lost at that crossing. Beyond that, you got a hard run until you reach the Blue Mountains where the trail just sort of peters out. Some time back, old Joe Meek tried to find a better passage through the Blues heading west. Don't know what happened to him and the wagon train. Some say the whole thing was lost. Others say Meek's living good in Oregon right now. Lord, why take the chance? Oregon's nothing but a wasteland with a hundred years to go before it improves. California has been settled and proved up for a hundred years. We have men here every summer from California to convince people to forget Oregon and take the California Trail."

"What about the gold?" demanded Elmer J. Johnson.

"Lots of people headed for the diggings," replied the clerk. "Even thinking about going myself. 'Cept I have a contract with ole Here Before Christ that runs another two months. Been trying to talk my way out of it a bit earlier."

"Many people going to the gold fields?" Mike Gorman pressed forward.

"Soon as the news was out, everyone headed in that direction."

"No one going into Oregon?"

The clerk shrugged. "You got a few diehards in

every crowd."

By now, the women and children were gathered around the clerk. They tried to crowd into the small store building until, finally, the clerk came from behind the counter and went outside. He went through the news about the gold strike again for latecomers. It would be another month before the information was printed in newspapers in Washington and Baltimore. More time would pass before the gold strike was mentioned on the floor of Congress, that event occurring on December 5. When the news finally hit the eastern states, the information had the power of a whirlwind. The republic was shaken to the foundation as people scrambled to be the first in the gold fields.

While the group discussed the news, a small party of rugged mountain men rode through the gates of the stockade. Their horses were trail weary, looking well spent and bedraggled. The group was led by a grizzled old man of indeterminate age. His deep blue eyes twinkled beneath his long white hair as he jumped off his horse. He stopped and gave orders for the other men in his party to tend to a string of pack mules accompanying their party. Before he turned his horse out to pasture, the old man pulled a heavy canvas sack off the animal's back.

Sam Lawson advanced toward the old man. "Hey, Caldwell! What brings you this far east?"

"Looking for supplies." The old man extended his hand. They shook.

"Sit down. Share some grub and tell me about what's happening in California." Sam said.

"Got some trading to do first," the old man grunted. He walked up to Martin Woodhull, the Hudson Bay Company clerk. "You got any supplies?"

"A few."

Caldwell threw his sacks on the ground. "Buy everything you got for a premium price."

"Well, now—" Caldwell blurted.

"I need shovels, picks, axes, flour, meal, sugar—whatever you got!"

"We're running low."

The old man kicked the two sacks. "There's gold in there, son! Real honest-to-god California gold! Don't tell me I've left the gold fields for nothing. We got to have supplies. I'll pay a hundred in gold for an ax! A hundred for a shovel! Same pay for a pair of blankets! An ounce of gold for a few sardines! A half ounce for a fresh egg! Give you three hundred in gold for a gallon of liquor! An ounce for a box of pills! A thousand dollars for a barrel of flour! Same for pork, sugar, coffee, pork, beef or whatever you got to sell!"

"You must be—" blurted an onlooker.

"Crazy! Not likely," cackled the old timer. "Money ain't nothing in California. We can get all the gold we want. Yesiree, all we want. But we need things to eat, tools to work with and shovels to dig that yellow stuff!"

The old man's name was Tom Caldwell. Fortified with a jug of whiskey, he stood in the compound and seemingly magnified the truth about California's gold. He offered gold to the emigrants for skillets, cooking pans, anything that could be used to pan out more gold. He wanted to buy saws, nails, axes, hammers, picks and even complete wagons. Why, that stuff back in California could be used to dam and divert the rivers, laying bare whole ledges of gold. They needed shovels to scoop up the precious metal. The miners were running low on food. They'd buy anything at a dollar a pound. More if it was something tasty like a delicacy. Caldwell wanted to buy oxen, packhorses, and wagons. They would pay a good wage to any man able to handle livestock and head for California.

"The old way's gone," Caldwell roared. "Ain't no use measuring life with a teaspoon. Why, people won't work for a paltry four bits a day. Not even for ten dollars a day! I used a beat-up old iron spoon and panned out eight hundred in gold in a morning. Took out four thousand before Wednesday one week. Why, everything a man has never dreamed about can come true."

Mike Gorman asked, "Are you rich?"

Caldwell whooped. "Ain't ever going to work no more. Lordy! There's gold everywhere in California. The whole human race can quit grieving and be happy. Ain't no need to worry. Mister" —he pointed his finger at Mike— "has life done you a few bad turns? You been disappointed? Getting tired of craving things you can't have? Worried about being rich enough to support yourself in your old age? Only one answer for that. Gold! Gold! Gold! I'll guide anybody who cares to join this millennial day in paradise! Take you west with us. We be leaving just as soon as we can get supplies and load up our pack mules."

While the others crowded around Caldwell, Jay Samuels went back to his wagon. The vehicle was worn and creaking by now, the paint worn away from felly, spoke and hub, the sides covered with dust, the canvas top stained with debris from the trail. He gazed at the rig with affection. The wagon spokes had been wedged to hold them tight. Each evening he had to pour water on the wood to keep it swollen tight. The rims were bound with hide, worn away at the edges where the iron gave no covering. He had reset the iron rims almost every day along the trail. He shook the nearest wheel to test the hub.

Jane came up. "You going to California?"

"Maybe," he said. "I ain't sure. One part of me wants to hurry over there to cash in on the gold fields. Another thing says a man shouldn't change his plans so sudden like. Maybe these people are lying. The gold could play out tomorrow. A man would be high and dry in California then."

"I don't know," Jane said wistfully. "No use holding to a plan if something better comes along. We've all come West to better our lot in life."

"I just don't know."

"You'll have to decide pretty soon."

He took her arm and led her around the wagon, out of sight of the other emigrants. "Going to California will separate us," Jay said.

Jane started. "We can get married before we go."

"True," he agreed. "But I wouldn't want to take my bride into the gold fields."

"I'm tough and strong as any man," Jane insisted.

"It wouldn't be right!"

Jane blinked back tears. "You're just saying that to run away from me!" Her voice was sullen.

Jay kissed the tip of her nose. "You could go to Oregon with Agnes. I could write when I get settled in California. You could come there when I've made my mark."

"Jay Samuels!" Jane stomped her foot. "I won't hear of that!"

"Or I can come to Oregon to get you."

Jane turned away, crying. She ran to her wagon, crawled inside and lay atop a large trunk and sobbed.

*   *   *

467

Sam Lawson struck a deal with Tom Caldwell and the Fort Hall clerks. The emigrants would be allowed to purchase their necessary supplies from the store at normal prices. Whatever was left on the shelves could be purchased by Caldwell and his Californians. Word went out for the families to purchase their supplies, whether they planned on going to Oregon or California. When their shopping was completed, Tom Caldwell and his men swept the remainder of the merchandise off the shelves. They loaded up their pack mules, then went out into the wagon train to barter for goods.

Twilight brought a wispy gray fog rising off the meadow floor. Steve Wellman went around to each wagon, calling for a council meeting after supper. Presently, a thin slice of silver moon shone through the clouds as the emigrants gathered for a meeting. Steve Wellman briefly outlined their situation.

"We can't waste time here because winter's coming on," he explained. "Tom Caldwell and his bunch are pulling out tomorrow. They'll guide anyone who wishes to go to California. No charge. I'll call out your name and you say where your plan on heading. Sam has a contract to take the train to Oregon. He'll guide you there as we originally planned."

Sam cast a baleful glance in Wellman's direction. "Let's all go to California," he suggested.

We'll see." Steve's eyes fastened on Mike Gorman's eager face. "What about you, Mike?"

The Irishman brightened. "I'm heading for the diggings."

"Bruce Middleton?"

"Nothing in Oregon for me."

Across the way, Melissa gave a tight gasp of disappointment. She started to say something, then her lips tightened. She walked wordlessly away from the group.

"Excuse me," Bruce Middleton told the crowd. "I got something to do." He headed out after Melissa.

Steve asked, "What about you, Josh?"

"Skip me for now. I ain't sure."

"Agnes Miller."

She stood up and spoke in a strident voice. "Oregon."

Sam growled. "I knew it! I knew someone would have to go to Oregon!"

Everyone laughed loudly at the guide's predicament.

"You signed to take us there," Agnes said pointedly.

"Be fair!" Sam pleaded. "I didn't know about the gold!"

"I'm going to Oregon," Agnes insisted.

Sam groaned. "All right. I'll see you get there."

"Elmer Johnson."

The man from Illinois stammered. "Well . . . I . . . my wife says we're going to Oregon!" He glowered at his mate, then retreated into the shadows.

"Brad Payne?"

The printer spoke quickly. "California. I can set up shop there as well as in Oregon. Sounds like there will be plenty of news to print."

"Lonnie Thompson?"

The young man who had come to the caravan with Uncle Durgeon Adkins smiled shyly. "California. That is if Mr. Middleton wants his extra wagon to go there."

"Eric Potter?"

"I'll ride along with Lonnie if we can go."

"Dan Pitzen?"

The gambler was wearing a gray frockcoat and trousers. Wellman wondered how he managed to look so clean and unsoiled.

"I have a few things to say about this California deal," Pitzen said. "As some of you know, I used to be a gambler on a riverboat. A very exciting life. But excitement always brings danger. Chances are, everyone who goes to California has the expectation of getting rich. You want to grab that quick, easy money. I've heard a lot of talk about gold the past few days. Most of it is plain lies! There may be riches in California—but you'll pay a hard price to get part of it. I've heard the oldtimers on the river talk about a gold rush over in the Carolinas. A lot of wildness took place there. Shoot-outs, claim-jumping and downright murder over a piece of ground or a poke of gold dust. Erica and I came out here to find a better life. We're going on to Oregon as we intended. Oregon may be a little slower than the action in the gold fields. That's just fine with us. We want to live the rest of our lives with dignity in a respectable community. We want to establish a home in Oregon and help this country grow."

The gambler's words were interrupted by a chorus of noisy cheers from the women.

" . . . No schools in California!" cried a young mother.

" . . . We started for Oregon. We'll go there!" added another woman.

" . . . We got young'uns to raise!" A young wife looked sternly at her awed husband. "We can't drag them off to hunt gold!"

" . . . Let's go where women and kids got a chance," yelled another mother.

Dan Pitzen's remarks had electrified the women. Under their prodding, the rest of the emigrants reluctantly gave up their dreams of instant riches. To a man, they voted for settling in Oregon.

After the meeting ended, Sam Lawson strolled over to where Dan Pitzen was surrounded by grateful wives. After the women had expressed their thanks, Sam smiled wryly at the gambler.

Pitzen cringed slightly under the guide's malevolent gaze.

"It wasn't my fault, Sam," Pitzen said. "Families should go to Oregon. The gold fields are no place for women and kids. A man who gets there and doesn't find gold will be in a fix."

"It won't be that bad."

"A few people got rich in the Carolina rush. Most died poor."

Sam persisted. "But all you have to do is pick it off the ground."

"You truly believe that?"

"Caldwell brought in two sacks this afternoon."

Pitzen indicated he was not impressed. He added, "Caldwell will need a wagonload of nuggets to pay the prices he was quoting. Who ever heard of three hundred dollars for a jug of whiskey? That's craziness."

Sam smiled slightly. "That does seem a bit out of line."

"When do we pull out for Oregon?"

"Get some sleep," Sam advised. "We'll get started early in the morning."

Vivian Middleton stomped around the cabin. She glared across the room to where Pegleg Smith sat at his rude wooden table. The mountain man had been drinking most of the afternoon. Now, he was eating yet another of her fresh-baked pies, letting the drippings fall down his bewhiskered chin.

"Eat it up, you ole coot!" cried Vivian. "I'm not

cooking another pie until you keep your bargain."

Pegleg cut another slab of pie, held the slice aloft. "Best I ever ate. Vivian, you're a great cook."

"No more!" She roared, clenched fists on her hips. "I want my pony. I've been here almost a week. You're nothing but a pie-eating old fool! Pie! Pie! Pie! I must've cooked twenty of those damned things for you."

"And every one better'n the last," Pegleg said.

"Where's my pony?"

"Injuns took him away for pasture."

"I want a horse to get out of here."

Pegleg shrugged. "All gone to pasture."

"Which direction?" she asked. "I'll go get them."

"Settle down, missy." Pegleg's voice became hard. "Don't act like a wife and brow-beat ole Pegleg. I get riled up, I might beat you over the head with my peg leg. Down't Independence the last time, I cleaned out a whole saloon of yahoos. Nearly beat 'em to death with my leg. Now"—he grinned—"I like a woman like you. Too much vinegar to be worth much between a man's blankets. Pegleg don't like the sour kind. You would yammer a man into killin' you. I've been thinking about your husband these past few days. Sure have, missy. At first, I figured he must've been harder'n nails to abandon you with the tribes. But ole Pegleg knows now that feller was right smart. Leave a vinegary woman in the wilderness. Bet that little filly he's got is sweet and tender. Make a man just drool to think about her!"

Vivian snorted. "No more pies!"

"I think tomorrow," Pegleg mused, "we'll try another gooseberry. I surely do love the taste of juicy berries."

"You ain't letting me go?"

"Not whilst the berry bushes are full," Pegleg confessed.

"That means you're holding me a prisoner."

Pegleg nodded in agreement. "Well, Missy, you figured things out. I figured a smart vinegary woman would get the lay of the land. Took you a while, it did. But I got some serious drinkin' to do. You best get out with my Injun women and pick some gooseberries."

Vivian glowered. "Go to hell!"

The mountain man's hard hickory leg thumped against the cabin wall. "I been beatin' women for a spell. Keeps a squaw in line. Missy, your job is to keep ole Pegleg happy. Quit doin' that and I'll sell you to a Shoshone brave. Make an enemy for life, but I can use the money. Step lively now and hurry back with some pie fixin's."

Sullen with anger, Vivian grabbed a wooden bucket and went to find Pegleg's Indian woman. Darkness was already falling, but she knew the mountain man would demand a fresh pie for breakfast. She knew Smith's character well enough to know he would punish her unmercifully if a pie was not baked by morning.

Dang Your Soul was the name Pegleg had affixed on the frightened Indian woman who lived with the mountain man. She was a quiet, taciturn woman of about thirty years. Both women had conspired for the last couple of days for Vivian to leave. Dang Your Soul told the white woman that Pegleg had sent the horses to a Shoshone village nearby.

"He no want you go," she said in broken English.

"Can't we steal a horse?" Vivian inquired.

"Pegleg know you want go," Dang Your Soul explained. "Horses tied up. Braves watch all time. Pegleg kill man who lose horse you steal."

The night air chilled the women as they walked away from the settlement. They followed a rutted road over to the Oregon Trail. Dang Your Soul explained that a large patch of gooseberries had ripened beside the trail in the past two days.

"Get fixin' stuff quick," she explained.

The two women slapped at mosquitos, picked berries and lamented about Vivian's captivity. They were intent on their conversation and did not hear the rumble of wagon wheels until the rig was almost beside them. Then, Vivian turned with a happy glance and saw a solitary prairie schooner rolling north along the trail. Dropping her bucket, she ran down the road and waited for the wagon to top a small rise.

The man on the wagon seat reined in his team of oxen. The flash of a gun barrel glistened in the moonlight. Vivian heard the click of a hammer being cocked on the rifle.

"Who're you?" the man inquired.

"Don't shoot!" Vivian ran forward. "I'm a white woman."

The gun did not waver.

"What're you doing out here?"

Sobbing, Vivian blurted out her story. She had really just got started on the recitation when the man cleared his throat. "I ain't got a week, lady. What do you want me to do?"

"Take me away from here."

The man slapped the wagon seat beside him.

"Climb on board."

"We may be followed."

The man held the rifle aloft. "Old Betsy will stop them!"

Vivian crawled up on the wagon. In the moonlight she caught a glimpse of the man's tired sunken eyes. He appeared ready to drop over from exhaustion.

"Lord, I never expected anybody coming along this late," Vivian said.

"Running late," the man admitted. "Had some trouble with my wagon. Tore a wheel off crossing a creek. All by myself and had a devil of a time fixing it."

"I'm Vivian Middleton."

The man grinned at her. "Clay Gill's my name."

THIRTY-FIVE

Agnes Miller was angry and worried. Melissa had gone off early in the evening without saying anything. Returning around midnight, the girl walked back into camp with Bruce Middleton by her side. When Agnes berated him for ruining Melissa's reputation, Bruce grinned sheepishly and put his arm around the girl's waist.

"Don't worry, Miss Miller," he said calmly. "Me and Melissa are getting married. We talked everything out. We're both for it. We'd like your permission."

Agnes was thunderstruck. She gazed at the couple with a look of dismay and wonderment.

"We're in love," Melissa explained.

Agnes turned to Middleton. "You're old enough to be her father."

"Age doesn't matter when you're in love," he answered.

"You're too old for her." Agnes felt betrayed.

Melissa giggled. "He's young enough for me."

Agnes fretted. "What if I don't give my permission?"

Bruce's expression was distressed.

"We sort of hoped you would," he answered.

"She's still high-toned and uppity," Melissa said, anger creeping into her voice. She moved closer to Bruce. "We don't need permission. You can't boss me forever."

"Agnes, we—" Bruce began.

"Leave her be," Melissa interrupted.

Agnes took a deep breath, inhaling the cool night air. She ignored Melissa's remark and turned to Middleton. "Your wife may still be alive," she told him. "I can't let Melissa marry a man who may have a wife. True, Vivian probably won't ever show up and the Indians probably killed her. But Sam never said she was dead. Did you see her die?"

Bruce shook his head. "No. She was alive the last time I seen her."

"Besides," Agnes went on, "You haven't spent enough time in mourning."

Bruce acknowledged the truth of her statement. "Sure, we're rushing things a bit. That's to be expected. Things happen fast out here. We ain't back home. The people there got time to wait. Things are set up and established. They can fiddle-faddle around. We could have waited longer if I was going on to Oregon. But I'm heading for California. Me and Melissa got to get hitched up. Otherwise, our trails split and we may never see each other."

Agnes shrugged. "You said it wasn't necessary to have my blessing. Since you're hell-bent to do it, I'll give you my permission. Just be kind to Melissa because she's a very special person. Sometimes full of the devil, doesn't always mind, but still a very nice girl."

Liquid joy shone in Melissa's eyes. She embraced Agnes and the two women cried. Bruce looked on foolishly, wondering what he should do.

Bruce and Melissa were married the next morning. Right after breakfast, Bruce crawled up into his wagon and dressed in his Sunday clothes. He came down wearing a black wool suit, white shirt with stiff collar, cravat and stickpin.

Melissa's wedding gown was her newest gingham dress, ruffled in back with a ribboned bow around the bodice. She entered the stockade a few minutes after the groom. She carried a bouquet of freshly picked flowers. Her hand rested on Sam Lawson's arm.

"Why pick me to give you away?" Sam growled in a low whisper.

Melissa smiled prettily, speaking out of the side of her mouth. "You're my stepfather," she whispered.

"Christ!" Sam blurted out. "I forgot about that."

The manager of the fort performed the ceremony, reading eloquently from a printed form supplied by Hudson's Bay Company. When the manager blessed the couple, pronounced them man and wife, everyone rushed in to congratulate the newlyweds. Tom Caldwell and the Californians wanted to open a whiskey barrel, kill and roast an ox, throw a real celebration for the couple.

"Never saw a prettier bride in all my born days," whooped Caldwell. "This calls for a real shindig."

"Maybe later," said Sam. "We got to get rolling."

Undeterred, Caldwell rummaged in his gold bags, came up with a nugget the size of a pullet egg.

"To the loveliest woman in the West," he said grandly, presenting the gold to Melissa.

After everyone had wished the couple a long and happy

life, the women went back to their wagons. The men slapped Bruce on the back, looked enviously at the bride and wondered how she was in bed. Later, after the caravan pulled away from Fort Hall, Melissa sat happily on the wagon seat beside her husband. Her small hands clutched the stems of her bridal bouquet.

Bruce chided, "You got to throw them away some time."

"Never!" Melissa cast a saucy glance in his direction. "I'll press them in a book. They'll be my keepsake until I'm dead and gone."

"No regrets?"

"None at all." Melissa sighed with happiness. "I've never been a wife before. Just wait until tonight. I'm going to pull you into our tent and . . ."

The caravan stopped briefly to view American Falls, a towering cascade of water in the Snake River. Everyone picked up samples of black rock that lay around the edge of the falls. Then the wagons pulled out into the sagebrush desert, leaving a trail of heavy dust. The distance to Cassia Creek was traversed in two days. They camped at this junction point where the California and Oregon Trails split.

Tom Caldwell explained that Cassia Creek led to the Raft River. "Then the road runs across the desert and into the Sierra Mountains," he told the emigrants. "It's a long jump and a dry one. The Oregon Trail don't offer much comfort. It's a bit longer, not so dry, but runs through some of the awfulest country that God ever slapped down on this earth."

Heated discussion arose that night among the families. Men tried desperately to change their wives' minds. The women held firm for Oregon. Defeated and disgusted, the men grumbled about Dan Pitzen and his speechmaking. All that yammering about respectability had caused the wives to vote for Oregon.

"Why," roared Joe Halsey, safely out of earshot of his wife, "Pitzen's nothing more than a tinhorn gambler. What's he know about decent folks living right?"

"True," Elmer Johnson answered prudently. "But we did set out for Oregon."

"Every furrow plowed in Oregon costs a lot of blood and bone."

"Same can be said for California gold."

Halsey eyed his companion suspiciously. "You taking up for Pitzen?"

"Just stating facts," Elmer replied. "Oregon looked real good until we heard about the gold fields."

Halsey picked up a long piece of sagebrush. He whittled away at the stem.

"Best booger in the caravan is ole Bruce Middleton," Halsey offered, enviously. "Got rid of his yammering wife. Bet there's some hidden stuff about her being left out there with the Indians. Specially when he come back with that hot little piece, Melissa. Got rid of an ole hag, trading her for a sweet tight little pussy. Yesiree, Bruce Middleton's the smartest of the bunch. Don't you think so?"

"She's awful pretty."

Halsey pointed his knife blade toward Jane and Jay Samuels standing a short distance away by the river bank. The young couple were heatedly arguing, gesturing with their hands.

"Poor Jane!" Johnson sounded sad. "Jay's headed for the gold fields. She's going on up to Oregon.

"Thunderation! She's interested in a Jew?"

"Seems like a pretty good man."

"Still a Jew," Halsey insisted. "They're crooks! Cheat a man in a deal."

"Probably good and bad ones," Johnson commented. "I met some good peddlers who come through Shawneetown. Hard-working folks! Always traveling from farm to farm, carrying everything on their backs. I don't know how they did it. Must've been bone tired at the end of a day."

"Their prices are always too high."

"How old are you, Halsey?"

"Thirty-five."

"How far from town did you live?"

"'Bout twenty miles."

"They probably carried whatever you need to your doorstep on their backs."

"Still too high." Halsey shaved the sagebrush stem into nothing. He closed his knife, slipped it into his pocket. "Besides, you saying you'd let your kids take up with a Jew?"

At that precise moment, Elmer J. Johnson became his own man. His mind flashed with images of that dreadful night in Shawneetown. He saw the jeering faces of men who were his friends—a blood-lusting mob thirsting for his blood. Friends! They were willing to kill for a single transgression. He was shocked to realize such violence had been directed at certain people for centuries. The Jews had been stoned since before the time of Christ. If they were not available to quench the blood lust, then the darkies, Irishmen, Mexicans, Chinamen or poor white trash would do.

Johnson stood up. He looked down at Halsey with a

481

contemptous expression.

"You're a sorry specimen of humanity," Johnson said.

Halsey was surprised. Shock registered on his face.

"Jesus! What'd I do?" he asked lamely.

Johnson pointed to the young couple. "I see Jane and Jay trying to work out a problem of love over there," he snapped. "You see something dark and nasty. There's a sickness in your brain, Halsey, a bad sickness."

"You like Jews?" Halsey was unable to fathom the anger in Johnson's tone.

"Live and let live," Johnson said. "Don't keep yammering about people. So Bruce and Melissa got married. Maybe they'll find a little happiness. Maybe not. You shouldn't set yourself up as the supreme judge of other people's business."

Halsey screwed his face into a painful expression.

He asked, "I've been doing that?"

"Sounds like it to me."

Halsey considered the matter for a long interval. He smiled sheepishly, then said: "Maybe you're right, Johnson. I have been kinda looking for the worst side of people. That's a bad habit, ain't it?"

Johnson patted Halsey's shoulders. "But one that can be broken. We got too many problems in this world without adding to them."

Halsey got up and the two men walked back into the wagon camp.

For the rest of the evening, Jane Miller directed her wrath toward Jay Samuels. She fumed and fretted, alternately became aloof, sullen, resentful, angry, loving and tearful. After a tearful goodnight kiss, Jane walked limply to her tent. She rolled and twisted in her bedroll and considered the unfairness of the world. She decided God was biased against good girls. Melissa was a good case study on that subject. She had always been crazy about men, constantly flirting, smiling and wiggling her hips to attract their attention. She'd often slipped away from the house in Natchez to meet with boys and, sometimes, older men. Jane had remained prim and proper, followed Agnes's instructions, and truly believed what the preachers said about wickedness. Their sermons claimed a wanton woman would be punished for tempting men. Virtuous women would be rewarded.

Jane had been shocked by the marriage. Bruce might be an old man, she figured, but he was a living, breathing husband. Jane couldn't imagine kissing an old man like Bruce Middleton. He must be at least forty years old! That was positively ancient. Nevertheless, Melissa was off to California with a new husband. In a few weeks, more than likely, she would be rich. She'd wear diamonds on every finger, lead Bruce around like a pet dog, and live like a queen in regal splendor.

And what had her life of goodness brought?

A suitor named Jay Samuels, who was leaving her and heading off to the California gold fields. All she could see in the future was the dirty old Oregon Trail, the company of loutish farmers and more of Agnes and her goody two shoes bromides. She knew it was going to happen! Jay would meet up with a rich hussy and he'd forget her. Just like that! A wicked woman would bat her eyelashes, flirt outrageously and get her man.

Then she recalled what Sam Lawson had said to her one day. She had cried after a wagon ran over a small, feisty little dog belonging to Polly Johnson.

"It isn't fair," she whimpered. "He was such a cute

little thing."

Sam had patted her shoulder. "Remember one thing and you'll get through life a lot easier. Nothing's fair in this world. Don't ever expect fairness. You won't find it."

Jane buried her face in her pillow. Sam had sure been right.

The next morning at breakfast, Tom Caldwell regaled the emigrants with a story about California. "This'll be your last chance to change your plans," he told the Oregon group. "You're going to miss some wonderful climate out in California. Like, I know an old man who is about two hundred and fifty years old. He is a rich old coot, having dug a lot of gold and silver out of the mountains. Some of these early settlers knew about the gold. They just kept tight-lipped about it, so's the whole world wouldn't catch on. Well, as might be expected, the old man's relatives got to fidgeting. They wondered when he would die and leave his property to them. So his relatives decided that they'd send him to England for a holiday, that'd he'd die over there and they'd get his property legal. Well he went, he died and the relatives held a big party celebrating their good fortune. Except the old man left orders for his body to be shipped back to California for burial. So when his coffin come back, they buried him in California like he asked. But as soon as he got a whiff of that California dirt, he came back to life again! 'Pone my honor if he ain't alive and mining gold out there right today!"

The emigrants laughed.

"Enjoy a tall story," chuckled Elmer Johnson.

"Pretty good one," Dan Pitzen agreed.

"It is the honest truth," Caldwell insisted with a straight face. "California does that to folks."

The wagons were packed. It was time to roll out, yet the emigrants were reluctant to make the split. Women hugged and said tearful farewells, the men joked and slapped each other's shoulders. Jane Miller stood by the edge of the column of wagons, tearfully clinging to Jay Samuels's coat sleeve.

"I'll never see you again," she whimpered.

"I'll be sure to write when I get there." He could barely contain the sadness welling up into his throat.

"You might get hurt. Maybe killed."

"Jane, I love you. I'll keep in touch." He bent and brushed his lips across her forehead. "Good-bye."

Crying aloud, Jane took one last look at his face. She wheeled and ran to her wagon and crawled inside the dusty canvas top. Moving with leaden feet, Samuels walked off and crawled up on his wagon.

Steve and Cynthia Wellman shook hands with Sam Lawson. They expressed their gratitude to the guide.

"We'll miss you," Cynthia said.

Sam sniffed. "I'll get these folks to Oregon and be right down to the gold fields. First thing I'll do is hunt you up."

"Do that." Steve's voice cracked with emotion.

"How you going to find us?" Cynthia wondered.

"Leave word with Caldwell. He's known to everybody. I'll find him, then get the news about you."

Mike and Molly came up and said a tearful farewell to Lawson.

"I'll send you a nugget, Sam," Mike crowed in a lilting Irish brogue.

Sam grinned. "I'll bring extra rations down from Oregon. You'll need something to eat when I get there."

Caldwell yelled from the other side of the column. "All heading for California, fall in line behind me."

Dr. Josh McDonald was in the Oregon column. When he heard Caldwell's shout, McDonald made a sudden decision. He pulled his rig out of the line and rolled in behind Caldwell.

"You going?" Lawson yelled.

McDonald laughed. "Might as well. I'm not tied down. Might as well see what a gold rush is like."

Steve Wellman pulled in behind the doctor's wagon. Next, Bruce and Melissa swung into line. They were followed by Mike and Molly Gorman's rig. Lonnie Thompson and Eric Potter could barely contain their excitement as they pulled Middleton's extra wagon into the California line.

Steve went back to catch Jay Samuels pulling his wagon into line.

"You're going to eat dust anyway," he told Samuels. "I'd feel better if you brought up the rear. Gladys and Hattie might have trouble. This way, you'll be behind them if something happens."

"They're going?" Samuels looked puzzled.

"Afraid so. Sam won't take them to Oregon. They're driving the wagon that belonged to the Ordmans."

Samuels pulled around as the two women moved into the column. Gladys handled the reins like an experienced drover; Hattie sat quietly beside her mother and silently prayed for God to talk to her. When Wellman got back to his wagon, Caldwell motioned to the other Californians. They rode horses and were leading several pack mules.

"California Ho!" cried Caldwell.

The wagons moved sluggishly down the trail. The Oregon Company remained fixed and watched their friends thread a dusty path through the sagebrush.

Finally, Sam galloped past the wagons for a quick visual inspection. He returned to the front of the column, waved his arms and yelled.

"Roll out to Oregon!"

THIRTY-SIX

Vivian Middleton paced the floor of the sutler's store at Fort Hall like an angry panther. The object of her ire was her husband, Bruce Middleton, who had gone and married that little bitch. Vivian ranted to anyone who would listen about that scoundrel's shortcomings and misdeeds. The Hudson Bay Company clerk, Martin Woodhull, Clay Gill and the manager of the fort were her audience. They listened with wide-eyed wonderment as Vivian delivered a long recitation of Bruce's rascality.

"Now he's gone and committed bigamy!" Vivian roared. "Took up with that piece of trash, swilling around like a hog rutting for slop!"

"Ma'am," said the manager. "He seemed like a good man."

Vivian speared him with a baleful glance. "A fine judge of character you are!"

"We didn't know," said Martin Woodhull. "Figured they wanted to get married. The other people in the caravan should have spoken up."

"They're in cohoots with him!" Vivian trembled with rage.

"Calm down," Clay Gill said in an authoritative voice. "You'll catch up with him someday. I'm heading for California. That's where they're going. The law will hang his hide."

"You sure they headed for California?" Vivian looked doubtful.

"Not positive," admitted Martin Woodhull. "People can change their minds right up to the Raft River cutoff."

Vivian simmered. "If that low-life said California, then he's probably high-tailing it to Oregon. Worthless! A mealy-mouthed coward who abandoned his wife in the wilderness to the Indians. Left me there to die! Throwed me out like a worn-out dishrag! Took up with that hussy and—"

"Vivian!" Clay Gill's voice snapped like whip. "Calm down! You keep jabbering like this and I'll leave you here."

Martin Woodhull spoke quickly. "Ma'am, we ain't got accommodations for ladies."

Vivian walked over and sat down on a cracker barrel. A few weeks before, she had been a well-fed and rounded matron. Now, travel through the wilderness had taken a toll of her body. She was as slender and lean as the day she left the farm and married Bruce Middleton. She sat desolately while Clay Gill dickered for supplies. The sutler's stores had been wiped out. Food was scarce except for the herd to feed the manager and clerks through the winter.

"I'll give you a few things," the manager said, at last. "Just enough to get by. And you'll have to shoot game along the trail."

Clay nodded in agreement. "Need some salt, a few boxes of crackers and whatever else you can manage."

Martin Woodhull spent the next hour rationing out the supplies and loading Clay's wagon. When the last box of food was stored inside the rig, Clay asked, "They running very far ahead of us?"

"They didn't pull out until this morning."

Clay's thin face grinned wolfishly. "Hot damn! Maybe we can catch up with that bunch. I'd like to meet her husband. Bruce Middleton sounds like a man who knows how to survive."

The clerk glanced around. He walked to the door of the store, saw Vivian talking earnestly with the manager. He came back to Clay and whispered conspiratorially. "Smart man, too. The lady in there is like a regular hellcat."

Clay nodded solemnly. "She does have a temper. Of course, her old man left her out there with the Indians."

"Might do the same myself if I was hitched up to her."

"She keeps acting up," Clay added, "and she'll be walking to Oregon."

He went inside, paid for the supplies with money stolen from the True Christian caravan. Vivian was still talking with the manager, who wore a tired expression on his face. He pulled her away from the counter, said a quick farewell and rolled out in pursuit of Vivian's wayward husband.

They continued along the trail until near dark, striking camp when Clay worried that an ox might stumble and cripple a leg. Vivian was quiet and wrapped up in her thoughts. She prepared a rabbit Clay had shot for dinner. After washing their dishes, she rolled up in a bedroll and thought about the unfairness of life.

About ten o'clock, she awakened when Clay threw a few pieces of wood on the fire. He came over and lay down near her.

"You better forget that husband," he said. "He's got a new wife. Ain't planning on supporting two, I'll bet."

Vivian groaned sleepily.

Clay's hand was suddenly on the mound of her hip. "A nice woman like you shouldn't pine for a rascal like him. There's a lot of other men in the world."

"Keep your hands off!" Vivian demanded.

"Damn it! I ain't going to," Clay roared. "I been carrying you for several days now, forcing my team like blazes to catch up with your worthless husband. Paying for the food! Taking you wherever you want to go! Now, I'm hornier than a hot hoot-owl! You got what I want and I aim to get it."

"You got a wife," Vivian said sullenly.

"Dead back in the desert."

"That's what Bruce thought about me."

"I ain't asking much," he said, pleasantly. "Just a piece of pussy."

"That's all men think about!" Vivian moved away from his hand.

"Is there anything else?"

"Honor, decency, love of country. A Christian life." Vivian wrapped a blanket tightly around her. "That's for starters."

Clay moved in. "I ain't giving up. Been thinking about your skinny legs all day. Love to have them wrapped around me."

Vivian frowned, then cast a curious look at him. "Don't be ridiculous! I'm a skinny old hag."

"You're a pretty woman."

"You really think so?"

"Sure you are," Clay lied. "Not like those sickly young girls. They're not worth a grain of powder. No experience. Give me a woman who knows what loving is all about."

"Pshaw! You're just trying to trick me."

Clay grinned wolfishly in the darkness. Just like trolling for fish, he thought. Tell them what they want to know. "Take you," he told Vivian. "You've been hurt and abandoned by your man. He's took up with another woman. Bet you never had any other man since you been married."

"Bruce is the only one I ever had."

"So maybe you ought to find out about things," he went on. "Try another man. See if I feel any different. Maybe I ain't as good. Maybe I'm better. At the very least, you owe it to yourself to find out. You need to find out if you're still a real woman." Clay moved closer and caressed her hair. Vivian lay still and accepted his touch. "You never thought of getting another man?"

"Bruce pestered me too much."

"A real fire-ball, huh?"

"Wanted all that French stuff."

"What's that?" Clay's ears became alert.

Vivian told him what her husband liked to do in bed.

Clay expressed his amazement. "Lord! I never heard of such a thing."

"Perverted. Against God and everything else," she remarked.

"So how do you like to do it?"

"Never liked it," Vivian said with sadness. "Never could figure out what men was so het up about."

"Bruce didn't know what he was doing," Clay explained. "I know a bit more than the average fellow about such things. My pap and some older men explained the facts to me. Pap was a real hell-hound after pussy. If it walked, Pap was willing to go after it. Even saw him rutting with a crippled girl one time. We was visiting some folks who had a kind of loony girl, who walked with a limp. Pap caught her out by the barn when nobody was looking. Blim! Bam! Faster'n a rabbit almost. Didn't even give the girl a chance to remove her undergarments. He was a hard old man. Nobody doubted that. But he taught me a lot about how to please a woman."

Vivian stirred, raised up on her elbow. She asked, "What pleases a woman?"

"First off, women think different than men."

"Praise the Lord!"

"They got all these buttons and hooks inside their heads. Don't do this. That ain't right. The children might be listening and the neighbors are surely peeking through the windows. So you have to sort of bypass them hooks."

"That sounds crazy. You can't do it."

"Whiskey works wonders for kinda fuzzing over the hooks." Clay jumped up and disappeared into the wagon. He returned with a jug of whiskey. "Brought this all the way from Missouri just for a special occasion."

Clay took a long draught of the whiskey. He handed the jug to Vivian, who shuddered when the liquid went down her throat.

"Awful stuff!" she remarked.

"Does the trick. Have another drink!"

Ten minutes later, Vivian was on her way to getting drunk. Her eyes were glistening, her speech slurred. She accepted Clay's amourous advances without protest.

Without guilt, she opened her dress and exposed her breasts. His lips fastened on a nipple and affixed themselves for a long interval. As his lips moved up along her throat, and then onto her wet lips, Vivian felt a warm sensation in her loins. At length, she pushed his head away from her. She stood up and spread her legs wide. She tossed away her deerskin dress and his eyes fastened on the dark, bushy hair at the apex of her legs.

"Beautiful!" Clay murmured.

"Like what you see?" Vivian stumbled through the sand, picked up the jug and took another long drink.

"A mighty fine woman," Clay agreed.

Vivian's nude body was colored gold by the glow of the campfire. Legs spread wide, hands on her hips, she looked directly at Clay Gill.

"O.K. mister!" Her words were slurred. "Let's get drunk and fuck!"

Clay laughed and headed for her.

Clay Gill was barely able to move the next morning. Once she got started, he reflected, Vivian Middleton was making up for a lifetime of hurt and want. She had gone at him like a hungry cat, tearing and clawing like a wild woman. The liquor had drugged her senses just enough, he figured, for the suppressed instincts to surface. Once her true sensuality was unleashed, Vivian Middleton couldn't get enough. They lay wrapped in the bedroll and rutted until the sun brightened the eastern skies. He had slept for maybe an hour when Vivian was tugging at him again, trying to build something out of nothing. He had grunted his displeasure, rolled away and slept until the sun's heat woke him.

They ate a quick breakfast, prepared by Clay, while

Vivian nursed a massive hangover. She drank enough water to float a steamboat, ate ravenously and then went to sleep in back of the wagon. Clay rolled out along the trail and kept pressing the team for more speed. Vivian awoke late in the afternoon and came up to sit beside him. She did not mention their lovemaking and somehow seemed embarrassed when he brought it up. He remained quiet after that, not wanting to trigger her wrath. They continued along the trail for several hours after dark, hoping to catch sight of a campfire from the caravan's camp.

On the third day out, around noon, they came to the point where the trail split. The embers of fires still smoldered at the campsite.

"They must have just left this morning," Clay said excitedly. "We're right behind them."

"But which way did they go?" Vivian wondered.

"Take your choice," Clay pointed to the trail along the Snake River. "That goes to Oregon the people at Fort Hall said. And over there"—he jerked his thumb westward—"is the route to California."

Vivian deliberated. Her chances for vengeance rested on a decision that had to be made without facts. "I don't know," she said at length.

"Take your time. I'll rustle up a hot lunch." Clay threw a few sticks on a mass of embers.

They were drinking cups of black coffee following their meal. Clay was restless, but did not interfere with Vivian's gnawing worry about the direction her husband had gone. Let her make the decision, he decided, and she can't fault me. As long as she's like a mink between the blankets, I'll take her anywhere. He stood up and paced around the campsite. Once, he paused and looked down the California trail.

"Must be my imagination," he told Vivian. "Thought I saw something move out there."

Half an hour passed before a covered wagon and ox team were fully visible. A solitary man was aboard the rig. His eyes were shaded from the sun by a wide-brimmed hat and, as he came closer, Vivian let out a happy cry of recognition.

"You know him?" Clay asked.

"Sure do."

She bounced happily about the campground when Jay Samuels pulled his wagon up. The young Jew's face dropped with surprise when he recognized her.

"Vivian," he said with wonderment. "What are you doing here?"

She smiled without mirth. "Trying to catch up with my husband."

Jay stepped down from his rig. He accepted a tin cup of coffee offered by Clay Gill. He asked, "Haven't we meet somewhere?"

"Might have seen me at the rendezvous in Independence." Clay purposely did not mention the True Christians, or the incident where Samuels's wagon had been attacked.

"Where's Bruce headed?" Vivian asked.

Jay Samuels hesitated. "He got married back at Fort Hall."

"I heard about that."

"The girl, Melissa."

Cunning glistened in Vivian's eyes. "She's such a nice girl. Maybe they'll be happy together. Clay and I want to visit with them, wish them a long and happy life."

"They're on the way to California," Samuels said. "I

was headed that way. Started for the gold fields. Figured I'd find my fortune out there."

Clay laughed. "Looks like you're headed in the wrong direction."

"No," Samuels replied. "This is the right way. I'm hurrying to catch up with the Oregon company."

"A girl?" Vivian asked.

"Jane Miller."

"She'll make you a good wife."

"That's what I decided."

Simmering inwardly, Vivian outwardly remained cool and calm. "A trip west sure changes things. We find out the true meanings of life."

After sharing their left-over food with Samuels, Clay and Vivian watched the young man head his rig toward Oregon.

"Maybe we ought to go that way," Clay ventured.

"I want to see Bruce squirm."

"You can't live for revenge forever."

"Just once will be enough."

Clay wondered. "We might go to Oregon, get our donor land and start a new life."

"It would stick in my craw, knowing he wasn't punished."

"What about us?" Clay inquired.

Vivian looked at him sharply. "Maybe you'd better spell things out."

"I got a liking for you." Clay looked down at his boot tips.

"Really?" Vivian sounded like a schoolgirl.

"Figure you're a pretty good woman. You had some bad times in the past few months. Maybe some hard times before that. That rascal just didn't appreciate you. He didn't know how good you could be."

Vivian came over and nuzzled up against him. "Clay, you sure say the sweetest things."

"What I mean is," he elaborated, "a lot of us make mistakes in life. I made a few. You've had your share of problems. Right now, we got a chance for a new shot at life. Something nice and different that maybe would work out. We head for California and you're going to be gnawing about getting even with your husband. That's going to occupy your every waking hour and maybe your sleep at night. You won't be fitten to be a good wife."

"But," she protested, "there's gold out there."

"I got no hankering to be rich."

"I do. Let's get started."

He lied. "I've been pushing the team awful hard. They need rest."

Vivian's eyes narrowed suspiciously.

"You never said nothing before." Her voice was strident.

"Animals need a rest. There's plenty of salmon in the river. We can hole up here a couple days."

"And then go on to California?"

"Wherever you want to go." Clay picked up his fishing pole. "I'm going to catch a couple fish for dinner. You crawl up in the wagon. Pull out that whiskey jug and get in a loving mood."

Clay kept Vivian drunk for eight days. She was insatiable in her sexual demands, almost wearing him out, but the pressure was pleasurable. When the jug got empty, he tapped a small keg hidden inside a trunk. He just went through the motions of drinking, staying alert in case somebody—white or Indian—came along the trail. Vivian drank like a dragoon trooper.

He encouraged her to stay drunk, reasoning that she'd want to head out when she sobered up. He couldn't see any personal profit in helping Vivian get her revenge. A smart man, his Paw always said, stayed out of other people's quarrels. Bruce Middleton had found himself a sweet little piece of young, tender meat. No need to fault a man for that. With a week's head start, Middleton and his new bride might never be seen again. That was the way Clay wanted it.

When he figured Middleton had a good advantage, Clay sobered Vivian up and set out on the California Trail.

"Lord," she complained the first morning, "I feel awful. How long did I stay drunk?"

"One day," he lied.

"Mouth tastes like death. Seems like I been drinking for a month."

Clay chuckled. "You was just enjoying yourself."

"Probably did some things I shouldn't."

"You was just fine."

Her face hardened. "You think we can catch them?"

"Sure, baby."

"I just want him to get his punishment."

"I ain't worried too much about him," Clay admitted. "My mind has been turning over the possibilities in California. Shoot! We might as well do a little digging. Maybe strike some gold like the rest. Take our riches and start a new life somewhere."

"That sounds fine." Vivian sighed and laid her head on his shoulder. "A new life would really be great."

THIRTY-SEVEN

Jay Samuels caught up with the Oregon company when they were camped along the Snake River. Sheepish and embarrassed, he brought his wagon into camp late that evening. The emigrants rushed outside the corral to greet him whooping and hollering at the top of their voices. Jane Miller heard the noise and came out of her tent. When she caught sight of Jay, she threw away her inhibitions and raced to him. She threw her arms around his neck and smothered his face with kisses.

"Jay! Jay!" she cried happily.

"Hi, Jane," he said, conscious of the grinning people crowding around.

"Welcome back." Sam extended his hand.

Elmer Johnson came up and slapped Jay on the back.

"Glad to see you," Johnson said. "Maybe not as much as that young lady, however."

Jane clung to Jay's neck with both arms. "You're back! You came back!"

"We're going to get married," Jay told the crowd.

"That is, if Jane will have me."

"I will!" she squealed.

"But not until we get to Oregon," he went on. "I want Jane to be married in a real church."

Sam chuckled. "Maybe she ain't willing to wait!"

"I'm the happiest girl in the world!" Jane beamed.

While the women went to warm up some food, Jay motioned to Sam Lawson. The two men went outside the corral. Jay told the guide about meeting Vivian Middleton at the Cassia Creek campsite.

"She's alive!" Sam whistled.

"Claimed she was abandoned by you and her husband."

Sam chewed his lower lip and deliberated. "It might appear to her like that. I skeddadled out when things got hot." He explained how Vivian had tried to leave Melissa with the tribe.

Jay listened to the guide's explanation. "I figured right," he said. "Decided it was best to talk with you before telling the others."

"You did the right thing." Sam told him. "Fact is, I wouldn't say anything else to anyone. Agnes would start worrying about Melissa. If Vivian catches up with the newlyweds, there'll be hell to pay."

"You feel that's best?" Jay asked doubtfully.

"We got enough problems on the trail. No use complicating things."

Jay accepted the guide's advice. They went back inside the corral where Jane had a heaping plate of food waiting. She watched happily as Jay ate.

The course of the trail ran along the great valley of the Snake River. The emigrants had heard about the great

501

cascades, high falls and rushing white water flowing through steep gorges. Sam kept the wagons on the high plateaus, dipping down only to cross numerous rushing creeks. Everything took time in the rugged wilderness. The caravan was lucky to average ten miles a day of travel.

The nights grew colder. Extra blankets were pulled out of trunks and added to bedrolls. Back home, Elmer Johnson said, the corn was in shocks, the wheat stacked, and farmers were making plans to butcher their hogs. His words brought back memories of fresh-killed pork, whetting the emigrants' appetites. They also recalled the taste of roasted buffalo ribs and wondered where the wild game had gone. Sam came in each night with a few rabbits, a handful of sage grouse and that was about it. The Snake River was full of salmon, but the gorges were often too steep and high to fish the stream.

They ground out the miles with a vague uneasiness. Each night, the families gathered around the campfire and talked anxiously about crossing the Snake River. The power of the river heightened their apprehensions. At last, they came to a steep decline that led down to water level. They halted and camped there for the night.

"Better rest up," Sam told them. "We're crossing tomorrow morning."

The strong green waters of the river were divided at this ancient ford by two islands at midstream. The strong, relentless current rippled swiftly past. A man could only guess at the depth. There was no ferry, no boat and nothing available to build one. Sam said it would be impossible to shore up the wagon beds so they would stay dry. Everyone knew that if a wagon was swept past the crossing point, then all hope was lost.

Sam called the men together the next morning. "We got a full day's work cut out," he explained. "This is probably the most dangerous point on the trail. But a lot of other wagons have crossed here ahead of us. They made it across, so we can do the same."

While the emigrants watched, Sam rode out into the stream to test the bottom. His horse was soon belly-deep in the rippling current, but the bottom was firm. Wheel marks could be seen on the first island. When Sam waved his hand, the first wagon rolled up to the river's edge. Two men were mounted on the wagon seat. Elmer Johnson and Jay Samuels rode beside the lead oxen, holding their yokes to keep the beasts surefooted in the water. The wagon plunged into the river and crossed to the first island. By mid-morning, every wagon rested on the island. They got there without an accident.

A dizzying flood of water lay ahead to the second island in the stream. The surface rippled and foamed and men swore it was too swift to cross. But, once again, Sam Lawson rode out into the river. He followed the bottom upstream, angled with a rising bar and drove his animal onto the second island.

"Follow the bar!" Sam yelled. "Don't drop off!"

The lead wagon plunged into the racing water and crawled out into the river. The oxen advanced, holding their footing, as the water broke over the sides of the wagon. The team followed the bar until the edge of the deep channel was attained. Their legs submerged, the foaming current pressing against their sides caused the oxen to balk.

"Get 'em moving!" Sam yelled. "Come on through! Don't stop!"

The riders pulled on the lead oxen's yokes. They

plunged, wallowed and yelled until the animals began to move. Then the lead ox caught sight of Sam on the island, moved out and dragged the rest of the team along. Wagon after wagon made the crossing. Trouble came when Jay Samuels's lead oxen panicked, rose up and lost its footing in the middle of the current. The animal bellowed mightily, its head plunging under the current.

"Get him up!" screamed Sam from the island.

Samuels saw his wagon teeter precariously. Everything he owned was in the rig. When Elmer Johnson failed to get the ox up. Samuels leaped off the wagon seat and rushed through the water. Pulling up with all their strength, they managed to help the beast find footing.

Samuels was wet and tired when his wagon pulled onto the second island. Jane ran up with a blanket to throw over his shoulders. She toweled off his face.

"I was worried," she remarked.

"Worried?" Jay laughed. "I was scared to death out there."

From the second island, the remainder of the crossing was easy. The water flowed fast but was only knee-deep. They camped on a hillock just beyond the river and built a large fire. They set about drying themselves and their belongings.

One wintry day, a wagon train rattled over an icy road winding down the Sandy River from the snow-covered Cascade Mountains. The caravan crossed the Clackamas River, then rolled past the fringe of a forest and broke into a clearing.

"There she is!" Sam roared from the head of the column. "Oregon City!"

The caravan rolled slowly toward the town. The oxen

moved haltingly, tongues lolling out, their necks rubbed to a bloody rawness by the sway of their yokes. Their hooves were scarred and cut. The emigrants sat proudly on the wagon seats and listened to their loose wagon wheels weaving on the hubs. Their canvas tops sagged over the poles. The barrels of grain, for both man and beast, were empty. The emigrants themselves were gaunt and hollow-eyed from the toil of the trail. Their shoes were worn thin, their trousers and dresses ragged and torn.

Sam led the wagon train directly into town, sitting tall on his horse. The residents of Oregon City came rushing from their homes and stores, shouting welcome to the newcomers. When they had passed through the main section of the tiny community, Sam signaled for the wagons to pull into a corral. The emigrants were experts now; each wagon moved easily into place. Men stepped down and unyoked their oxen. The weary animals dropped down onto the ground, sighing with fatigue.

Suddenly, their emotions caught up with the group. They looked around, almost unbelieving, at the neat homes they had passed. The Oregonians were rushing across the field to meet them, waving their arms, shouting greetings.

Sam walked down the line, slapping men on the back, roaring with delight.

"Told you we'd make it," he yelled.

The women wept. Men brushed tears from their eyes. They had safely crossed two thousand miles of wilderness, endured unimaginable hardships and turmoil. They needed now to start about selecting their donor land, setting up businesses, finding a way of earning a living in their new country.

An hour later, everyone was still celebrating the arrival of the wagon train. Sam withdrew from the festivities, took his bedroll from Agnes Miller's wagon and tied it onto his saddle. He picked up his pay from Elmer Johnson, who held the emigrants' fund for the guide.

"You leaving?" Johnson asked.

"Job's finished."

"Where you heading?"

"Figure I'll drop down to California and see what's happening in the gold fields."

Johnson brushed a tear from his eye. "Christ! I don't know what to say at a time like this. You know . . ." His voice trailed off.

"See you later." Sam slapped Johnson's shoulder and walked away.

He was riding out of the camp when a woman came running after him.

"Sam! Sam!" Agnes cried.

He stopped his horse and got down. Agnes came rushing up.

"You didn't say good-bye."

"I ain't very good at that."

"You're leaving for good?" Her lower lip trembled. "Look, I was thinking maybe that we could . . . well, you know . . . stay here for a while and work together."

He shook his head. "It wouldn't work. You're a good woman, Agnes. I'm just a mountain man whose time is past. I wouldn't fit in where there's churches, families and people trying to live good lives."

"But," she whispered. "I think I'm in love with you. This is the first time anything like that ever happened."

Sam grinned. "I think about you sometimes."

"Stay here! Give it a try."

Sam looked at her with longing in his eyes. "I'm tempted!"

"Then why not do it?"

"Settling down is against my nature." He turned away and put his foot into the stirrup.

"Just a second." Agnes came forward and threw her arms around his neck. "I ain't an expert at kissing. But I'm going to give you this to think about."

She planted her lips tightly against his mouth. They held the kiss for several minutes. Finally, Sam stepped back and took a deep breath.

"Whew! You've been practicing."

Agnes smiled. "See what you're missing?"

"Maybe I'll be back." Sam swung up on his horse and, without looking back, rode away.

Agnes stood and watched his departure. Tears streamed down her face. She whimpered: "You rascal!"

The next morning, the emigrants broke camp. They scattered in different directions, each seeking his dream in Oregon.

THE TEMPESTUOUS TOLLIVER SAGA

BY ARTHUR MOORE

THE TEMPEST (521, $2.50)
As struggling young America chooses sides in an inevitable Civil War, the passionate, strong-willed Tollivers, torn by jealousy and greed, begin their life-long battle for the magnificent Burnham Hill.

THE TURMOIL (490, $2.50)
While the Civil War ravages the land, the Tolliver men march to battle, and the women they leave behind fall victim to dangerous love and deception, uncertain if they'll ever see their loved ones again.

THE TRIUMPH (522, $2.50)
As the Civil War approaches its final days and the men, long separated, return home, the struggle between the Tollivers for possession of Burnham Hill is rekindled, with even more venom than before.

THE TAPESTRY (523, $2.50)
With the Civil War ended and Burnham Hill burned to the ground, the Tollivers who have scattered around the globe, reunite, continuing their fierce family feud as they rebuild their beloved plantation home.

Available wherever paperbacks are sold, or order direct from the Publisher. Send cover price plus 40¢ per copy for mailing and handling to Zebra Books, 21 East 40th Street, New York, N.Y. 10016. DO NOT SEND CASH!

SOMETHING FOR EVERYONE—
BEST SELLERS FROM ZEBRA!

FOUR FAST-ACTION NOVELS OF THE FRONTIER WEST

THE SPIRIT OF THE BORDER   (318, $1.75)
by Zane Grey
Lewis Wetzel was an Indian hunter, a self-styled avenger and the right arm of defense to the settlers of Fort Henry. To the superstitious Indians he was a shadow which breathed menace from the dark forests. . . .

THE HERITAGE OF THE DESERT   (328, $1.75)
by Zane Grey
Jack Hare was faced with a desperate choice: Either gun down the son of the man who had saved his life—or be killed himself!

THE TROUBLE AT PENA BLANCA   (330, $1.75)
by Nelson Nye
The ad read: "Wanted—A Tough Hand for Trouble!" But for Bendigo to do the job, he'd have to go back to Mexico where the Durango Militia, hot on his heels, had almost got him at the border. . . .

THE CISCO KID   (338, $1.75)
in "The Caballero's Way"
by O. Henry
Meet the *real* Cisco Kid, who was as heartless as he was handsome, who killed for the love of it and who escaped capture because he could shoot five-sixths of a second sooner than any sheriff or ranger in the service.

FIVE FAST-ACTION NOVELS OF THE FRONTIER WEST

GHOST OF A GUNFIGHTER   (559, $1.95)
by Wayne C. Lee
Dave Paxton finds himself in double trouble when he returns to
Monotony to avenge his uncle's death and discovers the murderer
is his look-alike.

MASSACRE AT WOUNDED KNEE   (542, $2.50)
by Abby Mann
Spurred by the brutal killing of an old Indian, young radical
leaders convince their fellow Indians to make a stand for their
rights. They begin a peaceful hunger strike which ends in a
violent, useless battle reminiscent of the age-old MASSACRE AT
WOUNDED KNEE.

RIDE TO REVENGE   (551, $1.95)
by Eric Allen
Jake Spaniard, a high-tempered young gunfighter from Whiskey
Smith, killed his pa's murderer and is out to shoot the man who's
tampering with his family's land.

RIFLES OF REVENGE   (568, $1.95)
by Lewis B. Patten
Lucille Robineau seeks revenge against the "Cattle King" who
caused her father to take his own life. She hires the meanest,
deadliest man in town to shoot him dead with his quick-fire
RIFLES OF REVENGE.

SHOWDOWN AT FIRE HILL   (560, $1.95)
by Roe Richmond
After being forced to kill a bandit who'd once been his friend,
Ranger Lashtrow wanted to lay down his guns. But deadly gun-
nies wouldn't let him run away, and he knew, sooner or later,
he'd be back behind a gun barrel—even if it killed him.

*Available wherever paperbacks are sold, or order direct from the
Publisher. Send cover price plus 50¢ per copy for mailing and
handling to Zebra Books, 21 East 40th Street, New York, N.Y.
10016. DO NOT SEND CASH!*